Praise for *Serious Moonlight*

atmospheric, multilayered, sex-positive romance from the talented Bennett."
—*KIRKUS REVIEWS*, STARRED REVIEW

"Romance fans won't be disappointed."
—*BCCB*

"Compulsively readable and enormously fun,
this is a first purchase for YA collections."
—*SLJ*

"Bennett creates a cast of vibrant supporting characters . . .
offers vivid descriptions of Seattle's landmarks along with nonstop suspense."
—*PUBLISHERS WEEKLY*

Praise for *Alex, Approximately*

★"A must for romance readers."
—*BOOKLIST*, STARRED REVIEW

★"An irresistible tribute to classic screwball-comedy romances that captures
the 'delicious whirling, twirling, buzzing' of falling in love."
—*KIRKUS REVIEWS*, STARRED REVIEW

"A sexier, modern version of *You've Got Mail* and *The Shop Around the Corner*,
this will hit rom-com fans right in the sweet spot."
—*BCCB*

"A strong addition to romance collections."
—*SLJ*

"Sympathetic characters and plenty of drama."
—*PUBLISHERS WEEKLY*

Praise for *Starry Eyes*

★"A sweet and surprisingly substantial friends-to-more romance."
—*KIRKUS REVIEWS*, STARRED REVIEW

"Vivid plots and endearing characters make this novel impossible to put down."
—*SLJ*

"A layered adventure–love story that's as much about the families we have
and the families we make ourselves as it is about romance."
—*BOOKLIST*

Also by Jenn Bennett

Alex, Approximately
Starry Eyes
The Lady Rogue
Chasing Lucky

Serious

Moonlight

JENN BENNETT

SIMON & SCHUSTER BFYR

NEW YORK   LONDON   TORONTO   SYDNEY   NEW DELHI

SIMON & SCHUSTER BFYR

An imprint of Simon & Schuster Children's Publishing Division
1230 Avenue of the Americas, New York, New York 10020
Text copyright © 2019 by Jenn Bennett
Cover photograph copyright © 2021 by Monique Aimee
Also available in a hardcover edition.
All rights reserved, including the right of reproduction in whole or in part in any form.
SIMON & SCHUSTER BFYR and related marks are trademarks of Simon & Schuster, Inc.
For information about special discounts for bulk purchases, please contact
Simon & Schuster Special Sales at 1-866-506-1949 or business@simonandschuster.com.
The Simon & Schuster Speakers Bureau can bring authors to your live event. For more
information or to book an event contact the Simon & Schuster Speakers Bureau
at 1-866-248-3049 or visit our website at www.simonspeakers.com.
Cover designed by Laura Eckes
Interior designed by Tom Daly
The text of this book was set in Adobe Garamond Pro.
Manufactured in the United States of America
2 4 6 8 10 9 7 5 3 1
First SIMON & SCHUSTER BFYR paperback edition January 2021
The Library of Congress has cataloged the hardcover edition as follows:
Names: Bennett, Jenn, author.
Title: Serious moonlight / by Jenn Bennett.
Description: First Simon Pulse hardcover edition. | New York : Simon Pulse, 2019. |
Summary: Eighteen-year-old, mystery-loving Birdie's new job at a historic Seattle hotel leads
her and her coworker Daniel to a real mystery about a reclusive writer who resides there.
Identifiers: LCCN 2018028885 |
ISBN 9781534425149 (hardcover) | ISBN 9781534425163 (eBook)
Subjects: | CYAC: Hotels, motels, etc.—Fiction. | Recluses—Fiction. |
Authors—Fiction. | Love—Fiction. | Narcolepsy—Fiction. |
Seattle (Wash.)—Fiction. | Mystery and detective stories.
Classification: LCC PZ7.1.B4538 Ser 2019 | DDC [Fic]—dc23
LC record available at https://lccn.loc.gov/2018028885
ISBN 9781534425156 (paperback)

For everyone who feels alone: you're not.

> "You see, but you do not observe."
> —Sherlock Holmes, "A Scandal in Bohemia" (1891)

I

He'd probably forgotten me already. It was a month ago. Practically forever.

He definitely wasn't here tonight. Just to be sure, I scanned the diner one more time, from the rain-speckled glass door to the PIE OF THE DAY chalkboard sign near the register, where the owner had carefully written: ANNE OF GREEN GRAPES, *featuring Yakima Valley chardonnay grapes and blueberries.*

All clear.

For the better part of May, I'd avoided coming to the diner, walking past the windows with my hood up, fearing he'd be here, and if we ever occupied the same space again it would rip open a hole in the universe and create the Most Awkward Moment in Modern History, and the diner—my haven in the city—would be tainted forever and ever.

But he wasn't here, and just because he worked somewhere nearby didn't mean he was a loyal patron of the Moonlight Diner.

And so what if he was? This was my home away from home. I'd spent most of my childhood living in a tiny two-bedroom apartment directly above it. This booth, with its tufted red leatherette seats? It was *my* booth. I'd learned the alphabet at this table. Read *Harriet the Spy* and every Nancy Drew mystery. Won dozens of games of Clue and Mystery Mansion with my mom and Aunt Mona. On the underside of the table I'd drawn crayon portraits of Ms. Patty and Mr. Frank, the diner's owners.

The Moonlight was my territory, and it wasn't cursed just because I'd met a boy here and done something stupid.

"I'd like to buy a vowel, Pat."

I glanced at the woman sitting across from me in the booth, drinking coffee, blinking at me through gold-tipped fake lashes. "Um, what?"

"I'm trying to solve this *Wheel of Fortune* puzzle in the elusive but always intriguing category of 'What is Birdie thinking about?' But I'm missing too many letters," Aunt Mona explained, gesturing like Vanna White at an imaginary game board with long fingernails that featured decals of bumblebees. They matched her 1960s yellow go-go dress (so much fringe), black lipstick, and towering golden beehive wig, complete with tiny winged bee pins.

Mona Rivera did *not* do anything halfway. Not when she was my mother's best friend in high school, and not now, at the ripe age of thirty-six. Most of her elaborate outfits were cobbled from vintage pieces, and she had an entire wall of wigs. She was somewhere between cosplayer and drag queen, and one of the best artists in the Seattle area. She was the bravest, most original person I knew and the most important person in my life.

It was *very* hard to keep secrets from her.

"You told me you weren't nervous about starting this job tonight, but if you are, it's totally normal," she said. "All your training has been during the day, and working at night is going to feel completely different. Graveyard shift is not for the faint of heart—trust me—and if you're worried about staying awake and worried about your sleep issues—"

"I'm not worried," I argued. Mostly not anyway. On one hand, I was a night person, so graveyard didn't bother me. On the other hand, it was my first real job. The first time since my grandmother died this past Christmas that I was allowed to take the ferry into the city alone. I would be spending the entire summer working in downtown Seattle, and I was excited. And a little nervous. And extraordinarily caffeinated—which, in hindsight, was probably a mistake. But on the Alertness Scale, which is a scale I just made up, I lean heavily toward the Always Sleepy side, as narcolepsy runs in my family, along with a slew of other weak genes. My mom used to joke that our Scandinavian ancestors must have gone through an inbreeding phase a couple of hundred years ago.

Aunt Mona frowned. "You haven't been listening to a word I've said over our celebratory Endless Hash Browns dinner, which is the finest of all the Moonlight's food groups."

"Agreed."

"So why are you watching everyone that comes through the door and making your Nancy Drew face?"

"I'm not making my Nancy Drew face."

"Squinty eyes, super alert. Ready to nab a criminal. Oh. I believe I know your Nancy Drew face, especially since I'm the one who coined it." Her gaze darted around the diner. "Who's the suspect? Are we talking robbery or murder?"

I'm a mystery fiend. Detectives, criminals, and clues are my catnip. When I was younger, Mona designed noir-style case files for me to fill out on my vintage Smith Corona typewriter, so that I could keep track of my ongoing neighborhood investigations. Case of Mr. Abernathy's missing garbage can? Solved. Case of the broken streetlights on Eagle Harbor Drive? Solved and reported to the city.

Case of why a sheltered, nerdy girl decided to flirt with a beautiful stranger who was *way* out of her league?

Completely unsolved.

If I had to profile myself, it would look something like this:

Suspect: Birdie Lindberg

Age: 18

Medical conditions: (1) Sleep problems, possibly inherited from grandfather. (2) Hospital phobia. (3) Bookworm disease. (4) Possible addiction to watching old *Columbo*, *Midsomer Murders*, and *Miss Fisher's Murder Mysteries* episodes.

Personality traits: Shy but curious.
Occasionally cowardly. Excellent with details.
Good observer.

Background: Mother got knocked up by an
unknown boy when she was a rebellious
seventeen-year-old, disappointing her
small-town parents. Mother dropped out of
high school, left her sleepy childhood home
on Bainbridge Island, and crossed Elliott Bay
into Seattle with her childhood best friend,
Mona Rivera. The two friends raised Birdie
together until the mother died unexpectedly
when the girl was ten. She was then taken in
by her grandparents on Bainbridge Island and
homeschooled, causing the suspect to develop
a profound sense of loneliness and rabid
curiosity about everything she was missing.
Her only refuge was Mona Rivera, who moved
back to the island to be closer to young
Birdie. When Birdie's strict grandmother
died six months ago of the same weak heart
condition that took her mother, Birdie was
sad but also relieved that her grandfather
realized she was eighteen and couldn't stay
trapped on the island forever and granted
her permission to get her first real job in

Seattle. Abusing her newly earned freedom,
the suspect promptly engaged in lewd and
lascivious acts with a boy she met in the
Moonlight after her first job interview.

"No suspects tonight," I told Aunt Mona, pushing away a plate of lacy hash browns indecently smeared with ketchup. "The Moonlight is free and clear of any ne'er-do-wells, hoodlums, and crooks. Which is good, because I probably should be heading to work soon."

She shook her head. "Not so fast. If there's no suspicious activity and you aren't worried about your first night on the job, then what in the world is going on with you?"

I groaned and laid my cheek on the cool linoleum tabletop, staring out a plate-glass window flecked with raindrops at the people beyond, who were dashing down the sidewalk in the twilight drizzle as streetlights came to life. Gray May would soon be turning to June Gloom, which meant more drizzle and overcast skies before summer truly arrived in Seattle.

"I did a stupid thing," I admitted. "And I can't stop thinking about it."

Bumblebee nails gently moved mousy-brown hair off my forehead, away from the ketchup-smeared rim of my unfinished plate, and tucked it behind a single lily I wore in my hair behind one ear. "Can't be that bad. Fess up."

After a couple of long sighs, I mumbled, "I met a boy."

"O-o-h," she murmured. "A *boy*, you say? A genuine member of the human race?"

"Possibly. He's really beautiful, so he may be a space alien or a clone or some kind of android."

"Mmm, sexy boy robot," she purred. "Tell me everything."

"There's not much to tell. He's a year older than me—nineteen. And a magician."

"Like, Las Vegas performer or Harry Potter?" she asked.

I huffed out a soft laugh. "Like card tricks and making a napkin with his phone number written on it appear inside the book I was reading."

"Wait. You met him here? At the diner?"

In answer, I held up a limp fist and mimicked a head nodding.

"Was this when you were interviewing last month?"

"For that part-time library job." That I *totally* thought was a sure thing . . . yet didn't get. Which was doubly depressing when I later realized that my misplaced confidence was one of the factors that led me to get carried away with "the boy" on that unfateful day.

"And you didn't tell me?" Aunt Mona said. "Birdie! You know I live for romantic drama. I've been waiting your entire life for one juicy story, one glorious piece of top-notch teen gossip that will make me swoon, and you don't tell me?"

"Maybe this is why."

She pretended to gasp. "Okay, fair point. But now the cat's out of the bag. Tell me more about this sexy, sexy cat—*meow*."

"First, he's a boy, not cat or a robot. And he was charming and sweet."

"Keep going," she said.

"He showed me some card tricks. I was feeling enthusiastic about the library job. It was raining pretty hard. He asked if I wanted to go see an indie movie at the Egyptian, and I told him I'd never been to the Egyptian, and he said it was in a Masonic Temple, which I didn't know. Did you? Apparently it was—"

"Birdie," Aunt Mona said, exasperated. *"What happened?"*

I sighed heavily. My cheek was sticking to the linoleum. "So we ran through the rain and went to his car, which was parked in the garage behind the diner, and it was pretty much deserted, and the next thing you know . . ."

"Oh. My. God. You didn't."

"We did."

"Tell me you used a condom."

I lifted my head and frantically glanced around the diner. "Can you please keep your voice down?"

"Condoms, Birdie. Did you use them?" she said, whispering entirely too loudly.

I checked to make sure Ms. Patty wasn't anywhere in sight. Or any of her nieces and nephews. There were almost a dozen of those, a couple of whom I'd gone to school with when I was a kid. "Do you really think that me, a product of unsafe teen sex, whose mother later *literally died* after getting pregnant a second time, someone who had to listen to a thousand and one safe-sex lectures from her former guardian—"

"Once a guardian, always a guardian. I will never be your former anything, Birdie."

"Her current guardian in spirit."

"That's better."

"I'm just saying. Yes. Of course. That wasn't the problem."

"There was a problem? Was he a jerk? Did you get caught?"

"Stop. It was none of that. It was me. I suddenly just got . . . weirded out."

One moment I was all caught up in feeling good. This beautiful, funny boy whom I'd just met was kissing me, and I was kissing him, and I think I may have just possibly suggested we get in the back seat instead of going to the movie theater. I don't know what I was thinking. I suppose I wasn't, and that was the problem. Because once we got back there and clothes started getting unbuttoned and unzipped, it all happened so fast. And in the middle of everything, I had a startling moment of clarity. He was a stranger. I mean, a *complete* stranger. I didn't know where he lived or anything about his family. I didn't know him at all. It got way too real, way too fast.

So when it was over, I bolted.

Ditched him like a guilty criminal fleeing a botched bank job.

Then I headed to the ferry terminal and never looked back.

"Oof," Mona said in sympathy, but I was pretty sure I heard some relief in her voice too. "Did he . . . ? I mean, was he upset about it?"

I shook my head and absently rearranged the salt and pepper shakers. "I heard him calling my name. I think he was confused. It all happened so fast. . . ."

"Maybe too fast?"

"He wasn't pushy or anything. He was nice, and I'm such a dud."

Mona made a chiding noise and quickly held up three fingers in a mock Scout salute. "On my honor—come on. Say it."

"Trying to be an adult here."

"Trying to help you be an adult. Say our pledge, Birdie."

I did the salute. "On my honor as a daring dame and gutsy gal, I will do my best to be true to myself, be kind to others, and never listen to any repressive poppycock."

When my grandmother was alive, she forbade swearing, cursing, and anything resembling rebellion under her roof. Adjusting to her rules after my mother died had often been draining. Aunt Mona had helped me cope by coming up with the Daring Dame pledge . . . and secretly teaching ten-year-old me a dozen words that contained the word "cock."

Aunt Mona and Grandma did *not* get along.

Satisfied with my Daring Dame pledge, she dropped her fingers. "I know it's hard for you to get close to people, and I know as much as you and Eleanor disagreed, she was still your grandmother and it hurts to lose someone. I know you must feel like everyone you love keeps leaving you, but it's not true. I'm here. And other people will be too. You just have to let them in."

"Aunt Mona—" I started, not wanting to talk about this right now.

"All I'm saying is that you didn't do anything wrong. And maybe if this boy is as awesome as you say he is, he could be understanding about how things ended if you gave it another chance. You said he gave you his phone number. Maybe you should call him."

"Must have fallen out of my book when I was running," I lied, shaking my head. I actually tossed if off the side of the ferry on my way home that afternoon when I was still freaking out about what I'd done. "But maybe it's for the best. What would I say? Sorry I bailed on you like a weirdo?"

"*Aren't* you sorry you bailed on him, though?"

I wasn't sure. But it didn't matter. I'd probably never see him again. And that was a good thing. It was one thing to say the Daring Dame pledge and a whole other to live it. Maybe I needed to build up some real-world experience before I braved dating. Perhaps I needed to put on my detective glasses and figure out where I went wrong.

But after all the mystery shows I'd binged, I should've known that detectives never investigate their own crimes.

2

The Cascadia was a five-story historic brick building on the corner of First Avenue in downtown Seattle near the waterfront. It was a luxury landmark hotel built in 1920 and was recently restored to showcase its Pacific Northwest roots while offering thoroughly modern amenities—at least, according to the website.

And I was going to work here.

Its unassuming entrance sat beneath an awning that sheltered the sidewalk. And beneath that awning, leaning against a hotel van parked at the curb, stood a Native American porter in a green uniform, perhaps a couple of years older than me. When I approached, he mistook me for a hotel guest, straightened, and opened one of two gold-trimmed doors. "Good evening, miss."

"I work here," I told him. "Tonight's my first shift. Birdie Lindberg."

"Oh." He allowed the door to swing shut. "I'm Joseph," he said, quickly looking me over until his gaze briefly lit on the pink-and-white stargazer lily pinned over my ear. "You're a Bat, right?"

"I'm the new night auditor?"

"You're a Bat, then," he said with a smile.

Right. I remembered now. Melinda was the night manager, and "Bats" made up the graveyard crew. My position was basically just a glorified front desk clerk who worked graveyard shift at the hotel and, after midnight, ran the software program that tabulated all the room bills and settled accounts. I was being paid a dime over minimum wage.

"Been through training?" Joseph asked.

"Last week," I said. "With Roxanne, during the day. I was hoping for midday shifts, but this was all that was open."

"It's almost always open. The only people who want to work graveyard are college students and nighthawks. Or people with no alternatives."

"This is my first job," I admitted.

"Well, welcome to the night crew, Birdie," he said with a smile, opening the hotel's gold entrance door for me. "Try not to fall asleep. There's free coffee in the break room."

More caffeine was the last thing my nerves needed right now, and I wasn't a coffee fan. I thanked him, blew out a quick breath, and stepped inside.

The Cascadia's Pacific Northwest style and vintage glamour was as dazzling as it had been the first time I'd stepped into the grand lobby. So dazzling, in fact, that it took me a moment to realize how different it was at night. No constant click of heels on the madrone wood floor. No dueling *ding*s of the two gold elevators near the entrance, with their tribal salmon design covering the doors. And no tourists pressing their noses to the lobby's giant aquarium, which housed a giant Pacific octopus named Octavia—maybe the best thing in the entire hotel.

As I walked past the softly glowing tank beneath a row of painted canoes hanging from the mezzanine, jazz floated over the lobby's speakers. A well-dressed couple headed up to their room for the night, and a single businessman sat on one of the soft leather sofas, staring into the screen of his laptop.

Amazing to think that any one of these guests could be famous or important. Agatha Christie stayed here when she was touring the world with her husband. President Franklin Roosevelt gave a secret fundraising speech in the ballroom. Rock stars. Presidents. Mobsters. The Cascadia had hosted them all.

The hotel even had its own murder mystery: beloved Hollywood starlet Tippie Talbot had died on the fifth floor in 1938. Foul play was suspected but never proven, and her unsolved death had made headlines around the country. Who knows. Maybe I'd uncover some new clues on one of my shifts.

Anything could happen!

I felt supremely lucky. All that talk about "the boy" with Aunt Mona faded softly into the past. Nothing could spoil this. It was magical. And it was time to get to work.

The registration desk was deserted, so I made a beeline toward the hidden hallway behind it, which led to the back offices. Inside the employee break room, a single housekeeper sat on a battered couch, watching TV with her eyes closed. So I hurried into the women's locker room and stowed my purse in my assigned locker. Then I shrugged into my forest-green hotel blazer, pinning a gold name tag to my breast pocket, and returned to the break room, ready for work.

During training I'd been cautioned about clocking in too early. And too late. Apparently the hotel was like Goldilocks and preferred their porridge *just right*. But as I stood in front of the old-fashioned time clock, wondering if I should use the same time card I'd already started for training, heels clicked behind me, and a strong chocolate-scented lotion wafted over the microwave-popcorn scent that permeated the employee lounge. When I turned around, the hotel's night manager stood in front me, balancing an enormous baby bump while standing on insanely high heels.

"I'm Melinda Pappas," she said, offering a hand to shake. Black hair was pulled back tightly into a flight-attendant bun, giving me the impression that she was all about professionalism and rules, and the dark circles hanging under her eyes told me she wasn't sleeping, perhaps due to her pregnancy.

"Um, I'm Birdie Lindberg," I said. "The new night auditor?"

She nodded. "You just missed a crew meeting. I added it to the schedule last night."

A burst of panic fired through my chest. I frantically glanced at the schedule and said, "I didn't know there was a meeting. I'm so sorry. I'm never late for anything, but Roxanne didn't mention that my shifts might change. My last day of training was—"

Melinda held up a hand. "It's fine. We had an incident with an animal rights group in the lobby yesterday. I'll brief you about it, but it's best to call in on your day off and get someone to double-check the schedule for you and make sure there aren't any meetings."

"Okay," I said. "I'm really sorry. Ma'am."

"I'm thirty," she said. "Not a 'ma'am' yet. Just call me Melinda. Come on. I'll introduce you to the rest of the Bats."

She gestured for me to follow her and proceeded to introduce me to the night staff one by one—kitchen staff, housekeeping, security . . . There were a lot of new names, but I was good with details, so I filed them all away, creating a mental map of their faces and roles as we made our way into the lobby.

"I assume you were trained about Octavia the Octopus," Melinda said, tilting her head toward the big tank, where a red cephalopod clung to the glass by two tentacled arms lined with white suckers. Bright coral, rocky caves, and several starfish kept her company. "If guests ask, Octavia was rescued out of Puget Sound after a boat damaged one of her arms, and we have a biologist on staff who takes care of her."

"We do?"

Melinda scrolled on her tablet. "*That* is what you tell guests. We have a biologist on call at the Seattle Aquarium who advises us if we need help, but there's no need to go into that with guests. And as I told the rest of the Bats in the staff meeting earlier, if any members of SARG come into the lobby, then you call me immediately."

"SARG?"

"Seattle Animal Rights Group," she said, rounding the registration desk. "They brought signs and made a big scene here yesterday, claiming we are killing goldfish and abusing the octopus by keeping her in captivity."

Melinda waved a hand toward a line of four round fishbowls that sat behind the desk. Each contained one orange goldfish that could be rented out by guests if they wanted a companion in their room. One of my duties included feeding any unrented fish at midnight and filling out the little standing cards in front of the bowls with goldfish names. When I found out about this, it was frosting on the proverbial cake, because I used to have fish at home.

"I thought the goldfish program was a big success," I said. In training, I'd been told that families loved it. Kids could choose which goldfish they wanted upon check-in, and one of the porters would carry it up to their room.

"It is," Melinda insisted. "No one's killing fish. Sometimes they get diseases or an overeager child scoops one out of the bowl or dumps orange juice in the water . . . So, of course, we must dispose of them occasionally. But it's not as if we kill them for pleasure. Goldfish don't live long anyway."

I knew for a fact that wasn't true, but no way was I saying so.

"And Octavia has a custom-built, half-a-million-dollar tank," Melinda said. "She's adored by locals and tourists, and she's perfectly happy living with her starfish friends. Every fall we release that year's Octavia into the Sound and catch another one."

"Wait, what?"

"They only live a year or so. We 'retire' them and catch a young one. But if guests press you about this, just say that this Octavia is the former Octavia's baby. And if anyone has a problem with the way we run things, they can talk to me. Got it?"

"Absolutely," I said, though I wasn't liking any of this information. But it was obviously a sore topic for her, so I was thankful to leave the fish issues behind for now and head out the front door with her when she was ready to introduce me to the final three Bats.

The first was someone I'd already met earlier: Joseph. Turned out, he not only watched the door, but he was also the bellhop and the backup valet, if any guests needed their luggage carried or their car retrieved from the underground parking, until the Bat shift ended and the morning crew's Roosters took our places.

At Joseph's side was a blond, college-aged bruiser named Chuck, who was loud, obnoxious, and a guard working under the security manager, Mr. Kenneth. "What up, femme?"

"Please refrain from using that term," Melinda scolded. "It doesn't mean what you think it does."

"It's French for female," Chuck argued around the gum he was smacking. "It's a term of endearment. And why does she get to use a nickname on her tag?"

I glanced down at my name tag. "It's my real name."

"Your mom named you Birdie? Is she some kind of hippie?"

"She's dead."

"Oh shit!" Chuck says. "My bad."

"Please refrain from using bad language on the property," Melinda said wearily.

He wasn't paying attention. "So, Birdie. Betcha didn't know that Joseph here was descended from Chief Seattle," Chuck informed me.

Joseph sighed heavily, pushing dark hair out of his eyes. "My family's Puyallup, from Tacoma. Completely different tribe."

"Who cares? Guests eat that shit up," Chuck said, grinning. "Right, boss?"

Now Melinda ignored *him*. "And over there is our driver," she told me.

The scent of her chocolate-scented lotion filled my nostrils when she waved her arm and shouted to get the attention of a boy about my age. He was lean and animated, standing on the other side of the hotel van, cheerfully chatting with a taxi driver and completely oblivious to Melinda.

"He's half-deaf," Chuck offered. "Must be nice. You can tune out whoever you want."

"His hearing is impaired," Melinda corrected in a low voice. "You need to be patient with him sometimes."

Joseph whistled sharply with his teeth. The van driver waved good-bye to the taxi and hurried toward us, slender legs striding, head down, hands shoved deep in the pockets of the same sort of zipped-up green windbreaker that some of the staff wore. He had dark, short hair . . . Wait, no. Long hair. *Really* long hair, wound up into a samurai-style, hipster topknot at the crown of his head.

Huh.

My heart started hammering furiously.

When people say they have a "gut feeling" about something, it's because our brains are constantly being fed information by our bodies. Our noses smell smoke, and then our brain tells us to get the heck out of the house. And at that moment, my body was telling me to stop, drop, and roll. It just took my slowpoke brain a few extra moments to realize why.

"This is the night-shift van driver," Melinda informed me as he approached. "Daniel Aoki, meet Birdie. She's the new night clerk."

When the driver lifted his head, his eyes widened, and he murmured, "Oh, fuuuuuuuu . . ."

Every muscle in my body turned to stone.

I knew that face. And lots more of him too.

This was the boy I'd met in the diner.

3

Son of a beekeeper!

I tried to process what was happening, but all I could do was stare and wonder if all of this was a bad dream. Just to be sure, I stealthily counted my fingers—a trick I learned from my grandpa. Looking at your hands is a good way to test wakefulness, because if you're dreaming, they sometimes morph into extra-long space-alien hands or the number of digits will be wrong. At the moment everything was as it should be. Five fingers. Nothing extraterrestrial.

I was awake, and all of this was really happening.

Okay. Deep breath. Maybe I was confused. This could be someone else who looked like him. A twin? I looked harder. Wide silver ring on middle finger. Tiny V-shaped scar on cheek. And on his head, one stray lock of hair hung loose around his face: it spilled over his shoulder and stopped in the middle of his chest, a million times longer than mine.

It was him, all right.

And the way his face lit up with joy when he recognized me made it all *so much* worse. Oh, that smile—so effortless and sincere. So big and wide, it lifted the keen angles of his cheeks and made his brown eyes squint. That was the thing that had attracted me in the diner, his easygoing, open manner. I'd never met anyone so comfortable with both himself and other people, so honestly cheerful.

This couldn't be happening. He was standing in front of me, and he had a full name: Daniel Aoki. I didn't want to know that. He was supposed to be my private, forgettable mistake, not my coworker!

"We call him Jesus," Chuck said. "If you saw him with his hair down, you'd understand. He does magic tricks for the guests that are probably just as good as turning water into wine." Chuck turned to Daniel and asked, "Hey, what's the Japanese word for Jesus?"

"No idea," Daniel said. "Don't speak it."

"But your mom does, right?" Chuck said.

"Isn't your mom from Spokane?" Joseph asked Daniel.

"Born and raised," Daniel said, unaffected by Chuck's boorish observations. Maybe he'd become numb to them. Maybe, like me, he was too busy trying to compute the chances of us ending up being coworkers, and how was this even possible? I wished he'd quit looking at me like that.

"You two know each other, or something?" Chuck asked after an awkward silence.

"No," I said at the same time Daniel replied, "Yes."

"Or maybe not?" he corrected as everyone stared at us. "Sort of? I mean, we . . ."

"Have seen each other around town," I said quickly.

Joseph glanced at the lily tucked behind my ear. "Dude. The flower girl?" he murmured to Daniel, slapping the back of his hand against Daniel's chest, making him flinch.

The breath in my lungs disappeared.

Oh God, oh God, oh God. This couldn't be happening.

Was I blushing? I think this was blushing. Or I was about to have a stroke. Inside my frantic brain, a dozen scenarios flashed. Of Daniel, bragging bro-style to Joseph and Chuck, talking me up as a laughable conquest. Or as the weird girl who freaked out and ran away. *Do I already have a reputation here? DO I?*

Things were being whispered. I think Daniel told Joseph to "shut the hell up, man," and then Joseph, grimacing, responded, "Oh shit."

Indeed. A huge, stinking pile of it.

"Well," Melinda said to me. "Now you get to see each other every night, because it's Daniel's job to make supply runs that *you* get to log at the desk."

"What?" I said, trying to make my brain work. I wished he'd stop staring at me.

"Time out, time in," Melinda said. "You log Daniel's comings and goings in the hotel's system. But we aren't an airport shuttle service, so everyone who begs for a 'quick ride' to the bank at two in the morning, inform them you can call a car."

"Unless they're on the fifth floor," Daniel corrected while I looked anywhere but at his face. "Those are the VIPs."

"Floor-fivers are all, 'I forgot to get my niece a Christmas present, boo-hoo,'" Chuck mocked, imitating wiping tears. "'I need a specific wine from a special year from some fruity gourmet merchant across town or my anniversary will be ruined.' You wouldn't believe what they ask for. . . ."

This certainly wasn't the same speech Roxanne had given me in training about going "above and beyond to create unforgettable moments" for guests, treating them like family.

"Please stop by my office before your break," Melinda told Chuck. And before he could protest, she excused us and herded me back into the hotel. I was in such a state of shock about Daniel, I could barely keep up with her high heels.

Despite the dangerous panic levels filling my brain, I immediately had to switch gears and concentrate on the actual *work* part of work, because Melinda was passing me off to the midshift desk clerk who was done with her "mental health break" and staying late to help me transition. She got me up to speed with all the outstanding guest issues of the day, reminded me to feed the goldfish, made sure I'd been trained on how to use the reservation system, and then—boom! She was clocking out, and I was left all by my lonesome.

In a luxury hotel lobby.

At night.

On the first shift of my first real job.

With my greatest humiliation standing outside the front door.

Once the shock of it all wore off a little, I realized that a secret part of me was happy to see him. Practically ecstatic. If I were an actual daring dame and not a wobbly wallflower, I might even have done what Aunt Mona suggested and attempt to talk with him. Apologize for running out on him. Explain that what we did was an anomaly for me. But as my shift ticked by, the longer I went without seeing him, the more I convinced myself that maybe he didn't want an explanation.

If I were to write up a profile on Daniel now, it would look something like this:

Suspect: Daniel Aoki

Age: 19

Occupation: Hotel van driver, graveyard shift

Medical conditions: (1) Hearing-impaired. (2) Distractingly good-looking. (3) Excellent smile. (4) Good kisser. (5) Good hands. (6) Re-e-e-eally good hands.

Personality traits: Knows a million card tricks and enjoys performing for people. Cheerful. Gregarious. Maybe too gregarious, as he seems to have blabbed to a coworker about what we did.

Background: Need to investigate further.

Trying to banish thoughts of Daniel, I put on a cheerful face and embraced the work that began trickling in like the soothing sounds of the river-rock waterfall that covered the wall behind the registration desk. I helped a guest find the downstairs restrooms. Helped another with the Wi-Fi password. Rerouted a call for room service to the kitchen.

See. I really *could* do this. *I am working! Like a real person!* Daniel who? That was a month ago. Who cared that he worked here? Not me. Not even worth starting a case file.

It was all good. Until I checked out a businessman who had a red-eye flight and needed his car out of the hotel garage. That's when I had to radio the Bats out front. Joseph answered, thank goodness, and the businessman lounged on a sofa in the lobby until his car was brought to the entrance. Then Daniel suddenly appeared, jogging past the gold elevators to inform the guest that his car was ready. The businessman wheeled out his carry-on, and the lobby was empty again.

Mostly. Daniel was heading toward the front desk.

I panicked, wishing I could duck down. But he'd already seen me.

"Of all the gin joints in all the world, she walks into mine," he said, flashing me that stupid-sexy smile that got me in trouble the first time around. The shock of seeing him had worn off, but my body was still overreacting. Pulse erratic. Thoughts fuzzy. Fingers tingling. I couldn't tell if it was panic or attraction, but I sure as heck didn't want him to see how much he affected me, so I bent behind the counter to straighten a stack of paper sleeves for room key cards and tried to sound casual.

"Guess the small-world cliché is an actual thing."

"What's that?" he said.

I stood up. "What's what?"

"I didn't hear you." He tapped his right ear. "Deaf in this one. Sometimes I miss things."

He'd failed to mention this when I'd met him in the diner, so now I wasn't sure what to say.

But he was unfazed by my silence.

"Happened a couple of years ago, when I was young and stupid. Still stupid, actually," he said, smiling sheepishly. "It's weird how it messes with your depth perception. Sometimes I miss pieces of conversation, and other times I can pick out crazy-specific sounds over vast distances. Like, when you're talking to guests up here? I can hear your voice across the lobby when the door opens."

"Mine?"

He nodded. "Clear as a bell. Something about the pitch of it. You're a dog whistle."

"Oh," I said stupidly, embarrassed.

Then it was quiet between us. Nothing but the waterfall tinkling.

"Okay," he said. "Wow. Shit. This is weird, huh?"

"A little," I admitted.

Should I apologize for running out on him? Should I try to

explain? Bringing it up here, out in the lobby, where everything echoed, made me anxious. What if Melinda were monitoring our conversation back in her office? Was that a thing they did here?

Ella Fitzgerald and Louis Armstrong were duetting over the hotel speakers about the pronunciation of potatoes and tomatoes. I tried to focus on their relationship problems and not mine and ignored Daniel. That was a little trick I did when I didn't know what to say to people—I just pretended they weren't there. I learned it by observing people in the city, a local phenomenon affectionately known as the Seattle Freeze. And it worked. When I froze people out, they usually got the hint and left.

Everyone but Daniel.

"So-o-o-o . . . ," he drawled, one finger sliding across the counter to tap near the keyboard. "I didn't know if you were aware, but you've got to make a note on the reservation that the guest took his car. It's for insurance, or whatever, so he can't sue us later and claim his car got jacked from our garage."

"Oh. Okay. Thank you," I said, trying not to look at his face as I opened a screen on the computer. *Code for valet service.* It was here somewhere in a drop-down menu . . . *Freeze, freeze, freeze.*

"That actually happened once," Daniel said, propping his elbow on the counter as if he had all night. "Some doctor got her car stolen after she left the hotel. Joyriders crashed it in Ballard. Her insurance wouldn't pay because she left her keys in the ignition, so she changed her story and said *we* left them in—that the car was stolen from our garage." He mimicked an explosion with his fingers near the side of his head. He was a hand talker. Lots of gestures. Lots of movement in general. "Hotel owner had to go to court. It was on the news and everything."

He reached for a rubber band that was near my arm. I tried to keep my eyes on the screen, but he was doing something with the rubber band. First it was wound around his index finger; then he opened his fist and it jumped to his pinky. Then jumped again, back to his index finger. He held up his hand and wiggled his fingers. "Jumping rubber band trick," he said. "Want to see how it's done?"

Yes, I did, actually. The mystery lover in me needed to know the *how* behind any and every puzzle. But I fought this urge and just said, "No, thank you."

"Hey," he said. "Birdie?"

I couldn't *not* look up. "Yes?"

"Hi." He smiled softly.

"Hi?"

"Nice to meet you again."

Rattled, I made a vague noise somewhere between "mmm" and "hmm."

"Sorry about earlier outside," he said, scratching the outer shell of his bad ear. "It threw me off, seeing you here. I didn't know what to say."

That made two of us.

"It's fine," I said.

"Is it? Because last time I saw you, I thought things were going good until—"

"Yes, I know," I said quickly, hoping he wouldn't continue.

"Right. Well, afterward, when you bailed, I . . . wasn't sure why, so I tried to chase after you. I thought maybe you'd gone back to the diner. But you weren't there, and the server had assumed we were doing a dine and dash on the check."

Crap. I'd forgotten to pay? Terrific. Had someone told Ms. Patty? No one mentioned it today when Aunt Mona and I came in, but then again, a new girl was working the booths. In a panic, I imagined my Polaroid being taped behind the diner register, on the board for banned customers, where it said in black Sharpie: *Do not serve these assholes.*

"Ye-a-a-a-ah, so I took care of it," he said, nervously tapping his fingers on the edge of the counter. "And then you were long gone."

My cheeks were getting warm again. "Um, I can—how much? I'll pay you back. I'm sorry."

"Don't worry about it," he said with a quick shake of his head. "I was more concerned about you running off." He looked around the lobby and leaned over the desk. "Did you see my ad?"

Ad?

"My listing." He blinked several times and scratched his temple. "Of course not. I thought maybe you saw it and . . ." He was talking more to himself than to me. "When we met, you said you'd just interviewed . . ."

"For a different job. At the library. I didn't get it," I said. "And I didn't realize you worked here, or I wouldn't have applied."

His brow tightened. "You wouldn't have?"

"I didn't mean . . . I meant that I wasn't stalking you, or anything. In case that's what you thought. It was just a weird coincidence."

"Oh. Guess that whole small-world thing really is true, huh?"

Did he realize I'd said that already? I couldn't tell, and this threw me off . . . made me feel as though *I* were missing half of the conversation. How could I not have picked up on his hearing issue at the diner? That was the type of detail I usually didn't miss.

"Let's just forget it and move on," I suggested.

"I regret it for sure," he said.

Wait: he regretted it too? Why? I mean, I know why I regretted it.

"Maybe it was a mistake, but I thought we had a connection. Our chemistry . . . I mean, Christ. In the diner? When we first got into the car? It was *so* there." He paused. "At least, I thought so."

Fresh panic rolled through me. He *seemed* sincere, but the detective in me was distrustful, and maybe that's because something was still niggling me from our earlier reintroduction outside the hotel's entrance. "Oh, really? Is that why you told Joseph about us?"

"I didn't!" he protested before giving me a shy look. "Not everything, anyway."

"But enough," I said.

"It's not like I gave him a play-by-play, Christ. Joseph and I are friends. I've known him since high school. He couldn't care less about what we did or didn't do."

"Did you tell that Chuck guy too?" I asked.

"I wouldn't tell Chuck the hotel was burning down. He's a jackass. I didn't tell anyone but Joseph, Scout's honor." He leans over the counter and speaks in a lower voice. "What happened between me and you was . . . not something that happens to me every day. Joseph's the one who suggested I do the classified ad."

What ad?

"Anyway, Joseph was just surprised when he saw you. *I* was surprised."

We were all surprised, apparently.

"He's embarrassed now," Daniel insisted.

He wasn't the only one. "Look, I should get back to work," I said, self-conscious and embarrassed. "This job is important to me, and I can't afford to lose it." I needed to prove to myself that I could be independent after my grandmother's isolating rules and restrictions. I needed to earn my own money that I could spend however I chose. I needed to be around people who weren't from Bainbridge Island. People who didn't know me as Birdie, the weird kid who was homeschooled. Or Birdie, the kid whose high-school-dropout mother died. Or Birdie, the kid who now lives alone with her grandfather while everyone else her age is graduating and getting ready to go to college and I was still trying to figure out how to be independent.

Maybe that was why I was attracted to Daniel in the first place. He didn't know me. Maybe if he did, he would wonder what he ever saw in me that afternoon.

"Let's just please put all of this in the past," I suggested to Daniel. "And pretend it never happened."

"You're serious?" An exasperated noise burred in the back of his throat. "I can't just . . . I mean, why would you . . . ?" He glanced over his shoulder. "Can't we just talk about it? Not here. Outside of work. We could meet up somewhere. Uh, maybe not the diner. That might be a little weird. What about after work? Before? Name the time and place, and I'll be there."

"I don't want to talk about it. There's nothing to say."

Couldn't he see how embarrassed I was? I should have worn a sign around my neck that said: PLEASE DON'T FEED THE SKITTISH ANIMAL, AS IT IS UNACCUSTOMED TO HUMAN CONTACT, AND WHILE IT MAY HAVE SEEMED FRIENDLY THE LAST TIME YOU VISITED, IT HASN'T QUITE ADJUSTED TO ITS GROWING HABITAT.

After a moment Daniel said, "What about fate?"

"What about it?"

"Don't you think it's *really* strange that we ended up being coworkers?"

"I think it's random," I said. "Like life."

A loud *beep* startled both of us. Two *beep*s. They came from our walkie-talkies.

"Uh, guys? We've got a problem. I think another pipe busted in the garage," Joseph's voice said, crackling over the radio. "It smells like sewage, and it's dripping on someone's BMW. Piss and shit *everywhere*."

"Not again," Daniel moaned. He set the rubber band on the counter and slid it toward me. "Please don't leave. We'll talk later. Right now I've got to find a pair of gloves and a hazmat suit. Who knew driving a hotel van would involve so much feces?"

He jogged away, and I was unsure how I felt about our conversation.

Maybe I should give this fate thing a second look.

Because I was pretty sure karma was doing its best to make me pay for what I'd done.

"The voice of Love seemed to call to me, but it was a wrong number."
—Bertie Wooster, *Very Good, Jeeves!* (1930)

4

The leak in the hotel garage kept everyone busy for hours. I saw Daniel only twice more, briefly, when he logged a couple of trips for the hotel van. And then, before I knew it, the morning-shift people—the "Roosters"—were filing into the hotel to take over. In the shuffle, I locked myself in a restroom stall and stayed there, rereading a dog-eared Elizabeth Peters paperback; I always keep a comfort mystery book in my purse for emergencies.

I know. It was cowardly. But the first ferry back to Bainbridge Island wasn't for another hour, and no way was I going to do what I'd planned: hole up two blocks away in the Moonlight Diner to wait. Not when Daniel was so eager to talk.

I needed the Moonlight to be my refuge after work. Seattle may be sleepless, but it wasn't open all night. And downtown was severely lacking in early-morning havens for commuters. I couldn't hole up in the hotel's restrooms every morning after work, three days a week, for the rest of the summer.

But that was a problem I'd deal with later. Right now I pinned on my proverbial Coward's Badge—waiting until I was certain Daniel had gone—before power walking all the way to the ferry terminal and boarding the *Wenatchee*. Then I collapsed in the first free seat I found, wrapped myself up in my jacket, and promptly fell asleep.

I used to think that was my superpower—being able to fall asleep almost anywhere, anytime. I've always needed a lot of naps to get through the day, probably because I have trouble staying asleep at night. But then my grandfather, a retired Coast Guard detective who shares my napping ability, fell asleep while piloting a boat three years ago. He crashed the boat and messed up his leg. That's when he got diagnosed with narcolepsy.

My grandmother was shocked. She'd always joked that we both had lazy genes and that it didn't come from her side of the family. Grandpa's doctor gave her a list of possible symptoms: Always sleepy. Irresistible and frequent bouts of sleep during the day, sometimes in the middle of working, eating, or conversation. Dream imagery and hallucinations before falling asleep or after waking. Temporary paralysis after waking. Occasionally losing muscle tone and seemingly "passing out" for seconds to minutes immediately after experiencing strong emotions, especially laughter.

Knowing that was all well and good, but there isn't a cure. All you can do is manage it. And if Grandpa could live with narcolepsy for fifty-plus years before it became too bad to handle, then

I figured that *if* I had it too—and maybe I didn't—I had plenty of time to sort it out. It was only sleep, after all. And I wasn't piloting boats or even driving a car. What was the worst that could happen? I'd fall asleep at the hotel registration desk? Hopefully not. I just needed to make sure I had plenty of sleep before and after work.

I'd be fine.

Like now. After sleeping through the half-hour ferry ride across the water, I promptly woke when the boat's melancholy horn blew. We were entering Eagle Harbor.

Home. I'd made it through work, and I'd made it through Daniel.

Sitting across the bay from Seattle, Bainbridge Island is an idyllic community that could be considered the Nantucket of the Pacific Northwest, dense with evergreens on land and sailboats on water. It's a sleepy, laid-back island—nightlife includes a couple of bars and a grocery store that stays open until eleven p.m.—but we get our fair share of photographers and style bloggers who like to use us as a romantic backdrop for pretty pictures. And every day tourists take the ferry over from the city to stroll through the harbor village of Winslow, our downtown area: waterfront seafood restaurants, local wine, art galleries, and a darn good ice cream shop.

There's not much else to see or do here. But if you're lucky enough to live on the coast like we do, you get top-notch views of the harbor and, in the distance, Seattle's skyline.

Those views were not to be underestimated. By the time I disembarked from my ferry and hiked the ten-minute stretch of sidewalk around the harbor, the sun was rising over blue water scattered with sailboats, and it was a welcome sight.

Our waterfront home sat five steps down from the coastal road, through a tidy yard with a greenhouse and a lily-surfaced koi pond with no koi. We used to have a giant white-and-red koi named Clementine in the pond. She was as big as my forearm and lived there since my grandma was a little girl. My grandma took care of her, then my mom, and then me, when I moved in here after Mom died. But Clementine got sluggish after Christmas, and then I found her floating in February. Sometimes koi can live a hundred years, but Clementine only made it to fifty. It was as if she knew Grandma died and didn't want to go on.

Grandpa and I weren't ready to replace her yet. Some people think fish are unemotional pets, but they get to know and trust you. Clementine would not only eat watermelon and orange slices from my hand, but she would circle the pond and stay near me when I'd help Grandma weed the flower beds outside the greenhouse. Fish have personalities; they're just quiet ones. I guess that's why I liked them. I could relate.

Our house has been in our family since it was built in the early twentieth century. Sometime before I was born, my grandfather painted it sky blue and updated the kitchen—except for the black-and-white checkerboard floor that I crossed now to set my keys in a little bowl on the counter.

After calling upstairs and getting no answer, I padded through the kitchen to look for Grandpa out back. Most of the homes around us had been extensively renovated or torn down and replaced with modern million-dollar masterpieces built by eco-architecture firms. Compared to them, our old Craftsman was an eyesore. But on a clear day, we had the same glittering views of the Seattle skyline and Mount Rainier, the same narrow rocky beach for a backyard—which was where I found my grandfather that morning.

"That you, Birdie?" Grandpa Hugo asked as the screen door slammed behind me.

Shells and rocks ground beneath my shoes as I made my way across the tiny beach to a pair of wooden Adirondack chairs. He sat there, watching the sunrise, as he frequently did. "The one and only," I said, taking his outstretched hand as he reached back and guided me around to the empty chair next to him. Below his wire-rim glasses, his smile was sincere, and his cheeks were rosy.

"You managed to avoid murder on the ferry," he said cheerfully.

"Both my own and others."

He was dressed as he always was: crisp white button-down shirt and pressed slacks held up by black suspenders, which he wore because a belt irritated his metal hip after the boating injury that sent him into early retirement from the Coast Guard—and made him dependent upon mild opiates and the footed walking cane that stood in the stand near his chair.

Despite the bum hip, he was healthy and sharp, and he looked good for his age—especially for someone who slept only a few hours at night. Before Grandpa's accident, I assumed his work schedule caused him to be sleepy, because he often worked at night, shutting down offshore smuggling operations around the Sound. After the accident, when he was officially diagnosed with narcolepsy, he said he was too old to change his ways and that the medicine his doctor wanted him to take made him feel weird.

If I had to profile Grandpa Hugo, it would look like this:

Suspect: Hugo Lindberg

Age: 59

Occupation: Former criminal investigator, US Coast Guard, base Seattle

Medical conditions: (1) Narcolepsy. (2) Metal hip and pins in left leg. (3) Nearsighted; wears glasses. (4) Comically afraid of big spiders.

Personality traits: Kind. Excellent with details. Good observer.

Background: Born on Bainbridge Island. Parents were Swedish immigrants. Married Eleanor May Gladstone in 1979. Loves paperback thrillers, model ships, and fishing. Has one close friend. Regrets kicking his pregnant teenage daughter out of the house after a major fight, which kept him and his wife estranged from his

granddaughter for ten years. Never quite got
over his daughter's untimely death.

"I texted you twice to let you know I was safe," I told him.
Once while I was holed up in the hotel bathroom after work and
again when I'd safely made it onto the ferry.

"And I got them. Much appreciated, Birdie."

"You made me breakfast?"

Orange juice, a carafe of hot tea, muesli cereal, and yogurt.
All of it was artfully arranged on an old wooden cable-spool table
between us.

"It was exhausting," he teased. "I could barely get the cereal
box open. Scoot your cup over and let me pour you some berga-
mot tea. Tell me all about your first night. Did you stumble upon
any cases that needed solving?"

Grandpa is nuts about mystery novels and noirs too. He tried
to get my mom interested in whodunits when she was my age,
but the whole teenage pregnancy thing drove a wedge between
them. After she died, when I moved in with my grandparents
here, I inherited some of her old mystery books. Which made
Grandpa happy. I think he was just so relieved to find a shared
interest with ten-year-old me, a virtual stranger with whom he'd
spent little time. Mom had just died, and being able to read and
talk about death, bodies, and murder in a way that was removed
and clinical was strangely comforting. Maybe for both of us.

And now that Grandma was gone, our love of mystery

continued to be common ground. We had an ongoing friendly competition to identify potential unsolved mysteries around the island. Petty theft. Disappearances. Affairs. Why Mrs. Taylor moved her car out of her driveway in the middle of the night. You'd be surprised what you can learn about your neighbors when you stay up late.

"What about that old Hollywood starlet's murder? Tippie Talbot. Any hotel secrets about her?"

"The room she died in was converted into a big suite with the room next door. Completely renovated. Doubt there's anything to find now."

"That's unfortunate. What else?"

"There's a mysterious sewage leak in the hotel garage," I informed him as heavenly steam rose from my mug. "According to the building plans, there isn't a sewage pipe down there. It's coming from an area of the garage that they can't access, and it would cost too much money to investigate fully, because they'd have to close the garage and tear out ceilings and walls. So they keep blindly spraying some sort of industrial-strength liquid rubber until the leak temporarily stops. Apparently, they've done this twice before."

The wind fluttered his dark gray hair. "Sounds unsanitary."

"I caught a whiff of it from the lobby a couple of times," I said, grimacing and shaking my head. "Anyway, that's all I got. Not an interesting case."

"No, it's not." He squinted at the orange sun peeking out from trails of gray clouds covering the sky. "You need a proper summer

mystery. One involving a big downtown corporation and a missing briefcase of money."

"An animal rights group has been protesting our goldfish
rental program, but I don't think that's much of a conundrum." I
took a sip of hot tea, strong and floral, trying to think of anything
else that might be intriguing. "Daniel said cars have been stolen
from the hotel garage and taken on joyrides.'"

"Who's Daniel?"

I hesitated. "Just some guy I work with. The hotel van driver."

"Interesting."

"What is?"

"Nothing. It's funny what you can tell about someone's
thoughts when you pay attention. The way their voice changes.
The way they avoid your eyes."

"I'm not avoiding your eyes." I was. "He's just a boy. It's complicated. I don't want to talk about it."

I shouldn't have mentioned him. I'm not even sure why I did.
If Grandpa knew what I did . . . His mind and spirit were far more
rational and modern than Grandma's had been, but he'd still be disappointed. And—worse—he'd question my ability to make good
decisions for myself. What if Daniel had been a bad person? Ted
Bundy was charming, after all. What if I'd ended up dead in a ditch
or stuffed into someone's refrigerator? It's not as if I hadn't thought
those things myself. But if Grandpa thought them, he would make
me quit the hotel job. Talking him into the idea of me working
the graveyard shift in the city wasn't easy—Aunt Mona had to get

involved, reminding him that I grew up in that neighborhood and that the walk from the hotel to the pedestrian bridge to the ferry terminal was only two blocks on a busy, well-lit, well-patrolled street. But he'd finally caved because he trusted my judgment. He had faith that I'd be mindful of my surroundings, that I'd be cautious—that I wouldn't be lured into a proverbial ice cream truck by a stranger with a fruity rainbow pop.

I was supposed to be smarter than that.

What neither of us took into account was the rush of excitement that came with my newfound freedom. Or my rabid curiosity. Or Daniel's infectious smile.

"Well, I'm sure Mona will get an earful about this Daniel boy. Lord knows you could never talk to your grandmother about these things when she was alive," Grandpa said, wistful.

"Too late now," I said bluntly. "She's gone."

"None of us are ever really gone, sweetheart."

I'd heard that from him a hundred times. My grandmother had been religious. However, Grandpa veered toward angel sightings and UFOs and people communicating with their long-lost Aunt Margie from Topeka. Too much talk radio was probably to blame. He used to listen in his room after midnight while Grandma was sleeping. Sometimes he'd let me stay up with him, reading mystery books and scrolling through my phone while he built model ships at his work desk.

That was the first time I realized how satisfying rebellion could be, even quiet ones.

"Birdie?" Grandpa said. "Did you hear me?"

"Sorry," I said, mentally wiping away my stray thoughts. "What were you saying?"

"Did you want to walk down to the supermarket with me?"

"Think I'll just crash, if that's okay."

"First days are tough. Tomorrow will be better." He touched the flower above my ear, a touch as soft as the wind, and the far-away look in his eye told me that he was thinking of my mother. His daughter. The person who kept us apart and brought us together.

"Look at you, being independent. You're growing up so fast. Too fast, maybe. But you're handling all of this just fine," he said. "Your mother would be so proud of you."

I hoped so.

When Grandpa left to go shopping, I gathered the remains of breakfast and headed up the creaky wooden staircase. The only full bathroom in the house sat at the top of the stairs; my bedroom was next to it. When Grandma died, Grandpa moved his stuff out of the master bedroom and into the spare room, across the landing from mine. That's where all his books and model ships were, and where he slept. And now that no one was on the other side of my bedroom wall, I finally felt as if I had some privacy.

Gray morning light suffused my room, softening the harsh lines of my canopy bed and brightening the wild colors of the paintings lining my walls. Aunt Mona was an artist—a really good one, who had her work sold in Seattle galleries—and she'd painted me a dozen whimsical portraits over the years. Sherlock Holmes. Hercule Poirot. Nick and Nora Charles. Columbo. And Nancy Drew.

She even painted one of my mother. That portrait hung alongside a couple of old photographs near my bedroom vanity set, next to a framed poster of Billie Holiday circa 1946, with her iconic white flower in her hair. That's where I got the idea to wear flowers myself. And now I unpinned the stargazer lily from my hair and set it next to a vase filled with a dozen more before tossing my socks in a laundry hatch that led downstairs to the laundry room—one of the perks of an old home. Then I grabbed the laptop from my desk, where it teetered atop my vintage Smith Corona typewriter, and stretched out on my bed.

Daniel Aoki. I pressed enter in the search field and began scrolling. Not much to see. Nothing in images, just some random guys with the same name. A few social media accounts popped up, and one of them may have been his—profile pic was a poster of Houdini and a brief bio: "Stop asking if I'm okay"—but it was private. I'd have to send a request to the account holder to see it, and no way was I doing that. The only other thing I found was his name listed at a Seattle comic shop for winning some kind of gaming event, but that was three years ago.

Who are you, Daniel Aoki?

And who was I that rainy afternoon in the diner, throwing myself at him like I didn't have a care in the world?

My gaze lit on a wall of bookshelves crammed with mystery novels, their jagged spines like crooked teeth. Most of them were dime-store paperbacks, but I had two complete sets of the entire Nancy Drew series—the original volumes, which used to belong to my mom, with unedited text, in which Nancy was flippant and daring, and the revised 1960s editions with yellow spines, in which Nancy became coolheaded and a little too perfect.

The original ones were the best.

I used to keep my grittier crime novels hidden in the back of my walk-in closet, because good girls weren't supposed to be reading about serial killers and sex and crime. When Grandma passed, I had a small breakdown over those hidden books, because it felt like I'd been keeping secrets from her. Being rebellious, just like my mom had been—at least, that's what I'd imagined she'd think if she ever found them.

Grief causes irrational thoughts.

Including me being convinced that the constant bickering I did with Grandma over the fact that I wanted to attend public school during my senior year may have contributed to her heart attack. Rationally, I knew this wasn't true, but that didn't stop me from reliving our fights inside my head as some kind of personal punishment. That was another reason I needed the job at the hotel. Living in a lonely house of grief for the last few months had begun to feel like a prison I'd never escape.

Latitude affects your attitude.

Scrolling on my laptop, I thought about the ad Daniel had mentioned, which he'd thought I'd seen. Was it still up? If so, how could I find it? My curiosity got the better of me, so I began combing through local blogs and news sites. Nothing online in *The Stranger*, Seattle's local alt-weekly city paper, and the *Seattle Times* classifieds was a bust. I spent almost an hour looking, until sleep was trying to pull me under. Stifling a yawn, I was about to give up and close my laptop when I stumbled upon a local forum for Missed Connections.

The forum contained hundreds of listings over the last week—how many people crossed paths in the city? I was dumbfounded. Most of them were strangers, spotted on public transportation. A few were just begging for kinky hookups. One woman fell for some guy she saw through a restaurant window—just the back of his head, but she knew it was true love.

Then I spotted a listing that sent my slumberous pulse racing:

> *Flower girl in Moonlight Diner.*
> *Tuesday night we talked in a booth by the*
> *window. You had killer eyes and were reading a*
> *detective novel. I showed you some card tricks.*
> *We left together in the rain, but you disappeared.*
> *Can we talk? I can't sleep, thinking about you and*
> *wondering what went wrong.*

I reread it several times before closing my laptop.

And for the remainder of the morning, I lay awake, staring at the ceiling while my thoughts ran in circles, racing the beats of my rebellious heart.

"Fellas, coincidence and fate figure largely in our lives."
—Special Agent Dale Cooper, *Twin Peaks* (1990)

5

Aunt Mona had taken me to Pike Place Market since I was old enough to stroll the tiled waterfront arcade. It was only a few blocks away from the Moonlight Diner, and even now, as we approached the iconic Public Market Center clock in the late afternoon before my third hotel shift, my mind still associated it with pleasure-filled Saturdays: watching fishmongers throw halibut for the delight of tourists; pressing my nose against the window of Beecher's as cheese was made; rubbing the snout of Rachel, the bronze pig at the market's entrance, for good luck. The market's acres of shops spread over multiple floors were a never-ending labyrinth of discoveries waiting to be found.

But this afternoon, I was tagging along while she picked up a check from a stall that sold her *People of Seattle* prints—quirky drawings of quirky residents.

I'd worked another shift at the hotel last night. A Daniel-free shift, as he wasn't scheduled. To be honest, after reading his

Missed Connections ad, I wasn't sure if I was relieved or disappointed that I didn't have to see him. Or what, if anything, I would say when I eventually did. But I thought about it. A lot.

After I'd woken up today, I called into work to check the schedule and found that a staff meeting was being held at seven thirty p.m. to discuss the ongoing sewage cleanup in the hotel garage, so I decided to take the ferry over a little early with Aunt Mona to waste time and perhaps get some advice.

"Okay, 'kay, 'kay. You're telling me that the boy who wrote this *unbelievably* romantic Missed Connections ad is your coworker? Rewind what you just told me," Aunt Mona said, handing me back my phone. Today she was wearing her Oscar Wilde "dandy" outfit: green velvet jacket with tails, tweed waistcoat, oversize neck scarf with twinkling pin, and heeled spats. A tiny top hat was tipped rakishly over one brow, and her wig beneath it might not have been out of place in Victorian England if it weren't a color that was somewhere between lime and shamrock. As she strolled, she tapped the tip of a sparkly cane on the floor as if she were Willy Wonka touring his own chocolate factory.

"Please don't make me say it again," I begged as we passed a movie-worthy gray view of Puget Sound through the dingy restaurant window where Tom Hanks talked to Rob Reiner in *Sleepless in Seattle*.

Aunt Mona blinked eyes trimmed in enormous fake green lashes and dramatic eye shadow. "You're telling me that this is the guy you did the four-leg frolic with in the back seat of a car—"

"Shh!"

"He works with you at the hotel? Holy smoke, Birdie, that's . . ."

"A nightmare?"

"More like destiny," she said, grinning at me like a deranged psychopath. The green lipstick didn't help.

"Don't start with that," I said, shoving my phone in my purse. "Daniel already said something about fate."

"*Daniel,*" she says, shivering dramatically with both shoulders, causing the LED-lit boutonniere pinned to her velvet jacket to blink. "Sounds so sophisticated. I need to see a photo."

"Keep on needing. I don't have one."

"I'm a visual person, *mi corazón*. I cannot give you my blessing until I see how hot he is."

"I'm not asking for your blessing. I'm asking what I should do. He wants to talk about what we did."

"The banging? The horizontal mambo? A little pickle-me, tickle-me?"

"Please stop," I begged, glancing around to make sure no one heard her.

"Stop being your prudish grandmother. She's gone, Birdie. It's okay to live a little."

"Like mother, like daughter, huh?"

Aunt Mona stopped in the middle of the market, hooked her cane on her forearm, and grasped my shoulders with both hands. "Your mother was a goddess. Not a whore. Not a sinner. You know this."

A sudden swell of emotion tightened my throat. I whispered, "I think I made a huge mistake."

"Look. So, you had sex. Big deal. I've told you a million times—virginity isn't something you lose. It's not a missing sock. It's a state of mind."

"It was weird and awkward."

"Because you ran away afterward?"

"No. It's why I ran. It was . . . not like what I expected. It wasn't magical. It wasn't . . . I don't know . . . Disneyland."

"Disneyland?"

"You know. Matterhorn. Churros. Fireworks. The happiest place on earth."

Mona laughed softly. "God, I love you, kid."

"Really?" I said, scowling. "Because it sure seems like you're laughing while I'm trying to spill my guts to you, which is what you're always begging me to do."

"You're absolutely right, darling. Forgive me." She slung an arm around my shoulder, and we strolled together while she talked. "Look. Sure, my first time was magical—"

I'd heard about it. In detail. Many times. I *really* wish I hadn't.

"But since then? *Pfft.* Do you know how much weird sex I've had in my life?"

"Don't want to know."

"Good, because I can't count that high. Sometimes it's good; sometimes it's awkward. Sometimes it's just plain bad. It's never the same. It's like . . ." Her mouth twisted as she searched for the right words. "Okay, think of it this way. You brought up Disneyland. . . . Remember when we went?"

A few months before my mom died. They'd saved money for two years. Ms. Patty from the diner even chipped in. We drove down through Oregon and California, and we couldn't afford to stay in an official park hotel, so we ended up in a motel outside that had roaches. But I didn't care. Those three days inside the park were pure joy.

Aunt Mona continued. "You had a great time. I had a great time. But your mom was miserable."

Huh. I'd forgotten that. She was sick with a chest cold that had developed into bronchitis and sat on benches hacking her lungs up while Mona and I stood in line for rides.

"Disneyland was a miserable experience for her. Maybe another time, when she wasn't sick, it wouldn't have been. And that's pretty much how sex is. Sometimes it's the happiest place on earth, and sometimes it's too crowded, and sometimes there are no fireworks over the castle, and that's something you need to address with the prince, and if he doesn't listen to your complaints, then you need to find a new prince."

"Good grief," I said, checking to see that no one was listening to us.

"If Daniel wants to talk about what happened, then maybe you should talk about it. Or maybe you should talk about other things? What's the worst that could happen? You get embarrassed? Even if it's not *wuv, twue wuv*," she said, quoting *The Princess*

Bride, "you never know what may happen. I mean, it could turn out that he's a really sweet boy whom you cherish as a friend for your entire life, and when he has a kid and dies suddenly, you might find yourself promising to look after that kid and one day giving it advice about another Daniel."

"Circle of life?"

"Circle of fucking life," she says, smiling through green lipstick. "Now, the only payment I ask for the gift of my advice is for you to secretly take a photo of him, so that I can confer my official blessing upon this union, which is my sacred duty as your unofficial godmother."

"Will you wear a Pope outfit?"

She thought about this for a moment. "I could alter my purple nun habit and pair it with a wizard staff."

"Good enough."

"Excellent. Now, the stalls will be packing up soon, so I'm going to fetch my check. You coming with?"

"Meet you downstairs in the usual spot in thirty?"

"Thirty it is." She pointed a gloved hand at me, doing a finger-gun motion, before swishing her dandy butt away to the art stall, cane clicking on the tiled floor.

Inside my head, I filed away everything she said and made my way through the market. A riot of cheerful neon signs greeted me as I rambled through the main level, passing stalls laden with tulips, vegetables, freshly smoked salmon, and Pacific Northwest cherries. I followed a neon arrow down a ramp to the lower levels

under the main arcade. Down here, windowless halls and creaking wooden floors led to an odd array of shops that seemed to
stand still in time while the rest of the world moved on.

One of those shops was always my primary destination when
I came here with Aunt Mona: Get a Clue Mystery Bookshop.
The hand-painted sign featured a magnifying glass and a Sherlock
Holmes deerstalker cap. It hung above a narrow door, the glass
of which was covered in smeared handprints. The middle-aged
owner knew more about mystery and thriller books than anyone
I'd ever met—including Grandpa Hugo, and he knew quite a bit.
I usually enjoyed talking to her, but she wasn't in today. Disap-
pointed, I browsed the overstuffed shelves and ended up buying a
used Raymond Chandler paperback from the shop's dull assistant.

When I left the bookstore, I noticed that some of the lower-
level shops were already closing, and I was about to text Aunt
Mona to tell her I'd meet her upstairs instead of in our usual
spot. But something just down the corridor distracted me: a
glass-encased old-fashioned animatronic fortune-teller machine.
It stood in front of a collection of vaudeville Carter the Great
stage magician posters that lined the front of a wood-paneled
shop front from floor to ceiling.

Pike Place's iconic magic shop.

A fixture in the market, the magic shop was one of the oldest in the country, crammed with novelty magic tricks and
gags—interlocking rings, invisible ink, fake dog poop, signed
photos from famous magicians. It was also where you could

buy a deck of marked cards, and that made me think of Daniel.

I headed toward the fortune-teller machine and peered inside the magic shop's propped-open door. A small group of people were watching the owner give an impromptu magic lesson. I used to love watching these performances when I was younger.

Hold on.

That wasn't the owner.

Daniel's long face turned toward the doorway, and before I could process what was happening, his eyes met mine and widened.

6

Without thinking, I jumped back and hid behind the fortune-teller machine. Why, oh why, had I made the mistake of walking over here?

Don't panic, I told myself. *He probably didn't recognize you.*

So why were people suddenly exiting the store? Was the magic demonstration over?

What were my options here? I could run, but I'd already done that once with him, and look where it got me: working in the same hotel. I considered taking refuge in the bookstore, but they'd shut off their lights already and were flipping over the closed sign.

Crap! Daniel was exiting the magic shop, looking around. No time to escape. How could I look . . . less obvious? Maybe I should get my fortune told by the animatronic machine? Yes. Okay. That was a good reason to be standing here. I rummaged around the bottom of my purse for coins. *Oh God, he's coming over here. . . .*

"Is this a stakeout?"

I glanced up from my purse and tried to act surprised. His dark hair hung loose around his shoulders like it had when I'd first met him in the diner. Since when was I into guys with long hair? Since when did I *know* any guys with long hair? The only one I could think of was Chippy Jones, the old bearded hippie who owned the kite store on Bainbridge Island and rode a two-person bike everywhere. Daniel was no old hippie.

"Oh, it's you," I said, sounding a little touched in the head.

"Hello, Birdie."

I started to reply, but my tongue felt thick in my mouth. A sickly sweat broke over my skin, as if I'd contracted the flu. Or food poisoning. Maybe the dropsy or some sort of milk fever—one of those vague, old-timey conditions.

"I made the joke about stakeouts because of your mystery-book obsession," he explained. "Detectives. Sleuthing. Stakeouts."

He remembered what I'd told him in the diner. Wait. Did he think I was stalking him?

"Not here for a stakeout." I removed my hand from my purse to show him . . . three pennies and some fuzzy lint, which stuck to my palm when I tried to let go of it. "I'm looking for quarters. For this . . . thing," I said, shifting my eyes to the machine.

"Really." He didn't sound convinced. Amused, but not convinced.

"I'm wasting time before the staff meeting. I was in there"—I used my lint-covered, sweaty hand to gesture toward the mystery bookstore—"only they're closing, and I decided . . . I didn't know you were here. I mean, I know you do magic, but I wasn't stalking you. I'm just here for the Great Swami."

"Oh, he's not great. He's just Swami."

"Whatever. I'm not stalking you."

He squinted. "You said that already."

"GD," I swore under my breath.

"GD?"

"Goddammit."

He arched a brow.

"There was a no-swearing rule in my house," I explained, thoroughly embarrassed. "It's just an old habit."

"Ah.

"And I have a perfectly logical reason for being here."

"Me too," he said. "I know the magic store's owners, and they let me do tricks for customers. Sometimes I perform outside the market entrance, next to Rachel the Piggy Bank."

Now I had to look out for Daniel whenever I wanted to come down here to buy a book? Terrific.

"I'm good with misdirection."

"Excuse me?"

"In my street magic. Misdirection," he repeated, holding out a hand and showing me his open palm. "You're looking here, which is why you don't see me taking this." He held up a ring of keys on one finger.

My house keys.

"Hey!" I glanced down at my purse. The front pocket gaped open. "How . . . ?"

"Misdirection," he said with a satisfied smile, offering me my keys back, which I carefully took, not touching his finger.

"Are you a pickpocket or a magician?" I asked.

"A skill is a skill," he said, mouth quirking up on one side. "I like to keep my options open."

I laughed nervously.

"Anyway, I need to practice with bigger groups. That's why I like performing outside the market. My mom would kill me if she knew, so let's keep that our little secret," he said before rethinking his words. "Or, I guess, add it to our ongoing list of secrets."

We looked at each other for a moment, and the air seemed to crackle between us. My chest grew hot. Surely he wouldn't bring up what happened between us here, in public.

I dropped my keys back into my purse and tried to think of a way to escape without looking like a coward. Maybe I could say I was sick. Not a total lie. I sure *felt* sick at the moment.

"You're shedding," Daniel said.

Was this another misdirection? I quickly glanced down at the black slacks I had to wear for work and was startled to feel Daniel's fingers on my hair. His touch sent tingles across my scalp. Then his hand moved back, and he showed me what he'd captured on his palm. "You lost a petal."

"Oh," I said, embarrassed, touching the lily in my hair.

He tilted his hand, and the petal floated to the floor, only to be trampled by a passing blind man and his guide dog.

After an awkward moment, Daniel tapped the glass of the machine. "So, you're in the market for a fortune, are you? Honestly, this guy kind of sucks and is bordering on offensive. Definitely an insult to actual religious gurus. If you want a penny fortune, the Elvis machine inside is way better. Come on. They'll let us in before they close."

He herded me inside the store before I could think of a good excuse to turn him down. The owner was behind the counter, counting bills inside his register till while the last remaining customers dawdled—a father and his young son, who couldn't decide which silly gag to buy.

"We'll only be a second," Daniel called out to the owner as he jogged across the floor toward the Elvis fortune-teller machine. "I've got two quarters, but it takes three."

"I thought you said it was a penny?"

"That's just what they're called, Birdie. Penny fortunes. Like a penny arcade—ever hear of that? Back in ancient times, they were a penny. Got another quarter?"

I wanted to protest, to tell him that I didn't need him to be the old-fashioned, gallant knight who pays for all my stuff. But in the end I gave in—mainly because the indecisive kid behind us had finally settled on fake dog poop, and I didn't want Daniel and me to be the last customers left in the store.

Daniel fed quarters into the coin slot, and Automaton Elvis came to life. He was dressed in white with a red scarf around his neck, and he sang a couple of lines about hound dogs; being built from the waist up, he had no gyrating hips, so you had to suspend your disbelief. After singing, the King informed us that he could see into the future, and I was trying to concentrate on that, and not on Daniel's face—which I could see in the reflection of the glass—because he was watching my reaction. And then it was over, and Elvis was spitting out a preprinted fortune card.

Daniel grabbed the card and read it out loud while we looked at it. "'I see that you will have a chance meeting with a dark stranger who will reveal great secrets to you.'" He waggled his brows and said, "I think Elvis means me."

"Uh-huh," I said, hoping I sounded more sarcastic than flustered.

"'If you collaborate, a bold and dashing adventure will be in your future,'" he continued reading, flicking the card's edge with his fingers. "It's right here in black and white, Birdie. I told you. Good old GD fate. Can't escape it."

Was he making fun of me? I couldn't tell. When he offered me the card, I took it from him and pointed at the text. "It also says, 'But beware of perilous pitfalls that lead to ruin.'"

He read the last lines, "'It takes a level head and determination to survive a run through the gauntlet. In great attempts, it is glorious even to fail, because in conflict you will find common ground together.' See that? *Together*. Elvis is giving us his blessing to seek adventure."

"Didn't Elvis die on the toilet?"

"Touché, Birdie," he said, amused.

Behind us at the counter, I spied the little boy standing on tiptoes to pay for his fake dog poop. "Guess they're closing up, so I better take off," I told Daniel. "I have to go . . ." Where? *Think, think*. But all I could say was, "Home."

"Wait, don't you live on Bainbridge? You have time to take the ferry and then come back before the meeting?"

"How did you know where I lived?"

"Melinda. I tried to catch up with you after work, to see if you needed a lift home or something." He paused, squinting. "I mean, not that I was trying to lure you into my car again. And not that I lured you the first time. I'm not some kind of creepy car pervert. I've never done that before. That was—"

I glanced at the people in the store and whispered, "Let's not discuss that now, please?"

"Sorry."

I cleared my throat and said a little louder, "So, thanks for the, uh, not-a-penny fortune. See you at work."

"Hey, wait! The night's still young," he said, walking backward in front of me as I headed toward the door. "Are you really going back on the ferry? We still have two hours before the staff meeting. Want to go grab dinner? What do you like? Mexican? Chinese? There's an awesome French bistro a couple of blocks away with these amazing hot sandwiches with melted cheese and a poached egg on top—they're super cheap."

"I can't," I said, scrambling for an excuse. "I misspoke earlier. I meant to say that someone is meeting me outside the market, to, um, take me to dinner. You know, before the staff meeting."

"Oh," Daniel said, looking vaguely wounded.

"My aunt Mona," I explained. "She's not really my aunt. She's just a friend of the family. Well, not that my family is big. It's just me and my grandfather now."

"You live with your grandfather?" Daniel shifted to my side and walked with me toward the upstairs ramp.

"He's a retired Coast Guard detective. My mom died when I was ten. My grandmother died this past Christmas."

"Oh, hey, I'm sorry."

I shrugged, trying to appear nonchalant. "My grandma and I had a complicated relationship."

"What about your dad?"

"No idea. Some punk kid she met on a high school field trip to the Pacific Science Center when she was seventeen. I don't think he ever knew he'd knocked up my mom."

"That's something we sort of have in common," he said as we hiked up the ramp. "My dad didn't want to have anything to do with me, so he basically gave my mom a big hunk of cash for an abortion, washed his hands, and said *adios*. My mom used the money to buy a Subaru."

My eyes flicked toward his.

"Yep, *that* Subaru. I inherited it when she got a new car a couple of years ago. Driving it is my private revenge. My father sucks. But whatever. His loss."

We walked together in silence through the dwindling crowds in the main arcade until Daniel tapped my bag. "What did you get at the bookstore? Another mystery book?"

"At a mystery bookstore? Imagine that."

"Who's your favorite detective?" he asked before quickly adding, "I like Jessica Fletcher. I've streamed every episode of *Murder, She*

Wrote. Angela Lansbury is the best. When I was a kid, I had a crush on her."

"On Angela Lansbury?" I said, incredulous.

He struggled to hide a smile. "So hot."

"You're making fun of me."

"I'm totally serious. I like old shows. Anyway, who's your favorite detective?"

He seemed genuinely interested, so I answered. "From fiction, probably Miss Marple or Amelia Peabody. In movies, Nick and Nora Charles from *The Thin Man*."

"*The Thin Man*? That sounds familiar."

"It should. It's just one of the best movies of all time."

"Is that so?" Daniel chuckled, but not in a mean way, so I continued.

"And my favorite TV detective is Columbo," I said. "Hands down."

"The cop in the trench coat? What's the actor's name?"

"Peter Falk. People underestimate him. They think he's just a bumbling idiot, so they let their guard down, and that's how he outsmarts them. He's the kind of detective I'd want to be."

I'd been drawn to mysteries since I was a kid, but I'd be drawn to detectives in particular since my mom died. Detectives were cool, calm, and capable. They were usually loners, helping people from a distance. Because the crime had already been committed, a detective could take the time to be careful and deliberate. They were underdogs that people miscalculated.

"You want to be a cop?" Daniel asked.

"No. I want to be a private investigator, not a police detective. For sure not a Coast Guard detective, like my grandfather. Their investigations are boring, mostly fishery violations and some minor smuggling. I prefer more scandal in my cases."

"A gumshoe, eh?"

"It's one of the reasons I was excited about working at the Cascadia. You know, that Agatha Christie stayed there, and the whole unsolved crime of that actress back in the 1930s, Tippie Talbot. So disappointing that they remodeled her room. If I were the owners, I would have decorated it with her Hollywood memorabilia. I bet old movie buffs would stay there if they played it up. Or crime aficionados. Maybe someone could have found a new clue and solved her murder."

"Like you?"

I laughed, a little flustered. "The thought *did* cross mind. My grandpa wants me to find a good mystery to solve there, but so far I haven't stumbled upon any dead bodies."

"Birdie Lindberg, private eye," he said, grinning at me. "You should be in security at the hotel, not a desk clerk."

Now I was embarrassed that I'd said too much. I glanced around, scouting for an escape route. In the distance, I caught a glimpse of a bobbing yellow beehive. "So . . . anyway. You don't have to stay. I'll just—"

"I know a real-life mystery going on at the hotel."

I stared at him.

"A real one." His eyes were bright and wide. He sniffled, rubbed his nose, and then leaned closer and said, "Have you ever heard of a writer named Raymond Darke?"

Of course I had. Raymond Darke was the most successful thriller writer from Seattle—as in, number one *New York Times* bestselling author, millions of copies sold. Grandpa used to read his books. "I don't really care for legal thrillers," I said. "And his characters are boring."

Daniel's mouth curved into a smile. "But you *do* know who I'm talking about."

"Everyone knows Darke. His books, at least. No one knows the actual writer. The mystery of his true identity is far more interesting than any of the plots in his books."

The official author photos on Darke's book jackets were silhouettes of a fedora-wearing man who never faced the camera. He didn't make public appearances or do anything other than e-mail interviews. No book signings. No nothing. All his books took place in Seattle, and his biography claimed that he lived here, but who really knew?

I paused and gave Daniel a hard look. "What's this got to do with the hotel?"

"What if I told you that Raymond Darke comes into the Cascadia every Tuesday night at seven? He has no luggage. He just goes upstairs for a few minutes, then comes back down and leaves without anyone realizing who he really is or why he's there."

"I'd say that sounds . . . sensational."

"As in good?"

"As in tabloid fodder."

"But what if it's true?" Daniel's face was open and honest. He seemed to believe what he was saying. Excitement flashed behind his dark eyes.

"That would be a national headline. Every magazine and newspaper in the country would jump at a chance to investigate Darke's identity if it were true."

"It is."

"How do you know it's Raymond Darke?"

He shoved both hands into his pockets and gave me a slow shrug. "I have my methods. And I can prove it to you. I've been trying to figure out why he comes to the hotel for a couple of weeks now. But if you're interested, maybe we can team up."

"Team up?"

"Just as friends," he cautioned. "Less than friends—coworkers."

What did he mean by that? My emotions were all over the place. A real mystery in the hotel? Involving a famous writer? It was almost too good to be true.

"Forget everything I said before. There's no need to talk about what happened between us," he said. "You were right. We'll leave the past in the past, as you suggested. Onward and upward."

"Um . . ." I didn't know what to say. Shouldn't I be happier about this? It's what I told him I wanted. I should be relieved.

He was doing that walking-backward thing again, heading outside and leaving me at the market entrance. "Just think about it. If you want to know more, hit me up at work tonight. Maybe we can investigate together and figure out what he's doing at the hotel every week. Maybe it's something nefarious and scintillating," he said, waggling his brows comically.

Before I could answer, a female Oscar Wilde stepped to my side. "Nefarious and scintillating? My favorite subjects."

Daniel blinked.

"Uh, this is my aunt Mona," I said.

"The aunt who's not an aunt?" Daniel said.

"More like fairy godmother," Aunt Mona said, extending a gloved hand. "Ramona Rivera. You can call me Mona. And you are . . . ?"

"Daniel Aoki," he said, shaking her hand vigorously. "I work with Birdie at the Cascadia."

"Oh, *yes*," she said, practically purring. "I've heard about you."

If there were an all-powerful being that ruled the universe, it would have surely heard my desperate prayer to please, oh please, have mercy and strike me down. I needed a natural disaster and pronto—earthquake, tornado, tsunami. Anything.

Unfortunately, no one answered my prayers. I was still standing and deeply mortified.

Daniel, however, was elated by this revelation. I mean, he completely *lit up*. Just for one lightning flash of a second. Then he almost looked embarrassed. Then . . . nothing. He scratched his chin absently and darted a glance at me under the cover of dark lashes.

Right. I got snippy with him about telling Joseph at work about us. Guess I told someone too. Yikes. Was he mad? I couldn't tell.

He told Mona, "I really dig your entire Mad Hatter look."

She primped her green hair, pleased. "Why, thank you. I created it myself."

"Well," I said, overloud, squelching any further conversation. "We'd better be on our way."

"Pshaw!" she said. "We have all the time in the—"

"*We'd better be on our way,*" I repeated, elbowing her in the ribs.

"It's cool," Daniel said. "I probably should go too. It was nice to meet you, though."

"The pleasure was all mine," she said dramatically.

He walked backward and called out to me, "Think about what I said and let me know. Remember what Elvis told you."

"Right. Fate." I tried for a casual laugh, but it came out sounding nervous.

"Maybe I was wrong about fate. See you at work," he said as he jogged away, leaving me alone with Aunt Mona.

"Oh, *my*," she murmured, watching him go. "And just what did the boy say that you are supposed to be thinking about, hmm?"

I shook my head. "Not a date, so don't get your hopes up."

"My hopes are always up, darling," she said. "And by the way . . ." She made a sign in the air and set a reverent hand on my head. "Blessing conferred."

7

The hotel staff meeting was boring and unnecessary. I spent most of it trying not to think about Daniel and what happened at the market, but it was difficult, because his eyes kept flicking toward mine from across the break room, and every time our gazes met, my pulse went a little erratic and my heart became a trapped rabbit, pounding on my ribs and begging to be set free.

Stupid, silly rabbit.

When our shift started, I was relieved to throw myself into work and was promptly inundated with late-night guest requests. One of them involved discussing a luggage issue outside the entrance with Joseph, which was completely awkward, because now he wouldn't look me in the eye, and that made me feel guilty . . . and I wondered just how much Daniel had told him. I thought about the expression on Daniel's face after Aunt Mona had opened her big mouth—*I've heard about you*—and then only a few moments later how he said that maybe he was wrong about fate. Did that mean he only wanted to be friends? Was that possible, after what we'd done?

Apart from me obsessing over interpreting Daniel's emotions, nothing else notable happened for the first part of the night, and when a lull came, I skipped my ten-minute break after feeding five unrented goldfish at midnight and instead used it to search archived guest ledgers.

I needed to see if Daniel's story about Raymond Darke coming into the hotel was plausible, so I searched records from this past Tuesday at seven p.m.

Huh. There was a check-in around that time, at 6:55. Not Raymond Darke, but a listing for "A. Ivanov." In fact, when I went farther back in the archives, this Ivanov appeared twice before, both times on Tuesday nights at 6:55 p.m. And last month, the same thing. And again, farther back, in the late winter.

His Tuesday-night check-ins were brief. He never stayed the night, but instead checked back out within the hour. A few of his stays were only fifteen minutes long.

Interesting. *Very* interesting.

I pulled up a web browser and googled A. Ivanov to find . . . everything. And nothing. It could be any number of students. An athlete. A dead painter. Several doctors. Or a whole lot of Russians. Without a first name, it was impossible to narrow anything down.

I scanned the information we had on him in the system. The room reservation was made over the phone every Sunday. The room number was requested—the same room each time, on the fifth floor. Our VIP floor, usually reserved for Emerald Service Loyalty Program members.

In our system, the man's address was listed as being in San Francisco. I googled that, and when the pinpoint on the map popped onto my computer screen, I stilled.

The company that owned the Cascadia was Seattle-based, but I remembered from my training that they had invested in two other hotels: one in Portland and one in San Francisco.

Mr. A. Ivanov's address? It was the same address as our San Francisco hotel.

If Daniel hadn't insisted this person was Raymond Darke and I'd stumbled upon this on my own, I'd have guessed this Ivanov was someone from hotel management, making routine trips to other hotels for one reason or another—perhaps one of those "secret shopper" types that companies hire to test their customer service.

And maybe he was.

Or maybe Daniel was onto something.

Could it really be? If so, it was monumental. Maybe not a 1938 unsolved murder, but Tippie Talbot was long forgotten and Raymond Darke was very much not. He was a celebrity of the book world. And he might be walking right under our noses every week.

A tiny thrill zinged through me. Ah, the intoxicating lure of a juicy mystery. Clues beckoned, and I was a weak, weak girl.

A couple of hours later, I was still daydreaming about possibilities while heading across the lobby when Daniel appeared from nowhere and briefly fell into step at my side. "I heard you earlier helping that lady who wanted to trade rooms. You did a good job keeping her calm."

A clean tea tree and mint scent wafted from his hair as he loosely tied it up, and for one kaleidoscopic moment, I was transported back into his car, and my hands were in his hair, and he was kissing me into a wobbly, weak pulp.

Terrified he might somehow know what I was thinking, I quickly said, "Are you spying on me now?"

"I can't help what I hear," he said, tapping his ear as we stopped in front of Octavia the Octopus. She was hiding inside her main cave tonight, but if you looked closely, you could see her red arms and white suckers. If you *pretended* to look closely, you could watch Daniel's reflection in the tank while he remained unaware.

"Besides," he said. "You spied on me at the magic shop."

"That wasn't spying."

"Stalking."

"Coincidence-ing."

He laughed. "That's not a real thing."

"It is when my favorite bookstore just so happens to be near your magic shop."

"How long have you been going there?"

"Years and years," I said, still watching his reflection in the tank's soft glow. "I used to live in the city."

"Right, right," he said, pressing the tip of his finger against the glass to leave a pale fingerprint that quickly faded. "You mentioned that in the diner. Well, I've been going to the magic shop since I was in diapers."

I snorted a soft laugh. "Is this a competition?"

"Don't you think it's weird that we've both been walking in that same corridor forever, maybe a few feet from each other? Maybe we've even seen each other before and just don't remember."

"Or maybe, as I said, it's merely coincidence. I thought you said you'd changed your mind about fate?"

"Yep, I did, didn't I?"

"You did."

"Must have meant it, then. I always say what I mean. What you see is what you get. Nothing coy here. No beating around bushes," he said, trailing a finger across the glass and stopping in front of my staring eyes. "I mean, since you're Detective Birdie Lindberg, you've probably figured that out already."

Was he teasing me? It felt like he was, because my frightened-rabbit heart began wailing on my ribs again. I took a risk and glanced at his face, but his eyes were hooded.

He cleared his throat and said, "So . . . have you thought any about my mystery proposal?"

"I have," I said, trying not to sound too eager. "I need to know why you think this man is Raymond Darke."

"You searched for him in the reservation system?"

"Of course."

His look of satisfaction was annoying. "Thought you might. Does that mean we're sleuthing partners?"

"Tell me what you know first."

"Nope." He shook his head, a smile behind his eyes. "Agree to solve the crime with me. Then I'll tell you."

"What makes you think a crime was committed?"

"Wouldn't you like to know?"

Yes, I very much would! A thousand brain cells were coming to life in my head, flicking on like a string of Christmas lights, eager and curious.

But all he said was, "I'll let you sleep on it. I'm off tomorrow, but we work together the next shift. You can tell me then. Better yet, let me see your phone."

"Um, I don't think so," I huffed.

"Fine. Give me your hand."

"Hey—"

"May I?" He used his teeth to remove the cap of a marker and tugged my fingers toward him, scrawling a string of digits onto my palm while he bit down on the marker cap. "There. Now you can text me."

"If this doesn't wash off, I'm going to strangle you. Is this permanent?"

"Nothing's permanent, Birdie. Ask Mr. Kenneth to show you security footage from the elevators last Tuesday from 7:00 to 7:05 p.m. Look for a white guy with dark glasses and a baseball cap. He carries a shopping bag." Daniel dramatically replaced the marker cap, hammering it down with the heel of his palm, and headed toward the hotel entrance. "Text me. Any day, anytime. Or don't. It's up to you. Maybe you just like to watch detectives solve crimes on TV. Maybe you aren't interested in solving one yourself."

"That's not going to work."

"No?" he called back.

Probably not.

I shuffled to the registration desk and stood there for several moments, staring at the marker on my palm and watching the front doors at the hotel entrance to make sure he wasn't coming back. Then, when the lobby was empty, I stealthily slipped back into the employee wing and made my way to the security room.

It was at the end of the back hallway, past the break room and managerial offices. After checking to ensure that no one was following me, I peered through the open security door and spotted Mr. Kenneth lounging in his chair, feet kicked up.

"Hey, hey," he said jovially, waving me inside. "What can I do for you?"

"I was wondering if you could pull up some footage for me?"

"With pleasure." He pushed a ham sandwich to one side of his workspace. "Date, time, camera location."

I relayed Daniel's suggestion.

"Elevators . . . Give me a second here. System is slow. Ah, here we are," he said. "This is time elapsed, so let me know when you want me to pause it or slow down. Seen something suspicious?"

"A guest complained that her shopping bag was stolen by

another guest," I said, proud of myself for thinking on my feet. And Mr. Kenneth's unsurprised, slow nod made me think that this kind of thing happened often enough. I bent down to watch the footage rolling on the computer. It was a split screen that showed the interiors of both elevators. One went up and down twice, ferrying guests from the upper levels. The other was empty and still. I looked at each face, but none matched the description Daniel had given me. Until—

"There!" I said.

"Him?" Mr. Kenneth paused the screen and blew it up. "That your man?"

"That's him, all right." Sunglasses. Blue baseball cap. Middle-aged and white. A little portly, reddish nose and cheeks. And he was carrying a striped shopping bag.

I stared at the screen for several seconds, trying to match up the silhouette in the photo on Raymond Darke's book jackets, wondering if this truly was the famous author.

"I've seen him before," Mr. Kenneth said, squinting at the screen. "You know, I think Aoki asked me to look up some foot-age of him."

Uh-oh.

"Might be the same guest?" I said.

"You think this man here stole the bag?"

"Actually, no," I said, trying to invent an excuse on the spot. "The guest who was complaining said it was, uh, a Macy's bag. That's not it."

"Nope. Macy's doesn't have stripes. And this one here looks plastic. Like it's from a bookstore, or something."

"Ah. False alarm," I told him.

But inside my head, all the gears began turning.

Looked like we had an honest-to-God mystery on our hands.

So what was I going to do about it?

8

I hoped to see Daniel in the break room after my shift ended, but he wasn't there. After wasting as much time as I could without people in the break room starting to question why I was hanging around, I headed back to the lobby and made small talk with the incoming desk clerk about tasks that needed to be done. Daniel was still nowhere to be seen, and the clerk asked me to take some spare uniforms to housekeeping that had been stashed under the registration desk, so I went downstairs to the laundry room. They were still in the middle of shift change, so I sat at the end of a big folding table and waited for someone to log in what I'd brought. I waited so long, I dozed off.

For a while. A housekeeper woke me up, which was embarrassing.

It probably had nothing to do with narcolepsy. I was just exhausted, getting used to working nights; it could have happened to anyone. So I told myself not to obsess about it.

But because I'd fallen asleep, I missed both Daniel and the first ferry and was forced to wait for another. By the time I got back to the island and walked home from the terminal, it was well past seven a.m.

As I headed down the steps toward our front door, I spotted Grandpa in the greenhouse . . . and someone else. He waved me inside, a blurry figure behind rain-spattered glass. I hesitated before changing course. Humid air and compost filled my lungs as the rickety door slammed shut behind me.

Grandpa cradled a small tomato plant connected to a clump of dark soil. Next to him was his longtime friend, a retired Seattle police officer named Roger Cassidy, known simply as Cass. He was tall and willowy, and a good decade older than Grandpa, his once bright ginger hair now pale. He also had a prosthetic hand, after losing his before I was born—he was shot in the line of duty.

"Birdie," he said, smiling broadly.

"Hi, Cass. Didn't expect to see you here so early." He lived alone on the other side of the island in a small house that faced Bremerton. He'd never married or owned any pets. I sometimes wondered if he was lonely. Ever since my grandmother passed, Grandpa and Cass had been spending more time together. It was as if her death had broken an invisible barrier around our house, and now half the town was knocking on our door, checking in to see if we were managing.

"I was picking up coffee downtown and thought I'd drop some off for Hugo, found him out here a few minutes ago." He raised a paper coffee cup. "Just back from your new job?"

"Indeed, I am." I moved Grandpa's metal walking cane a few inches so that he wouldn't knock it over. I'd texted him earlier this morning from the hotel, so that he wouldn't worry, but he never answered. "Sorry I'm late. I missed the first ferry."

"And you're mizzled," he said, using his own slang for the misting of rain clinging to my hair and clothes.

"I'm always mizzled. What are you doing out here?"

"Staking the Marnero tomatoes," he said, brushing dirt off his gardening gloves. "Your grandmother would have a fit if she knew I'd neglected her plants."

My grandmother had loved to cook and had spent half her days out here, growing herbs and vegetables and a few orchids. Before she'd married my grandfather and had my mother, she'd done missionary work in East Africa and Bolivia, and she'd said those trips awakened her interest in cooking new things. Curries. Fried breads. Fragrant rice dishes.

When she was alive, especially over the last couple of years, all we did was fight. But now that she was gone, all I could remember were good things. It was as if my mind were intent on making me regret not appreciating her more when she was alive. The same thing happened when my mom died. Anyway, I guess that's why I'd avoided coming out here the last few months, to avoid thinking about it too much. And I guess Grandpa had too. A lot of her plants were dead. At least the orchids were blooming.

"Any reason why you were late?" Grandpa asked.

"I just . . . lost track of time."

He didn't ask why, so I didn't elaborate.

"Anything interesting happen at work?" Cass asked. "That's the hotel where that starlet died. What was her name?"

"Tippie Talbot," I said.

"She was only twenty," Grandpa added. "Did one picture with Cary Grant, I think. Birdie says her room was torn down. Any other animal rights protests?" he asked, briefly filling Cass in on the octopus and goldfish scandal.

"No protests. No sewage main breaks. It was super boring tonight. I'm not even sure why they need an auditor, to be honest. It's pretty much all automated. A monkey could run the program."

"Those are the best jobs," Grandpa said, eyes crinkling at the corners. "No stress. No responsibility. Enjoy it while you can. One day you'll be wishing you were back there, doing monkey work."

"Ooo-ooo, ahh-ahh," I hooted, doing my best monkey imitation.

They laughed, and Grandpa began rolling up the chicken wire he'd been using around the tomato plants. "Actually," I said, "something interesting *did* happen today. I heard some gossip about Raymond Darke."

Cass perked up. "The writer? Doesn't he write the stuff you read, Hugo? Thrillers?"

"What gossip?" Grandpa asked.

"Someone I work with claims Darke checks into our hotel every week for an hour."

Grandpa pushed up his glasses, leaving a streak of dirt on his nose. "You're joking."

"I'm not. Hold still." I used my thumb to wipe away the smudge. "I combed through the hotel's records, and someone named Ivanov checks in every week. Same room." I told them about the home address being the same as our sister hotel in San Francisco and about the man with the baseball cap in the elevator.

"Very odd," Cass murmured. "But why does your coworker think it's Darke? Every journalist in Seattle would sell their left foot for a chance to reveal the man behind the books."

"Daniel says—"

"Daniel," Grandpa repeated. "That's the boy you mentioned before? You two are becoming fast friends, huh? Mona texted me last night. Said she met him . . ."

Ugh. "She did."

Cass laughed. "I know that look. Hugo, stop pestering her."

Grandpa held up his hands in surrender. "Not pestering. Continue, Birdie. Continue."

"There isn't much left to tell you. Daniel claims to have proof it's Darke. He just can't figure out why he's checking into the hotel. He wants me to help him figure out why."

Grandpa nodded. "I see. He knows you're a mystery hound, then?"

"Yes."

He shared a conspiratorial look with Cass that I ignored. Then he shoved the roll of chicken wire underneath a potting table. "You know, it's strange you bring this up, because just last night they were talking about Darke on *Rainier Time*."

His favorite local radio show, which ran late at night.

"A listener called in, talking about the detective in Darke's books—"

"Paul Parker," I said. "Stupidest detective name ever."

"Like it or not, it's a million-dollar name for Darke," Grandpa said with a smile. "Anyway, the listener was talking about how Darke's detective is a fan of opera music and that all the book titles are based on opera names. They say writers usually write what they know. I would be greatly surprised if Mr. Darke didn't have a real-life obsession with opera. I think I even remember reading an interview with him—he almost never gives them, you know."

I made air circles with my hand, hurrying him along. "And?"

"What's that on your palm?"

"Looks like a phone number," Cass said.

I scrubbed a thumb over the ink, feeling my cheeks warm.

"Wouldn't be from your friend Daniel, would it?" Grandpa asked.

"It's just the manager's number," I lied. "You were saying about this Darke interview?"

"Oh, right. I was going to call into the show about it, but I wasn't a hundred percent sure, and before I could look for the magazine, they were already talking about something else. But I seem to remember Darke mentioning in this interview that he collects opera records. Actual records, like they used to make."

They still did. Lots of people collected vinyl, and some records were worth a lot of money.

If Darke collected records, then it stood to reason he browsed vinyl shops in Seattle. I wondered how many of those there were. I knew of at least one in Pike Place, but I didn't recall seeing any opera records there. Besides, if a man was trying to keep a low profile, he probably wasn't browsing in a place that was so busy and filled with tourists. Maybe a smaller store with less foot traffic. A store that employed someone who shared his passion for music.

Inside my head, I couldn't resist typing up a suspect profile for Darke:

Suspect: Raymond Darke

Age: Early fifties?

Occupation: Mystery author

Education: Graduated from the University of Washington (according to his public biography)

Physical description: Caucasian. Slightly overweight. Possible rosacea? (Red nose)

Personality traits: Wealthy. Famous. Desire to stay out of the public eye; values privacy. Wears blue baseball cap and sunglasses in public . . . to hide his identity?

Other details: Books show a familiarity with
legal procedure. Opera fan. Vinyl record
collector. (Further investigation required . . .
with Daniel?)

"Does any of that help?" Grandpa asked.

"Possibly. I'll do some snooping. But right now I'm going to
get some sleep."

"I'll be curious to know what you find," Cass added.

Grandpa gave me an approving nod. "This is an excellent summer mystery you've found, Birdie. Much better than the toxic
leaking sewage pipe—and probably better for your health."

Funny, but it felt twice as risky.

9

Daniel's phone number on my hand didn't wash off with soap. I had to tear the bathroom apart, hunting down rubbing alcohol, to remove the ink—and even then, the numbers were still faintly visible when I woke the next afternoon. That irritated me. I thought about using those numbers to text Daniel a piece of my mind about his tattooing them on my hand, but I decided to wait until I saw him at work, where I could also tell him about Darke and the opera record lead. But when I got to the hotel, I realized it was Daniel's day off. I wasn't sure if I was irritated or disappointed.

Maybe a little of both.

Unlike the previous night, the hotel wasn't busy at all. Two of the staff called in sick, but Melinda seemed too tired to care. Maybe pregnancy was wearing her down. Or maybe it was Chuck, who insisted on telling everyone on staff some stupid dirty joke, which was bad enough, but he kept getting the punch line wrong.

I just ignored him and read my emergency purse book behind the desk in a desperate attempt to pass the time and stay awake.

When the night finally ended and the shift change came, I was exhausted from boredom and starving for hot food. After swapping out the Cascadia employee blazer for my favorite navy gabardine trench coat, I headed down the marble lobby floor and exited the hotel.

Chilly night air was wrapped in a light fog that had rolled in from the bay; it smelled of brine and clung to the tops of buildings and streetlights like smoky halos. A light drizzle was starting, so I tugged up the buttoned-on hood of my coat and scanned the street. *Be aware of your environment*, Grandpa always warned me. First Avenue was quiet, only a few cars and a street cleaner. I spotted a familiar elderly homeless man who Joseph said was friendly, and under a fog-ringed streetlight, perched on a newspaper rack like a raven, I spotted someone else.

Daniel?

I blinked, but he was still there, smiling beneath a black hoodie. I couldn't trust that. Maybe I'd fallen asleep in the employee break room and this was just a mirage. I sneaked a look at my hand and flexed my fingers. One, two, three, four, five—

Not a dream.

"Hello, Birdie," he called.

"What are you doing out here?" I called back. "You're not on the schedule."

He jumped from the newspaper rack, landing gracefully on

black Converse low-tops, and walked over to me. "I was running an errand."

At four thirty in the morning?

"And I thought you might want company on your way to the ferry, what with all the crazy kooks you could encounter out here at this time of day," he said. "Are you mad? If you don't want me here, tell me to leave and I'll go. I'm only realizing just now that I could be perceived as one of said kooks."

"*Are* you a kook?"

"A good-intentioned kook?" he said, shrugging slowly with his palms upward. "A lovable kook? Definitely not a chain-saw-wielding maniac."

"That's probably what a chain-saw-wielding maniac would say."

"Touché, Birdie," he said, snapping his fingers as if he hadn't thought of that. "If you'd rather not risk it, I totally understand."

I looked at him, then glanced at the vehicles parked by the curb. "I'm not getting in your car again."

"My car isn't even parked here. Come on. Let me walk you to the ferry."

"It doesn't run for another hour."

"Then where were you headed?"

I hesitated, eyes shifting down the block. "Um . . ."

"Oh!" He slapped his hand against his forehead. "Duh. Moonlight, right? Don't look at me like that. It's just logical. You told me you lived above it when you were a kid, and it's the only thing open around here this early besides the Murder 7-Eleven on Pike and Third."

That stretch of Third Avenue was off-limits, according to my grandpa. Too many shootings. And stabbings. Though, strangely, it might not be as bad as Hatchet 7-Eleven, south of the city, for reasons easy to surmise.

"That's why I go to the diner when I don't want to head straight home after work," he continued. "Coffee sounds *pretty* fucking good right now."

How could I get out of this? Did I *want* to get out of it? My hands were getting sweaty again, which was some kind of bizarre medical miracle, because it was downright cold out here. I busied myself, cinching the belt of my coat tighter around my waist.

On one hand, going to the diner with him could be weird because of what happened the first time we were there together. On the other hand, I really wanted to talk to him about Raymond Darke.

On the third hand, somewhere inside I was inexplicably happy to see Daniel, and maybe that was a problem, because now I was back to hand number one.

"Come on," he said with a gentle smile. "Let's have late-night breakfast together. Completely chill. Just two coworkers hanging out who've definitely never been handsy with each other."

"Oh my God," I whispered as heat radiated across my chest.

"We can even go dutch to keep everything nice and equal." He tilted his hooded head to catch my eyes, and the expression on his face was kind and good-natured. "Besides, we should talk about you-know-who and our investigation."

"Which I haven't agreed to."

"More reason to talk. What do you say?"

I glanced up and down the block before answering. "All right. Just breakfast. Then I need to get to the ferry. My grandfather will be expecting me. His best friend was a cop, and if I'm even a minute late, he'll have half the Seattle PD looking for me."

He squinted with one eye. "I *think* I should be offended that you'd feel the need to tell me that, but hey. If I were a girl, I'd probably be saying the same thing. You deal with shit I don't, so I get it. And you can leave whenever you want or tell me to get lost, and I'll skedaddle."

"Skedaddle?"

"Didn't I tell you? I'm a lovable kook *and* a great skedaddler. Maybe the best."

"Is that so?"

"You should see my trophies."

"Do they say Top Award for Best Skedaddler?"

"A few of them. Some say Ultimate Skedaddling Champion of the Universe, but, you know, I don't enjoy bragging."

"Seems exactly what you enjoy doing."

He laughed and waved me to his side.

We strolled down the sidewalk together, the soles of our shoes slapping against rain-slicked concrete. The city was impossibly empty, a sleeping giant; we were just Lilliputians, tiptoeing around its borders.

"How did you get here?" I asked.

"I drove." His hands were shoved deep into the pockets of his jeans, elbows locked. Head buried in his hoodie. I could see only snatches of his face as he talked. "I don't park my car in the hotel garage. My mom is friends with someone who works for Diamond Parking, so I get a free reserved space at the garage behind . . . well, you know. Where we went before."

"Oh," I said, hoping he didn't hear the creak in my voice. "Uh, I thought employee parking was free at the hotel."

"It is, but if you'd seen the things I'd seen down there—rats, roaches. The constant threat of raw sewage. Oh, and not to mention that the part of the garage where they make us park is a safety hazard. A support is damaged. One day an earthquake's going to hit and the whole thing will cave in."

"Are you serious?"

"I'm not taking a chance. Plus, it smells like piss under there."

"Doesn't half of downtown?"

He laughed. "You are not wrong, Birdie. Old piss and seagull shit. *Eau de Seattle.*"

An ambulance blared in the distance as we crossed the street and headed toward the diner's neon moon. Through the windows, the Moonlight didn't look busy exactly, but it wasn't empty, either. Daniel reached over my shoulder to get the door, holding it open for me, and then we stepped inside.

Old Motown music played on the jukebox in the corner as I quickly scanned the restaurant. Two cops sat at the counter, drinking coffee. A couple who looked as if they were on the verge of a hangover scarfed down pancakes in a booth in the corner. Three other tables were occupied, and I could see the cook in a cloud of steam beyond the pass-through window, where a single order slip hung from a clip. No one I knew was working this morning.

"Hey, our booth is open," Daniel said, tugging his hood off. Static electricity made his glossy black hair stick to his jacket until he freed it and pulled it around his shoulder.

Our booth? That was *my* booth.

He looked at my face and tugged his ear absently. "Places like this with a lot of background noise and terrible acoustics make it harder for me to hear. Everything gets jumbled, especially at tables out in the open. I'd rather sit at a booth where it's more private. Is that cool?"

I nodded and slid into one side, then stuck my nose in a menu that had been propped between the window and a napkin holder. A few seconds into my browsing, Daniel's finger hooked around the top of my menu. He pulled it down slowly until he could see my face. "You know what you should have?"

"Endless hash browns?" They were the cheapest and best thing here.

"And pie."

I made a face. "It's not even five in the morning."

"*Au contraire, mon ami,*" Daniel said, slinging his arm onto the back of the vinyl seat. "It's always pie time somewhere. And I'm not sure if you knew this, but this diner makes the best pie in the entire city."

I did know that. It was my mom's favorite. She ate Moonlight pie almost every day. The first time I came back here after she died and I moved to Bainbridge, I ate so many slices, I vomited in the restroom. I guess that's why I'd never eaten it since. Sometimes it felt as if grief were a tightrope, and I spent half of my time trying to stay balanced; I never fell off, but I also never made it to the other side.

Daniel pointed to the Pie of the Day chalkboard and read aloud, "'PUT A BING ON IT, featuring a mixture of Bing and Rainier cherries, topped with brown-sugar crumble and a ring of caramel.'" He kissed his fingers, chef-style. "Did you know they have a freakin' commercial pie warmer behind the counter?"

I did. When I was a kid, I'd helped Ms. Patty fill it up on rainy days. She always said it was a sin to serve apple pie cold.

"Do it, Birdie," he said. "I'm going to. Breakfast pie is the best pie. It's GD terrific."

"Am I ever going to live 'GD' down?" I mumbled.

"Never. I'm using it whenever possible. It's goddamn adorable."

A college-aged server walked up to our table and paused to look at us. "Oh, it's you two again," she said, sticking a pencil over her ear into strawberry-red dyed hair. Her name tag officially identified her as Shonda, but an added sticker above that read: CAP'N CRUNCH. "Gonna run out on me like last time?"

I wanted to melt into my seat and slide under the table.

Daniel just grinned at her. "Shonda, oh, Shonda. The Moonlight's best server—nay! The best server in all of Seattle. You know that was just a mistake. Have I not been coming here for months? Am I not your favorite customer?"

"Anyone who tips me correctly is my favorite customer," she deadpanned.

He laughed. "Okay, but last month *was* a mistake, and I paid up, remember?"

"I remember," she said. "Lovers' quarrels make people crazy, I suppose."

"Nah. We're just coworkers," Daniel said quickly. "We aren't assholes, promise," he said, lifting his chin toward the Polaroids of Moonlight criminals.

She stared at him, one hand folded on her hip.

"Look. We're good for it." He pulled out a crumpled twenty-dollar bill from his pocket, flattened it, and set it by his napkin. "I'll have a slice of Put a Bing on It and coffee. Extra cream. Your tip will be the stuff of legends."

The server gave him a long-suffering sigh before looking toward me. Could she tell I was mortified? Did she know what we did last month? "I swear I know you from somewhere else," she said, squinting at my face. "Oh, wait. Have I seen you in here talking to Ms. Patty?"

I nodded. "I grew up in one of the apartments upstairs. She babysat me a lot."

"Oh," the server said. "You're the kid. Dovie."

"Birdie."

"Sorry about your mom. Ms. Patty said she was like a daughter."

"Thanks," I said. Condolences made me uncomfortable, so I blindly stared at the menu and ordered without thinking. I was relieved when she left.

"Thanks for covering," I mumbled to Daniel.

"It's fine," Daniel reassured me. "You okay? You sort of clammed up when she brought up your mother."

"I guess I just get tired of everyone feeling sorry for me. Death is sort of personal. Talking about it so casually with strangers, like, you know—hey, it's a scorcher out there, and by the way, sorry to hear about that person dying—it can be . . . exhausting."

"Totally get that."

"And, you know, it's been ten years since my mom died, and I feel like it shouldn't bother me as much as it does sometimes."

"But your grandmother died how long ago? Six months?"

"Give or take. I should be a pro at condolences by now, huh?" I said, trying to lighten the mood.

"I don't think anyone masters them," he said with a soft smile that was strangely comforting. "And they're always given with a touch of pity, which is the worst."

I nodded, a little surprised he got it. Then I remembered the social media account matching his name online, and the one-line bio that accompanied it, *Stop asking if I'm okay.* Maybe it was more than just generic teenage angst. I hesitated and then asked, "Has someone close to you . . . ?"

He shook his head. "Nah. I just hate people feeling sorry for me. It makes me feel weak."

Oh. I guess he was talking about his ear, but he didn't seem to want to keep talking about it, so I just nodded and gazed out the rain-spattered window. Moving headlights created blurry trails up and down the street.

"I wasn't running an errand."

I flicked my eyes toward Daniel. "Excuse me?"

"I lied," he said, rearranging his silverware. "I came all the way up here to see you. Not in a stalker way. I just . . . I don't know. I don't know," he repeated.

"Oh," I said stupidly. Part of me was panicked and thinking: *Does he want to have the Talk? He agreed it would be weird to talk about it here.* Yet I was also thinking: *He came here on his day off to see me?* And a dozen heart-shaped bubbles filled my head. Maybe he just wanted to talk about Raymond Darke. If so, why was he acting so flustered?

And now that was exactly how I felt. So I just asked, "Where do you live?"

He crossed his arms and rested them on the edge of the table, leaning forward. "A couple of blocks from Alki Beach in West Seattle. I grew up across town, just east of the International District. Graduated from Garfield last year."

"That's a big high school." Their football team was always on the local news. Jimi Hendrix went there. And Quincy Jones. If my mother had never died, and we'd continued to live in this building, it would have been my high school.

"Did you like it?"

He shrugged. "It was fine. I liked our old neighborhood. A lot of my cousins lived there. But we left after graduation, when my mom decided to move into the Nest."

"I don't know what that is."

He groaned. "Cohousing. It's, like, this entire block of private land with twenty families. They each live in separate houses or condos, but there's a common house in the center, and that's where all the residents meet and make decisions. It's some Danish concept from the 1970s. A lot of old hippies live there, but they're trying to be 'diverse'"—he made air quotes with his fingers—"so that's why my family got chosen for a house. We're the token non-white family. Yay," he said without enthusiasm, raising his fist.

"That's . . . interesting? I mean, the housing concept."

"It's cool when you want a free meal in the common house. It's not cool when you want to crank up music and chill, because one of the crotchety community elders will come over and tell you to *turn it down, sonny boy!*" he said in a cartoonish old-man voice. "And then you'll be shamed in the monthly residents' meeting. But whatever. It's fine. I save money. I just have to listen to my mom trying to get me to go to fake school."

"What's fake school?"

"I'm not built for college. It's a boring story." He gave me a dismissive shrug and sighed. "Anyway, I just wish Alki Beach wasn't so far from work."

"I can see it from my house."

"You can?"

"On clear days," I amended. "I can *just* make out the lighthouse on Alki Point."

"No shit?"

"No shit."

He laughed. "I love how prim and proper you sound when you swear. It's adorable. So, if I stand by the lighthouse and wave, you could see me?"

"It's like five miles across the water, or whatever, so no. But I can see Mount Rainier on clear days."

"So cool. I've only been to Bainbridge Island once. My family wanted to see the Japanese memorial wall."

I intended to tell him that I'd been to the opening ceremony for the wall but was interrupted when our server reappeared. She'd brought a carafe of coffee, a cup of hot tea, a plate of hash browns, and a shamefully large slice of pie. I kept my head down while she distributed everything and poured coffee for Daniel. When Shonda left, I extricated the limp bag of tea leaves from my cup and concentrated on inverting the ketchup over my hash browns, watching its snail-slow descent down the bottle's neck.

"You have to smack it with the heel of your hand," Daniel said.

I glanced at him over the ketchup bottle. "I'll do it my way, thank you."

He snorted, smiling, and after a moment drawled, "*S-o-o-o.* Did you talk to Mr. Kenneth in the security room?"

My heart sped. "I did."

"And you saw the footage from the elevator."

"Yep."

"And? What do you think?"

I tilted the ketchup bottle and gave it one shake. "I'll tell you when you tell *me* how you know this man is actually Raymond Darke."

"It's eating you up, isn't it? I can tell."

"You can't tell."

"I can. Good magicians need to be able to pick up on non-verbal clues to be able to guess how their mark will react, and I don't mind saying that I'm pretty fucking good at it. You try to be all cool and collected, but I can read you like a book, Birdie Lindberg. Whenever we talk about mysteries, you get really alert and your eyes do this funny, squinty thing."

"That's my Nancy Drew face," I said, feeling a little sheepish. "That's what Aunt Mona calls it."

He grinned and pointed at me over the table. "Aha! So I was right."

"Maybe."

"Tell me I'm right. I need to hear it from your lips," he said, and it almost sounded flirty.

Or maybe I was just remembering how it was between us the day we met.

"First tell me how you know it's Raymond Darke," I insisted.

He chuckled and rubbed his hands together as if he was as eager to tell me as I was to hear it. "Okay, so the reason I know is because I drove him from the hotel to the Safe." When I shook my head, he clarified. "Safeco Field. He had tickets to a Mariners game. It was after his first visit to the hotel. He was in a hurry to get to the stadium for some party in a private suite—you know, one of those club-level rooms that rich people and corporations rent out?"

I nodded and shook the ketchup bottle again, hoping I wasn't making my Nancy Drew face.

"Anyway, normally most hotel guests like to chat with me in the van," Daniel said, cutting the corner off his pie with the tines of his fork. "Those who don't, they just want the music turned up while they scroll on their phones or whatever. But this guy didn't want either. No music. No talking. And then he took a phone call, and that's when I put it all together."

Daniel's eyelids fluttered when he put a forkful of pie in his mouth. "So good. Seriously, Birdie. You need to try this."

I was sort of wishing I'd ordered a piece. "How did you put it all together?"

"The call was from his agent. They were talking about sales of a book. He was angry because his royalty check was wrong. He claimed his publisher owed him money, and apparently the agent was sick of his shit, because there was some yelling involved. This guy is a real prick, by the way. And anyway, long story short, the book titles he mentioned? I looked them up later. They were Raymond Darke books."

I set the ketchup down on the table; it wasn't coming out, and I didn't want to do it the way he suggested, because he'd probably gloat about it until the end of time. "You mean to tell me that the Thomas Pynchon of legal thrillers, a man who has successfully guarded his identity from the press for twenty years, just slipped up and let a van driver know who he was?"

"You'd be shocked what I hear in that van. Shocked. I once heard some Amazon bigwig order two male prostitutes on his phone."

"No way."

"Yes way. And once a congressman berated his wife in front of me—said nasty, horrible shit you wouldn't say to your worst enemy while she cried. I almost wondered if I should call the police. Like, if he treated her this way in public, what did he do to her at home? But see, that's the thing. It's not *really* in public, because I'm not a real human being to a lot of these people. I'm just the driver—a servant to do their bidding. They'll never see me again, so why bother holding back?"

"Wow."

"It's the way of the world, Birdie."

Indeed. I asked Daniel for the names of the books, and he rattled them off without thinking. I recognized one of them, and when I started to pull out my phone and look the other one up, he said, "It hasn't come out yet. Click on the first link. I think it's *Entertainment Weekly*. They revealed the cover a couple of months ago."

He was right. I glanced from my phone to his face. "Are you sure he was Raymond Darke, and not just some manager or something?"

"It was Darke," he said. "I would bet my life on it."

We sat in silence for several moments while I considered what he'd told me. "Is Darke Russian? I couldn't tell from the security footage, but the name in the registry was Ivanov."

"Nope. Not Russian—I mean, not that I could tell. He just looks like . . . I don't know. A random middle-aged American white dude. Maybe he has Russian ancestry. Who knows. But I'm thinking Ivanov is another fake name. Not his writing pseudonym, but maybe an identity he uses."

I mentioned the address on file being the Cascadia's sister hotel in San Francisco.

"I noticed that too. That's the first thing I looked up, because I thought, whoa. Maybe I can track down his house, see how he lives. But no. I feel like he's trying to cover his tracks."

"But why not a local address? Why use one from another hotel—*that* hotel? The average person couldn't know that the hotel in San Francisco is owned by the same people. Something's not right about that."

"Something's not right about the whole thing. What does he do up there? Does he meet someone? I asked housekeeping, but they said the room is spotless after he leaves. Is he dealing drugs? Running arms for a Russian mobster?"

"Maybe it's research for his next novel," I said.

Daniel considered this. "I don't think so. Whatever he'd been doing upstairs in the hotel room seemed to have made him upset. He told his agent that he needed his royalties ASAP because he'd just forked out an enormous sum of money, and he was being swindled, and then the agent seemed to ask about it, but he said, 'Never mind. It's personal.'"

Okay, that didn't sound like research.

I told Daniel about the opera theme running through Darke's books. "His fictional detective, Paul Parker—"

"Stupidest name ever."

I couldn't help but smile. "That's what I said."

He held his fist over the table, and after a short hesitation, I bumped it with my own. He seemed *far* too happy about this, and my cheeks were warming *way* too fast, so I quickly got back to my point before he pointed out that I was blushing.

"Anyway," I said, "Paul Parker loves opera in the books. He has a massive collection of opera records. I breezed through a couple of his older books yesterday—they were on my grandfather's bookshelves. And the details about opera are way too emotional. The way he describes music? It's more than just a random character detail. It's obvious Darke knows what he's talking about."

"He knows opera." Daniel paused. "Wait. You mean he likes opera himself? Like, personally? Not just the character."

"I think it's a definite possibility. And I was thinking . . ."

"Yes?"

"Well, if you want to figure out why Darke is coming to the hotel, we could try to follow him next Tuesday. That's risky, and it depends on our schedules, but beyond that, it's still a few days from now. In the meantime, if you want to understand why someone's doing something, you need to understand them. That means finding out what they're like. Where they live, where they go, who they see."

"We don't know where he lives, though. The San Francisco address in the hotel registry is bogus."

I leaned closer. "But we *do* know there's a chance that Darke buys opera records somewhere in town. And I researched that. There's a record store on Capitol Hill that boasts having the best selection of classical music on vinyl in the city."

"All I know is Spin Cycle on Broadway."

"This is smaller. Tenor Records. I think it's all classical and jazz."

"Whoa! Genius," Daniel said. "Should we go there? Is that what you're saying? You're agreeing to partner up with me?"

"*Just* for sleuthing purposes," I clarified.

"Strictly business between coworkers," he agreed. "This has nothing to do with fate."

"No fate," I confirmed.

"And no flirting, no touching."

The way he said this, it was almost a question. Was he teasing me? Maybe I was imagining it. I was trying to think of a response when his foot bumped against mine under the table. And then the side of his leg.

"That was an accident," he argued when I glanced at his face.

But he didn't sound sorry, and he wasn't moving. His leg was warm and heavy. Tingles erupted from the place we were joined. I should have moved away.

I didn't.

After a moment, I picked up my fork to dig into my hash browns. But when I looked down, instead of potatoes, a half-eaten piece of pie sat in front of me. Daniel had swapped plates.

He smiled at me with his eyes. "Misdirection, Birdie. It gets you every time."

"I like detective stories—and detectives. Brainy is the new sexy."
—Irene Adler, *Sherlock* (2012)

IO

Daniel was right: the pie was good. Like, life-changing, I-just-found-religion good. How in the world had I avoided it all this time? No wonder my mom had eaten it as if it were nutrition personified.

In fact, I was still thinking about it when I took an early ferry into the city the next day. I was also thinking about Daniel's leg touching mine under the table. I couldn't figure out why it felt more taboo than what we did in the back seat. Maybe I was just on a mystery high. Or a pie high.

Maybe both.

After daydreaming my way through a short bus ride from the downtown ferry terminal, I ended up in front of Elliott Bay Book Company in Capitol Hill. I'd been here before, and it was an excellent bookstore—two expansive stories with lots of light spilling over crisscrossed beams, wood floors, and row after row of cedar shelves. Any other day, I'd spend hours browsing. But I was headed to the café in the back of the store, where I was supposed to be meeting Daniel. I'd given him my phone number last night under the heady influence of Rainier cherries and brown-sugar crumble, and we'd been texting to coordinate our plans. When I looked around, I worried that I'd misunderstood.

Then I spotted him at the counter.

Like me, he was wearing the hotel's required "uniform" of black pants and white shirt—it was two hours before we both had to clock in—but instead of the green Cascadia zip-up he wore when driving the hotel van, he had on a slim leather jacket with a diagonal zipper that clung to lines of lean muscle on his arms and chest. Inside my head, I had a brief, hallucinatory flash of that chest without a shirt on and quickly banished it.

As if he could sense me, he turned around and his eyes immediately found mine.

"Hello, Nora."

I glanced behind me.

"You're supposed to call me Nick," he explained. "Or I could be Nora, if you want. I'm not picky."

I stared at him.

"I watched online clips from *The Thin Man* last night," he said brightly.

"Oh," I said, unexpectedly pleased. "You did?"

"I felt it was my duty to get in the right frame of mind for sleuthing. I have no idea what the movie's about, but Myrna Loy was insanely hot, and they're both total boozers. I liked it when she found out her husband had already had five martinis and she wanted to catch up with him."

"'Bartender, bring me five more martinis,'" I said, loosely quoting Nora in the film.

"'And line them up right here!'" he finished.

I laughed. "It was the 1930s. Drinking was a sport."

"Well, this isn't a martini, but it will have to do," he said, extending an arm to hand me a steaming paper cup. "Black tea. Since you are apparently a coffee hater, which is a little blasphemous in this town. But if you truly prefer it, I will defend your right to drink this brown tap water."

"Perfect," I said, smiling. "Thanks."

He nodded toward my head. "Different flower."

"Tiger lily. We have all kinds of lilies growing in our yard. My grandmother was a big gardener," I explained. "She said it was holy work."

"Is that why you were homeschooled and couldn't swear? She was religious?"

"No. I mean, yes, she was religious, but I think it had to do more with the fact that she drove her teenage daughter away, and they didn't speak for years, and then she died. I think she was just trying to keep me on a short leash out of overprotective fear, if that makes sense."

Daniel stared at me for so long with a dazed expression, I feared I'd said something wrong. But how could that be? Maybe it was just that he hadn't heard me. It *was* a little loud in the café (music, cappuccino steaming, cups clinking), and I wondered if this was one of those environments that made it hard for him to pick out sounds. So I pointed toward the front door, and we walked outside together.

What little sun we had was low in the sky, and Capitol Hill was windy, which made walking and talking hard. But we didn't have far to go. We turned on Pike and crossed Broadway, made famous by Sir Mix-a-Lot and his posse, when he wasn't proclaiming his love for big butts. This enclave of the neighborhood was a collection of restaurants and yoga studios, lots of rainbow flags.

"I sort of pictured you living here," I said. "When we first met."

He tugged his ear and shifted to the other side of me. "This is my good ear," he said, and then asked me to repeat myself. When I did, he said, "You thought I lived here? Why?"

"Seems like hipster central. Or maybe Ballard."

"Me, a hipster?" He laughed and then twisted his head at a comical angle. "Are you serious? Birdie, Birdie, Birdie. I take Saturday nights off from work twice a month to play in Magic tournaments."

"Magicians have tournaments?"

"Magic the Gathering. You know, the card game?"

I thought back to when I'd researched Daniel online, and some event from a comic book shop had popped up—not that I was going to tell him I'd been stalking him online. "Like Dungeons and Dragons?" I asked.

"Same crowd of nerds, so close enough, and I was a dungeon

master when I was a kid. Basically, if there's a wizard in it, I've played it. I like my games dark and full of demons." He glanced at me. "I bet your religious grandmother would have hated me anywhere near her granddaughter, huh?"

He *had* heard me earlier in the bookstore. "She was Lutheran, not a member of a crazy cult," I said, grinning. "Sure, she thought that Bobby Pruitt down the street was trouble because he listened to heavy metal, but we weren't Amish, or anything. We had Internet and TV."

"So, though you couldn't swear, electricity wasn't satanic science for you either. That's what you're saying."

"That's what I'm saying. I just wasn't aware of tournaments for games like that."

"There's a pro tour every year—the World Magic Cup. You travel to other cities and win big cash. Like, tens of thousands. And you get to go to cool cities, which I'd love to do."

"Because you're not a hipster with a man bun; you're a nerd."

He feigned insult. "I'll have you know, this is a topknot, not a man bun. But, yeah, I'm *such* a nerd. Throw in magic tricks and the fact that I'm nineteen and still live with my mom. Now you've built yourself a raging nerd monster." He thumped his chest with one fist and roared.

I laughed so hard, hot tea splashed on my hand.

"Are you laughing at my dorkishness?" he said, eyes merry.

"In a good way. You might be the biggest nerd I've ever met."

"It's good to be number one in something," he said with a

smile, holding out his coffee cup for me to clink. When I did, he lifted his chin toward a storefront. "I think that's our destination."

The record shop was part of a block-long building, its neighbors being a fish-and-chips shop and a gay nightclub. A leafy tree growing out of the sidewalk hid the store's unassuming black-and-white sign—TENOR RECORDS. If it weren't for the album covers plastering the glass door, we might have missed it.

"Put down your martini and let's get to some sleuthing, Nora," Daniel said, full of infectious cheer. A bell tinkled when he opened the door, and we stepped inside.

The narrow store was a claustrophobe's nightmare. Clunky record racks stretched from the register to the Employees Only door in the back corner. Every inch of wall space was filled with albums pegged to display racks and vintage cardboard flats of old covers—operas and concerts from every decade, every language. And between the two outer walls, instruments hung from the ceiling by fishing wire: violins and bows, clarinets and flutes. It was like a scene from inside the Great Hall at Hogwarts.

"Whoa," Daniel said, looking around as a string quartet played Mozart over the shop's trembling stereo speakers. "We seem to be the only customers."

And no employees. We were alone. "Maybe someone's in the back? Let's look around."

Daniel and I strolled down an aisle, scanning the bins of records until I spotted the opera section, and he began flicking through the covers. Most of them appeared to be old and used.

I caught snatches of words in vintage fonts: scenes and arias, Decca, Maria Callas, Pavarotti. Metropolitan Orchestra. *Tosca*, *La Traviata*, *Antony and Cleopatra*. It was like reading a book in a foreign language.

"Look at this thing," Daniel murmured, hefting a giant boxed set of records emblazoned with raised silver letters. *Der Ring Des Nibelungen*. "This is one opera? Christ. Fifteen hours? That's insane."

"I'd probably fall asleep in the first hour." I picked up a copy of arias from Verdi's *Aida*. On the front was a photo of an enormous Egyptian temple set, the two opera singers inside it looking like ants. "Rome Opera House. I had no idea the sets were so elaborate." I opened the gatefold to see more of the Egyptian temple inside.

"It's like Broadway on crack," Daniel said, standing closer to inspect the photograph with me. "You think this is what Raymond Darke listens to?"

At that moment, a single clerk emerged from the back offices, a pale, gangly man who looked to be in his early twenties, possibly younger. One side of his short blond hair was shaved, and the other flopped over his eyes. Tattooed musical notes along both wrists peeked out from his shirtsleeves when he stretched to straighten the top of a rack of sheet music. Then he headed toward the front register, stopping only when he spotted us.

"You guys need something?" he asked, pushing hair out of his eyes.

Daniel closed the *Aida* album, tucking it under his arm as he approached the clerk. "Hey, man. What's up?" he said, casual as can be. "We were trying to track down someone who may be a regular customer here and wondering if you might be able to help us."

"Uh . . ." The clerk looked at Daniel, then me. Then Daniel again. "Maybe?"

"He's a white dude in his early fifties. About this tall," he said, holding up his hand. "Looks like he enjoys wine—has a reddish nose and a potbelly. Wears a blue baseball cap. Frowns all the time."

The clerk shrugged. "That sounds like half our customers, honestly."

I added, "He's well off. Would likely drop a lot of cash on collectibles. Rare vinyl, that sort of thing."

"Yeah, we've got a couple customers who do. They pretty much keep the store afloat."

Daniel whipped out his phone, and after pulling up a few screens, turned it around to show the clerk a photo. It was pixelated and a little blurry, but I recognized it: our mystery man in the hotel elevator. Daniel had snapped a picture of Mr. Kenneth's security footage at work.

The clerk's eyes brightened. "Yeah, that's Mr. Waddle. Bill Waddle."

Waddle? Was that another alias? Daniel and I shared a look before I asked, "Can you tell us anything about him?"

"Uh, well. We order a lot of imports for him."

"Like this?" Daniel said, holding up the *Aida* album.

The clerk nodded. "Yeah, he's into Verdi. But that particular pressing isn't rare enough for him. He likes hard-to-find things. He's been trying to track down a rare recording of *The Mikado* for about a year, but only ten copies were pressed. It's worth a grand, easy."

"Does he come here often?" I asked.

"A couple of times a month, I guess," the clerk answered. "Sometimes to browse. Sometimes to pick up special orders."

"You wouldn't happen to have an address on file?" Daniel asked bluntly.

I was instantly nervous. I wasn't expecting Daniel to ask that. It wasn't part of the plan we'd discussed in the diner last night. We were just supposed to be getting a sense of Raymond Darke. What he likes. Where he goes. Who he was. We knew where to find him—at least, in theory. If we wanted to see him, we could wait until he came into the hotel again on Tuesday.

The clerk made a funny sound. "That's private information. Sorry. I don't even know if we have it, but if we did and I gave it out, I'd get fired. Why do you need it?"

"Honestly?" Daniel said. "We're just trying to help out a friend."

We were?

Daniel continued. "He took something from our friend, and they want it back. It was probably a mistake. He might not even realize he has it. Anyway, this Waddle guy is a total dick, and I'd be happy if I never saw him again. I'm just trying to do someone a solid."

What a vague, terrible story. This guy would never buy it.

Except, he did.

The clerk laughed, and his shoulders relaxed. He leaned one hip against the counter and crossed his arms. "I'm so glad you said that. He makes me run around like a chicken with my head off, pulling this or that album, only to leave them piled on the floor when he's finished. Nothing makes him happy. According to him, we never have what he wants, and we open too late, and all of this is always my fault somehow. Meanwhile, his two yappy bulldogs get free rein of the store, and they slobber on everything. He's just a nightmare."

"Dude," Daniel said chummily. "That's *just* how I pictured him. And I'm in customer service, so I'm completely understand your pain. Miserable people are the worst. And this guy does not like his life. You can tell."

"You're right about that."

"Is there anything you can do to help?" Daniel asked.

"I can't give you his address," the clerk said. "But I *can* tell you that he's always bragging that he's woken up before the sun for thirty years. If you want to talk to him, he walks his slobbering dogs every morning at sunrise. Kerry Park, in Queen Anne."

My inner Nancy Drew did cartwheels while Daniel gave me a secret, triumphant look.

Maybe this whole partnering-up idea was a good idea after all.

"Unless you are good at guessing, it is not much use being a detective."
—Hercule Poirot, *The Mystery of the Blue Train* (1928)

II

When you're investigating something and a piece of information is dropped into your lap, you can't just ignore it. We sure didn't. Which was why we made plans to go to Kerry Park after work the following day. We could have done it the same night we went to the record store, but Daniel suggested I give my grandfather a heads-up beforehand that I'd be staying out late. "Make sure you tell him that I'm trustworthy and try to paint me as a saint. I wouldn't want him to hate me," Daniel said. The fact that Daniel worried what an old man thought about him probably would have put him in Grandpa's good graces, but I didn't tell him that.

I did, however, tell Aunt Mona, when I stopped by her house on my way to work the next day. She lives in the island's small downtown area, inside a tiny, old movie theater. Her great-grandparents built it in the 1930s, when they first moved here from Puerto Rico, and it was the first theater on the island to show "talkies." I suppose "theatrical" was sort of a Rivera family gene, because her parents later went on to manage a local open-air playhouse when we were living over the diner.

Anyway, after bigger theaters were built around the island, this one briefly became an art-house cinema that showed indie movies in the 1990s before shuttering permanently. Aunt Mona converted it into her art studio after my mom died, and eventually made it her home. It still had its original marquee—topped with its name, THE RIVERA—and sometimes I helped her change out the plastic letters to announce her upcoming gallery showings . . . or to spell out rude messages to the local government when Mona got angry about potholes or a controversial bridge being built.

I passed the ticket window under the marquee—where a crowd of cardboard standees stared out at me, old movie characters who once stood in the lobby—and rang the doorbell. Paint covered the double doors on the inside of the glass, brightly colored faces, and a sign told random tourists that this was private property and that the owner could see them on video. She couldn't.

One of the doors flew open, and a bright pink head popped out. "Darling!"

"Bubble-gum princess?" I asked, trying to see what she was wearing.

"Bubble-gum nurse," she said, showing me her shiny PVC uniform and matching cap with sparkly red cross. She even had a name tag that said NURSE MONA.

But despite her cheery outfit, she looked . . . worried. Something was off. "Is this a bad time? You're not sick, are you?"

"No. Just feeling blah." She stuck out her tongue.

"Not sure if it helps, but I come bearing gifts," I said, showing her a bakery box the color of her wig. "They were out of almond croissants, but I got one orange and three *pains au chocolat*."

She sighed. "I love you madly."

"I know."

"But *extra*, because all I've been thinking about this morning is Belgian chocolate."

"Oh!" Now the way she looked made sense. "Cramps?"

"Exactly. Yes. I woke up with cramps."

"Ugh," I complained. "Your uterus must have sent out a Bat-Signal to mine because I started my period last night."

"Darling, sometimes I feel like my uterus controls the entire island. Get inside so we can stuff our faces before I have to leave." She opened the door to let me in and then locked it. I headed across the lobby, dodging mismatched furniture and her needy cat—Zsa Zsa Gabor, a solid white Persian who couldn't be petted enough—and set the bakery box down on a purple dining table. Steps away, the theater's original concessions stand had been converted into a kitchen, but it still had a working popcorn machine and soda fountain, which I thought were the bee's knees when I was twelve.

And it wasn't the only thing Aunt Mona had renovated. The women's bathroom had been converted to make room for a bathtub, and the men's was now a giant closet with an entire wall of wigs. The projection booth was her bedroom. The theater itself—where she painted and sculpted and sewed fabulous clothes—had all but two rows of seats torn out and skylights installed in the ceiling. The screen still worked, though, and she'd upgraded to digital projection; I'd watched many a movie with her when my grandmother and I were fighting. After I moved in with my grandparents, Grandma tried to forbid Mona from seeing me at all until Mona threatened to take her to court and sue for guardianship. Then Grandma only let her visit me on the weekends in our house. But after I ran away three times in one month—I always came here—Grandma finally relented and allowed me to bike over to Mona's theater.

I used to think Grandma illogically blamed Mona for my mom's death. In her eyes, Mona was the weird kid and therefore a bad influence who turned my mom against her. But now I understand that she resented Mona because she got to help raise me when I was younger and Grandma didn't. Not once did Grandma ever admit any blame in our family's estrangement, but I knew she felt it. She carried that guilt with her to the grave.

I never wanted to be that stubborn.

"Where are you heading today?" I asked Mona as she stood on tiptoes in pink stockinged feet to fetch plates.

"Don't ask me."

"Too late. I'm asking," I said, plopping down on a mismatched dining chair covered in tiny strawberry people—also a childhood favorite. The wall next to me was adorned in old Broadway posters that she'd "liberated" from the backstage area of her parents'

old open-air theatrical playhouse on the other side of the island—
Jesus Christ Superstar, Cats, Rent, Fiddler on the Roof, Cabaret, and
several others. Mona said she used to despise musicals when she
was growing up—she had a vicious love-hate relationship with
her parents—but now that she was older, she could admit that
they fueled her early love of costume.

"Go on, tell me," I encouraged.

She feigned sobbing. "You're going to judge me."

"I won't."

"Even if I told you I was meeting Leon Snodgrass?"

I swung around in my chair. "Ugh. Ugh! *No-o-o-o!* What?"

"I told you not to ask!"

"How did this happen? I thought he moved to Texas."

"He's back in town for the summer."

"He cheated on you," I reminded her.

"Technically we were on a break. I saw someone else too."

"Out of revenge! He's a stockbroker who plays golf. He wears
monogrammed shirts, and he's allergic to Zsa Zsa Gabor," I said
as the cat wound around my ankle. Leon Snodgrass was the bane
of my existence. A year or so ago, it seemed as if every time I came
to the theater to hang out with Mona, there he was, being boring
as ever. She needed a wild spirit—someone like her. Not a drab
numbers guy who was always using dated slang "ironically" and
making stupid jokes.

Aunt Mona sat down next to me on a chair painted to look
as if it were covered in dragon scales. "I know. But he was so nice

when I saw him on the harbor yesterday. He has a new yacht."

"Gross."

"He named it the *Spirit of Mona.*"

"Are you serious?" I pretended to heave, puffing out my cheeks.

"I know. I know!" she said, scooping up a chocolate-filled pastry. "But how can you turn down a guy who's named a boat after you? It's sort of romantic."

"More like sort of creepy."

"He says he's changed. Maybe he has. Maybe I have. I don't know. Besides, it's not a date. He asked me to meet him at his grandmother's house on Hidden Cove to look at her painting collection. They want to know what it's worth."

"You're not an art dealer."

She shrugged. "But I have an eye for it and knowledge of the market. I don't know . . . It's probably a waste of time, but at least Grandma Snodgrass will be chaperoning us, so I won't do anything regrettable. Speaking of regret, how's our beautiful boy Daniel?"

"He's not *our* boy. Or my boy. He's his own boy." I gave her a hard stare. "You told Grandpa Hugo about meeting him in Pike Place?"

"It may have come up. Promise, cross my heart, that I won't tattle again."

Unlikely. Ever since my grandmother died, Aunt Mona and Grandpa practically had become bosom buddies, which was weird, because things had always been tense between Mona and my grandparents. As she ate her pastry, I told her about the conversation I had with Grandpa and Cass in the greenhouse, filling her in on the Raymond Darke intrigue . . . and the breakthrough Daniel and I had in the record shop.

"This is all sort of fascinating. And essentially you're telling me that you're playing Nancy Drew with Daniel. I can picture it all now—*Oh, Daniel. Help me solve the riddle of the hidden staircase!*"

I licked chocolate off my finger. "Don't make it sound lurid. We're just investigating a man who comes in the hotel. And we may possibly be going to Kerry Park after work."

"*O-o-oh*, super romantic."

"It's a stakeout."

"Super-duper romantic, especially if your name is Birdie Lindberg."

"At five in the morning."

She made a face. "Now you've killed it for me. I'll never understand your sleep issues. I know you hate doctors because of what happened to your mom, but you need to see somebody and get this sleep stuff worked out."

"There's nothing to work out. Sometimes I have trouble sleeping, and sometimes I have trouble staying awake."

"Hugo said the same thing and look what happened to him and his men."

When Grandpa fell asleep piloting a boat, it wasn't just him it affected. Two other people were injured. This is why I'll never drive a car. I'm terrified of falling asleep at the wheel and hurting other people.

"Has anything been getting worse lately?" she asked. "You haven't had anything weird happen at work, have you?"

I knew what she meant: what Grandpa called "going boneless," better known as cataplexy. It's this thing that happens to some narcoleptics. Basically, you lose control of all your muscles and sometimes collapse. People think you've fainted, but you're conscious. It's just that you can't move. And it's triggered by the stupidest things. A burst of laughter. Excitement. Anger. Any intense emotion, really. It's completely unpredictable, and it had happened to me three times. Twice since Christmas.

"I'm fine," I told her. "Don't worry. I haven't fallen asleep on the job." I mean, *technically* I fell asleep in the laundry room *after* my shift. "And I haven't gone boneless for several months. Since . . ."

"Eleanor's funeral."

"Right," I said. "Since then." Unbelievably embarrassing. I didn't cry that day—not once—through the entire service. And then boom. Paralyzed, right in front of her grave. A hundred people thought I'd fainted. Good times.

"Does Daniel know?" she asked.

"No one at work knows. Why would I tell them? I told you, it's all going fine."

She sighed heavily. "All right, I'm backing off. But I think you should tell Daniel. And I definitely think you should talk to him about what happened in the back seat of his car."

"That's a big N-O. Besides, he doesn't want to talk about it anymore, either. We agreed to leave the past in the past. We're investigating this Raymond Darke thing strictly as coworkers."

"Oh, *really*? Where's that flower girl ad he wrote you? Pull it up. I want to read it again."

I protested, but she insisted. It was bookmarked on my phone, not that I kept looking at it or anything. But while Zsa Zsa Gabor rubbed her snowy-white kitty face against my leg, I got out my phone and pulled up the Missed Connections site.

Huh. Daniel's ad was no longer there.

He'd taken it down.

Before our excursion to Kerry Park, I had to wait on Daniel after our shift ended, because he wasn't back from taking a customer to the airport. I'd been fighting off the intense need to take a nap since leaving Aunt Mona's place, so the combination of these things was a little disastrous. One minute I was sitting on a sofa in the hotel lobby, stifling a yawn while cracking open my dog-eared emergency purse book, and the next thing I knew, I woke to find Daniel's face floating over mine.

I yelped.

"WAKE UP." His arms were on either side of my head, braced on the back of the sofa.

"Wasn't asleep." My tongue was thick around the words, slurring syllables. "Just drifted off."

"That's the same thing."

"Says you."

"You always fall asleep in public?"

I hesitated, thinking of my earlier conversation with Aunt Mona, and decided to test the waters. "Sometimes on the ferry," I admitted. One of the ferry employees had woken me up on several occasions, which was embarrassing, because I worried he thought I might be a drunkard or a heroin addict. "And I've never stayed awake during an entire movie in a theater."

"Ever?"

"Movie theaters make me drowsy," I explained. "At home it's different. I can move around. And it's not dark."

"Huh. I've never fallen asleep in a theater."

He was making me feel self-conscious. It didn't help that his face was a few inches from mine and I could smell his minty, tea-tree oil shampoo on a tendril of hair that fell against his shoulder, having slipped from where he'd tied it up in a knot at the base of his neck. "Sleep and I have unresolved issues," I mumbled.

"Are you too tired to do this, or—"

"I'm fine," I said irritably, shooing the air with my hand to encourage him to move. "If you don't mind . . ."

He stood up, eyes darting to the floor. "Must have been this riveting read of yours that's to blame."

"Holy crap," I muttered, scooping my open book off the floor. Technically, I wasn't supposed to be out here. Employees weren't allowed to linger in the hotel's public spaces during their off-time. "Did anyone notice?"

"No, but I almost took a photo." When he saw the look on my face, he said, "That was a joke, jeez. Now, are we going on this stakeout, or what? I've had an *intense* amount of caffeine tonight in preparation, so don't make me waste perfectly good jitters."

"Glad one of us is alert." I shoved the paperback in my purse and glanced at my phone. We still had forty-five minutes or more until dawn, so I walked outside with him and tried to shake off my fatigue.

Daniel had parked his car in the loading area. Seeing it again made me cringe, but I didn't want him to know this, so when he chivalrously opened the door for me, I quickly slid into the passenger seat. It smelled the same as I remembered, like the ubiquitous pine-tree air freshener hanging from the rearview mirror, synthetic and sweet. Daniel jogged to the driver's side and started the engine.

"I was sort of worried you wouldn't get in my car ever again," he said, briefly flicking a teasing look in my direction.

"The back seat, no. But the front is neutral."

"*So* neutral," he agreed, nodding slowly. "As long as you keep your hands to yourself—"

"Me?"

"We both know who suggested going back there in the first place."

I started to protest, but he was right. It had been my idea.

We'd left the diner, intending to go see a movie. Our clothes were wet from the rain, and I was shivering as we hiked up the parking garage stairwell. When we got to his car, Daniel offered me his coat, but it was damper than mine, and we both started laughing. And he kissed me. And I kissed him. And kissed . . . And when he pulled away and said we should cool off, I suggested we skip the movie. He made a joke about his back seat being big, and the next thing I knew, we were in it.

I guess we both got carried away.

I may have been a virgin, but it wasn't the first time I'd kissed a boy. That honor went to Will Collins, who used to live in a town house on the way between my grandparents' house and Aunt Mona's theater. I was sort of friends with his sister, Tracy. He used to play basketball in the parking lot, and sometimes I stopped to watch. Last summer, when Tracy was at swimming practice, he kissed me by the fence. Then again, two days later, for much longer. Secret basketball make-out sessions became a regular thing for a few weeks. Then one day I saw him and Tracy helping their dad load a rental moving truck, and that was the end of my first and only summer romance. And that was my last attempt at pursuing new relationships in general, for friendship or otherwise.

Until Daniel.

Daniel gestured to his pants with a sweeping hand. "I know how irresistible these black chinos are. Every lady loves a man in uniform, and mine radiates subservience and minimum wage. Don't be tempted."

I huffed out a laugh.

"Now, I'm not shirking my part in our past entanglements. I mean, clearly I have no willpower around pretty lady detectives. Which is why it's best you don't cross this line," he said, drawing an invisible boundary over the parking brake.

"Maybe you should put the armrest down."

"Can't. It's broken. You'll have to pretend there's a wall here."

"What did you say?" I shouted, cupping my hand around my mouth. "I can't hear you over this wall."

He mouthed something back to me and did a mime-trapped-in-box routine, which made me laugh. Then *he* laughed, and we were smiling at each other a little too hard, and for a moment it felt like that first afternoon in the rain. Breaking the spell, I looked away and hoped he couldn't read my feelings on my face. *Calm down, Birdie*, I told myself. This wasn't a date, for the love of Pete.

After a moment of awkward silence, he whipped out his phone. "All right, so, anyway. Let me just get some car music going, and then we can leave." Soft light beamed up at his face as he scrolled through songs. "I'm on a major David Bowie kick right now. Like, full-blown crush."

"Oh?"

"He was so brilliant and revolutionary, a shape-shifter of music. You want pop? Avant-garde? Rock? Soul? Gender-bending alien glam? He did it all. Right now I'm mostly listening to his earlier stuff. *Hunky Dory, Aladdin Sane*, the Berlin trilogy. Also, the last album he made before he died, *Blackstar*. He knew he was dying of cancer when he made it, so it's a swan song. And the whole thing is trippy and depressing and defiant all at the same time. Like me."

Depressing? Daniel was the most cheerful person I'd ever met.

"How about some *Ziggy Stardust*? It's a perfect album."

He pressed his phone screen and put the car in gear. The speakers shook out fuzzy, guitar-driven cinematic music that sounded as if it started on the ground and rose up into the night sky.

It rattled around in my rib cage as he sped his car down the dark street, all the way through Belltown and up into Queen Anne, the most elevated neighborhood in Seattle, whose affluent streets were loaded with big, old Victorian houses and big, old leafy trees.

He pulled the car over near a curb and parked. Apart from the occasional passing vehicle and distant siren, it was quiet up here. Nothing but sleepy homes on one side of the street and a well-known public space sitting on a hill over the city.

Kerry Park.

The park itself was smaller than small—just a couple of narrow stretches of grass divided by a nondescript urban sculpture and bordered by a handful of benches. But as we approached a short retaining wall, I realized why people said it boasted the best view in the entire city.

A classic view.

I could see Seattle's city lights from the beach in our backyard on Bainbridge Island, but *this* was the skyline you saw in photos and postcards. Jagged tops of skyscrapers jutting up from the black basin. A hint of the Olympic Mountains in the distance behind them. And in the middle of it all, the iconic flying-saucer-topped Space Needle, symbol of Seattle.

"Look at that," Daniel said, not bothering to hide the awe in his voice. "Isn't it fucking amazing?"

"It certainly is," I murmured. At night, from here, downtown looked as if it were wrapped in Christmas lights—white and rose gold, twinkling and shimmering against the black bay water.

He turned around and surveyed the park. At the far end, a professional photographer had set up a camera on a tripod and was preparing to take pictures of the skyline. Another couple ambled down the sidewalk.

"Should be easy enough to spot a pudgy asshole with two bulldogs," Daniel said, sliding onto a slatted wood bench seat built into the wall. "Wish I'd brought some coffee."

"Coffee?" I said, glancing at his bouncing leg as I sat on the bench next to him. He whistled softly and gestured to his other side. It took me a moment to realize he was trying to get me to sit on his "good" side, so he could hear better. We swapped places, and I said, "I thought you were already intensely caffeinated."

"Well, *now*, sure. But what if we're here for hours?"

"Dawn's not that far away. If he shows up when the record-store guy said he should."

"True." He rested an elbow on the wall as he craned his neck to look out over the city. Then he said, "Hmm. Need a way to pass the time."

I glanced at his face.

His eyes flicked to mine. "Not *that*."

"I wasn't implying anything," I argued as my pulse went a little haywire.

"Good, because I don't think most detectives do that on stake-outs. Maybe Nick and Nora."

"Well, they're an exception," I said, chuckling nervously.

"I was thinking more in terms of a game."

"What kind of game?"

"How about," he said, mouth curling up at the corners, "we play a little Truth or Lie?"

12

I lifted a brow at Daniel. "I think you mean *dare*? Truth or Dare."

Back when I was living over the diner with Mom and Mona, when I was going to public school, I used to play Truth or Dare with kids on the playground at recess. It almost always involved someone trying to climb branches of an overgrown tree that bent over the schoolyard fence.

"Nope. Truth or Lie," he insisted. "This is how we play. We each get three turns. On your turn, you ask me a question. Something that you want to know about me. And I can either answer truthfully . . . or I can lie. You decide if you believe me, or you can challenge my answer. Like, I might ask you what your favorite song is."

"Okay."

"What's your favorite song?"

"Right now?"

"Right now, Birdie."

"I don't have one."

"Everyone has a favorite song. Mine is 'Under Pressure' by Bowie and Freddie Mercury. Or is it? Do you think I'm telling the truth?"

"Yes?"

"You're right. I am. Point to you. That's how you play."

"I don't get it. How do you win?"

"Knowledge is winning, Birdie," he said with a grin. "Just ask me a question. It must be something you genuinely want to know. And my answer has to be completely fabricated or all truth. No middle ground, no avoiding answering. After I give you my answer, you decide if I'm lying."

"Like cross-examination?"

"Just like that. I should have called this game Interrogate Me. That's more appealing for lady detectives such as yourself."

"Hold on. Did you make this game up just now?"

"Is that your official question? You only get three. Don't waste them."

I laughed. He laughed.

Fine. I guess we were doing this.

I tried to think up a good question, occasionally surveilling the park, until something popped into my mind. "Okay, I thought of one. Ready?"

"Hit me."

"How did you lose your hearing? That's my official question."

"Ah," he said, leaning back casually. "It's a funny story, actually.

See, my mother, Cherry—that's her name. She was a magician's assistant. You know, the pretty thing onstage who gets chopped up in boxes."

I squinted at him. Was he already lying?

He continued. "She performed every weekend with a semi-famous Seattle magician in the 1990s. They started out in small clubs until they got some notoriety. Then she met my father and got pregnant, and no one wanted to see a pregnant assistant get stabbed by swords in a locked box, so she was forced to stop. And, of course, you already know that my father was a soulless waste of flesh who felt she got in the way of his career, and how could he tell his über-white conservative family that he'd knocked up a young Asian girl? So he dumped her, and she pressed the pause button on magic to have me, and then her stage partner—the magician—died in a freak airplane accident, so she quit it alto-gether."

"Interesting," I said carefully, unsure if he was telling the truth. "But I don't see how this answers my question."

He raised his index finger. "Getting to that. My mother may have quit magic, but she kept all their stage props. And when I started showing an interest in performing, my grandfather encour-aged me—Jiji. My mom's father. That's what I call him. And before you know it, I was trying to impress everyone, and . . . Do you know about Houdini's water torture cell?"

"Uh, the escape trick?"

"Exactly. Magician is restrained and lowered into a tank of

water, and while a curtain falls over the tank, he escapes. Well, the summer before my senior year in high school, I fixed up an old water cell and filled it up in my backyard. Some other guys helped me. It was going fine—I knew how to execute the escape—but the trick lock at the top of the cell was stuck. I panicked and accidentally hit my head on the glass. One of my friends used an ax to break open the tank before I drowned . . . but I perforated my eardrum. Got a bad infection. And that's how I lost the hearing in my right ear. It's also why I'm not allowed to do any magic or escape tricks. Like, ever again. I mean, there are other reasons for that, but . . ." For a moment, it sounded as if he were going to say more but quickly decided against it. "Anyway, there you go."

I stared at his face, trying to decide if I believed him. It was an outlandish story, but then again, he *had* told me he wasn't supposed to be performing magic tricks at Pike Place. "What other reasons?"

He shook his head. "It's nothing. All in the past. I mean, unless you want to use up another question. . . ."

Did he *want* me to ask? I couldn't decide. The detective in me longed to pry, but a strained uneasiness settled between us, as if I'd stumbled onto private land with a big KEEP OUT sign.

"What do you think?" he said after several seconds of silence.

"About . . . ?"

"About what I just told you. You asked. I answered," he said, gesturing to himself and then to me. "Now you have to decide if I was telling the truth."

Right. Okay. Maybe all of that tenseness was in my imagination. Best to take off my detective hat and focus on what he'd told me—not what he hadn't. After replaying his entire story in my head, I decided to go with my gut. "I think I believe you."

He nodded, looking satisfied. "Good. It was the truth. Point for you. My turn. How did your mom die?"

I wasn't expecting a serious question. It took me a long time to decide if I wanted to tell him the truth. "She died of a weak heart."

"Wait, what?" Daniel said. "That's not a thing. You mean she had a heart attack?"

"You tell me," I said, crossing my arms. Maybe I liked this game now.

"Hmm. You said your mom died when you were ten, and you also said she got pregnant with you when she was about your age. That would have made her, what? Twenty-eight when she died?"

I nodded, expecting the usual tightness in my chest that always seemed to come when I talked too much about her death, but . . . it didn't happen. Oddly, I sort of *wanted* to talk to him about it. "Yes," I said. "She was twenty-eight."

He made a noise and then exhaled heavily. "Okay, I'm going to say your story is . . . true."

"Do I have to confirm?"

"You do."

"Okay, it's true. Technically."

"What do you mean? You lied?"

I hesitated. It was easier to talk about things in the dark, out here where it felt as if we were on top of the city, far away from everything.

"Do you know what an ectopic pregnancy is?" I asked.

"I've heard of it, maybe?"

"It's when a fertilized egg implants in the wrong place, like on the inside of a fallopian tube. So the baby starts growing there, and the tube eventually bursts and bleeds, and it's super painful, and if it's not removed in time, you can die. But my mom didn't know she was pregnant. She thought it was food poisoning. But it got worse, and Aunt Mona—she lived with us—was working. And I didn't know what to do, so I went and got Ms. Patty from the diner, and we called an ambulance. It took them forever to see her in the ER, and once they figured out that she was bleeding and were prepping her for surgery, Mona finally got there. But before they could operate, Mom had a heart attack."

"Jesus," Daniel murmured. "That's awful, Birdie."

I forced myself to shrug, to keep my emotions in check. "It was just dumb luck. Just one of those things that happens. But it's why I hate hospitals."

"I don't blame you. I'm really sorry."

"The weird thing is that my grandmother died of a heart attack too. They both had congenital heart defects. So, as I said, weak heart. Which make you technically right when you guessed."

He reached out, and I felt the gentle weight of his fingers on mine, a whisper of a touch.

I squeezed his hand in answer and then let go. "I'm okay. Let's keep playing."

"All right," he said. "One point to me. We're tied. Your turn to ask a question."

I was relieved that he wasn't making a big deal out of my revelation. It made me relax a little. I pushed hair out of my eyes while a brisk wind blew through the park. A purple tinge was bleeding into the night sky. Dawn was coming. Still no sign of our stakeout target, so I continued. "Back in the diner, you said your mom was trying to talk you into going to fake school. What does that mean?"

"Pfft," he said. "That's barely a question."

"You have to answer, right?"

He sighed heavily. "Okay, fine. Here goes. My mom wants me to go to clown school."

I blinked several times. "Clown school?"

"Red noses. Painted faces. Big shoes."

"There's a school for that?"

"She says I act like a clown, so maybe I should turn that into a professional career."

"Um . . . no. Not true. Lie."

He laughed. "Fine. But she did tell me that once, so it wasn't completely a lie."

"A point for me, and now you've got to tell me the truth."

"Fine," he said, pretending to be upset. "Here goes. After the Houdini fuckup, I sort of had a hard time. I went through some stuff, and yadda, yadda, yadda, I missed a bunch of school, my grades bit the dirt, and I graduated by the skin of my teeth. I didn't apply for college because . . ."

"Because?"

"It was a bad time in my life."

I waited for him to explain.

He considered his words carefully, starting and stopping a couple of times before settling on, "I did a stupid thing."

"Okay . . . ?"

"I was mad at the world for losing my hearing," he explained. "Which was ridiculous, because first of all, it was my fault. And second of all, once I started . . ." He paused to think, head turned toward the city lights. "Once I started getting my shit together, started working full-time at the hotel last summer after graduation, made some . . . adjustments. I guess you could say things slowly got better. But over the last year, I've been thinking, hey— do I really want to end up working at the Cascadia for the rest of my life? No. I do not. So, I'm trying to figure out what to do. I mean, yes, I'd like to do magic for a living, but I don't want to end up being the sad magician that does kids' birthday parties or gets paid in free appetizers to entertain people in chain restaurants, and I hate Las Vegas, so where does that leave me? Pickpocketing?"

"Might be lucrative. But then there's the jail time."

"Exactly. Anyway, my mom wants me to go to wood tech school."

"Huh?"

He gestured loosely. "There's a vocational school that teaches you how to build things. Carpentry. Boats. Furniture. There's a woman who lives in our community—"

"That Nest place you told me about."

"Yep, that's the one. And Katy is one of the residents there. She built all our picnic tables, cabinets . . . even remodeled two of the houses. She's a genius. Anyway, she's been teaching me stuff, and I'm pretty good at it. And that's why my mom says I should learn a trade instead of going to college. I don't know. It's weird to think about not going to a regular university, or whatever."

It sounded as if he was fishing for an opinion, so I said, "Just because you take a few classes doesn't mean you have to commit to it forever, right?"

"I suppose, but I'm sort of a commitment type of guy." He gestured loosely with his hands. "Anyway, I'm still not sure."

"I get that. I'm not sure what I should be doing either."

"Are you going to college?"

"I want to," I said. "But I don't have a diploma."

"There aren't homeschool diplomas? I don't know how that works. Your grandma taught you? Did you have a regular sched-ule like people in school? Was she teaching you the same stuff we were taught? Did you study and have tests?"

"Tests. Lessons. Regular school schedule. Grandma was a high school teacher before my mom died, so she knew what she was doing. In some ways, I probably got a better education than a lot of kids, because it was one-on-one without distractions. But in other ways, not so much. I mean, I *wanted* to go to public school. She wouldn't let me. My grandparents argued over it. She won. And then she died before she could issue me a diploma, so technically, even though I scored high on my SATs and made good grades—"

"She graded you?"

"It wasn't hobo school. There were grades, like I said. And tests, which I passed. But I don't have a diploma, so I never officially graduated. Which makes things complicated for college applications."

"Whoa. That's wild. I've never met anyone who was homeschooled. I have a million more questions."

I smiled. "I thought we only got three. And that was your second question for me. By the way, I should get a point for catching you in the clown school lie. And let the record show that I believed you were telling the truth about wood school."

"And I think *you* were telling the truth about hobo school—or homeschooling, as you claim."

"I mean, I can hop a train and heat a can of beans over an open fire like no one's business."

"Is that right?" he said, teeth flashing at me in the dark as he grinned. "If I went to wood school, I could probably make you a stick for your hobo sack."

"A bindle?"

"They have a name for that?"

"You'd know this if you'd gone to hobo school."

He laughed loudly. The photographer on the other side of the park turned to look at us while I shushed Daniel. And for a moment I became paranoid. Someone was walking around the sculpture in the middle of the park—was it Raymond Darke?

It wasn't. But it sobered us up.

We were quiet for a long stretch of time, each buried in our own thoughts. My mind went back to when he said he'd done a stupid thing. I desperately wanted to know what that was, but I didn't want to press him if he wasn't ready to share it. He was so open about everything; maybe that was off-limits for a good reason. So my mind drifted to other answers I wanted from him. One answer in particular.

I cleared my throat and said, "You agreed with me when I said that what happened the first time we met was a mistake. So why did you post that Missed Connections ad?"

Every casual line on his body straightened at once. "You saw the ad?"

"Only after you told me about it. Before you took it down."

"Well, I'd found you, so there was no reason to keep it up."

Oh. "I just assumed you'd changed your mind. About us. You said all that stuff about fate, and then you said maybe you didn't believe in fate." And maybe after he spent more time around me at the hotel, he realized I wasn't his one true destiny. Not that I thought I was. I still barely knew him, and he barely knew me.

He started to answer, changed his mind, and started over again.

"I told myself if you answered the ad, it was a signpost."

"A . . . ?"

"Signpost. Do you ever feel like the universe is trying to communicate with you? If you just listen hard enough and pay attention to things around you? I know that sounds a little wacky, but it happens to me. Streetlights blink when I walk under them, or I see things I've dreamed about . . . It's hard to explain, but I think sometimes they're signs. And if I follow them, they lead me to important things. Or important people. And I think I was supposed to meet you for a reason."

I didn't know what to say to that, so I tried to keep the conversation light. "This sounds a lot like fate."

"Fate will find a way, Birdie."

"Are you trying to quote Jeff Goldblum? It's 'life.' *Life* finds a way. Jurassic dinosaur apocalypse, not destiny."

"Can't we have both?" he said with a smile. "Look, I'm not trying to get heavy here. I'm just saying, maybe I was supposed to meet you because of Raymond Darke. Or maybe it was for something bigger." He tugged his ear several times. "As for the other thing, I agreed that us having sex was a mistake because it was. Clearly. It was . . . pretty awful."

Ah, there it was. My old friend humiliation and its accompanying red face.

"No, no, no," he said quickly. "I didn't mean . . . I meant, yes, it was awkward at the end, but it started out good. Right? It's just . . . Why didn't you tell me you were a virgin?"

Ugh. He knew? I didn't want to think about how, but I definitely never told him. Why did I even ask about this? Rewind! Cancel!

After a strained moment, I reconsidered what he'd just asked me and got a little angry.

"Are you *blaming me*?"

He held up both hands. "Not at all. It just . . . can be different the first time."

"I'm not an idiot. I'm aware of women's bodies. I have one." I was most definitely aware of the pain and the smear of blood that haunted me until I got home, until I cried in the shower and later threw away my underwear—making sure it was well hidden, as if it were a piece of murder evidence. I think I halfway expected Grandma Eleanor to rise from the grave and tell me I was just like my mother. As much as I loved my mom, sometimes I felt I'd never be free of her mistakes . . . or free of Grandma judging me for them, because my mother wasn't alive to carry the guilt anymore.

Daniel sighed. "This is coming out all wrong."

"What are you trying to say, then?"

"That . . ." He drew in a fast breath and said, "We were racing like the world was burning down. Like we might get caught. It should have been somewhere else—somewhere private. In a bed, with candles. Or after a date at the top of the Space Needle," he said, gesturing loosely toward the lit-up white tower in the distance.

"Space Needle?"

"Something more romantic. I don't know," he said, throwing up his arms.

"I don't need all of that romantic stuff."

"Well, maybe I do," he said, a little indignant. "All I'm saying is that I feel awful about how everything played out, and I'm an idiot for not picking up on the clues, but I guess I'm a shitty detective. And I liked you too much. I was greedy and stupid and not thinking. But also, you wouldn't talk to me."

"You didn't say anything! I thought, okay, he's finished. I guess that's that."

He made a face and held up a finger. "Um, I didn't finish. For the record. I stopped. There's a difference."

A renewed surge of embarrassment raced through my body. "Well, I'm sorry I didn't realize that," I said angrily. "Do you want some sort of good-guy prize?"

"What? No!" He growled in frustration, pressing the heels of his palms into his eyes. "I don't want a prize. I'm trying to say that I'm sorry that it sucked, and I feel responsible. I wish you'd stayed and talked to me. I wish I'd had the sense to talk to you more before we started. I wish . . . I don't know, Birdie. I feel like an asshole, and I wish I had a time machine so that I could go back and change everything. Because it could have been so much better. We could have gone to the movies that night. We could have gotten to know each other first." He blew out a long breath through his nostrils. "All I'm saying is that I wish you had talked to me instead of leaving."

"What do you want me to say about it now? That I wasn't thinking when we got in your car and that I freaked out because I realized halfway through it all that you were a stranger, and it was just way too intense? That I'm not good at heart-to-heart talks because I'm terrified of getting too close to anyone—because everyone I care about always leaves me, so why bother?"

He stared at me, eyes wide, body rigid.

The underside of my eyelids prickled. *Do not cry. Do not cry.* I pushed myself off the bench and paced in front of the wall, just to clear my head and put some distance between us. He didn't follow.

Everything he'd said replayed inside my head on a loop. And now that I was able to calm down a little, I wished I hadn't said what I did. It wasn't fair to him. See, this was why I didn't do this kind of thing. I wanted to erase everything I'd just said and go back to the first part of Daniel's game, when it was easy and breezy and my heart didn't feel as if it were studded with broken glass.

Maybe it wasn't too late to apologize.

But before I could rally the nerve to turn around and find out, I spotted someone walking two dogs. A husky man. With a baseball cap.

It was the man from the elevator. I'd bet my life on it. The clerk at the record store had been right. Bill Waddle, opera fan, walked his dogs at dawn.

Was it possible that right now I was looking at the actual Raymond Darke?

All the hairs on my arms lifted. My brain closed the door on our emotional talk and switched into investigation mode—something that was much more comfortable, frankly.

I spun around to signal Daniel, but he was right in front of me. Startled, I let out a little cry, which carried across the park. The photographer looked at us again. So did the man walking his dogs.

"Oh no," I whispered. "I think that's him. He sees us."

"Shit," Daniel murmured. "Move here. Okay, that's good."

Now my back was to the man. "Is he still looking?" I whispered. "Is it Darke?"

"It's definitely him," he whispered back. "I'm going to put my hand on your shoulder. Don't freak. Just act casual. I don't want him to recognize me."

Duh. Me, either! I wanted him to come back to the hotel on Tuesday night, so I could trail him and find out what he's doing there every week. I didn't need him seeing me here now and getting spooked if he recognized me later in the hotel. No detective worth their salt would be so sloppy.

Daniel rested his hand on my shoulder. Several tense seconds ticked by. I watched Daniel's face while he watched Darke under lowered eyelids, and my thoughts began to wander. He smelled nice. Maybe that was his hair. It fell over one shoulder and down his chest, and it was right in front of my face. Close enough that if I leaned forward a few inches, I could stick my face in it. It would be soft, and—

What was the matter with me? Soft hair? These were probably a serial killer's thoughts. And for the love of Pete, why was I even thinking about this? Hadn't we just had a fight? My feelings were certainly raw enough.

His hand was shifting to the back of my neck. I became light-headed, thinking about all the movies that had scenes in which people faked a kiss to avoid being seen. Was he planning to do that?

Did I want him to?

It didn't matter, because his hand suddenly dropped to his side. Right. Ha. Yeah. No kiss was coming, so I could forget that silly notion.

"He's not looking anymore," Daniel murmured. "Let's move before he leaves the park."

Grabbing my hand, Daniel jogged toward the metal sculpture. I tried to run without making noise. The damp grass muffled our footsteps, and we slowed when our shoes hit concrete. The sculpture cast a big shadow, but it was getting lighter outside, and everything had that funny haziness of dawn. Dark . . . but not. Almost morning, not really night. I could see Raymond Darke clearly—could see the lolling tongues of his two beefy dogs. If I could see him, could he see me?

"Should we trail him?" Daniel whispered. "He might be headed home. We could see where he lives. How far could it be? Those mutts don't look like they were bred for long-distance walks."

"I don't know. . . . I think it's a bad idea. What if—"

A man stepped out from a shadow at the edge of the park. A uniformed cop. Darke stopped and talked to him. One of the bulldogs was pulling on his leash, trying to get around the cop's legs. Holy crap, those dogs looked mean. Like they could tear someone's hand off.

Suddenly the bulldog lunged and began barking. His brother joined in, a chest-deep cacophony that sent my adrenaline soaring: *the dogs were barking at us.*

For one terror-filled moment, I pictured the bulldogs breaking their leashes and running to attack us. But it was so much worse: the author and the cop both turned around, and Darke pointed in our direction.

"Oh, shit!" Daniel whispered loudly. "We gotta leave. Now!"

The cop shouted something at us that I didn't catch because we'd turned around in tandem and strode away. Not fast enough to be running—that would look suspicious. But fast enough that my calves burned, trying to keep up with Daniel's longer stride. I didn't know where we were going. Wasn't his car in the opposite direction?

We crossed the street and walked half a block before we could head around a building and catch our breath. Was the cop following, or had we lost him? I didn't hear anyone coming. Maybe we were being ridiculous.

"We weren't doing anything illegal," I said, more to myself than to Daniel.

"I think he might have seen my face. Fuck," Daniel swore.

"The cop?"

"No, Darke." Daniel seemed even more upset than I felt. "This was stupid. I'm not even sure what we accomplished by coming here."

We'd learned nothing about Darke. Possibly blew our cover. Nearly got attacked by rabid bulldogs. And, oh, that's right: our terrible attempt at sex that I'd been desperately trying to forget? It was now back out in the open and more painful than ever.

If we'd accomplished anything, it was that we'd dug up a giant pit of misery beneath our own feet and both fallen inside.

My worries didn't diminish when he drove me back downtown in silence. No David Bowie. No arguing. No nothing. It wasn't until couple of hours later, when I was back at home and getting ready for bed, that a light shone from the top of our proverbial misery pit. I got a text from Daniel. It said:

TRUTH OR LIE, BONUS QUESTION:

Do u think we'd be together now if we never went to my car that day?

I reread it several times and finally typed out my answer:

I'm not sure.

Then I turned off my phone and went to sleep. Let him figure out if I was lying.

Maybe I'd need to figure that out myself.

13

After the disastrous trip to Kerry Park, nothing more was said about that night. Not about our emotional talk before the man and his bulldogs showed up and not about his Truth or Lie text—or my reply, which he never answered. Our communication breakdown was helped along by the fact that our work shifts didn't line up the next two nights. I was both relieved and bothered, because it felt like we'd left everything unfinished, and that made my thoughts go in strange directions.

Maybe he regretted what he'd said. Maybe after my reply to his text, he decided none of it mattered and perhaps I wasn't worth the trouble after all.

Why did that make me feel panicky? Why could I not stop thinking about all of it?

And worrying.

And wishing we could talk more about it.

No way was I bringing any of this up with Grandpa, and

later, when I tried getting advice from Aunt Mona, she was no help. She was too busy planning a date with waste-of-space Leon Snodgrass, who had convinced her to let him take her out on the *Spirit of Mona*. I hated him and his dumb yacht, and I couldn't understand why she was falling for something so saccharine.

Just when I was starting to go a little crazy about everything, Daniel texted out of the blue to remind me about Darke's weekly visit to the hotel and proposed that we pick back up on our "case," as he called it. I was thrilled. We were still partners! I hadn't driven him away. It was surprising how happy this made me. How relieved I felt.

Daniel and Birdie the couple might be a failure. But Nick and Nora the detective team were still okay.

After a couple of back-and-forths, we decided we would try to stealthily listen in on what happened inside Darke's room. No bulldogs. No cops.

He suggested we meet up somewhere outside the hotel before work tonight, and we decided the ferry terminal was as good a place as any.

On my way to the Bainbridge ferry terminal, I stopped to buy a warm cinnamon roll from my second-favorite bakery on the island. The woman who came up with the Cinnabon recipe lived here on the island, so it seemed only fair that we had amazing cinnamon rolls. I originally intended to get one for me, but at the last second I found myself thinking of Daniel and asking for two. I carried them like wounded birds nested inside their mini bakery box and headed toward the terminal.

It was only a few minutes before the ferry departed—early-evening rush hour for commuters—and I was cutting it close. If I was going to witness Raymond Darke at his usual Tuesday check-in at seven p.m., this was the last boat I could take. I hurried inside the waiting area, preparing to sprint up the ramp—

Only to stop short.

Standing in front of me was an unexpected sight.

Daniel.

"Hi," he said, raising a hand.

My heart thudded against my ribs. "What are you doing here?"

"Are you mad?"

"Why would I be mad?"

"That seems like a trick question."

"I'm just . . ." *So very confused.* "I thought we were meeting at the terminal in the city."

He squinted one eye closed. "I was bored at home, and I thought I'd see what the ferry ride was like . . . and I tried to guess which ferry you were taking today, but I was wrong." He made a funny, self-deprecating face. "So, anyway, I guess I'm idiot because I've been stuck here for more than an hour. And I've read all the Department of Transportation pamphlets. Did you know six million people ride the ferries here every year?"

"I did not."

"And there are seals in the marina."

"The big one is Herbert," I informed him. "Fletcher Bay has otters."

He lightly kicked at the glossy floor with the rubber heel of his black Converse low-tops. "I tried texting earlier this afternoon, but you didn't answer, and that made me afraid you'd changed your mind and weren't coming into the city early. I came out here to hopefully change your mind, but . . . I didn't really know where you lived, exactly, and you haven't changed your mind, because . . . here you are." He laughed nervously. "So clearly this was not well thought out, much like most of my life."

My heart did a few leaps and jumps. I juggled my bakery box and struggled to retrieve my phone, only to find three unread messages from Daniel. "Crap," I said. "My ringer was off. I guess I didn't check it after we first texted about meeting up. I never heard them."

"Oh, good. I mean, in my head you'd blocked me."

"Not yet."

"Fair enough." He flashed me a smile before gesturing toward my hand. "Why do you do that counting thing with your fingers? I've noticed it a few times now."

I looked down at my hand as if it were a foreign object I couldn't comprehend. "Oh," I said, embarrassed. "It's silly. Just this little trick I do to make sure I'm awake. I have a lot of sleep issues."

"Like falling asleep in public."

"Like that," I said, shifting my cinnamon roll box. "The finger counting . . . Have you ever wondered 'am I dreaming?' in the middle of dream, but you weren't sure how to tell?"

"Sure?" he said, slightly skeptical.

"Well, what you can do is either find a clock or read something, or you can look at your hand. If the clock dial is melting, or you can't read words, or you have too many fingers . . . you're probably dreaming."

"Huh," he said. "I didn't know that."

"Reality check."

"Did we pass?" he asked, eyes glinting. "Are we in a dream?"

"I'm not. Are you?"

He counted his fingers. "All there, as it should be. Thank God, because being stuck in this terminal is a little nightmarish. I'm hoping you're feeling sorry enough for me to let me keep you company on the way back. I mean, sure. This briny island air is good for the lungs," he said, thumping his chest with the back of his fist as he inhaled deeply through his nostrils. "But I don't think I can stick around for a third ferry."

Daniel was wrong: I didn't feel sorry for him. I felt . . . happy to see him. Surprisingly happy. Our unfinished argument back in the park that night had felt like the giant Fremont Troll had left its home under the bridge across the city and was clinging to my shoulders, but now that I saw with my own eyes that we were going to be okay, that ugly bridge troll was suddenly several pounds lighter.

"I'm glad you came out here," I said shyly, surprising both of us. "I even brought you a peace offering."

"You did?"

I nodded. "Come on. The ferry waits for no one."

We hurriedly boarded the green-and-white *Tacoma*, making it aboard right at the two-minute cutoff before sailing. It was more crowded than usual, but even so, there were a dozen nooks and crannies to find peace and quiet. And after we passed through the main floor, which looked a bit like an airport waiting area, we stopped off at the food counter to purchase hot coffee and tea. Then we found an empty booth near a window that overlooked the sundeck and settled in for the half-hour ride to the city.

June Gloom was in full effect. Not even a sliver of sunshine peeked through gray clouds, and all the kids running around the breezy outdoor deck on the other side of our window were armored in windbreakers and lightweight hoodies. But at least it wasn't drizzling, and as the ferry glided away from the island, I pointed out my house on the beach. When it passed from view, Daniel waxed poetic over the ferry's amenities: "It has hot tater tots *and* Wi-Fi?" This was far better than sitting in traffic for half an hour, he informed me.

Having never sat in much traffic, I wouldn't know. But we compared commutes, and before I knew it, we were chatting nonstop. About his family and mine. About work. About all the shops he'd seen walking around the marina and downtown, wasting time that afternoon between ferries.

And about the glory of Bainbridge cinnamon rolls.

"Dear God," he murmured, licking icing off the side of his finger.

"Few things are better," I confirmed.

"Almost as good as breakfast pie at the Moonlight."

"I needed the sugar," I admitted. "I didn't sleep well."

"You never sleep well," he said, squinting at me.

Honestly, I was starting to think that the graveyard shift at the hotel was making my sleep problems worse. It was the first time I'd been forced to stick to a rigid schedule beyond my grandma's homeschooling lessons, and I felt as if I were existing in a world between sleep and wakefulness.

"Do you ever have dreams where you wake up, or you think you do, but you're still dreaming?" I asked Daniel.

"Once, when I was a kid."

"Well, that's been happening to me a lot lately. I've always had crazy dreams. Really vivid. Sometimes when I'm dozing off, I start dreaming so fast, I can't tell if I'm still awake."

"The finger counting," he said.

I nodded, a little sheepish, and then continued. "Early this morning something different happened. I dreamed that I woke up and couldn't move. I was completely paralyzed. I could open my eyes, but that was it. And the worst part was, there was a creature sitting on my chest. I couldn't really see any details, but he was like this big, heavy shadowy . . . demon. I was so terrified. And when I tried to scream, nothing came out. Then I really woke up."

"Oh! It's like that spooky gothic painting," Daniel said, snapping his fingers repeatedly as he tried to remember. "It came up in art class . . . *The Nightmare*. Some dude, Fussolini or Fuseli, or something. You know the one?"

Now that he was saying it, yeah, it sounded familiar. "A woman is lying on a bed?"

He nodded. "That's the one. Some weird troll-like demon is sitting on her while she sleeps."

"Well, call me a work of art, because it happened. And it scared me to pieces."

"Maybe it's a dream message. Is something weighing on you? Do you feel crushed?"

Only by imaginary bridge trolls clinging to my neck. "I feel . . . full of delicious cinnamon roll. Does that count?"

"Maybe you'll dream about turning into a pastry tonight," he said.

"Maybe *you'll* dream about a giant pastry girl crushing your chest."

"Birdie, I dream about that every night," he said with a grin.

We finished our hot drinks and ditched our booth, heading out on the deck to lean over the railing and enjoy the salty breeze. It was so easy to talk to him now. Why? I wanted to believe it was because we weren't fighting about our regrettable back-seat adventure anymore, but I had the sneaking suspicion it was just the opposite.

I think it was because we *had* talked about it.

Getting all of it out in the open had made what happened between us . . . more tolerable? More *something*, because I could relax—so much so, the half-hour ferry ride passed in a snap. When the IVAR'S ACRES OF CLAMS sign and the rest of the Seattle waterfront district popped into view, I was genuinely surprised.

After the ferry pulled into the terminal and dropped its front gate, we disembarked with the rest of the crowd, never stopping our conversation. One moment we were laughing about how we ran from Darke's dogs and the cop—it seemed funnier now that time had passed—and the next thing I knew, we were turning onto First Avenue, and the hotel was right in front of us.

"Fifteen minutes to spare," Daniel said, shoving his hands into the pockets of his hoodie. "Still think our plan is kosher?"

"Better than our plan in the park, which was a disaster."

"Let's hope he doesn't bring those damn dogs this time," he said. "Come on."

It was strange to be in the hotel while there was still an abundance of daylight, though most of the midshift "Hawk" crew was familiar, because we took over for them when their shifts ended. And Daniel seemed to be on a friendly basis with everyone, because he had no problems sweet-talking the porter and desk clerk to text him when a Mr. Ivanov checked in around seven. And after confirming that the manager on duty was in the back offices, we stepped into one of the gold elevators, and Daniel used his key card to give us access to the fifth floor.

I'd been up here only once before, during training. All the

floors had the same basic layout, the same gold lighting and forest-green carpeted hallways, but this floor had original paintings instead of prints. A display of local Salish tribal wood carvings. No Coke or ice machines to make noise: fifth-floor guests had a dedicated employee on call to run back and forth for all their needs. It also had a recessed alcove with two plush wingback chairs. And the potted trees that flanked the alcove provided anyone sitting there with a bit of shelter from guests entering room 514.

The perfect place to spy on Darke.

We waited nervously for several minutes until Daniel's phone buzzed with an incoming text. "The eagle is heading to the nest," he told me in a hushed voice. "I repeat, the eagle is heading—"

"We aren't spies."

"Speak for yourself. I'm deep undercover."

"You're sitting behind a potted plant."

"I'm sure James Bond has utilized a potted plant or two for cover."

"Oh, so you're James Bond now?"

He gestured at himself. "Suave, dashing. Can fistfight on moving trains. And this skinny weakling body is irresistible to the ladies."

"Did you say *resistible*?"

He clutched the front of his shirt and made a pained face. "My tender male ego . . . shattering . . . into a million pieces."

I extended my leg and playfully kicked at him, but he caught my foot and trapped it between his knees. I had to stifle a laugh and tried to squirm my way loose. "Let me go or I'll kick you in your tender male ego."

"You wouldn't dare."

"Oh, I *so* would!"

He held on to my foot harder. "Don't make *me* pull out my 007 spy-gadget thingamabob and obliterate you right here behind this potted palm tree. It will—"

The elevator *ding*ed.

We froze. I came to my senses and scrambled out of his grip. He signaled me with a finger in front of his lips and craned his neck to see through the tree branches. In the distance, someone was talking, probably on the phone. It was brief, and something was odd about it, though I couldn't quite make out why—too far away—but now the person was getting closer, approaching us. Fabric swished . . . and then paused.

I carefully turned to my side and peered through the potted greenery. A tall, pale man in a suit with slicked-back hair was inserting his key card into the door lock. It beeped pleasantly, and then he was heading inside, rolling a black carry-on suitcase.

When the door closed behind him, Daniel said, "Who the hell was that?"

I thought for a moment before realizing. Of course. "It's Ivanov."

"That's who checks in? It's not a pseudonym? That's . . ."

"That's who Darke is meeting," I finished.

And sure enough, the elevator *ding*ed a second time, and along came a second man: Raymond Darke. No mistaking him or his blue baseball cap. But he was accompanied by a blond woman with sharp eyes and model-long legs, striding beneath the hem of a wispy dress. She was younger than Darke, perhaps in her early forties, and something about the way she carried herself conjured images of multimillion-dollar mansions and black-tie parties.

Darke stopped at room 514 and knocked on the door three times. It opened, and the man inside greeted the couple with a peculiar accent.

Russian?

Daniel and I listened intently while the door closed again. Daniel was filming the hallway with his phone, and after a few moments he signaled that he wanted to move closer to the room. Two fingers pointed toward his eyes, then me, then the hallway—he wanted me to be lookout.

He crept to the room, ducking out of the sight of the peephole, and pressed his ear to the door for what felt like an excessively long time. Long enough for my neck to ache from swinging it back and forth down the hotel hallway. And long enough for my imagination to run wild. What was going on inside that room? Were they filming high-class porn? Was she a prostitute? A lawyer? A film agent? Maybe he was discussing high-stakes foreign rights for his books.

Or were Daniel and I on the right track when we joked about Russian arms deals? Was Ivanov a Russian mobster? Had Daniel been closer to the truth than we knew, joking about James Bond?

WAS THIS SOME KIND OF INTERNATIONAL SPY RING?

Just when I didn't think I could take it anymore, Daniel lunged away from the door and took four quick steps. He slipped behind the potted tree alongside me as Darke and the woman exited the room.

I stared at their retreating backs. We couldn't follow them. Not that I needed another reason not to do so after the incident in the park. But attempting to trail *two* people seemed so much more dangerous—especially when one of those people could recognize Daniel's face.

So, what now?

I gave Daniel a wide-eyed look. He gave me one in return, and then picked up my hand and placed it over his sternum. His chest rose and fell; his heartbeat pounded fiercely under my palm. Not like my frightened-rabbit heart, but strong and sure: *Thump, thump. Thump, thump.* He lifted both brows at me, as if to say, *See? I'm about to die of a stroke.* Or maybe, *See? We've lost our minds, getting involved in an international spy ring.* And when I didn't move my hand away and his eyelids grew heavy, it almost looked as if he were trying to say: *See? There really was something between us.*

He let go of my hand, so I moved it away from his chest quickly, embarrassed, but soon realized that he was only trying to focus on the hotel room again, where Ivanov was now leaving with his suitcase. When the man's lanky figure turned the corner to head toward the elevators, I whispered to Daniel, "Did you hear anything? What were they doing?"

"Only voices. The doors are too thick. I'm sorry, but it's a bust."

"Nothing at all?"

"The woman laughed once toward the end. They sounded happy. That's it."

I tried not to allow disappointment to sink in too deep. And then an idea hit me. "Let's follow Ivanov out of the hotel."

"Seriously? After the park incident, with the entire Seattle-fucking-PD after us?"

I rolled my eyes. "It was one cop, and we never even knew for sure he tried to follow us."

"I know for sure that Darke saw my face, and maybe you haven't noticed, because you don't stare at me often enough with yearning and devotion, but I'm a little recognizable."

"Tuck your hair inside your hoodie and make it disappear, Mr. Magician. We still have an hour and a half before our shift. Maybe we'll spot a car tag number, or something."

"A car tag number," he said, incredulous.

"Come on, Nick. Are we solving a GD mystery, or aren't we?"

A slow grin split his face. "Nora, my dear, you know I can't resist it when you use profanity."

"All right, then," I said, high on adrenaline. "Let's follow this mother shucker out of the hotel."

14

One elevator was still in use when we darted down the hallway. We took our chances that Ivanov was inside that one and called up the other. Meanwhile, Daniel texted both the desk clerk and the midshift van driver and asked them to keep an eye out for Mr. Blue Baseball Cap and "a tall Vladimir Putin fucker in a suit."

By the time we'd made it back down to the lobby, we'd learned three things. (1) Darke and his female companion had left the hotel in a private rideshare that was idling outside at the curb. (2) Ivanov had used express checkout from inside the room— skipping the front desk completely. (3) Ivanov had *just* left the hotel on foot . . . but not before he asked the porter out front for directions to Pier 54.

That was all we needed. We raced around the corner of the Cascadia, and before you could hum the latest James Bond theme song, we spotted him waiting for a crosswalk light. He was on his phone, using a Bluetooth earpiece.

"Who *is* this guy?" Daniel said in a low voice.

No idea, but we kept a cautious distance while the man chat- ted nonstop on his phone, gesturing to no one as he quickly crossed the street. I mentally struck "arms dealer" off my list of possible careers for this guy. Not that I personally knew any, but Ivanov had the aura of a dealmaker. A stockbroker, or a real estate go-between. I hated to let Daniel down, but this big mystery he'd stumbled upon was probably something boring. Maybe Darke was just buying a big piece of property. He *was* a millionaire. Didn't they do things like that?

Ivanov ended his phone call waited for the signal before cross- ing Alaskan Way to the waterfront. As we followed, Pier 54 came into view, which was basically a tourist trap, like all the piers here. This one had a boat charter booth and a couple of sailboats, and a little farther down, Ivar's Acres of Clams—a Seattle institution I saw every day from the ferry.

"Maybe he's got a hankering for fish and chips?" Daniel said.

Nope. The man was headed straight for the end of the pier. "Ye Olde Curiosity Shop."

"Should we go inside?" Daniel asked, glancing up at the dark- ening sky and the drizzle that was now falling. "Ivanov doesn't know our faces."

"And he doesn't have guard dogs."

"Fuck it," Daniel said enthusiastically. "Let's do this."

The Curiosity Shop had been one of my favorite places in the city when I was a kid; Mom and I must have come here a hundred times. One-part museum (actual mummies), one-part carnival side show (Fiji mermaid taxidermy hanging from the ceiling), and one-part novelty gift shop (vampire hunter kits), it was a popular tourist attraction. If you wanted a totem pole or a necklace with your name carved on a piece of rice, this was your store. Or you could just browse the glass cases filled with turn-of-the-century oddities.

I hadn't been in here for years, and the shop itself had moved between a couple of locations on the waterfront, but it smelled the same as I remembered, pleasantly musty. And at the moment, it was moderately crowded; a lot of families with loud kids gawked at an antique hinged educational aid nicknamed Medical Ed.

The crowds were good for us, since we were trying to avoid Ivanov's attention. He looked around a little, scanning the jam-packed shop, and then made a beeline for the Javari shrunken-head display.

Curiouser and curiouser . . .

Daniel and I pretended to be browsing while we listened in to a conversation Ivanov was having with one of the store's clerks. "Are these heads real?" he asked in a heavily accented voice.

The clerk answered, "Some of them came from the Heye Foundation in New York before the government banned the trafficking of human remains. A few may be monkey heads. Those were often sold to Northern tradespeople. Monkey or human, the process is still the same—Javari tribesmen in Peru would remove the skull from the back of the head, sew it up, and boil it to shrink it down."

I puffed up my lips to stop myself from gagging. Daniel pretended to chop my head off with his hand, and I swatted him away.

"However, the heads for sale are made from goatskin," the clerk informed him, showing him a line of gruesome heads hanging from a pole, each about the size of a fist.

"Fascinating," Ivanov said. "I have a twelve-year-old son who loves morbid things, so he will be happy if I bring him one back."

"Where are you from?" the clerk asked.

"Kiev."

"Is that the Ukraine?"

"Indeed, it is," Ivanov said.

Not Russian! Daniel and I shared a look.

"That's a long way away," the clerk said. "Here on business?"

Ivanov nodded. "Both here and in San Francisco—that's where I'm headed tonight. I've been in the States for a month. I'm homesick for my wife's cooking."

"Being away from home is hard," the clerk said.

"Yes. I'm ready to return, but I've got a couple things to tie up before I go. San Francisco this week, then back here to Seattle, then home, finally."

The clerk talked about jet lag and how that kind of traveling was tough on a body.

Ivanov studied the shrunken heads more closely and said, "The next time I come through Seattle, I won't be in this area—it will be more of a quick jaunt uptown for a show before I fly home to

Kiev in July. Because I'm downtown today, an associate of mine suggested I stop here while I wait for a rideshare to the airport."

"Nothing says Seattle like a shrunken head," the clerk agreed with a smile.

Ivanov was buying up several of them, and then he got a text and informed the clerk that his rideshare car was pulling up, so he needed to hurry. We watched him pay for his heads and rush out, shoving his purchase under his coat to shield it from the rain as he entered a car. Then he was gone, and we stood outside, unsure what to do next.

I flipped up the hood of my jacket. "He's Ukrainian."

"And he's been here for a month—also in San Francisco. That may explain the address he used to check in, and it *definitely* matches up with all of Darke's visits to the hotel. They started about a month ago."

"I wonder if Darke was the 'associate' who suggested he come to buy shrunken-head souvenirs."

"Maybe. I mean, this is more information than we've discovered so far, but . . ."

"It still doesn't tell us much," I said.

"He said he wouldn't be coming through Seattle again until July and not in this area."

"Uptown for a show. We have an uptown?"

"He probably means Lower Queen Anne. Seattle Center, all that," Daniel said, dismissive. "I'm more concerned that he won't be coming to the hotel again. I mean, is that what he's saying?

Whatever was happening in the hotel is finished? Darke won't be coming back? This is over?"

Exactly what I was wondering, only he sounded more upset about it. "Don't be discouraged," I said. "Mysteries aren't solved overnight. We can stake out the hotel for Darke again next Tuesday. Maybe this is just one piece of it. Maybe Ivanov is just one player."

We flattened ourselves against the wall of the building, standing under an overhang. Then Daniel crossed his arms over his chest and said, "You know what we should do? Get back to the hotel before room 514 is cleaned. Snoop around. See if any clues were left behind."

"Isn't that against company rules?"

Daniel's smile was mischievous. "Not if we don't get caught."

It took us a few minutes to hike it back up to the hotel. And after checking where the manager on duty was (in the back offices), we made another trip to the fifth floor—this time with someone from housekeeping named Beth. She was a *little* too friendly with Daniel, all smiles and coy jokes. But then she used her master key card to let us into the room and assured us no one had been inside to clean. Then she closed the door and promised to keep an eye out for management while we looked around.

"Let's see what we can find," Daniel said, rubbing his hands together. "I'll search on that side, and you search here."

"All right." I glanced at the bed. Made, of course, the foot draped with a Pendleton wool Nez Percé–tribe woven blanket. My side of the room looked utterly untouched. Room service menu propped on a console table. Curtains opened to a rain-speckled view of Puget Sound and the sprawling waterfront docks we'd just left.

I checked the bathroom. All the toiletries were in their places except the hand soap, which someone had used to wash their hands. Toilet paper was still folded into the silly triangular point that's *supposed* to be a sign to guests that the room's been cleaned . . . but really just lets you know the housekeeper's fingers have been there, possibly right after they were wiping down the germy toilet.

"You and Beth known each other a long time?" I called out from the bathroom as I checked inside the jetted tub.

"Huh? Oh, I used to sometimes work in the day when I started. So, about a year, I guess."

"She likes you."

"She's just friendly. We dated once. Sort of a bomb."

That bothered me more than it should have. "Isn't that against hotel policy—fraternizing with other employees? How many coworkers have you dated?"

"Yes," he said, sounding irritated. "Much like what we're doing now, it's against the rules. But it depends on what you consider a date."

"Hooking up in the back seat of your car?" I said, unable to control the annoyance in my voice.

He was quiet for a long moment. "That wasn't a date. And you're the only one, if that matters."

"Why would it matter?"

"I don't know, Birdie. You tell me. You're the one who brought it up."

I didn't respond to that. He was right. I was being petty. And we were having such a nice day together, so why was I trying to sabotage it? I glanced though a stack of bath towels and called out, "I'm not finding anything in the bathroom."

"Oh, shit. No way! Birdie, check this out."

I popped my head out of the doorway and spotted Daniel standing in front of the sofa, holding something. When I got closer, he turned around and held it up.

"Is that . . . ?"

"The bag Darke was carrying," he confirmed. "All the times I've studied it in the security footage . . . I never noticed this. Look at the front."

Excited, he handed me a black-and-white striped plastic bag. It was wrinkled and creased, as if it had been balled up. An unassuming logo was printed on the front—so small, anyone might miss it. A stylized music note surrounded by the words TENOR RECORDS.

"Oh, wow!" I said. And then it hit me. "It's empty. It wasn't when he was carrying it in the hallway. And he left it behind."

"Whatever was in that bag, he gave it to Ivanov. So, I'm thinking cash."

"Where was it?"

"In the trash," Daniel said, pointing to a gold trash can near a desk. "They must have sat here on the sofa and chairs—a pillow from the sofa is on the floor."

I nodded and smoothed out the bag, peering inside. A piece of paper was stuck to one side. "Did you see this?"

"What is it?" He tugged one corner and we read it together. It was a printout, one that was hard to read; the ink was light, and the font was strange. The edges of the page were jagged, as if they were perforated.

"Dot matrix," Daniel murmured. "Who even has a printer like this that still works?"

"Someone from the Ukraine, apparently." All the headings at the top were Cyrillic. But the bottom half of the paper contained a spreadsheet, and inside its columns were English letters.

"It's a list of names," Daniel said, reading aloud, "Oleksander. Aneta. Danya. These are all names, yeah? What's this column?"

Initials. Maybe abbreviated surnames. And then another with either an *M* or an *F*. "Male or female?"

"Probably. And this column has dates, I think."

"They're in the European format," I said. "See? All this year."

Except one from last year, which was crossed out with a blue pen, and two more that had future dates. Neat blue checkmarks had been added to one of those names with future dates, and one dated last month. Both males.

"What the hell is this? A prostitution ring?" Daniel said. "I was joking before, but Christ. My mind is going straight to sex trafficking or mail-order brides."

"Illegal immigration?"

Daniel nodded. "Okay, yeah. That sounds *way* less scary. But it doesn't make sense. Why is Darke involved in . . . whatever this is?"

I didn't know, but inside my head I compiled all the information we'd learned today into a quick profile:

Suspect: A. Ivanov

Background: Ukrainian; married; at least one child

Age: 40s?

Occupation: Unknown. Involves him flying to the United States for multiple private meetings (Seattle and San Francisco) with clients in hotel rooms.

Medical conditions: Unknown.

Personality traits: Punctual and efficient (regular short meetings with "associate" in pricey hotel room every week). Fond of twelve-year-old son. Fond of wife's cooking. Friendly and chatty to store clerks.

Other details: Returning to Seattle in July. Left behind mysterious spreadsheet in hotel room after meeting with client Raymond Darke. (What does this say about his secretive hotel meetings?)

Daniel and I stared at the printout for a long time, tossing theories around. None of them seemed reasonable. The only thing we could agree upon was that we'd finally made real progress. Ivanov might be headed back overseas soon, but our investigation wasn't dead in the water. We had a tangible clue in our hands, and that was exhilarating. I just wasn't sure what this clue was or how it added up in the bigger picture.

"It either matters or it doesn't," Daniel murmured out of the blue.

"What does?"

"Why you asked me earlier about dating people from the hotel."

Ugh. I was hoping he'd forgotten that. Why did I bring it up? "It doesn't."

"No?" He folded up the printout. "So, you don't care how many people I've dated?"

"No."

"No?"

"I don't give two hoots about it."

"Hoots? Oh my God, Birdie. You're priceless."

"Two *whatevers*," I said, frustrated. "Damns."

"Shits," he corrected. "You don't give two shits."

"That's right. I don't give two shits. Two shitholes. Two bear balls."

"Yikes," he said. "You *really* don't care about Beth."

"Should we keep the bag? I think so. Could be evidence. You

take the bag home, and I'll hold on to the printout. I'll see if I can translate it," I said, taking it from him and stuffing it inside my purse. "And, no, I don't care about Beth."

"Because you have no interest in my love life," he said.

"No," I said firmly, turning to face him. "I do not. I was just being nosy."

He nodded slowly. "And I have no interest in yours. You could be pining away for Joseph, for all I care."

"Joseph? He won't even look me in the eye."

"Or Chuck."

I made a face. "Not if he was the last boy on earth."

Daniel shrugged. "I'm just saying, it doesn't matter to me. I get it. You're not interested."

"In what?" And why were we still standing so close? We were done reading the printout.

I backed up a step.

Something flickered in his eyes. Leonine, limbs loose, he stepped forward and erased the distance I'd put between us. "You're not interested in me."

"Oh." How was I supposed to answer that?

"And you don't care about us," he said, as if "us" were a thing that existed anymore. "You've made that clear."

"I . . ."

His face was awfully close to mine. I'd forgotten that he was just the right height, not too tall, not too short. "We have no chemistry. That's why it didn't work between us. It was a mistake."

"A mistake," I agreed. I just wish I sounded surer of it.

"And you definitely don't want to try again. I mean, you can't rewind time, and there's no do-overs, right? We're like soured milk. Just throw it out and buy a new carton. Nothing to salvage."

"Well, I wouldn't go that far." I wiped my hands on my pants. For the love of Pete, WHY DID I SWEAT SO MUCH AROUND HIM?

"But you don't believe in second chances."

"I never said that."

"Did so. In that reply to that Truth or Lie text I sent you."

"You asked me if we'd still be together if we hadn't gotten into your car the first day we met. I said I wasn't sure."

"And you were lying."

"I was?"

"That's my guess."

I felt as if this were a trap, and I wasn't running at full brain capacity with him standing so close. "Obviously we can't physically go back and erase what we did, so I guess if you're asking how to do everything all over again differently . . . ? I wouldn't know where to start."

"Where to start?" he murmured. His gaze circled my face. "Well, if I were to hazard a guess—and I'm just spitballing here—I think I'd say something like, 'Hi, my name is Daniel.' And you'd say, 'I'm Birdie, the most adorable name ever, just like me.'"

I chuckled nervously.

"And then you'd say, 'I like to solve mysteries.' And I'd say,

'Cool. Want to solve one with me?' And you'd say, 'Oh, *Daniel*. That sounds dynamite.'"

"I'd never say that."

"Sorry. I meant, 'That sounds *GD* dynamite.'"

"I sort of want to strangle you right now."

The corners of his mouth curled ever so slightly. "I hear that a lot. So, anyway, you'd agree, and we'd start solving a mystery, much like this one. And I'd say, 'I love investigating with you, Detective Birdie. Look how great we are at solving things together.'"

"We've solved nothing, just for the record."

"Shh. This is my fantasy, not yours. Then I'd say, 'Uncovering criminal activities is exciting, but how will we ever figure out what it all means? Wait, I have an idea. Maybe we should go out tomorrow night to discuss what we've found, because I checked the schedule, and unless Melinda gets a wild hair up her ass to have another pointless staff meeting, we're both off.'"

"Uh . . ." My voice squeaked and crackled when I asked, "That's what you'd say?"

"Absolutely."

"I see. And what would I say?"

He lifted his hand to my hair and gingerly touched the petals on my lily. "You'd say, 'Wow, Daniel. You're the sexiest guy ever and the coolest detective partner of all time—so much better than that jerk Watson. Of *course* I'll go out with you tomorrow night at seven thirty.'"

"That's awfully specific."

"Then you'd let me pick you up at the ferry—the Colman Dock one here in the city, not on the island. Just to be clear."

"At seven thirty."

"At seven, actually. We'd need time to get there," he explained, eyes on my hair as he traced a line down from the flower to my neck. "So, yeah. We'd go out and do a fun thing right here in the city, for which I've already reserved two tickets, just in case you'd agree."

"Oh," I breathed, feeling shaky. "Tickets to what?"

He picked up my hand and placed it over his heart. It was racing as fast as it was when he was spying in the hallway. As fast as mine. "Can't tell you that until you say yes."

"Are you asking?"

"Will you say yes? I think you should." He leaned forward until his nose was touching the lily and inhaled deeply. Waves of chills raced over my scalp. And across my arm, radiating from where his warm hand pressed over mine, which hum-hum-hummed with the faint but insistent echo of his heartbeat. "Just two friends, enjoying a pleasant night out. In public. Nothing can happen."

He was confusing me, touching me like this, saying we're only friends. . . . "We were in public the first time around. And look what happened then."

He huffed out a little laugh that shook his chest and reverberated through my hand. "True. We do have a history of not being able to control ourselves. Never fear. We'll have a strict hands-off policy for this date that isn't a date."

"No hands."

"Mostly no hands," he assured me. "But *for sure* we'll keep our pants on this time."

"Oh God," I mumbled.

He pressed my hand more firmly against his chest. "Birdie?"

"Yes?"

"Seven o'clock tomorrow?"

Before I could answer, a triple-fast knock rapped on the door. We pulled away from each other as the lock *beep*ed. Beth's face poked inside the room. "Manager is on his way up here with two guests. Out, out!"

Heart hammering, I dashed toward the door, only to stop short when Daniel blocked my exit with his arm. "You didn't answer."

"Are you serious?" I said impatiently, utterly panicked. "Let me out!"

"Please, Birdie. I'm begging you to go out with me. Please, please—"

"Fine. Yes, whatever!"

He nodded firmly. "You won't regret it. Let's go." He released the door and urged me forward into the hallway unexpectedly. I had to lunge to avoid Beth's housekeeping cart, and in doing so, tripped over my own feet, barely catching myself from falling on my face.

"Oof!"

"Sorry!" he said, steadying me. "Oh, almost forgot. Wear purple tomorrow if you can."

"What?" I said a little too loudly.

"Oh my God, you two. Shut the hell up!" Beth whispered angrily. "If we get caught, we're all in deep trouble."

"Nah. We'll just be fired," Daniel whispered cheerfully, beaming at me with a big, stupid grin on his face.

Beth made an exasperated noise. "How do I let you talk me into this kind of shit? Sometimes I really want to strangle you, Daniel Aoki."

You and me both, Beth. You and me both.

"Fate is by far the greatest mystery of all."
—Lady Julia Grey, *Silent in the Grave* (2006)

15

What do people wear for dates that aren't dates? I didn't have a clue. That made me anxious. And several hours before I had to leave to catch a ferry the next night to meet Daniel, a slow-rising panic was filling my body. I hoped Aunt Mona knew what she was doing.

Critiquing my reflection in a floor mirror, I stood at the back of a boutique shop—Junk and Disorderly Vintage Clothes, just down the street from Mona's theater, which separated their racks of vintage clothing by era, 1920s to 1990s. Aunt Mona squatted on the floor in front of me, checking the length of my hem, while Grandpa Hugo sat on a bench outside, chatting with a couple he knew from across the island, whom he'd stopped when he spotted them passing by.

"Perfect," Mona said.

I twisted to peer at the paper tag pinned to the back of the bodice. "Better be. It's insanely expensive."

"Can you really put a price on something that looks this good?" she said, standing up to admire it from a fan of fake eyelashes that were made from tiny bird feathers. Today's wig was a silver bob. "Besides, it's my treat. You know I can always find money for new clothes."

She'd bought most of mine since I was old enough to walk. I smoothed my hand down the fabric of a casual 1950s dress. It had a narrow belt and a pleated skirt that looked "supremely Nancy Drew," according to Aunt Mona. It was also the only thing in the store right now in my size that was purple—mauve, close enough—for whatever reason Daniel had in mind.

"If we had a week or two, I could make you something fabulous," she said.

Likely it would be covered in sequins and have insane accessories.

"I love this," I said. "Honestly."

"Oh, good!" she said, clapping the tips of her fingers. "I needed a little joy today."

I looked at her face more closely. "Why? You haven't seen Leon Snodgrass again, have you? I thought you were going out on his stupid yacht tomorrow."

"Still am. Just to talk."

"About what?"

Her eyes darted away. "Nothing. To catch up, that's all."

"Why don't I believe you?" Maybe it was the little worry line that creased her forehead. Maybe it was because I had no faith in

Leon Snodgrass. For all I knew, he was planning to seduce her and whisk her away to Texas, or wherever he was living now. Aunt Mona leaving the island one day had always been a secret worry of mine, and now that I was working in the city and soon facing decisions about being an adult, I *double* worried about her leaving. I just always thought she'd be moving back to Seattle—not to the other side of the country.

I wasn't sure I could handle that.

"Is there something you aren't telling me?" I asked.

"Ugh," she complained, letting her head loll back as she squeezed her feather-deckled eyes shut. "You're worse than my own mother, Birdie."

"You don't speak to your mother."

"No, *mi corazón—she* doesn't speak to *me*. There's a difference."

"I feel like you're keeping secrets," I said. "That violates our sacred pact to always be honest with each other." I raised three fingers. "It's the second part of the Daring Dame pledge."

"On my honor." She held up three fingers, then took my hand, petted it, and sighed. "Sometimes when you say things a certain way, you look and sound just like your mom, and it makes me extraordinarily happy. Remember when I sold my first painting, and we were going to go out to that fancy seafood restaurant and celebrate, but you'd sneaked that entire jar of Nutella? It was all over your face."

"You called me a brownnose for weeks. Ms. Patty, too."

"Your mom was so calm when she was trying to get the truth out of you—'Birdie, I get the sinking feeling you've already spoiled your dinner,'" Mona said, doing a pretty good imitation of my mother.

I chuckled, remembering standing in the kitchen of our tiny apartment, knowing I was in trouble. "I truly had no idea how you guys knew. I'd buried that jar in the trash pretty well. And, you know, to this day, I can't even hear the word 'hazelnut' without getting a little queasy."

Mona's laugh was deep and throaty as she tugged at the bodice of my dress, looking me over. "Honestly, me either. I had no idea a girl that small could vomit so much. You were a live-action parenting course. I should get some kind of medal for all the stuff I learned from living with the two of you."

"Hey," I said, squinting. "Don't think you can distract me with memory-lane stories. What's going on with you? I'm genuinely starting to worry, and when I worry, things get blown up to epic proportions. In my head, you've got three days to live, and you're leaving on a plane to Jakarta tonight with Leon without even so much as a good-bye."

She snorted a little laugh. "If I had three days to live, I definitely wouldn't spend it on a plane with Leon. Stop worrying. It's nothing like that what-so-evah," she said dramatically. "Look, it's not a three-days-to-live situation, but I don't need gossipy island busybodies listening in on my personal stories here." She waved her hand toward a couple of elderly shoppers who were most definitely listening to us, scattering when they realized they'd been caught. Then Mona said in a lower voice to me, "I promise we'll do girl talk soon, okay?"

"But—"

"Stop. Worrying."

Maybe I was being silly. I considered the possibility that I was projecting my own stress and worries onto her, blowing things out of proportion. Maybe I was just being selfish, wanting her to shine all her glorious, sparkly light onto me and me alone—and not on Leon Snodgrass.

I sighed. "Fine."

"That's better. Now, on to more pressing things . . . Our Daniel is meeting you at what time?"

"He's not ours."

"Maybe not yet, but we can dream, yes?"

No problems there. Over the last twenty-four hours, all I could think about was how his heartbeat felt under my hand. Last night at work, I thought about it so much that it distracted me from doing my job correctly. I incorrectly programmed not one but *two* room keys. I had Joseph fetch the wrong car from the garage for a guest. I made errors when I ran the auditing program and had to get Melinda to override it so I could run it again. Chuck witnessed that fumble and christened me with a new nickname: Dopey. As in stupid Snow White and her stupid dwarfs.

"Hey," Aunt Mona said, frowning, "this isn't part of your mystery case, is it? Whatever it is you're doing with Daniel tonight?"

"I don't think so? But that reminds me . . . We found a clue. Hold on." I rummaged around in my purse and pulled out the spreadsheet we found in the hotel. "Raymond Darke left it in a hotel room. We're not sure what it is. I've tried matching the Cyrillic characters to an alphabet online, but it's impossible. The font on the printout makes the script look different, and some of the letters are connected, and I can't for the life of me make it out."

"Is this Russian?"

"Ukrainian."

Her brows lifted. "Really? I know someone who speaks Ukrainian. David Sharkovsky—he's that Seattle gallery owner."

"The guy who bought your first painting?" Which in turn led to my Nutella overdosing. I'd heard about him but had never seen him. "He's the guy who sold your *Young Napoleon Bonaparte* painting, right?" It was quite the conversation piece, and her biggest single sale of an original painting.

"That's him. He's sort of an asshole, but I'll bet he could translate this for you. If you want, I could try to arrange a meeting. Maybe you, me, and our Daniel could have lunch?"

"Are you serious?"

"I'll give him a call and let you know tomorrow. As payment, you can promise to have a good time tonight."

"I can't promise that. I don't even know what we're doing."

"Birdie," she said, throwing her arms around my shoulders to hug me, "one day you'll realize that the not knowing is the best part of life."

Maybe for someone brave like her. Me? I wasn't so sure.

After parting ways with Aunt Mona, I walked home with Grandpa Hugo and spent the rest of the afternoon fluctuating between anxiety and excitement. Sure, Daniel said this was a date that wasn't a date. I shouldn't place too much importance on one night. Or maybe at all. It felt like we'd done everything backward. If you were baking a cake and rushed to the end of the recipe, stuck it in the oven, and then several minutes later realized you forgot the eggs, wasn't it too late to add them?

Maybe we weren't a cake with missing eggs, but I honestly didn't know what we were or what I wanted us to be. I tried in vain to work it out on the ferry ride into the city that night, but my mind completely emptied when I stepped outside the terminal. Because that's where I found Daniel, sitting on the hood of his Subaru.

When he turned his head and spotted me, a giddy sense of elation zipped through my chest. He dropped to his feet with feline grace and smiled at me as if I were the sun. I smiled back from across the street, waiting for cars to pass before I crossed, heart hammering erratically. And then my feet were moving, and I was breathing, and it was all okay. I could do this.

"Hi," he said.

"Hi."

"I worried you'd change your mind," he said.

"But here I am."

"I should have trusted in my own mantra. Fate finds a way."

"Let's not bring fate into this, Jeff Goldblum," I teased.

He held up his hands in prayer and bowed. "That man should be canonized as a saint."

"I'm starting to think you've got a bigger crush on him than Angela Lansbury."

"Please keep my secrets, Birdie."

"We'll see," I said, moving out of the street so that I didn't get hit by a car before the date even started, which would absolutely be my luck.

"You wore purple," he said, nodding toward my dress and the cluster of orchid blossoms on a single stem, pinned above my ear. I'd stolen it from a large potted orchid my grandmother never in a million years would let me touch. Cutting it was a small rebellion. Daniel opened the diagonal zipper on his thin leather jacket to expose a short-sleeve shirt—typical Northwest flannel, except it was dark purple and black. "See?" he said. "We match perfectly."

"And that's not weird because . . . ?"

He grinned. "All in good time, my dear Birdie. Ready? Parking's going to be rough, so we better shake a leg."

"Where are we going?"

"You'll see," he said, running around to open the passenger door for me.

A couple of minutes later, we were heading away from the waterfront as the sky darkened. I was telling him about Aunt Mona's Ukrainian gallery owner and how she was trying to get us a lunch meeting with him to see if he could translate our mysterious spreadsheet—to which his response was, "Seriously? That's brilliant!" Right about that time, what started as a ho-hum drizzle on my window quickly changed over to real, actual rain.

Daniel flicked on his windshield wipers and suddenly it was pouring. Like, cats and dogs and herds of buffalos. It almost never storms here. Misting and gray skies for days on end, until you feel as if you'll never see the sun again? Absolutely. Storms, however, not so much. And because it's so rare, when it actually *does* happen, it's either thrilling or apocalyptic. Right now, it was both. When lightning flashed, Daniel joked, "Ominous start to a first date!"

"You told me it wasn't a real date," I said in a loud voice to be heard over the onslaught of rain on the windows. I couldn't see the road through the metronomic swish of the windshield wipers, which was mildly worrisome.

"I changed my mind!" he yelled back, hunched over the steering wheel and squinting. "Now help me watch for the interstate overpass so I don't miss the turn."

When an accident blocked the road, Daniel navigated down several side streets, and I was completely turned around. Then the rain slacked off. And after a block or two, when it was down to a tamer, less explosive rainfall, I asked him where we were. First Hill. I wasn't sure if I'd ever been in this part of the city. Nothing looked familiar, just a lot of hospitals and apartment high-rises. And tucked away behind some trees at the corner of a brisk intersection that housed a pizza place and a drugstore sat a stately Victorian mansion.

We drove around the block once, until a car serendipitously pulled out of one of a handful of private spaces behind the mansion. Spotting it, Daniel quickly parked there before someone else could nab it. "How lucky are we? I was starting to worry that we would have to walk blocks in the rain," he said, shutting off the engine. But when I asked him for the hundredth time where in God's name we were going, he just told me to trust him and make a run for it with him.

"Now, Birdie!"

We jumped out of the car and jogged through the rain, pulling our jackets over our heads and splashing through puddles on the crooked sidewalk. I screeched when a spray of splash-back from a car's tire hit the hem of my dress and sprayed my shoes. Daniel hurried me through an iron gate and up a private sidewalk shrouded by trees, and then we were dashing beneath a covered entry, shaking off water like drowned rats.

A fancy sign by the front doors read:

BY INVITATION ONLY.

TONIGHT'S PRIVATE EVENT BEGINS AT 7:30 P.M. SHARP,

AT WHICH TIME THE DOORS WILL BE LOCKED.

GOOD LUCK. YOU'LL NEED IT.

Clearly this wasn't a normal home with people living inside, but a restored historical house rented out for private functions. Was this some sort of stage magic performance? A party?

Daniel ushered me into a foyer with a high ceiling. A chandelier winked above us as we crossed the marble floor, passing doorways to other rooms. We headed to a tiny reception desk that sat in the crook of a grand staircase, where a tall, big-chested man with umber skin and a rich voice greeted us.

"Welcome to the Boddy mansion. I'm Mr. Wadsworth," he said, nodding politely. His dark gray tuxedo looked like something out of *Downton Abbey*. He gestured with white gloves. "Are you here for the dinner?"

"I have a reservation," Daniel said. "Aoki."

The man checked a tablet and smiled. "Ah, the Plums. Of course. You're assigned to my group. Let me just get your name tags and envelope."

Boddy. Plums. Why did this all sound wildly familiar? While the man bent behind the desk, Daniel retrieved a dark purple clip-on bow tie from his pocket and fastened it to his collar. "Is it straight?"

I nodded dumbly, and when Mr. Wadsworth stood up, he said approvingly of Daniel's bow tie, "That's more like it. Now, what names should I write on your name tags? Professor and Mrs.? Professor and Mr.? Both professors?"

"Professor Nick Plum and Professor Nora Plum," Daniel said.

I stared at him.

"Is this . . . ?"

Daniel bit his lower lip and squinted at me before saying, "Live-action Clue game."

"We're . . . ?"

"About to solve a murder mystery," Daniel said. "And eat dinner. Hopefully before the murder, because I'm famished."

"What are you afraid of, a fate worse than death?"
—Professor Plum, *Clue* (1985)

16

"Clue for Couples," the butler elaborated, handing me a stick-on name tag, on which he'd written *Professor Nora Plum* in neat script. And after giving Daniel his name tag and asking if he'd been to one of these events before—Daniel had not—Mr. Wadsworth informed both of us, "Tonight's killer has already been chosen randomly. It will be up to you to figure out whodunit," he said dramatically. "This is your character envelope. It's crucial that you don't open it until instructed during dinner, and absolutely do not show the contents to other players. Now, please feel free to join the other guests to your left in the ballroom."

"The ballroom," I repeated, thinking of the board game. "Is there a billiards room, too?"

"Absolutely. Mr. Boddy's mansion is here in its entirety, and you'll be free to explore later. For now, please confine yourselves to the ballroom. Dinner will be served in . . . let's see . . . fifteen minutes. I look forward to being your guide tonight, Plums. Enjoy!"

Daniel and I shuffled across the foyer toward an open door. He nudged my shoulder with his and spoke close to my ear. "Is this okay? Did I totally blow it? You're not saying anything, and—"

"I'm so excited," I whispered.

"You are?"

I nodded.

"Whew! I was worried there for a second. Like, maybe you hate surprises. Maybe you hate Clue or you've never played it."

"I love Clue! I used to play with Mom and Aunt Mona all the time."

"Well, this is kind of like a dinner murder-mystery thing? U-Dub's drama department does them to raise money. Lots of people from my high school used to go to these all the time. It's like *Rocky Horror*, you know? People cosplay and get into it."

God. Aunt Mona will die with excitement when I tell her. "That's why the purple," I said. "Professor Plum's color in the game."

He grinned. "Yeah."

"I like your bow tie."

"It smells gross. I couldn't find a purple one, so my mom dyed one of my grandfather's. Does it make me look smart and studious?"

"A-plus. Superhot," I confirmed.

His eyes flicked down my dress. "Not so bad yourself, Plum. I'm damn lucky to be married to you."

"Now we're married? This wasn't supposed to even be a date."

"Let this be a lesson. This is what happens when you believe a magician," he said. "You think it's not a date, and the next thing you know, *abracadabra!* You're married to a professor suspected of murder."

I snapped my fingers. "Misdirection."

"Gets you every time," he answered with a grin.

We walked into a small ballroom to find several other couples mingling. Most were adults, but there was another teen couple. A middle-aged man wearing a khaki uniform and a pith helmet was the first to greet us.

"The Plums have arrived," he said, toasting us with a glass of champagne.

"Colonel Mustard, I presume," Daniel said.

"Freshly returned from Africa, old boy. Big game, that's what I like to hunt. The bigger the better," he said, utterly committed to his character. He held up a hand to someone across the room. "You must excuse me. Miss Scarlet is trying to seduce my wife. Be seeing you."

A bearded, burly college-aged boy in a campy French maid's outfit circled the room with a tray of hors d'oeuvres, and after informing us that his name was Apollo, he then introduced several of us to each other, all in character. Many guests were repeat attendees, so when we met others who were first-timers, I was thankful to find we weren't the only ones who weren't in full-on cosplay. A few characters had been added—Dr. Orchid, Miss Peach, Prince Azure—to make a total of nine couples. We'd barely had time to meet everyone, when a young man in a black suit entered the room carrying two giant shopping bags.

"Good evening, everyone," he said, stopping the conversations. "I'm Mr. Boddy, owner of this elegant and very fine mansion. I invited you all here tonight." After a burst of applause and cheers, Mr. Boddy proceeded to tell us that we all had something in common, and could we figure out what that was? Colonel Mustard's wife, who was a little tipsy, shouted, "Blackmail!"

This *clearly* irritated the actor playing Mr. Boddy, who broke character for a few seconds. He then proceeded to give a dramatic speech about how we were all ruthless people with dark secrets— and look! He had some gifts befitting our dank, despicable souls. He withdrew stacks of boxes from the shopping bags, and after he exited the room to more applause, proclaiming, "I'll see all of you villains at dinner!" each couple chose a box. Daniel shook ours before opening it. It was our murder weapon; we got the candlestick.

While everyone was still buzzing about the prop weapons, the butler returned to herd us across the foyer into a dining room. Under another glittering chandelier, a long table was set with china and silver and fresh flowers. "Everyone, find your place cards," Mr. Wadsworth instructed. "And before you're seated, please place your weapons on the tables lining the walls."

We followed instructions and found our places at the table, which happened to be across from the only other teen couple— the Peacocks. They smiled at us, but I caught them staring at

Daniel and whispering, and that made me uncomfortable.

After a salad was served, Mr. Wadsworth encouraged each couple to open their envelopes without showing the contents to others. Ours contained: a "detective notebook" to check off clues; brief motives for our characters (Mr. Boddy was blackmailing us because we'd smuggled artifacts from South America, and we'd lose our university teaching jobs if anyone found out); and a single white card that read *innocent*.

"I'm almost disappointed," Daniel whispered. "That Mr. Boddy is sort of a dick, and I was hoping to off him tonight."

"Why did we smuggle artifacts? Wouldn't we be more concerned about going to jail than losing our jobs? This motive is incomplete."

"We probably needed the money from selling black-market artifacts to raise money for our sick child's surgery."

"We have a kid?"

"We have ten. Little Timmy may never walk again."

"He's not the only one," I mumbled. "Ten kids? Good grief."

"You couldn't stay away from me. I tried to resist, but the smell of chalk dust and blackboards excited you, so we were constantly having sex in the classroom where we taught."

"Well, that was enough to get us fired, right there."

"It wasn't in front of the students," Daniel said, feigning disgust. "God, Nora. Get your mind out of the gutter."

Dinner was a jumble of dishes and animated conversations. An anticipatory revelry crackled in the air. Everyone seemed happy—some more than others, depending on how hard they'd hit the cash bar. The only thing casting a pall over the otherwise cheerful table was the teen couple, who were continuing to make me nervous with all their staring. Finally, when dessert was served, the boy spoke up.

"Hey," he said to Daniel, signaling him with his hand. Both had to lean in to hear over the laughter and chatting surrounding us. "Did you go to Garfield?"

"Yeah," Daniel said, shifting a vase of flowers to see the boy better. "I graduated last year."

"I thought so. We're seniors," he said, referring to his partner. "We thought you looked . . . familiar."

The girl blinked rapidly and said, "You're not that kid who—"

"Shh," the boy scolded, bumping her. And then it sounded like he said, "Don't ask that here."

"Never mind," she mumbled to Daniel.

A tension grew in the silence that hung over the table. Maybe they were talking about his failed stunt with the Houdini water torture cell? Surely that wasn't what was causing all this weirdness. Then I remembered what Daniel said during Truth or Lie: *I did a stupid thing.*

What did he do?

Daniel was staring at his silverware. It crossed my mind that maybe he hadn't heard them; the table was loud, and perhaps his good ear hadn't picked up on their muttering. But then he volunteered, "I know what you're talking about, and yeah, that was me."

The boy looked away. The girl fidgeted with her hands in her lap and then said, "I'm sorry. That was rude. I was just curious. I didn't mean to . . ."

"It's fine," Daniel said.

"I shouldn't have—"

"Really," he insisted. "It's cool."

"That's good," the boy said. "Sorry again."

Daniel shook his head dismissively, and when he glanced at me, his look was awkward and self-conscious. And then he turned back to examining the silverware, distant and lost. I'd never seen him look that way. Now I was both dying to know what the couple had been talking about and wishing they'd never said anything, because the good cheer between me and Daniel was suddenly sucked away, and all the raucous laughter around us rang hollow.

Without thinking, I reached under the white linen tablecloth and put my hand on Daniel's. He looked up from the table, and the hard lines on his face softened.

And that's when the power went out.

Blackness fell over the room. Utter darkness. I couldn't see the table or the guests.

Gasps and a single scream echoed around the room. I panicked, thinking the storm had picked up again outside and knocked out the electricity. Was it thundering? That's when I realized two things: (A) the thunder was a recording being played over speakers, and (B) the scream was coming from Colonel Mustard's wife, and it was a scream of joy—not terror.

A bloodcurdling cry erupted from the far end of the room, and then there was a loud *thump*. Someone cried, "Murder!" And several people laughed. Then there were footfalls everywhere—behind us, to the side . . . across the room. Someone bumped into the back of my chair. What was happening? Were people running around in the dark? Upstairs, too?

"Everyone, stay calm!" Mr. Wadsworth's voice boomed somewhere in the blackness. "It's just the storm." People snickered. "We'll have the power back on shortly. Until we do, please stay in your seats." And then he said in a lower voice, "Mrs. Mustard, I can smell your perfume. Please remove your hand from my leg."

Daniel gripped my hand harder, and on instinct, I did the same. Before I realized what was happening, he'd slung his arm around my waist and pulled both me and my chair closer. I leaned into him, arm tucked against his chest. Then I was breathing in the warm skin of his neck, smelling the dye in his bow tie and his minty shampoo.

He whispered, "Okay?" into my hair. I wasn't sure if he was inquiring about my well-being or asking permission, but we sat like that together, listening to scurrying and giggling and people calling out "Marco!" and "Polo!"

The lights came back on without warning. I pulled away from Daniel while people began shouting, and then Mr. Wadsworth was telling us what we already knew.

"Someone killed Mr. Boddy!"

The actor playing Mr. Boddy was nowhere to be found, nor

his dead body, but whatever. I could roll with it. And naturally, under the threat of us all going to jail for the murder, we had to uncover the real killer by searching nine rooms for clues. There was a flurry of activity, and Mr. Wadsworth and Apollo the Maid were herding us all back into the foyer, dividing us into upstairs and downstairs groups, and spouting off a long list of rules. The gist of it seemed to be that each couple would take turns searching each room for five minutes. One prop weapon and one character card were hidden in each room, and we had to find them to deduce the murderer.

Easy.

Except it wasn't. Because after we'd all been assigned rooms and Mr. Wadsworth signaled that our first five-minute search period had started, Daniel and I ended up in the study: a desk, a conference table, a giant globe, a seating area. And clues were nowhere to be found.

"What does the character card look like?" Daniel asked in frustration. "How big is it?"

"No idea. Why can't we even find the weapon? Where could it be hidden?"

Daniel stopped. Looked at the desk. And slapped his forehead. "Shit!" He raced to the desk and began opening drawers. "Aha!" he said, holding up a toy gun. "The murder weapon was not a gun. Check it off the list, Nora."

"That's a water pistol. The gun was a revolver. It was brown."

Daniel cocked his head. "They hid red herrings to throw us off?"

They did. Which was sort of brilliant and maddening at the same time. But not half as maddening as the conversation at dinner between Daniel and the couple from his high school, which was now stuck in my brain like a splinter embedded in skin: small but painful, constantly nagging. I just wasn't sure if I wanted to bring it up, and I suppose I hoped Daniel would, to spare me the awkwardness of asking him.

But he didn't. Not in the study, where we found zero clues, and not when Wadsworth called time and made us shuffle to the billiards room. There, we found Miss Scarlet's character card, hidden in one of the pool pockets. I crossed it off on our little detective notebook sheet before we were shuffled again, this time into the library, where a small fire burned in the fireplace.

"*N-o-o-o*," Daniel moaned. "The character card could be in any one of these books? There must be a thousand."

"Better look fast," I said, searching behind books on the lower shelves. But my mind wasn't on the task at hand. "Hey. So. At dinner . . . those people from your school."

He sighed heavily. "Yeah. I was hoping you'd forget that."

"I'm sorry," I said. "I don't mean to pry. It's none of my business."

Another sigh. "It's not that. It's . . . I wanted tonight to be nice, you know, and I just don't want to spoil it."

"Say no more. I won't bother you." I'd just stew on it, imagining the worst, until I exploded. It must have been bad, whatever this thing in his past was, because those kids from his school were freaked out; the way they were acting, it was as if they'd heard a crazy story about him, passed along like an urban legend. Maybe he did something stupid like steal a car. Maybe he got arrested. Maybe he set the school on fire.

The more I tried not to think about it, the more it bothered me—both the not knowing and the fact that he didn't want to share it with me. That stung, and like a turtle, I withdrew into myself for protection and disengaged from the Clue for Couples mystery to ponder over the mystery that was Daniel:

Suspect: Daniel Aoki . . . if that is his real name.

Age: 19—or so he says

Occupation: Hotel van driver, graveyard shift

Medical conditions: (1) Stubborn. (2) Avoider. (3) Doesn't trust his date with his secrets, even though random people from high school know them. (4) Is probably a chain-saw-wielding maniac, and I've just been hoodwinked by his charm and wit this entire time. (4) WHY WON'T HE TELL ME WHAT HE DID?

"Okay, that's a million times worse," he said after a few moments of silence.

"What's worse?"

"That thing you're doing." He wiggled his hand at me.

"I haven't said anything."

"No, but you just turned on some kind of emotional force field and shut me out."

"Did not."

"Did too. It's like ten degrees cooler in here."

"You're being dramatic."

"Or are you being passive aggressive?"

Crap. I think I was, and I didn't want to be. Aunt Mona sometimes accused me of the same thing, that I'd learned it from living with Grandma; few had mastered the art of passive aggression like Eleanor Lindberg.

I pretended to push a button in the air. "*Bzzzt*. Force field off. I'm really sorry. Let's forget it."

Daniel groaned. "No one who ever said 'let's forget it' really meant that. What you really mean is 'I am upset that you won't tell me.' And I get that, believe me. I'd be upset too. But it's really, *really* not a conversation I want to have here. Can I promise to tell you some other time in the future? Please?"

"Of course," I said. "Seriously, it's fine."

"You sure?"

I nodded, and he relaxed a little, which made me relax too.

Trying to put it all out of my head, I continued searching the room. My hand slid past something on the bookcase. I looked under a shelf and spotted a button. "Um, hey. If you found a mysterious button on a bookshelf, would you press it?" I asked Daniel over my shoulder.

"Are you serious? Hell yeah, I would. Show me."

We looked at it for several moments, until curiosity got the better of me and I pressed it. The bookcase slid sideways into the wall like a pocket door, revealing a small room behind it, about the size of a walk-in closet.

"Secret room!" I whispered.

There wasn't much to see, only a few shelves on one wall. And—

"Bingo. The lead pipe and Miss White's character card," I said triumphantly. But before I could fumble around in my jacket pocket for our detective list, the shelf began closing behind us. "Oh, crap! Make it stop!"

But it didn't. The door shut, leaving us trapped in a tiny, dark closet.

"There has to be a release button, or something," I said.

His hand patted around the wall. "There is."

"Well, press it!"

"Only if you promise to stop being angry with me."

"This isn't anger—it's panic."

"There's nothing to panic about. It's a closet. Are you phobic about small spaces?"

"No, but I'm reconsidering."

He chuckled.

"Where's the button?"

"Right here." He took my hand and pulled me closer. Really close. I couldn't see him, but I could feel his arms circling my back.

"Hey," I protested weakly.

"Oops," he said, not sounding sorry in the least. "God, you feel nice. I swear, you're the softest human being that ever existed."

"I bet you say that to all the girls you get trapped in secret rooms with."

"You may not believe this, but you're my first fellow trapee."

"Sure this isn't some crazy pickup trick?"

"Now that you say it, I think I read about this in one of those bro guides to getting girls. Is it working?"

"Panic is the best aphrodisiac."

"Are you really panicked?"

"Depends on how much air we have."

"So much air. All the air you could want."

"Okay, fine," I said. "I'm not panicked."

"Good," he said, holding me a little tighter. Which felt . . . pretty nice, actually. "I've got a great idea. Want to hear it?"

"Do I have a choice?"

"I'm going to kiss you again."

"Here?"

"Right now. A do-over kiss. Pretend we've never done this before. Okay?"

Maybe I should have pulled away. A minute ago I was upset he wasn't confiding in me. Now here I was, shamelessly pressing my body against his, which was what got us in trouble the first time around.

"Birdie," he whispered into my ear, sending tingles across my skin. "I need an answer."

"Um . . ."

His lips brushed against mine and hovered there, hesitating, breath warm. My hands trembled. And now I was afraid *he* was going to change his mind and pull away.

So I kissed him.

Just a small, testing press of my mouth to his. But. His lips didn't move. For a moment I wondered if I'd misread him, or maybe everything he'd just said was all in my imagination. It certainly *felt* like a dream. And then, and then—

Oh *God*, did he kiss me back.

His mouth was on mine. Warm. Open. Eager. He kissed me like he meant it—like he was trying to say a thousand things to me at once. Like he'd been lying awake and thinking about kissing me again since that first day we met in the diner, even after he'd gotten to know the real me.

Like we belonged together.

Somewhere outside our shelter of darkness, a voice was shouting. It was Wadsworth, calling time. We broke apart, breathing heavy, still tangled up in each other's arms.

"Dammit," Daniel murmured, letting go of me.

My knees gave out a little. "Oh!"

"Whoa," he said, holding my waist tighter. "You all right there?"

I clung to him as a breathy laugh escaped my lips.

He chuckled. I wasn't even sure what was so funny, but I was smiling and swaying in the dark, and my hands were filled with his shirt.

Suddenly there were voices on the other side of the bookcase. "Crap!" I whispered, pushing away from Daniel.

"Hello?" a voice called.

Daniel pressed the button, and the bookcase opened, flooding my squinting eyes with light. I blinked it away and refocused on the couple standing in front of us. The stupid kids from Daniel's school. Daniel looked at them. They looked at us. And then Daniel's fingers went to his bare collar.

I glanced down at my hand; I was fisting his purple bow tie.

So much for our hands-off policy. At least our pants were still on.

"The clues are inside the secret room," Daniel told the couple as we skirted around them. They mumbled something I didn't catch, but it sounded judgmental.

Go on. Stare, I thought defiantly. Maybe they'd add me to whatever scandalous gossip they whispered about Daniel.

And maybe I didn't give two shits about it.

"If you work hard enough at something, it begins to make itself part of you."
—Inspector Chen Cao, *Death of a Red Heroine* (2000)

17

We didn't win Clue for Couples. I don't know about Daniel, but I blamed our loss on what happened in the secret room. Because after that, I spent our clue-searching time replaying the kiss inside my head in disjointed, staccato fashion. And because most of the other rooms didn't afford us much privacy, we didn't repeat the kiss or even acknowledge what we'd done. Problem was, even though we had plenty of chances to acknowledge it, we *still* didn't. Not during the game. Not after Colonel Mustard and his drunken wife figured out who'd killed Mr. Boddy. Not when Daniel dropped me off at the ferry.

I suppose that's not entirely true. He did give me a peck on the cheek that lasted a little longer than it should have, even though we were standing outside his car at the ferry terminal while pedestrians walked around us. Or maybe it was just in my frazzled imagination. Maybe it was a normal peck on the cheek, one that you'd give a close friend. I told myself it didn't matter. After all, for a date that wasn't really date, it was pretty wonderful.

Besides, Daniel probably felt as awkward as I did about every-thing. That's why he wasn't acknowledging the kiss. Or kissing me like that again. *Or* giving me any kind of indication about his feelings when I texted him after getting back home, as he asked me to do:

Me: Hey, I got home. All safe.

Him: Thanks for letting me know.

Me: You're welcome.

Him: Have a good night.

Have a good night? Not even a polite "I had a nice time tonight," or maybe an "I enjoyed kissing your face off." Did he regret the kiss? DID HE REGRET THE ENTIRE DATE?

I didn't know. I had no experience in any of this, and I wasn't prepared for the overwhelming rush of emotions that came with the unknown. I was worried. I was baffled. And even as I whipped myself into a state of mild hysteria over his bland-as-milk texts, some other part of me was experiencing a poignant *longing-pining-aching* for Daniel, and all of this turned my thoughts into a big, jumbled mess.

I was a wreck, and because my body had become accustomed to staying up all night for work, I couldn't sleep. All night. All the next day. I dozed off for a couple of hours early the next evening and nearly missed my ferry in to work.

When I stumbled into the hotel with seconds to spare, it was with zombielike grace and heavy bags under my eyes. I had no business being at work. And I was both dreading and longing to see Daniel, so naturally I avoided him in the employee break room (pretended not to see him). And in the lobby (busied myself with greeting a guest). At the registration desk (literally ducked down and hid when he walked past).

But there's only so much successful avoidance a zombie can manage in a hotel before their luck runs out. And like Cinderella, my luck ran out at midnight. That's when I was busy standing on a stepladder in front of Octavia the Octopus's tank, opening up a hidden hatch to dump a small bowl of thawed, raw shrimp into her water. The person who normally did this was out sick, but I didn't mind. I liked taking care of Octavia and the rental goldfish.

"Hey," Daniel said, the otherworldly light from the tank rippling over his face as he looked up at me from the bottom of the stepladder. "Shrimp duty?"

"Yep," I replied curtly.

"I wonder if Octavia realizes it's frozen shrimp from Thailand and not the shrimp from the Sound."

"No idea," I said, watching Octavia suction the headless shrimp bodies as they fell into the water. "But I'm starting to think the animal rights group may have some valid points. Giant Pacific Octopi are intelligent. Did you know that they can solve mazes quickly and unscrew jar lids in order to get to food? Octavia is probably bored out of her mind in this tank."

"Joseph said the last Octavia stopped eating and hid in the main cave before they replaced her. Maybe she missed the freedom of the ocean and was upset about being taken away from her other eight-legged friends. Maybe she had trust issues."

I flicked a glance at him. "Maybe."

We both watched this Octavia curl a suckered arm around one of the shrimp.

"S-o-o-o," he said. "I've got to take the van on a food run for Melinda. Her feet are swollen, and she can't leave the back office. So, she asked if I'd pick up Chinese."

"Justin will log your trip in the system," I told him, motioning to the floating supervisor who was coming to fill in for me. "He's relieving me for my lunch break."

"Right now?" Daniel asked.

"Yes."

"Come with me," Daniel whispered.

My pulse sped. I blinked down at him, then glanced at Justin.

"It won't take longer than your break," Daniel added. "Ride along with me."

"In the hotel van?" I whispered back. "Is that allowed?"

"It's not *not* allowed. I'd like to talk to you in private—not in the middle of the lobby where nosy Chuck and everyone else in the Cascadia can hear. Please?"

"All right," I said. "Meet you out front."

In a daze, I closed the hatch on Octavia's tank and hurried to the back to wash my shrimpy hands and clock out. A minute later, I was hopping into the hotel van with Daniel. It was bizarre to be alone with him again. And good. Too good. My heart started hoping again, and then that terrible *longing-pining-aching* feeling fired up, and it was so much worse, because it was happening while he was sitting next to me.

Sitting but not talking.

Not really. After we'd covered how our nights were going—uneventful—and that we both didn't sleep well—he yawned three times—an awkward silence congealed between us, and all my hopeful feelings retreated. I waited for him to say something, but he didn't.

"I thought you wanted a private conversation," I finally said, unable to endure the strained silence any longer. "If you were going to keep ignoring me, it would have been easier back in the hotel."

"Me? *Me?*"

"You," I confirmed.

"You hid from me at the start of our shift!"

"You told me to have a good night!"

He looked askance at me. "What?"

"You're confusing me. I thought our date last night was good. I thought it was . . . at least going okay. You're the one who wanted a do-over. *You* asked *me* out. And I don't know what's happening with us now. I didn't sleep all day because I was waiting to hear from you, like, to say something—anything! One minute you're kissing me like you meant it—"

"I *did* mean it!"

"—and the next minute you're telling me good-bye like I was your nerdy little cousin from far away, whom you'd never see again, but people were watching, so best be polite and give a platonic peck on the cheek."

"My cousins are all brats, so I damn sure wouldn't be giving them a fucking peck on the cheek, just for the record," he said. "And second, if you want to know the truth—"

"That's all I'm asking."

"—then, okay. I was upset about seeing people from school. And freaking out that, hey, if *they* were acting that way, how are you going to act? Maybe once you got to know all my deep, dark secrets, you'd think I wasn't worth the trouble."

I wanted to ask exactly what that trouble was. But he was speaking as if he were talking to himself, animated, wrist slung over the wheel, simultaneously steering the van while flicking his hand up to gesture. "So, there's that. And everything wasn't all peachy when I dropped you off at the ferry, you know. You acted sort of distant, and that made *me* feel weird. And when you texted, you were all matter-of-fact, so *I* was all matter-of-fact. And as far as what I was doing earlier today before work, I have a monthly appointment that I can't miss. Like, no excuses. And after my appointment, I was feeling better and more confident about everything, but then I got to work, and you were hiding from me. So . . . there you go."

Oh.

Huh.

He'd said . . . a lot. And I was sorting it all out in my head, but it was taking too long, and I kept getting stuck on the appointment thing; I doubted it was for a mandatory pedicure. But before

I could think too much about it, he was pulling over to the curb in front of a Pioneer Square restaurant crowned with neon dragons, so I just said, "You weren't sorry we went out?"

Daniel shifted the van into park. "Even with the drama, it was the best date I've ever had."

"Yeah?"

"Yeah," he said.

"It was the only date I've ever had, but it was still the best."

"Only?" He swiveled in his seat and stared at me with a look of concern.

I felt my cheeks getting warm. "I've had relationships," I said, thinking of last summer's fling with Will Collins under the basketball hoop. "Just not official, we're-a-couple-in-public dates. My grandmother was insanely strict and overprotective."

"I . . ." His face went through several contortions. "I don't understand that, like, at all. And it—"

"It's weird," I said quickly. "I get it."

"Weird is fine. Trust me. Weird and me are like this," he said, crossing his fingers.

I chuckled, nervous.

"It's just . . ." He imitated a bomb noise and made an exploding gesture at his temple. "My brain is like, whoa. You better do things right with this girl, because you're normally a huge screwup. And that's a lot of pressure."

"Well, that's dumb," I mumbled.

"Umm . . . ?"

"It's dumb," I said again. "I don't like when you push me away or keep secrets. It makes me anxious, and I need you not to do that. I want it to be like it was between us that afternoon on the ferry ride into the city. Remember?"

"I remember," he said softly.

"Everything felt natural and good, and I wasn't worried you were keeping things from me. I want that. And"—I took a deep breath—"I want what we did in the secret mansion room too. I think? Maybe you're right, and maybe it could be better than it was the first time between us. I don't know. But if we can't have everything, if it's either just a sex thing or a Nick and Nora partnership thing between us, then I guess I choose Nick and Nora. But I don't understand why we can't have both. Why is it so hard? Is this normal? Can't it be easier than this?"

But what I didn't say was that deep down I was worried the problem was me. Because deep down I was worried that there was something he wasn't saying. Maybe it was the secret that the kids at Clue for Couples had brought up. But what if it was something else? My frightened-rabbit heart cowered in the corner; it did *not* want to think about this too much.

He blinked at me. And then he said—

"Okay."

"Okay?"

"Okay," he repeated, exhaling and nodding several times.

I honestly had no idea what he was agreeing to and was just about to ask him when he leaned over the wheel to see around me. He waved to someone outside my passenger window, a bespectacled middle-aged woman in an apron who was holding the door open for a customer and smiling at us. "That's Annie, the owner. Hold on. I have to pick up this food. Don't go anywhere."

I wasn't sure where he expected me to go after midnight on a street full of bars. I sat there, deep in thought, going over everything he'd said, and tried to fill in some of the blanks on my mental profile of him.

Suspect: Daniel Aoki

Age: 19

Occupation: Hotel van driver, graveyard shift

Medical conditions: (1) Deaf in one ear due to Houdini escape trick accident. (2) Distractingly good-looking. (5) Excellent smile. (4) Good kisser. (5) Really good kisser.

Personality traits: Knows lots of card tricks and enjoys performing for people. Gregarious. Maybe not as gregarious toward me as I wish he'd be; sometimes withholds information.

Background: Lives in West Seattle, Alki Beach neighborhood. Mother (Cherry), whom he lives with, was magician's assistant. Secret woodworking talent; his mother wants him to go to a trade school.

Unsolved mystery: Has a standing appointment for some unknown reason every week. Something

happened in high school that is the subject of
gossip, but he STILL won't tell me what it is.
Why? (Ongoing investigation.)

A few minutes later Daniel returned with tightly tied bags of takeout that not only Melinda but several others at the hotel had ordered. He handed me a small bag containing a box of egg rolls. "A gift from Annie," he explained. And I looked out the window to see the woman standing in the doorway of the restaurant. I held up my hand in thanks and she waved in return.

"Does everyone in the city like you?" I mumbled.

"It's not easy being this awesome," Daniel said, giving me a smile that held a little shyness in it. And with a van full of Chinese takeout and an undefined agreement between us, we headed back to the hotel, both of us deep in thought. Right before we got there, I remembered a text I'd gotten earlier from Aunt Mona.

"So, hey," I said. "Remember that Ukrainian art gallery owner I was telling you about? The one my aunt knows? He said he'd take a look at our spreadsheet tomorrow afternoon. Want to come along?"

Daniel's brow furrowed. "Does he know we stole it from Darke's hotel room? How much did she tell him?"

"Nothing," I said, surprised that he was so concerned. "I warned her to keep it on the down-low. We can make something up about why we need it translated."

His shoulders and brow relaxed in tandem. "Okay. Then, yeah. That sounds good. Excellent, actually. Just let me know where and when and I'll be there."

"Truth walks toward us on the paths of our questions."
—Maurice Blanche, *Maisie Dobbs* (2003)

18

That "where and when" turned out to be three o'clock the next afternoon in front of the Moonlight Diner.

Aunt Mona—dressed as a 1960s *Mad Men* secretary, complete with tangerine wig, typewriter nail decals, and cat-eye glasses on a beaded chain—took her boxy Jeep on the ferry and drove us to pick up Daniel there. Standing at the curb on the side of the diner, he spotted us right away. Perhaps it was the life-size smiling skeleton painted on the hood, lying in a field of giant flowers, which covered everything but the car's windows and tires.

Just a guess.

"Hey, sweet young thing! We're looking to party," she shouted from the driver's seat after rolling down the window. "How much?"

"Oh God," I mumbled, slumping lower in the passenger seat as I scanned the sidewalk to make sure no one else heard that.

But Daniel just grinned. "I'd do almost anything for a slice of pie."

"It's true," I confirmed.

"Lucky for you, we've got a dozen apple pies in the back seat," she said. "Get in."

The sky was overcast, but it wasn't drizzling as we headed north toward Lake Union. And that's about how I felt things were with me and Daniel at the moment. He was cheery and friendly toward Aunt Mona, gushing about her car and asking a million questions about it as he sat in the middle of the back seat, leaning between our seats to talk. And he was cheery enough toward me. But there was something I couldn't put my finger on that wasn't quite right. Maybe it was the same thing he accused me of during Clue for Couples: an invisible barrier had been erected between us.

Or perhaps I was just being overly sensitive.

Mr. Sharkovsky, the man we were meeting, lived on an eastern arm of Lake Union called Portage Bay. It had a large enclave of floating homes—actual moored houses that didn't move, not houseboats. The most famous of those houses was Tom Hanks's home in *Sleepless in Seattle*, but that was on the western side of the lake. Here, Aunt Mona took her car down a series of hilly, mazelike streets through a residential neighborhood that dead-ended near the water. We turned into a drive that snaked between several upscale homes tightly packed around the waterfront, and near the end of the drive, we parked in one of three private spaces.

"That's his, there," she said, unbuckling her seat belt.

Sharkovsky's floating house was slate gray—a three-story, boxy building that was modern with Eastern *shōji*-style windows that looked as if they were made of translucent paper. Very posh, very stylish. Very art dealer.

As we exited Mona's car, she answered an annoying ringtone, and while she was telling someone on the other end of the call in a hushed voice that she couldn't talk, Daniel nudged my shoulder with his.

"Hey," he murmured. "I thought we were doing this alone. You know. Nick and Nora. Not Nick and Nora and Mona."

I blinked at him, a little confused, as a chilly wind blew off the lake and scattered my hair in my eyes. Did he think this was another date, or something? "I said in my text we'd pick you up at the diner."

"You didn't say Mona."

Didn't I? I resisted the urge to check my phone and prove him wrong. I suppose now that I thought back to the texts, they may not have been clear. "I don't drive," I argued. "I thought—"

"It's fine," he whispered as Mona was ending her hushed phone call. "I don't mind her company. She's super cool. I just thought this was . . ." He shook his head and started again. "I just had something I wanted to tell you. You know, privately. I never got around to it yesterday."

Yesterday? It took me a second to put two and two together that he was referring to last night, when he'd asked me to ride along in the hotel van—he'd said that he wanted a private conversation then, too. Then we started talking about Clue for Couples and his bland good-bye kiss, and . . . Had he wanted to discuss something else? How had I not realized this?

Before I could respond, Mona put away her phone and looked over at us, a strained smile on her face. Had she heard what we were saying? I suddenly felt caught in the middle and slightly confused about how I'd gotten here.

"Ready?" she said.

"Let's do this," Daniel said cheerfully, as if nothing in the world were wrong. And to me, he whispered, "It's cool. We'll talk later. No worries."

Right. That was what you said when there *were* worries.

What did he want to talk to me about?

The entrance to Sharkovsky's house sat on the nicest dock I've ever seen, behind a screen of potted bamboo trees. We stood next to a boat moored to the side of the house while Aunt Mona rang the doorbell. Then we were ushered inside by a middle-aged housekeeper, who led us through a living room with minimalist, cold furniture and walls covered in large paintings.

Daniel whistled at the artwork. "These must be worth a pretty penny, huh?"

"More than the house itself," Aunt Mona replied in a low voice. "And it's worth millions, much like Sharkovsky."

I didn't really care. I was too busy worrying about what Daniel wanted to talk about in private. But there was no chance to do that now, as the housekeeper was informing us that Sharkovsky was on the roof patio and beckoned for us to follow her. One after another, we climbed an open set of modern, narrow stairs, getting small peeks at the other floors as we passed. On the second landing, Mona halted her ascent and stared down a short hallway into what looked to be a bedroom.

"I can't believe it," she mumbled, a little dazed.

"What's wrong?" I asked, trying to lean around her so that I could see what she was looking at. But the housekeeper had noticed we'd stopped, and she wasn't happy.

"No, no! That is a private area, please," the housekeeper admonished.

For a moment Mona had a look in her eyes I couldn't identify, and I thought she might fail to comply. But the housekeeper shouldered through us and quickly shut the bedroom door before gesturing upstairs and saying, "Please, madam."

Aunt Mona relented, but not happily, and as I tried to figure out what that was all about, we continued climbing two more flights and exited through a door at the top that led onto the roof—if it could have been called that at all. More potted trees, a hot tub, an al fresco dining table and grill, and an abundance of outdoor seating packed the small space. A glass railing surrounding the scene helped to buffer the wind while giving guests a clear view of the shoreline, where dozens of other houseboats floated.

I'd met a lot of gallery owners over the years; Aunt Mona often dragged me along to installations. Most of them were upper-middle class, far wealthier than the artists they represented, but none were like the person lounging in front of us.

Sharkovsky was a dumpy, middle-aged man with a severely receding hairline and overly tanned skin. Either he spent a lot of time on beaches in warmer climates, or he had a tanning bed. But all that tanned skin was on display beneath a kimono robe that hung loosely open, revealing a bare chest, a potbelly, and silky black boxer shorts.

He held out both arms. "Mona, my love," he said in a big voice.

"Hello, Sharkie," she said, accepting kisses on both cheeks. In heels, she towered several inches above him. "You've remodeled."

"I added the patio up here a few months ago," he said, gesturing around him to a gray, urban landscape. "Best place to enjoy the view. That's the University District across the water."

He patted a portable massage table that had been set up near the hot tub. Nearby, a patio heater chased away the chill. "You'll have to pardon my rudeness. I have a masseur coming for an appointment in half an hour, so I can't talk long. I'm having trouble with my back."

"Sorry to hear that," she said, frowning at him with shockingly bright Tang-colored lipstick. "But we don't need long. This is my goddaughter, Birdie, and her friend Daniel."

I didn't want to shake his hand. Something about him rubbed me the wrong way. Maybe it was the fact that he already seemed to be oiled up for his massage. Folding my arms over my stomach, I lifted my chin in greeting and hung back while Daniel did the vigorous male-versus-male handshake.

"Please, make yourselves comfortable," the man said to us, sitting in a rattan patio chair and crossing one sandaled foot over his bare knee. "Tell me about what you're working on, Mona."

"This and that," she said, taking a seat across from him. "Nothing as grand as *Young Napoleon*."

"It's hard to top that." His smile wouldn't have been out of place in a used-car lot. When you got this high up in the art world, it wasn't so much for the love of art as for the love of money. And Sharkovsky projected a vibe of part greasy salesman, part sleazy socialite. Even sleazier, now that Daniel and I were seated together on a bench that gave us an unwelcome view inside the man's kimono.

"I'll always be grateful to you for finding it a good home," Aunt Mona said.

He lifted his hands and shrugged as if to say, *Hey, it's what I do.* "When you're ready to make more money, I'll take a trip to the island and see what you've been creating in that quirky little studio of yours."

"You'll be the first person I call," she said, but it sounded more like: *I want to rip your throat out.*

What in the world was going on between them? I glanced at Daniel, and he slid me a questioning look.

After a tense silence, Sharkovsky said, "So, you said these kids had something for me to translate."

I rummaged through my purse and pulled out the copy of the spreadsheet I'd made at work. After Daniel's anxious response when I proposed coming here, I decided it was best to clip out the actual spreadsheet part and only show him the header. After all, it was mostly just a list of names and dates, and we could figure that out ourselves; we needed him to tell us the name of the company.

"This is it," I said, handing the piece of paper to the man. "We were hoping you could tell us what this all means."

He picked up a pair of reading glasses that were sitting atop a book he was reading and put them on before inspecting the paper. "It has the name and address of a company in Odessa."

"Texas?" Aunt Mona said.

"The Ukraine," he replied, sliding her a critical glance over his reading glasses. Then he read off the address, which Daniel quickly typed into his phone. "The name of the company is ZAFZ. It doesn't say what that stands for, but everything is online these days, so I'm sure you can look it up."

"Does it say anything else?" I asked while Daniel frowned at his phone.

"It was printed two weeks ago, and it also says Ivanov—that's a surname. Whoever he is, he has a title. Facilitator."

"What's a facilitator?" Aunt Mona asked.

"Someone who facilitates . . . something?" Sharkovsky said, shrugging. "No idea. What's this for, anyway?"

"School project," Daniel said quickly. "International finance. This is a bonus project."

Sharkovsky stared at him as if he didn't believe a word coming out of his mouth.

"Does it say anything else?" I asked.

He glanced at it again before handing it back. "Not that I can read, sweetheart. If you want my opinion, it looks like it's something the two of you need to keep your noses out of. It's best to mind your own business when it comes to people's financial affairs."

That prickled. Embarrassed, I accepted the paper, folded it, and shoved it back into my purse while Daniel clicked off his phone's screen. He wasn't happy about Sharkovsky's condescending tone. At all. I could practically feel the annoyance radiating off him.

The art dealer's phone rang. He glanced at the screen and said, "Sorry, but I need to take this. I'll only be a second. Help yourselves to refreshments," he said, gesturing to a tray of vodka bottles, ice, and tumbler glasses. Then he pushed off his seat and answered the phone while padding to the opposite end of the roof.

As soon as he was out of sight behind a screen of bamboo trees, Aunt Mona swung toward us. "Come on," she whispered. "We need to get downstairs before that housekeeper comes back."

"What?"

"He lied to me! You think I'm going to let that stand? That's against the gutsy gal motto."

Alarm bells blared in my head. This had to do with whatever she'd seen from the landing downstairs. If I had a "Nancy Drew" inquisitive look, then Mona had a "Joan of Arc" defiant look, and I'd seen it plenty of times—usually when she was about to suggest something stupid, rebellious, and possibly illegal.

She jumped from her chair and grabbed my hand, tugging me to my feet. "Come on! Daniel, you too."

Even more confused than I was, Daniel leaped to follow as Aunt Mona led us back into the house, taking two stairs at once—which, I must say, is *pretty* impressive when you're wearing orange leopard-print heels. When she hit the final landing, she turned and entered the short hallway that had piqued her curiosity during our initial climb to the roof.

"What are you doing?" I whispered hotly, heart racing madly. "These are bedrooms."

"*His* bedroom," she clarified after sticking her head into the second doorway. Then she disappeared inside.

Thoroughly embarrassed and well on my way to a massive stress-induced stroke, I turned around and gave Daniel an apologetic look. He glanced up and down the stairwell, and then we both followed Aunt Mona.

It was a massive bedroom. All white. Plush, shaggy rug. An excellent view of the lake. But Aunt Mona wasn't concerned with any of that. She stood stock-still in front of a massive painting that covered half the wall.

I'd seen it before. I'd watched it being painted.

Young Napoleon Bonaparte. Seven feet tall, wearing a grungy Seattle flannel shirt and his famous bicorn admiral hat.

"But . . . I thought he sold that for you?" I said. "For a crap-ton of money."

"Oh, he *said* he did, but now I think I've figured it out," she said. "See, he had a thing for this painting. He'd hounded me about selling it to him before he finally agreed to display it in his main gallery. It hung for months with no offers or interest, and I was about to give up hope when a 'private' buyer came forward to take it off Sharkie's hands—only, he'd offered half the asking price, which Sharkie claimed was hugely inflated anyway."

Aunt Mona was desperate to sell and took the offer.

"Don't you see?" she said, gesturing wildly toward the painting.

I shook my head. Daniel just glanced back and forth between the painting and Mona, wide-eyed. Probably wondering why in the double hockey sticks he got involved with a weird girl and her crazy family, no doubt. I wouldn't blame him for thinking that. Not one bit.

Mona groaned in frustration. "Sharkie didn't sell this painting to an outside buyer. He kept it for himself and paid me half the asking price. He ripped me off!"

"Jesus," Daniel whispered.

"Jesus is fucking right," she mumbled. "And if Sharkie thinks he's getting away with this, he can think again. Help me get it off the wall."

"What? You can't be serious!" I whispered. "That's stealing."

"All right, Eleanor Lindberg," she chided.

I resented that. It also made me doubt myself. I did *not* want to be like my grandmother.

"Look, Birdie. The bastard cheated me. I painted this. Me!

It's mine. He swindled me out of thousands of dollars. So now I'm getting it back," she said. "Are you helping me, or not?"

Oh God. She was serious. The last time she got this fired up, I had to play lookout while she stole an American flag from the front of city hall and replaced it with one that read FASCISTS.

"You were supposed to be helping us with our case!" I whispered. "We didn't come out here to help you seek vengeance."

"No one plans vengeance," she argued.

"Yes! They do!" I said, exasperated. "It's a planned act of revenge."

"For you maybe. For me vengeance just happens."

"Did you know about this painting when you suggested we consult him about the spreadsheet?"

She squeezed one eye shut. "Maybe I suspected it? Two birds, one stone?"

"I'm so angry at you right now!"

"That's fair," she whispered. "But are you going to help me, or what?"

I started to tell her no, but Daniel spoke up.

"I'm in," he said. "Why not? That guy's an asshole."

"Oh God," I whispered, glancing down the hallway to the stairwell.

Cool and calm as could be, Daniel pushed his hair back over one shoulder and got on the opposite side of the painting. "It's on hooks," he told Aunt Mona. "We can lift it off if we go straight up. On three . . ."

With dueling grunts, they pushed the painting up and off the hooks. Then they argued in whispers about the best way to get it out of the room. It had to be turned sideways—even I could see that. And at this point, it was too late to keep my hands clean. So I helped them flip it around and guide it on its side out of the bedroom. It *barely* cleared the top of the doorframe. Getting it over the stairwell railing and down the last flight of stairs was even trickier. But we managed.

When we guided it down the final step, a small noise startled me. I turned around to find the housekeeper, holding a stack of towels in both arms.

"What are you doing?" she asked, eyes wide. But she didn't wait for an answer. She just trotted around the painting and called up the stairwell, "Mr. Sharkie! Mr. Sharkie!"

"Go, go, go!" Aunt Mona shouted.

She and Daniel carried the painting outside while I held the front door open, and then the three of us . . . well, it wasn't running exactly. More like quick shuffling. All the way down the dock, until we got to her car. I dug Aunt Mona's keys out of the glittery handbag threaded on her arm and popped open the back of her Jeep.

"It won't fit!" I said.

"Back seat down," she said breathlessly. "It'll fit. I put it in here when I took it to the gallery."

"Mona!" a voice bellowed from on high.

We all looked up to find Sharkovsky leaning over his glass roof railing, kimono billowing in the wind.

"Bring it back, Mona!" he yelled.

"Fuck you, you crook!" she yelled back. "I'm telling every artist in Seattle what a lying snake you are, and then I'm suing you for the rest of the money you owe me!"

Several people were watching us: a guy on a bike, an elderly man from his window, and a woman who appeared to be Sharkovsky's masseur, getting out of a nearby car. They were all so embarrassed by the scene, no one would look us in the face. That seemed about right.

I flipped the back seat down and helped Daniel and Mona shove the enormous painting into the Jeep. A good foot or so stuck out the back.

"Don't panic!" she told us. Being an experienced hauler of big artwork, she quickly bungee-corded the back hatch down with Daniel's help, and after realizing we'd just eliminated Daniel's seat for the ride home, we all piled into the front in a panicked flurry—Aunt Mona driving and me on Daniel's lap.

One minute I was trying to make myself small and unobtrusive while balancing on his legs, and the next, Aunt Mona was tearing out of the parking space and Daniel was pulling me back against him.

"Snake!" Aunt Mona yelled out the window at Sharkovsky as he limped across the dock, shouting obscenities at her. She turned out of the drive like a bat out of hell, and the last thing I saw was his graying hair blowing erratically in the breeze.

Aunt Mona raised both her hands. "Vengeance is mine!"

"I can't believe we just did that," I mumbled.

Daniel high-fived her, and for a moment the car was feral with wild emotions. Most of Mona's were centered on victory and revenge; most of mine were anger and embarrassment. I'd told her about the conversation I'd had with Daniel in the hotel van last night—she knew I was taking baby steps with him. This all felt selfish and outrageous, and I couldn't believe she was acting like this was a super-fun way to spend an afternoon. She was too old for this kind of stunt. It was humiliating.

But I didn't say any of that. Not in front of Daniel. To be honest, I was a little peeved at him, too, because he seemed perfectly happy to be her partner in crime.

This was *not* how I wanted things to go today.

By the time we got back to the diner, all the adrenaline in the car had worn off. Aunt Mona made a weak attempt at apologizing to both of us, but Daniel wouldn't accept it. He said it was "fun." And while she parked at the curb and called another fellow artist to brag about what happened, I exited the car with Daniel and talked to him on the sidewalk.

"I'm so sorry," I told him after shutting the door and making sure Mona couldn't hear us.

"Don't be sorry. Seriously. That was unexpected, and your godmother is a trip."

"She's something, all right," I muttered.

He chuckled and gave me a gentle smile. "It's fine. Seriously."

"I'm just . . . I don't know. This didn't turn out like I wanted. I'm sorry I gave you the wrong impression about her tagging along, and I'm sorry about her nutty shenanigans. To top it all off, we didn't even learn much about the spreadsheet."

"Stop apologizing. It's all good," he said, lightly brushing the back of my fingers with his.

"Are you sure?"

"Positive. And at least we got some info about the spreadsheet. We got the initials of the Ukrainian company, and we know Ivanov's title."

"What about the address that Sharkie translated when we were on the roof? I saw you pulling it up on your phone when he read it off."

"Doesn't exist," he said, shaking his head. "I'll text it to you, and I'll try it again later, but the map is just defaulting to the city."

"Maybe it's like a black-market thing."

He nodded and absently scratched his arm, glancing at Mona through the car window. "So, hey. About what I said earlier . . . You want to meet me for dinner tomorrow before work?"

Uh-oh. Was this the private talk he wanted?

"You have some place in mind?" I asked.

"Do you like sushi?"

"Sushi?"

"The food of my people," he joked. "Rice, nori, fishy goodness?"

"Not sure if I've ever had real sushi, but I like California rolls. And I like fish."

"That's a start," he said. "I know a place that you'll love. I promise. And we can talk. About things."

Things. Exactly what he meant by that, I wasn't sure.

But I didn't think it was about the Raymond Darke spreadsheet.

19

Daniel texted me directions to a small, triangular plaza near a statue of Chief Seattle, south of Denny Way. Making my way past a herd of blue-badged Amazon employees that had strayed too far from their corporate campus, I got there in time to meet him for dinner the next day before work.

The monorail track ran above, and just a few blocks away, the ever-present Space Needle was casting a long shadow over a criss-cross of streets. I exited a city bus, and as traffic sped by, I spotted Daniel a few steps away, hands stuffed in his pockets.

"This must be the nexus of the city," I joked.

"I've heard if you say 'candyman' three times at the Chief Seattle statue, Kurt Cobain's ghost will appear."

"Is that so?"

He smiled at me, just a small smile, but it was unguarded and hopeful, and seeing it caused a battalion of butterflies to wage war inside my stomach.

Were we okay? Were we not? Clearly he didn't ask me here to discuss our investigation. Was he going to tell me about the stupid thing he'd done in high school? Or had he changed his mind about our snatch-and-run with Aunt Mona yesterday and decided my weird family was too much for him to handle?

I tried to divine his intentions, becoming hyper-observant of his body language. His hands were in his pockets. Did that mean he was nervous because he was about to tell me we needed to cool things down?

Can you break up with someone whom you've only been out with once?

I was being paranoid, surely. It was just that he seemed . . . different. Tense.

Remnants of rush-hour traffic sped down Denny Way. We shuffled silently under trees lining the plaza, and after crossing the road, he ushered me down a sidewalk lined with casual restaurants and into a door marked TILIKUM SUSHI.

The restaurant was cozy and unadorned. A few tables were scattered around the perimeter, but it was what sat in the center that held my attention. Two chefs in black uniforms were cutting up fish in an open kitchen that sat in the center of a square wood counter. And around that counter, like a lazy train, a conveyer belt of slow-moving dishes glided past customers.

"Kaiten-sushi," Daniel explained. "Have you had it?"

I shook my head.

"Sometimes conveyer sushi isn't the best because it's basically fast food. But this place is awesome. I know the owner."

Of course he did. A few customers huddled around all four sides of the counter, mostly tech bros and lawyer types in suits. We sat down at a couple of free stools, and the chef, a Japanese man in his twenties, grinned when he spotted Daniel. "Yo, magic boy," he said.

"That's magic *man* to you," Daniel corrected. "Don't embarrass me in front of the lady."

"I'm Mike," the chef told me, holding up a sharp knife. A red bandanna cap covered his head, and his mustache curled up on both ends, à la Salvador Dalí. "And for the record, he embarrasses himself."

"This is true," Daniel said, smiling.

"How's Cherry?" the chef asked.

From a stack below the conveyer belt, Daniel pulled off two china cups without handles and set one in front of me. "Too old for you."

"I've dated older. And younger," he said, smiling at me. "How old are you?"

"Right in front of my face?" Daniel shook his head, and as he scooped green powder into our cups, he said to me conspiratorially, "Don't listen to this guy, Birdie. He's all talk, no game. And his sushi skills are shit."

The chef pointed the tip of his knife at Daniel. "Those are fighting words, Aoki."

"Fine. He's actually one of the best," Daniel told me. "He

worked for Shiro's, but he opened this place last year. Before all that, he used to live across the street from my auntie, and he hung out with all my cousins. He's been shit-talking me since I was a wide-eyed, tender boy."

"You serial pickpocketed me when I was in culinary school," the chef argued. "That was my beer money, man."

Daniel held my cup under a tap that jutted below the conveyer belt, pulling a lever. Steaming water streamed from the tap, making the powder inside the cup swirl. When he set it back down in front of me, the floral scent of green tea wafted up. "It's not my fault that you were the easiest target," he told the chef.

"Still am, probably. At least there's a counter between us. You ordering off the menu?"

"Nah. We're good. Do your thing."

The chef nodded, reaching over the conveyer belt to hand us rolled-up hot towels on little oblong bamboo trays. "Let me know if you need anything." Then he left us alone, returning to the giant gray-scaled fish he'd been carving, revealing rosy pink flesh as he sliced.

"That's tuna," Daniel told me.

"I think it's still moving," I murmured, unsure about all of this. Everything smelled and looked strange. Little signs that sat near the plates on the conveyer were in Japanese and English. It was overwhelming. Especially considering that I couldn't discern Daniel's intentions in bringing me here. "I've never had raw fish," I told him.

"Let's start out slow, yeah?" Daniel said, leaning his shoulder against mine and smiling down at me with his eyes.

"Okay," I said, trying to dispel my anxieties.

Nodding, he proceeded to explain everything in detail. The purpose of all the little bottles and jars and tiny plates sitting in front us. Where to put my chopsticks. The difference between nigiri and maki rolls and stuffed temaki cones. Between us, he set up a little station of soy sauce, wasabi paste, and pickled ginger slices, and we watched the conveyer belt until he spotted what he wanted me to try first.

"Tuna roll," he said, taking down a small plate from the belt. "It's basic. Nothing weird."

"It's raw?"

"Think of it as super fresh. Do you know how to use chopsticks?"

"Sort of." I wasn't very good at it.

"Then use your fingers. It's totally acceptable. See?" He wiped his fingers on one of the hot towels we'd been given, and I did the same. Then he dabbed a bit of green wasabi on two pieces of tuna roll and showed me how to dip it in soy sauce before eating a piece himself. "Mmm," he said, chewing. "See? Try it."

I steeled myself and popped one into my mouth. It was . . . salty. Briny. Soft. And—

"Oh God," I murmured as my eyes watered and my nose began burning. Should I swallow this or spit it out? Was I going to gag?

"Wasabi," Daniel said, laughing. "Swallow. It will go away. Have some tea."

The tea was too hot. I nearly burned my tongue. But at least the terrible nose burn was fading.

"Well?"

"I can't taste anything."

"Try again," he said, giving me a look that riled up those fluttery butterflies in my stomach again. "Sometimes things are better the second time."

I tried a second piece, this time without the wasabi. And it was . . . weird but good. He pulled down other plates from the conveyer belt—a salmon roll, a spicy tuna roll, some shrimp nigiri. Pretty little bites dressed in pink and orange roe. And before I knew it, I was eating everything and liking quite a bit of what I tasted. I even began enjoying the burn of the wasabi. It was crave-able.

Throughout the meal, our conversation meandered but never slowed. We talked about work. Octavia the Octopus and the local animal rights group. Card tricks. Books. The painting we helped Aunt Mona steal. And Ivanov's spreadsheet, of course. Neither one of us could find a speck of information on the "ZAFZ" company that Sharkovsky had translated for us. Daniel even tried enabling a Cyrillic keyboard on his laptop, hunting and pecking until he found the symbols for the address . . . Nada. Zero. Zilch.

Our Raymond Darke investigation had hit a dead end.

But despite that disappointment, it was pleasant to sit together like this, making small talk and enjoying each other's company. Touching shoulders. Smiling at each other. Like nothing was wrong.

Was there something wrong?

Was Daniel still tense?

"See?" he told me as our little plates stacked up. "I promised you'd like it."

"You were right," I agreed.

"Sometimes that happens." He smiled, but it was nervous, and that's when I absolutely felt a change in our easy dinner conversation. After a long silence, he said, "Okay. So, I promised you that we'd talk about that thing those kids at Clue were asking me about, and I guess there's no use putting it off."

"Okay," I said, my emotions all over the place. I was relieved he hadn't said, "Let's call the whole thing off," but I couldn't ignore the feeling in the pit of my stomach. That strange, buzzing trepidation that comes in that moment when you're pretty sure you're about to hear something bad, but you aren't sure *how bad*, and all the possibilities are so much worse than knowing for sure.

Daniel pulled out his phone and began searching for something. When he found it, he handed his phone to me.

It was an article from the *Seattle Times* dated a year and a half ago: SUICIDE STILL A GROWING PROBLEM AMONG WASHINGTON STUDENTS.

The first paragraph of the article talked about a high school senior at Garfield High who'd tried to overdose and was found in the school library by a janitor. The janitor heard a suspicious noise: the boy, who was seizing after ingesting a large quantity of fluoxetine, had knocked over a bust of Shakespeare. If it weren't

244 • JENN BENNETT

for the intervention, the boy would have died. He was instead rushed to a local hospital and was "now recuperating at home with his family."

"That was me," Daniel said quietly. "Joseph at work? He was the janitor. He graduated the year before from another high school and had just started doing janitorial work at Garfield. And like the article says, if he hadn't found me, I'd be dead."

A terrible tightness gripped my chest.

This was . . .

Not what I expected.

Half my thoughts were scrambling to fit this into what I knew of Daniel, reversing and replaying bits of conversation. This never came up in my online searches for him. And of course it didn't: he was an unnamed minor in this article. And I guess this wasn't the thing he was going to plaster all over his social media accounts either.

I was lost for words.

"It was at the beginning of my senior year," he explained. "I'd lost my hearing that summer and missed some school at the start of the year because of it. I got really depressed. My mom was worried and took me to our family doctor. Instead of referring me to someone, he just wrote me a prescription for an antidepressant and sent me on my way. Antidepressants take time to work, and they aren't all alike. I didn't understand that at the time. I was impatient and hurting, and I thought maybe I was just . . . unfixable." He shifted in his seat and cleared his throat. "It just felt like I was living in a bubble, and that bubble just got smaller and smaller. It wasn't until I started seeing a therapist afterward that things got better."

"The monthly appointment you can't miss," I murmured.

He nodded slowly and rubbed the heels of his palms over his thighs several times, as if he were trying to summon the courage to speak again.

"Before it happened . . . I was having trouble adjusting to the hearing loss, I blew up at a teacher and got stuck in detention, and I'd just taken my SATs for the second time, and my scores were still terrible." He stole a look at my face, blinking rapidly, but didn't look me in the eye. "All that sounds flimsy now, but at the time? I was . . . in a bad place, mentally. I fell into a black hole. It's hard to explain if you haven't been in that state of mind. I don't know. . . . It wasn't a cry for help, or anything. I really thought I wanted to die."

I never in a million years would have guessed this about him. He seemed so happy. So gregarious. So full of life—

But also hiding something. I thought back to when I'd searched for his Missed Connections ad and found the social media profile that said "Stop asking if I'm okay." And when he offhandedly described himself as being "depressing" when he was talking about David Bowie's music. The way he talked about the Houdini incident when we were playing Truth or Lie, and how I felt as if he weren't telling me something. His monthly appointment that he said he couldn't miss . . . and what happened at the Clue game.

"Those people who went to your school," I said. "This is what they were talking about?"

He nodded. "*Everyone* talked about it. And the more they did, the crazier the stories got. I was my own urban legend. I heard I slit my wrists and bled all over the floor, and if you looked in a certain spot, you could still see the stain."

I moaned, a little horrified. I could feel his leg anxiously shaking against my stool.

"Anyway, I'm not trying to make you feel sorry for me," he said. "Things got better slowly. My mom moved us into cohousing with her parents and found me a good therapist. I had to try two more medications before we found one that's been working for me. I mean, it's a process. Compared to how I felt back then, I feel a gazillion times better, but I don't want to . . . get into a bad place again. So, I still see Dr. Sanchez every month, just to make sure things are staying steady."

"That's your therapist?"

"Yeah. It's just . . . ," he started, and then hesitated, searching for the right words. "I know it's a lot to process. I don't need you to save me or anything. I'm doing good—really, I am. But this is part of my past, and I can't erase it. I thought maybe I could. That first night at the diner? You didn't know me, and that was kind of liberating. For a moment there I was someone else. I didn't have to talk about my ear or the stupid shit I'd done, and here was this pretty girl with killer eyes who laughed at my jokes, and she liked me. . . ."

I still like you. I tried to say it out loud, but it got stuck in my throat.

"It felt so good to just act on instinct, to just . . . live. And then you showed up at the hotel, and suddenly it felt so much bigger."

"Fate," I said.

His eyes softened. "Fate. I got so wound up in it, so wound up in you, that I forgot again. Well, not forgot, exactly. I don't know. I guess . . . I told myself that it didn't matter. It was in my past. I was better. It was fine." He sighed. "Seeing those kids at the Clue game? That made me realize that I can't escape it. There will always be people who knew me before it happened, and some of them will be cool—like Joseph."

I thought of Joseph, standing guard by the hotel's entrance. Maybe standing guard over Daniel, too . . . "That's how you met each other?" I asked.

"Strange way to start a friendship, but yeah. Joseph kept in touch, checking up on me. And when he got a job at the hotel, he found out there was another opening and put in a good word."

Once again I was stunned into silence while I digested everything he was telling me.

Chef Mike was hamming it up with customers on the other side of the counter, showing them the head of the big tuna that he'd just severed. I pretended to watch casually, but I couldn't help wondering, after all that talk about them growing up together . . .

"Yeah, Mike knows too," Daniel said in a low voice, reading my face. "And he's totally cool about it. But for all the people who understand, there's just as many who treat me differently. Some talk shit behind my back, saying I'm weak, or whatever. Some of my friends at school stepped back because they felt like they were barely holding themselves together, and trying to prop up someone else was only going to bring them down. And then there are the lookie-loos—the ones who are fascinated by scandal, but only from a distance."

"The people at the Clue game," I said.

"Exactly." His smile was tight and humorless. "It's just . . . always there for me, in one way or another. I've gone through every emotion—guilt, denial, regret, shame. Most of the time I just wish I could forget it ever happened and move the fuck on, but I'm always being reminded. And sometimes my mom is overprotective because she's scared it will happen again, so there's her to deal with. I know she's just doing the best she can and that I probably hurt her the most, but she makes it worse than it needs to be. I can't even lock my bedroom door because she'll break it down to make sure I'm not trying to do it again. She's gotten better lately, but occasionally she has a freak-out if she can't reach me, like, *immediately*."

It sounded a little like how my grandmother had treated me. I guess we sort of had that in common.

He sat back on his stool, arms crossed over his chest, and sighed. "This is probably a lot of information, huh?"

"It's a little surprising." A lot, actually, but I didn't say that, because I didn't want to make him feel awkward about having told me.

"I guess . . ." He hesitated and tried again. "I guess that I just wanted to get all of this out in the open. Am I freaking you out?"

"No," I insisted. "I'm sorry. I'm . . . overwhelmed. Trying to process. But I'm glad you're telling me." Was that the right thing to say? "I don't mean I'm *glad*. Grateful?"

Ugh. I sounded like an idiot. Why was this so hard?

"I get it," he said. "It's just that . . . I don't want you to think that I'm struggling all the time, or anything. I'm doing everything I can to make sure I don't slip into another black hole, and I'm definitely in a much better place now than I was two years ago. Tons better. You don't have to tiptoe around my feelings." He scratched the back of neck. Tugged on his ear. Then blew out a hard breath. "I'm . . . not good at talking about this. I don't know. . . . I guess my biggest fear is that you'll start looking at me differently—that you'll start seeing depression instead of me. It's not easy being in a relationship with a person who's got this kind of dark baggage."

I made a dismissive sound, but somewhere in the back of my mind, part of me was wondering if I could. Which was awful. And upsetting. Why would I even think that?

"Trust me. I know from experience. And I'm not just trying to protect you. The more attached I get to you, the worse it will be for me if you decide you can't handle it."

I turned my head to look at him. "What are you saying?"

"I'm giving you an out. If all of this scares you, and you don't think you can handle it, I get it."

"Daniel—"

He held up a hand. "Don't answer now. Before you decide anything, maybe at least think about what I've told you, sleep on it, and see how you feel over the weekend. Okay?"

He looked at me, and I looked at him, searching his face. He was serious.

"If you find you can't handle it and need to bail, just text me," he said. "It's easier that way. I can be professional at work, so don't worry about that. I won't hassle you."

A pair of talkative customers walked into the restaurant and plopped down on the two stools next to mine, shattering our privacy. But it didn't matter, because I was lost for words. My chest hurt, and my throat felt as if it were trying to choke me. Was he encouraging me to stay away? It sounded that way. I was confused and hurt, and that felt selfish, because I wasn't the one who'd been sad enough to almost die by suicide.

We left the restaurant together, both of us quiet as we took a bus downtown to get to work. Once I got over the immediate shock of it, I wanted to hug him. Hold him. Touch his hand. Anything. I wanted to let him know that I was grateful he trusted me enough to tell me, but I didn't know how to say it— especially not in a public space, surrounded by strangers. So I did nothing. Said nothing. I held myself together like some kind of walking, talking robot with a cold, mechanical heart. All the way back to the hotel and all through our shared shift, I tried not to think about it. Told myself it was no big deal. I fake smiled and fake nodded and faked my way through the night like a pro.

It wasn't until I got home that my mechanical heart stopped working, and I fell apart.

I couldn't have said why exactly. I was just shaken up and sad. He was supposed to be sunshine. That was what I thought the night when I first met him in the diner. But underneath, he was rain and gray skies. The sober realization that he'd struggled and been in so much pain shattered me into a thousand pieces, over and over again, and I cried until I ran out of tears.

I'd lost my mother.

I'd lost my grandmother.

The possibility of losing someone else was overwhelming.

Maybe *too* overwhelming.

The realization of this made me feel as if I'd been shoved off my feet and all my emotions had toppled out during the fall. Now came the hard part: picking those pieces up and fitting them back where they belonged.

"That's the thing about people. They always find ways to surprise you."
—DCI John Luther, *Luther* (2010)

20

I couldn't sleep that morning. Not really. It was hard for me to tell if it was worry-induced insomnia because I was still upset over Daniel's revelation, or if my usual sleep issues were getting worse. Maybe both. But when I finally sat up in bed around noon, it was to the sound of a loud thump somewhere outside my bedroom door. Tracking down the source of the noise, I found Grandpa Hugo in the upstairs hallway, dragging an old suitcase out of a closet.

"What's going on?" I asked, yawning.

He stood up on his walking cane and smiled at me. "Didn't mean to wake you."

"Eh, I wasn't sleeping well anyway. What are you doing with that old thing?"

"Packing for Yakima River Canyon. Cass's sister bought a cabin near Ellensburg, and he invited me to come along for some fly-fishing."

"Huh," I said, surprised. "Fly-fishing?"

"Rainbow trout. You haven't seen my rod, have you? The smaller one?"

"It's in the attic. I'll get it down for you. When are you leaving, and how long will you be gone?"

"Two weeks."

"You're leaving in two weeks?"

"Staying for two. Maybe less if the fish aren't biting. I'm leaving in a couple of hours."

"What?" I felt like I was hearing him wrong.

"I know it's last-minute." He scratched the back of his head as if he were uncomfortable, like he used to do when I was younger and he had no idea how to relate to me, a stranger who'd come to live in his house. "But Cass asked me a few days ago—that morning in the greenhouse when he came over. I told him no. You'd just started this job, and I didn't want to feel like I was abandoning you. But you seem to be adjusting to your work schedule just fine, and I woke up this morning and decided, what the heck?"

"You're leaving?" I repeated, still shaking off sleep.

"Do you not want me to go? I can call it off. It's—"

"No. I mean, I'll be fine. Of course you should go."

"Are you sure? Eleanor always helped make these decisions." His brow wrinkled. "Everything's topsy-turvy these days."

"I'm sure. When you were my age, you were joining the Coast Guard. I think I can manage a few days by myself."

Probably. I'd never been left alone for that long. Grandma was always here when he went on trips with Cass, and Grandpa was always here when she went to visit her family upstate.

"It's only a couple of hours from here," he said, adjusting his suspenders, "so if you had an emergency, I could come right back. But Mona said she'd look in on you and make sure you were feeding yourself."

He wouldn't be so gung ho about depending on her as some kind of angelic caretaker if he'd known what we'd done at Sharkovsky's house. But I didn't say this.

"If it would make you feel more comfortable," he said, "you can stay at Mona's while I'm gone."

Whoa. I used to fight both him and Grandma to be able to do that. It was weird for it to be such a casual offer now. "I'm eighteen, not a child, Grandpa."

He smiled. "I wouldn't leave if I thought you were, Birdie."

"Who's driving to Yakima?"

"Cass."

Better a one-handed man than Grandpa behind the wheel. Long-distance drives and narcolepsy were a terrible pair.

"Are you okay with all this?" he asked. "Work is fine? And everything is okay with that friend of yours at work?"

"Daniel."

"I remember," he said with a wink. "Mona likes him. I wish you'd bring him home and let your kind grandpa meet him."

"Maybe when you get back." If he was still in the picture. My stomach knotted as pieces of our sushi-dinner conversation flitted through my head.

"Everything *is* okay," Grandpa asked, "isn't it?"

I handed him his walking cane and picked up the suitcase, heading into his bedroom. "What if someone confessed something to you, and it's not necessarily bad. . . ." I struggled to dance around what Daniel had told me over sushi, trying to find the right words. "But it's really heavy, and you're having a hard time coming to terms with this revelation, but you're not sure why."

"Depends on the revelation."

"Let's just say, on the scale of revelations, it's not as if you thought they were a cultured psychiatrist who appreciated gourmet food but later found out they were Hannibal Lecter."

"Not a cannibal killer, then?"

"Definitely not," I said, giving him a quick smile. "It's . . . more like you thought their life was perfect, and then they confessed some things to you about their past, and now you're not sure if you can handle the weight of those things."

"No one's perfect, Birdie."

"I know that."

"And when you pin impossible ideals on someone, nobody wins. That was what your grandmother never understood. Judging other people unfairly doesn't define them; it defines you. And in the end everyone will be disappointed."

"I'm not judging at all. I'm just overwhelmed." And I was a little scared that I wasn't strong enough to handle Daniel's emotional burdens.

"Most of us are just living our lives, trying the best we can.

Accepting people for who they are is hard, but in the long run, it's easier than sitting around, wishing they were something they're not."

I wasn't sure he was getting what I was saying, but I also didn't feel comfortable telling him everything.

"You're going to be fine," he said confidently, as if he hadn't been listening to a word I said and was only now deciding that his fishing trip was a kosher idea. "In the meantime, if you get any good Raymond Darke leads while I'm gone, be sure to text me."

I assured him I would.

I thought about everything he'd said while I climbed the attic ladder to retrieve his fishing gear, and I realized he was right about one thing: expecting Daniel to be a magical sunshine boy was unfair to both him and me.

Maybe I just needed to put on my detective hat and think about all of this logically.

It wasn't that I was scandalized by Daniel's suicide attempt or his battle with depression. What made me nervous was that even though he said he didn't need saving, he also talked about all the people who'd bailed on him because they couldn't handle his emotional baggage. He never tried to pass any of it off as unimportant or trivial. It was a big deal, and he knew it when he told me—so big that he couldn't tell me that night after Clue. So big that he pretty much was handing me an out, relationship-wise, suggesting I text him if I didn't want to continue.

He needed someone he could lean on during dark times.

Could I give him that? How could I commit to being his rock when I'd never been in a real relationship before? I couldn't even maintain a long-term friendship with anyone—and hadn't since my mother died. On top of that, I didn't even *know* anyone in a healthy relationship. Mom dated a million guys whom I almost never saw. Mona's dating record was less prolific, but none of them stuck—except stupid Leon Snodgrass, the bane of my existence. Even Grandpa and Grandma, when she was still alive, seemed to merely tolerate each other. He had work and his hobbies, and she was busy controlling every aspect of my life.

And what if I failed Daniel? What if I didn't know the right things to say if he ever started struggling again? I was afraid I wasn't strong enough for him. Not cheery enough. Just plain not . . . *enough*. And what if my inability to help led to him falling down a black hole? What if he tried to hurt himself again and no one was there to stop him?

I could lose him like I've lost everyone else in my life.

That terrified me.

I tried not to let irrational fear cloud my thoughts. Maybe I was just getting ahead of myself with all these future what-ifs. We'd only been on one real date. Technically. Minus all the sleuthing.

And the sex.

The unspoken thing lurking ten steps behind us in the shadows, always present.

Sure, we'd talked about it a little at Kerry Park, but what did we even learn? That it was a mistake? That we had communication problems? Daniel seemed to think we could start over, but what if we dated for a while and then found out we were just bad in bed together? Does that happen?

Aunt Mona was my go-to adviser for matters like these, but when I texted her about Grandpa's trip, hoping I could swing by and talk to her about everything tumbling around in my head, she said she was busy meeting with a lawyer and would call later. If she was going to get in trouble for stealing that painting . . . I just couldn't handle her problems right now. I had enough to worry about.

I wished someone could tell me what to do about Daniel. I wished I believed in something, so I could ask for a sign. Fate. God. Myself. Elvis.

Elvis. I laughed out loud.

So ridiculous.

Yet what did I have to lose?

I rummaged through my desk drawer until I found what I was looking for: the not-a-penny fortune-teller card I'd gotten with Daniel in the magic shop.

> *I see that you will have a chance meeting with a*
> *dark stranger who will reveal great secrets to you.*
> *If you collaborate, a bold and dashing adventure*
> *will be in your future. But beware of perilous*
> *pitfalls that lead to ruin. It takes a level head*
> *and determination to survive a run through the*

gauntlet. In great attempts, it is glorious even to
fail, because in conflict you will find common
ground together.

Not the most precise advice, but maybe not the worst, either. I slid the edge of the fortune card into the mirror above my vanity table. My thoughts were all over the place, zipping and bouncing around like bees without a hive. And that's when I realized one thing: no one but Daniel had made me feel so much in such a small amount of time.

And I didn't want to walk away from that.

"We all try to forget what hurts us. It is sometimes the only way we can continue."
—William Monk, *A Sudden, Fearful Death* (1993)

21

I circled the drugstore aisle two times. My first time around, a chatty mom was browsing while talking on her phone while a screaming toddler ran behind her. The second time, a man was walking through. I waited until I was certain he was gone, and then I darted into the aisle.

My eyes scanned the colorful boxes on the shelves.

Fiery Ice. Studded. Sensitive. Extra Sensitive. Bare. Second Skin. Natural Lamb. Perfect Fit. Snug. Quickdraw. Colossus. Glyder. Extra Safe. Triple Safe. Armor of the Gods.

"Good grief," I mumbled. Why were there so many choices? And half of them had dire warnings on the box about allergic reactions. MAY CAUSE IRRITATION AND/OR BURNING and WHEN TO SEEK MEDICAL ATTENTION. *Maybe this is a mistake. It is probably a mistake. Give me a sign if this is a huge, horrible mistake.* Maybe I should have gone somewhere off the island to buy these. What if I saw someone I knew?

I needed to calm down. Grandpa had left for his fishing trip an hour ago, so I for sure wouldn't see him. Everything was fine. I could do this.

Another customer was approaching the aisle. I took a step to the side and pretended to be browsing . . . tampons. Terrific. When they passed, I grabbed the first box I could get my hands on. It was some kind of variety box, but it didn't have a burning warning. Good enough, surely. I booked it so fast to the front counter, I was breathing a little heavy when I slapped the box in front of an older woman with white hair. I probably should have gotten something else to buy, so that the box wasn't sitting there all alone and conspicuous. But it was too late now, and the cashier raised her brows to me as she scanned it. "Good for you, honey," she said. I didn't answer. I just prayed the government wasn't tracking my bank card purchases like Aunt Mona says they do. Then I took the flimsy bag and strode out of the store as fast as my legs would take me.

I was young. I was free of parental guidance. I had the night off from work and a box of condoms. I was living my best life.

Trial one complete.

Now for trial two.

Locating Daniel's cohousing community was easy. Getting there by ferry and bus was a struggle and took me a couple of hours. Once I got to West Seattle, I hiked through gray residential streets under a grayer sky, passing houses packed like sardines, a sea of cracked driveways, blue recycling bins, and wooden privacy fences. But at the end of a short cul-de-sac, I spotted a small parking lot beyond a private drive.

The Nest.

Tucked away in a few acres of green, the cohousing community was somewhere between modest and upper-middle class. Most of its two-story houses were painted in bright colors. They ringed a much larger building in the middle—the common house Daniel had told me about. Parking was in the front lot. I walked through it and passed a panel of mailboxes as I hiked down a wide sidewalk that meandered through the property. It was lushly landscaped, and there was an extensive garden near the common house, as well as a playground filled with loud kids.

As I strolled, it hit me that I didn't know which house belonged to Daniel's family. Each house was numbered, but apart from a red painted horse-shaped sign near someone's door that said VELKOMMEN, along with several Danish flags, there were no indicators of family names.

A plane flew overhead, somewhere above the trees. It was noisy here. And colorful. A couple of bikes sped by me. And when the rumble of the plane passed, I found myself looking at an elderly man with rosy cheeks, white hair, and wearing a pale blue beret.

"You look lost," he said, smiling, with a slight Scandinavian accent.

"Yes," I agreed. "I suppose I do. This is the Nest?"

He nodded. "That's right. Founded in 1972 by my parents. They brought the idea of cohousing with them from Denmark.

Every child should have one hundred parents—that was the motto. We have twenty-eight parents here and seventeen grandparents. That's close enough," he said with a laugh. "I'm Mr. Jessen, the community Elder. You interested in living here?"

"No. I'm actually looking for someone. The Aokis?"

"Ah," he said. "You have a private lesson with Cherry?"

"Uh . . ."

His brow furrowed. "She didn't log it."

"Log it?"

"She usually gives lessons in the common house. I'm almost positive that the room she uses has a bridge game booked. Mrs. Griffith is sick, but the game will probably still be happening. And it's best without her anyway, because Bob has been getting a little flirty."

Um, okay. Mr. Jessen was clearly the community gossip.

"Did I hear that you have a private lesson with Cherry?" another male voice said behind me.

I turned to face a stocky Asian man with a heavy beard, cradling a metal bowl filled with lettuce greens in the crook of his arm. He was dressed in jeans, sandals, and a sky-blue Hawaiian shirt covered in volcanos and palm trees. A leash was clipped to one of his belt loops; on that leash was the biggest cat I'd ever seen. Alarmingly big. Like a small bear.

"Jack," Mr. Jessen said, adjusting his beret. "This girl is looking for you."

"Me?" he said.

"She has a lesson with Cherry," Mr. Jessen said. "But the room in being used. We talked about this at the last meeting. The sign-up sheet is mandatory. I don't mind Cherry giving private lessons—"

"I'm not here for a lesson," I said, exasperated. "I'm looking for Daniel."

Discerning eyes flicked to the flower in my hair. "O-o-o-h," the bearded man said in a low, excited voice. "You're her. You're the girl."

"I am?"

"Nancy Drew."

"Birdie Lindberg," I said, feeling a little self-conscious.

"Birdie Lindberg," Mr. Jessen murmured, as if he were committing it to memory.

I asked the bearded man, "Are you Daniel's . . . ?" He looked younger than Grandpa Hugo. Definitely not as old as Mr. Jessen. Was his ear pierced?

"I'm his Jiji," he said, hand on his heart.

"Jiji," I said, smiling. "His grandfather."

His grin looked just like Daniel's. "That's right."

The enormous cat lifted her face in my direction and sniffed the air. She was bigger than a lot of dogs and had an insanely fluffy ruff around her neck; the furry tail was longer than my arm. "This is Blueberry," he told me. "She's a Maine coon. Don't let her size fool you. She's a sweet and tender lady." He flicked a tart look at Mr. Jessen.

"I'm just glad she's taking to the leash," Mr. Jessen said. "Just remember to keep her away from the playground. We don't want another incident."

Jiji looked as if he were biting back words. He closed his eyes for a moment and then turned to me and said, "You're here to see Danny?"

Danny? That was jarring.

Before I could answer, Mr. Jessen interjected, "Daniel normally goes to the comic shop to play that game on Saturday nights. Has he left already?"

"I should have called," I said, suddenly uncomfortable.

Jiji waved a dismissive hand. "He hasn't been to one of those games in weeks. Have you had dinner?" he asked me, nodding toward his bowl of leafy greens.

It was dinnertime? How had I not been aware of that? I guess once I started working at the hotel, my entire sense of normal time got screwed up.

"Baba roasted chicken," he said. "You eat roasted chicken?"

"I do?" I said, not knowing who Baba was.

"Everyone does. It's the best. Come on." He waved me toward him and held out his free elbow, and I couldn't refuse. What was I supposed to say? No thanks—I only came here to find out if your grandson wants to have sex with me again as some sort of half-baked relationship test that may or may not tell us anything about our potential relationship?

Be cool, Birdie. Be cool.

I slipped my hand around his forearm, and he led me as if I were his prom date, the big cat trailing behind us. Mr. Jessen was trying to tell us good-bye, but Daniel's grandfather just ignored him.

"Don't bother being polite to Old Man Jessen. If an asshole could wear a beret, that's what it would look like," he said under his breath as we strolled down the sidewalk, heading left when it split around the central common house. "Some people don't handle retirement well. He spends his policing us. Like I give a good goddamn about all his sign-up sheets. I weed the garden more than anyone here. I don't need a schedule." He glanced back at Jessen and gave him the stink eye. "Now he's got Blueberry in his sights. It wasn't an incident. If anything, we're the victims here. Mrs. Berquist's spoiled punk boy was trying to pull Blueberry's tail."

"Never pull a cat's tail," I said.

"It's just common sense," he agreed. "Of course, Blueberry swatted at him, and he got scratched on the arm. Whoop-de-do. It's not as though the boy needed stitches. Spray some antiseptic on it and then put your punk kid in time-out for harassing my cat."

"I've never seen a cat walk on a leash," I said. "She's very well trained."

"She took to the leash in one afternoon. Smartest cat you've ever seen," he said, beaming back at her. "Oh. Here we are, Birdie. This is us."

We stopped in front of a turquoise house. He let go of my arm to unhook Blueberry's leash, and the cat moseyed through a propped-open screen door on some sort of outbuilding attached to the side of the house. It looked as if it originally may have been a carport or garage but had been converted into a small workshop. Jiji ushered me inside. The scent of sawdust was heavy. My gaze roamed over a workbench. Saws. Pegboard filled with tools. And on a couple of sawhorses, an upside-down table was drying; the wood stain was still wet.

"Did Daniel build that?" I asked.

"Sure did. That's for Mr. Fontaine," he said, as if I would know who that was, and then waved his hand around the workshop. "Danny did all of this. The shelves on the walls, even. I helped him get started, but he's surpassed my knowledge and skills. If he'd slow down and measure things, he'd be even better." He sniffed the air. "Smell that? Roasted chicken's done. We'd better hurry."

Jiji stopped near another door and slipped off his shoes, placing them in a cubbyhole alongside others. With his hand on the door handle, he paused and looked back at me. "Baba does not allow shoes in the house."

"Oh?" He clearly expected me to follow suit. I felt odd, taking my shoes off, but he gave me a thumbs-up sign and a smile that looked far too close to Daniel's, so I stored the shoes, and we went inside the house.

Barefooted, I stepped onto cool tile in a large kitchen. Pots and pans hung from a rack on the ceiling over an island, where two whole roasted chickens sat, crispy and golden, their seductive perfume filling the air.

At the oven, two dark-haired women were arguing over what looked to be an enormous pan of green beans. One was short and wore red-rimmed glasses. The other was tall and thin, barefoot beneath black, stretchy pants and an off-the-shoulder baggy shirt. They were debating the saltiness of the dish in front of them.

"Too much miso, Mama," the younger woman was saying.

"You can never have too much miso."

"Tell that to my bloated face tomorrow."

"Ladies, look who I found outside," Jiji said gaily, as if I were a long-lost soldier, returned from war.

The women turned around. The shorter one looked me up and down over her glasses. The tall one's brows rose up into her hairline. "Who is this?"

"Guess," Jiji said, setting his bowl of greens down. "You'll never guess. Look at the flower. Tell them who you are, dear."

"I'm looking for Daniel."

"Birdie?" the younger woman said. She was stunningly pretty and had attractive, splotchy freckles all over her face.

I nodded.

She looked me over quickly and then stretched her arm toward me. "I'm Cherry, Daniel's mom."

"I've heard a lot about you," I told her, shaking her hand.

"This is my mother—Daniel's grandmother." Cherry gestured toward the other woman.

"You can call her Baba," Jiji said.

"Everyone does," the grandmother agreed. "You're the girl from Bainbridge Island with the house on the beach? You live with your grandparents?"

"With my grandfather. My grandma passed away a few months ago."

"Oh, I'm sorry to hear that. And your mother died too?"

Cherry made a face at her. "Don't be a gossip, Mama. She works at the hotel with Danny."

"I know that much," her mother answered, pretending to be irritated. The two of them stuck their tongues out at each other, and Baba laughed. Then she asked me, "Are you here for dinner? Daniel didn't let me know. But we've got plenty."

"Daniel didn't know," Cherry said, studying me harder. "He's . . . well, he's been waiting to hear from you, I believe."

He was? That made me uncomfortable. How much had Daniel told them about me? About us? Part of me was humbled that he'd mentioned me at all, but a deeper part of my brain was terrified. Did they know about what we did?

Why didn't I think this through? I shouldn't have come here.

"You're not here to break it off with him, are you?" Baba asked in a low voice.

"She's not breaking it off with him," Jiji said, and then turned to me. "Are you?"

"That's none of our business," Cherry said. "Jesus, enough with the gossipy questions. You two are as bad as Old Man Jessen."

Both of them grunted and said things under their breath.

"I didn't mean to barge into your dinner," I said.

"*Pfft.* We always have bargers," Jiji said, dumping his greens into a colander in the sink. "No one wants to eat in the common house. Who puts tofu and salmon on pizza?"

"Waste of perfectly good fish," Baba agreed as Blueberry wound around her legs.

"Besides, that's why we have two chickens," Jiji said. "One for me, and one for everyone else."

His wife slapped his fingers, which were reaching for a stray bit of crispy chicken skin. "Are the salad greens clean? You're holding us up."

Cherry wiped her hands on a kitchen towel. "Never mind them, Birdie. I'll take you to Daniel. He's in here. Follow me."

We walked through a living room with high ceilings and a second-story loft overlooking it. The walls were covered in framed magic posters and shelves lined with props—vintage decks of cards, top hats, wooden balls, stuffed rabbits . . . even an upright box with a painted sarcophagus. And so many photos . . .

"Oh, wow." I stopped in front of one of the larger framed photographs, an image of a magician and his assistant standing by a large poster that read: THE GREAT ALBINI AND BLACK BUTTERFLY. Cherry pointed to the woman in the photo.

"That was you? Black Butterfly?"

"My stage name," she said.

Wow, she was young. "I'm surprised you didn't go with Cherry Bomb."

She pointed at me, excited. "That was exactly the name I'd picked out originally, but Michael—my partner—was worried it didn't sound mysterious enough. Honestly, I think he was concerned that Cherry Bomb sounded too splashy, which would take the spotlight off him."

"How long did you perform?"

"Four years? I started right after I graduated from high school. We were getting booked at all these great clubs, and I was such a baby, I couldn't even drink. This photo was taken at the Velvet Elvis, which used to be a club in Pioneer Square. One night it was Mudhoney or the Murder City Devils. Next night it was us. We did shows with the Jim Rose Circus after they were on *The X-Files* and *The Simpsons*." She sighed. "But then I had Daniel, and you can't take a baby on the road."

I stole a look at her. She truly was extraordinarily pretty. When she glanced at me, I quickly looked away and continued scanning the room. Fake swords, jeweled turbans, and puzzle boxes. Their house put the magic shop in Pike Place to shame. But there were also posters of non-magic theater productions—was that *Rent*?

"You give people lessons now?" I asked.

"Dance lessons," she said.

"A dancer," I murmured.

"Theater. Videos. Commercials. Mostly musicals on cruises these days. If you ever find yourself on an Alaskan Disney cruise this fall, I'm in *Frozen*."

Wow. Why hadn't Daniel told me any of this? His mom was fascinating. We talked a little more, walking past memorabilia, but before she stepped around a folding screen that separated the living room from the dining room, she suddenly pulled me aside and whispered, "Look, he's been through hell, and he's everything to me. If you break his heart or do anything to hurt him, I won't be happy. Understand?"

Heat flashed through my chest and rose to my cheeks. I stuttered while forming an answer, but because I wasn't quite sure what that answer was, I never got it out. It didn't matter. She wasn't waiting for a reply. She gave me a tight smile, as if to say, *I'm only kidding . . . or am I?* Then she ducked into the dining room and waved her arm, saying, "Hey! Someone's here to see you."

Across the dining room, I caught a glimpse of dark hair and a single earbud, its mate swinging loose. Then Cherry was shifting out of the way, and there was Daniel, wearing low-slung jeans, a black T-shirt that said CHAOTIC GOOD, and a startled look on his face. He'd been setting the table, and nearly poked himself in the eye with a fork when he snatched the earbud out of his ear.

"Hey," he said.

"Hey," I answered.

Jangly, tinny guitars still floated from one side of his headphones. He struggled to pause the music while his mother hovered at my back. I glanced at her, and she murmured something about getting the food ready and left us alone.

"What are you doing here?" Daniel asked, and then quickly blinked several times. "I mean, not that I'm upset about it. I'm just . . ."

"I thought I'd . . . I mean, I didn't realize you'd be eating dinner."

He relaxed a little. "My grandparents would eat at three thirty if we let them."

"Ah." I scratched my arm. "They seem nice."

"You met everyone?"

"Even Blueberry. That's one big cat."

"A big fucking cat," he agreed. "She follows Jiji everywhere. Sleeps in the bed with them. It's ridiculous. They bought a king-size mattress to accommodate her."

"Wow," I said. Maybe my weird family had some competition.

After a moment he tugged on his bad ear and said, "You must be a better detective than me, because you actually found my house."

"It wasn't all that hard. I mean, I lucked out and ran into your grandfather after I bused my way out here, but it wasn't hard to find the street address. Not that many hippie communes in Seattle, surprisingly."

He chuckled. "This place, I swear. It's the worst, and the best. It's weird. I don't know. I think we'll eventually get kicked out. The guy running everything hates us. He likes rules, and we're rule breakers. Water and oil."

We stood on opposite sides of the table.

"Hey, Birdie?"

"Yeah?"

"I thought you worked tonight."

"Melinda changed the schedule two days ago."

"Oh." He straightened the silverware on the table. "So, why are you here?"

I hesitated, looking over my shoulder into the living room. Muffled whispering floated around the walls. This wasn't exactly the best place to have the conversation I wanted to have. So, I just said, "After sushi, you told me to text if I changed my mind about things."

"But you didn't text," he said carefully.

I shook my head slowly. "I didn't."

His eyes searched my face, but if he was going to ask me anything more, it was lost under the sound of laughter coming from the living room; his family was headed our way.

"We should talk later," Daniel said quickly.

"Alone," I added.

"That I can arrange," he said with a soft smile.

"Romance and detective work won't mix tonight!"
—Nancy Drew, *The Bungalow Mystery* (1930)

22

Dinner with the Aokis could be summed up in two words: boisterous and passionate.

During the many overlapping conversations that took place,
I learned several things about their family. That Jiji and Baba
were retired. That Jiji's father was forced to live in a Japanese-
American internment camp in Puyallup during WWII. And
that they visited Japan for the first time on their anniversary
last year. I also learned that Cherry was a background dancer in
a national Coke commercial when Daniel was three, and that
Baba really *had* watched every episode of *Murder, She Wrote*
with Daniel.

But after an hour of nonstop dinner conversation, I was
thankful when Daniel spoke up and said, "We're going to eat and
run, people. Birdie has to get back on a ferry soon, and I need to
give her a key card for the hotel, which is why she came out here."

"It is?" Jiji said, looking at me with surprise.

Sure. Why not? No one even gave me a chance to answer, so I dodged that bullet.

When we left the dining room, I thought Daniel might be taking me up to his bedroom so we could talk. Next thing I knew, he was urging me out the kitchen door and we were both slipping back into our shoes.

"Sorry about all that," he murmured after we trekked through the workshop and headed outside. "I knew if we didn't get out now, we'd be stuck there for hours."

"Where are we going?"

"I'm house-sitting for a retired couple across the quad here. I've been sleeping over there and taking care of their birds while they're in California, visiting their daughter. It's this way. Come on."

He led me across the grassy quad to a one-story home painted a strange, vivid shade of green. Then he unlocked the side door and off came the shoes again.

"Is this a Japanese thing or an Aoki thing?" I asked.

"Both. Shoes are filthy, Birdie. Why would you track dirt inside your own home—and dog shit and bacteria and everything else you've been carting around on the soles of your shoes? Plus, when you take off your shoes, you tell your mind that you're entering a safe space. Leave all the stressful, negative shit you've accumulated outside."

I hadn't thought of it that way, but it made sense. I took off my shoes again, and then we set them inside the door and stepped into the house.

My mouth dropped open.

This house wasn't just green on the outside; it was green *everywhere*. Green kitchen, where we stood. Appliances, counters, and avocado motif wallpaper. Green plants in every window. Green forest mural painted on the walls of the living room. Green shag carpet. Green jeweled lamps. And a bookshelf filled with spines of green books.

"What is happening?" I whispered.

Daniel closed the door behind us and laughed. "Welcome to Green Gables. It's perpetually stuck in 1980."

A green peninsula counter ringed with barstools separated the kitchen from a big, open living space. Daniel flipped on the lights, and it made the green glare so much worse. And that's when the birds began chirping.

"Meet Dipper, Nipper, Chipper, and Kipper," Daniel said, leading me to a wall of elaborate birdcages with four green parrots inside.

"Do they talk?"

"Not as much as you'd hope. This one says 'Dottie' sometimes—that's her owner. Dottie and Roman. That's them," he said, pointing to a photograph of a couple in their fifties with armfuls of birds. "They're super kooky and really nice."

I glanced at the giant old TV in the corner and a stereo that looked as if it had been manufactured as a prop for a cheesy science fiction movie. "Who would want to break in?"

"Only someone who would realize the error of their ways and

immediately run right back out. But Dottie and Roman knew I needed a break from my family, so they convinced my mom to let me sleep here until they get back in a couple of weeks. The first few nights, I had nightmares about *Charlie and the Chocolate Factory*, only all the candy was green."

A laptop sat on a coffee table in front of a giant green couch scattered with blankets and a pillow. Clothes were piled in a chair and on the floor. Daniel hurriedly moved the blankets to the far side of the couch. "Wasn't expecting company," he said, apologizing. "Here. Have a seat."

Holding my purse in my lap, I sank into the funky sofa. And sank and sank . . . "Whoa." I tried to pull myself up, and the springs bounced. "It's like a playground ride."

He laughed. "Yeah, it's got some mean spring to it. There's a foldout bed inside, but it smells like mildew and has a metal bar under the mattress that's a backbreaker."

I petted the velveteen fabric. "Would you call this shade of green Puke or Infection?"

"I think it's more of a Rotting Dill Pickle," he said, sitting next to me. Not close. Definitely putting some safe space between us. "So-o-o. You wanted to talk?"

Did I? I wasn't so sure anymore. All of this had drained my bravery levels. And the random parrot chirps were making me anxious. "How do you sleep with all that racket?"

"That's what you wanted to talk about?"

"No." It was hard to look at his face, but that was okay, because best I could tell from stolen glances, he wasn't exactly looking at me, either. "I . . . uh . . . had some time to think about everything you said. I've tried to be honest with myself. It's not as if I don't have any doubts or worries about it, because I do. And I've been trying to sort them all out."

"Okay," he said, crossing his arms over his chest. "Let's talk about them."

"Remember when you texted me that Truth or Lie question? You asked if we'd still be together if we hadn't gone to your car that first night."

"Yes."

"And when we were on our stakeout in the park . . . you said it could have been better between us."

"I did say that, yes."

"Well, I was thinking about it. We'll never know about the first thing. But I've been thinking that you're right about the do-over." I fumbled around in my purse and gingerly set the box of condoms on the coffee table as if it might explode. And then, because I was nervous, I suppose, I couldn't stop my mouth from running. "At first I wasn't sure if we should commit to anything if we weren't sure. Like, what if we aren't . . . compatible that way? Then what do we do? Go back to being friends? Never speak again? But then I realized that we didn't have to wonder." I exhaled a long breath.

Silence.

I continued. "What you went through . . . what you survived? It's upsetting and painful, and I can only pretend to imagine what it was like. Or how hard it still may be at times. But I'm so glad you told me—that you trusted me enough to share it. And none of what you said scares me off or makes me want to stay away. Not for the reasons you said."

"But for other reasons?" he asked, his face scrunching up.

"No!" I blew out a hard breath. "None of this is coming out right. It's only that . . . I'm worried, just a little, that I may not be what you need, and now your mother is threatening to maim me if I break your heart—"

"What?"

"But then she hugged me after dinner, so I don't know if that still stands." I laughed, but it sounded *way* too forced. "So, anyway," I said, rubbing my palms on the knees of my jeans. "I was thinking about all of this, and I found that Elvis card, remember? And it's basically saying relax and go forth and have an adventure. Just do it! Run the gauntlet! So I thought, well, maybe I'm over-thinking everything. That first afternoon we met in the diner, we just went with our instincts, and it was all great until I started thinking about what we were doing too much, which made me freak out and leave your car. And Mona is always telling me to relax and enjoy the moment—to stop worrying about the future and consequences and every possible bad thing that can happen. So maybe we should just do that?"

"Do what, exactly?"

"Sex. It will be *so* much better this time. I'm sure of it now. I won't freak out." *It will be great, and everything will be so much better between us, and Daniel won't get depressed, and I won't fail him, and he won't leave me.*

Right?

More silence. One of the birds chirped.

He wasn't saying anything, but the confused way he looked at me told me everything I needed to know. I buried my face in my hands and groaned. "Now that I say it out loud, I realize how dumb it sounds. I'm sorry. I don't know what I'm doing, and I'm really tired, so all of this is sleepy-brain logic, and that's never good logic, and—"

"Birdie? Stop it. Look at me." He tugged my arm until I faced him. "You're just freaking out about everything I told you yesterday. And that's okay. It's natural."

"I'm not spooked—if that's what you're thinking. I mean, I'm worried, because I always worry." Because I can't handle anyone else leaving me. "But I don't want to be that way anymore. I want to stop worrying."

"And that's why you want us to have sex again? You want us to run a sex gauntlet?"

"Elvis said that, not me."

He almost laughed. Not quite. "You know an actual gauntlet is punishment, right? You're basically equating us having sex with surviving some sort of horrible punishment."

"I didn't mean that!"

"Are you saying that if we have sex again and it's not perfect, you're done?"

"No! But we don't need to worry about that, because it will be great. Like sushi."

He squinted at me, brow lowered.

"The wasabi burned my nose and I wanted to spit it out, and then I tried it again, and it was really good."

"I see." He was quiet long enough to make me squirm and then said, "I confessed a really big part of my past to you yesterday. I've been sitting around, waiting for you to absorb it. Worrying that you would decide I wasn't worth the trouble. Hoping that you wouldn't. And now I'm not sure, but I feel like you want both of those options. You want a way out."

"That's not what I want!"

"Are you positive?"

"I'm just saying that maybe if we relax and have fun together, then neither of us will get hurt."

"So you want a friends-with-benefits sort of thing?"

"No. Maybe? No!" I threw up my hands. "Honestly, I don't know what I'm doing. Everything you told me yesterday scared me a little, and it shouldn't. So, I thought the problem must be me. That if I lived in the moment and quit being so cautious, that everything would work out. But the truth is, I don't know how to have a relationship. Not friendship, not friends with benefits, and not anything else. I feel like you're light-years ahead of me, and it probably wasn't like this with other girls."

"Jesus, Birdie. How many other people do you think I've been with?"

"I don't know. I just assumed—"

"One."

"One?" I repeated, not quite believing him. He was Daniel. He was beautiful and charming. Talking to people was as easy as breathing for him. He only had one girlfriend? How?

"Her name was Emily. And what do you want to hear? That it was great? It was—" He stopped. "It was someone I had a crush on before the incident. Afterward, she felt sorry for me. I'm not saying she wasn't attracted to me, but her need to . . . comfort me was greater, if that makes any sense. I didn't understand that at the time. I thought she liked me. Imagine my surprise, after we saw each other for a couple of months, when she moved on to someone who had their shit together, and I had to sit around with my heart broken, trying not to fall into another black hole."

Oh. I didn't expect this.

Maybe we weren't as different as I thought.

Maybe we'd both been let down by other people.

After a long silence, I said, "I'm sorry you went through that. I guess I assumed my life was more messed up than yours."

"It's not a competition."

"I'll see your overdose and bet you the death of a parent."

For a moment I was scared I'd been too jokey. Then his shoulders relaxed, and he smiled the sort of smile that made me feel like I was receiving the queen's blessing. "Who needs normal?" he said, eyes twinkling. "Not us."

"Normal is for the weak."

Warm fingers clasped mine and held tight. "Forget all this stuff. Remember what you told me in the van? I want that too. All of it. And I think we can. But I can't guarantee it, and I don't expect any sort of guarantee from you, either. I just need acceptance, that's all."

"*That* I can give you. But I need you to try not to die on me, because I'm getting really tired of that happening." I was trying for light and jokey, but a wave of emotion caught me off guard, and my eyes brimmed with tears. I blinked them away, wanting to smile and cry at the same time.

"Hey," he said, looking back at me with glossy eyes. "I'm pretty sure I can manage that."

"Okay," I said.

"Okay," he agreed.

He softly stroked his thumb over my knuckles. I couldn't stop my fingers from clasping his. Such a little thing, holding hands. But a warm, electric current flowed between us where we touched, and it suddenly felt as if things were going to be okay somehow.

"I feel pretty stupid now," I said after a moment.

"No reason for that. I mean, I do want to have sex with you again," he said, glancing at the box on the coffee table. "But for future reference, you can't just toss condoms at me and expect me to be in the mood. I mean, sure. The variety *is* tempting," he said, amusement in his voice. "I've always wanted to try a glow-in-the-dark flavored condom. Kiwi? And they're green, so I'd match the room."

"Good grief," I whispered, mildly horrified. "I just grabbed something."

"And I appreciate that," he said, struggling to hold back a smile. "Safe sex is good sex."

I snorted. "It wasn't last time."

"Okay, fair point," he said, grinning. "You know what? I think we should—" An obnoxious ringtone startled us both. He dug inside his pocket. "Shit. This is my mom's phone. How did that happen? I must have grabbed hers off the dinner table when I was rushing."

"Does that mean she has yours?"

"Probably. Stay here. I'll go run this over and get my phone before she breaks the door down here. Meanwhile, make yourself at home. There's Coke in the fridge. Let's . . . put all of this on hold for a minute and think about our options, agreed?"

"Agreed."

"Don't go anywhere," he instructed. "I'll be right back, yeah?"

I didn't want him to go. I wanted him to finish the sentence he was in middle of before the phone rang. *I think we should . . .* Should what? Wait until we're less emotional? Turn off the lights and see if these condoms really do glow in the dark? Run a taste test on the kiwi flavor? SHOULD WHAT?

Now I was nervous. I pushed off the old couch and meandered into the kitchen. A cold drink sounded good. I could use the sugar to power through the fog that was hanging over my brain. My eyes roamed over a collection of bizarre cookie jars—mostly frogs and leprechauns—until I spotted a Mason jar filled with sugared gummy squares on the counter. I wondered if they'd been there since the 1980s, so I opened the lid and cautiously sniffed. Smelled like sugar and fruit. Looked homemade. And when I took one out, it wasn't petrified, so I tested a small corner. Cherry. Nice. I grabbed a couple and ate them while opening the fridge. And after snagging a Coke and wiping sugar-sticky fingers on my jeans, I went for one more piece of candy. But when I opened my mouth to pop it inside, the door swung open.

"Don't eat that!" Daniel yelled, lunging toward me.

I dropped it on the counter, terrified. "Why?"

"Did you eat any already?"

I nodded.

"How many?"

"What's wrong?" I said, utterly alarmed. "You're scaring me."

"How many, Birdie?"

"Two? I don't know."

"Just two?"

"Yes! Are they bad? Is it bugs? Poison? *What's wrong?*"

Daniel gritted his teeth. "They're medicated," he said, and when I stared at him dumbly, he clarified. "As in cannabis."

> "I try hard not to make the same mistake more than three or four times."
> —Stephanie Plum, *Three to Get Deadly* (1997)

23

Oh. My. Good. Gravy.

"I just ate . . . weed candy?" I massaged my throat as if I could get it back out.

"If you only ate two, you should be fine," Daniel assured me. "They aren't strong."

I'd never even had a swig of beer! "What are these even doing here? They didn't taste weird. How was I supposed to know?"

"I didn't know you'd be coming over! I forgot they were even sitting out."

I was horrified. And close to a full-on panic attack. "I've been drugged."

"For the love of Christ," he muttered. "You haven't been drugged."

"Can I throw them up? Should I go to the ER and get my stomach pumped? I've never even been in a hospital!"

Daniel put both hands around the sides of my neck, holding me firmly in place, and whistled. "Calm down. You don't need to go to the ER. The candy isn't some back-alley edible. Dottie and Roman's son-in-law grows marijuana, and their daughter made these—the one who just had the baby. They aren't strong. I promise."

"How would you know?" I gasped audibly. *"You've had them."*

"Quite a few. Dottie left them here for me. It's my payment for watching their place."

I scolded, "Daniel!" Which unfortunately sounded *way* too much like my grandmother for comfort. And he just laughed at me. Laughed! "Does your mother know?" I asked.

"Hell no," he said. "She'd kick my ass. But Jiji had three of them a few days ago. And my therapist knows."

I was having trouble processing this. My grandpa enjoyed a cigar now and then, but he wouldn't dare eat weed candy. He referred to smoking marijuana as "toking the grass" when our rich neighbors had parties and we could smell it on our stretch of beach. "Don't people get hospitalized for eating too much pot candy?" I asked.

"Maybe a few dumb-dumbs who eat whatever some rando gives them at a party. Do you know how many people fatally overdosed on weed last year? Zero. It's always zero. Look, my grandfather's eaten this candy," he argued, stroking his thumb along my jawline. "Joseph's eaten them. I've eaten them. They're perfectly safe."

"Then why were you freaking out when you saw me eating one?"

"I don't know. I guess because you might have downed half the jar and gotten way too stoned, and that's never fun. And because you're . . ."

"What?"

"I don't know." He shrugged.

"I'm naive."

"I didn't say that."

"But you thought it."

"Not in a bad way. I just don't want you to be upset. And I don't think you should be. Seriously, you're going to be fine. You're not going to hell or the hospital."

"What you're saying is that I don't need to try to throw them up?"

"That would be silly. And a waste of perfectly good edibles. Besides, you may never even feel it. One gummy barely makes me feel relaxed. Worst that can happen is you just get a little buzzed in about an hour."

"An hour?"

"Or two."

"Two hours?"

He kept one hand on my shoulder while reaching to flip open the candy jar's lid. "How many did you have? Two? I'll catch up with you." He mimicked a transatlantic, 1930s Hollywood accent. "I'll have two martinis, bartender. Line them up right here."

"Don't you dare quote Nick and Nora to me at a time like this!"

He held up two gummy squares and popped both into his

mouth. "See? We're even stephen now." He chewed, swallowed, and stuck out his tongue to show me. "Ahhhh."

I relaxed a little. "Are you sure it's okay?"

"So sure," he said, amused. "Look, why don't we put our earlier talk on hold and just enjoy each other's company. We can curl up on the couch and watch a movie."

I was definitely not in the mood to discuss heavy topics anymore—and especially not sex; I was too busy dreading the candy's effects. After some more circuitous talking, in which he assured me several more times that I was okay, he took me out the back door for some fresh air on a small patio. And while we sat outside in the setting sun, I drank a soda—which made me feel better.

Eventually, I was calm enough to go back inside. It had been an hour, and I didn't feel anything, so maybe Daniel was right. Maybe I freaked out for no reason. We browsed the house's time-capsule video selection and picked out some weird fantasy film called *Labyrinth*. "It's got Jim Henson puppets and a kidnapping and David Bowie playing the Goblin King," Daniel informed me excitedly, showing me the back of the videotape sleeve.

"It sounds insane."

"It is. You will love it."

We put it in and sat on the couch together. Then he scooted me around and lay back against me, kicking his socked feet up on the armrest. Which felt . . . charmingly intimate.

Slowly, like a light dimming, my limbs began to loosen. He'd said that I'd relax eventually, but I wondered if it had more to do with his pleasant weight on me and the scent of his hair falling over his shoulder and less to do with the candy. Was I feeling something? Maybe. I was less panicky about it. I tried to enjoy it and concentrated on the TV screen. What was this movie even about? Some chick running around inside a goblin maze trying to save her baby brother? But suddenly there was David Bowie in a crazy wig, looking like a mad vampire, and then a little later . . . wow. What was I seeing?

"Those tights are pornographic," I said.

Daniel laughed. "It's a famously epic film bulge."

"That's not a bulge. It's a sentient entity."

A sentient entity? Oh my God, I think I'm high.

"Ha-ha!" I laughed so loud, it made Daniel jump.

And then the worst possible thing happened: my muscles stopped working.

I was about to have a cataplexy episode.

No, no, no! Not now!

The blood left my arms. Then neck, then face. And I was absolutely frozen. I could still hear. I was conscious. It probably wouldn't last long—a few seconds. A minute at most. But I couldn't tell Daniel this because I couldn't talk. My jaw had fallen open, which was utterly embarrassing, and my face was twitching.

And Daniel was freaking out, shouting my name, shaking me.

I zoned out for a moment, and then—all at once—my muscles

suddenly thawed. I closed my mouth and moved my arms to stop him from shaking me.

"I'm okay, I'm okay!" I told him.

"Oh my God," he said, anxious. "I thought you passed out. Your entire body just drooped all at once."

"It's happened before a couple of times, usually when I laugh really hard."

"What?" he said, mildly hysterical.

"Stop. It's fine," I said, still trying to shake off the tingling feeling. "My grandpa calls it going boneless, because it feels like your bones disappear. It feels a little like when you're on an elevator and there's a strange moment when you can't tell if you're moving or if the walls are moving."

He stared at me, blinking. Completely dumbfounded.

"It's not a big deal," I said. "One time it happened to me when I was sitting in Madison Diner, and I laughed really hard, and the next thing I knew, people were picking me up off the floor. I slid right out of my seat," I said, whistling. "I could hear everything they were saying, because they were talking about calling an ambulance. It never lasts long."

"Birdie?" he said carefully. "Do you have . . . narcolepsy?"

"Wha-a-at?" I said, sounding like some kind of stoner in a bad teen movie.

"Oh my God, you do!"

"Maybe? Not officially. I don't like doctors, so I've never been checked."

"Jesus! It all makes sense now. That's why you're sleepy all the time. Why you fell asleep in the hotel lobby before we went to Kerry Park."

"It's possible I may have inherited a few pesky sleepy genes."

"Hello! That's called narcolepsy!"

I sighed heavily and tried to sit up a little, but I was still feeling weak, and Daniel was sort of in my face, blocking me from moving too far. "Yes, it's possible I have narcolepsy. Grandpa got diagnosed when he was in the Coast Guard, but only after he fell asleep piloting a boat and screwed up his leg. Before that, he just sort of managed it on its own." I shrugged and stretched my neck, trying to revive my muscles. "One doctor thought he had epilepsy and another thought it was insomnia. I guess it's easy to misdiagnose."

"Is it serious?"

"More like seriously annoying. I've only had a few cataplexy episodes—that's what just happened. Sometimes I zone out when people are talking and miss a few words of a sentence. Grandpa calls that blanking out, but I think of them as mini naps. They only last a couple of seconds. Not even long enough for me to put my head down."

"That's not what was happening when you fell asleep in the lobby."

"No. That was pure exhaustion. Sometimes I get so tired out of the blue that I know I've got to sit down somewhere and take a nap. And sometimes I hallucinate a little when I'm falling asleep, and it feels like I'm still awake, so I get confused."

He blinked several times. "The finger-counting trick."

"Ye-a-a-ah," I drawl. "But that's all."

"That's all? Oh shit! When you were telling me about that nightmare you had about the demon sitting on your chest—like the famous painting."

"That's only happened to me that one time."

"But you haven't seen a doctor about all of this?"

"There's not a cure. What's the point?"

"Don't be stupid. You need to see a doctor."

"Paging Doctor Danny," I called out.

"Jesus Christ," he murmured. "You're stoned out of your goddamned mind."

"I feel *really* good," I said, unable to stop smiling.

"I can tell."

"Well, pat yourself on the back for being right about the candy," I said. "It's totally fine."

"Why haven't you told me about your narcolepsy?"

"Honestly?"

"Honestly."

"I'm sort of embarrassed about it," I admitted. "I've talked with people online who have it, and they all say not to tell anyone because, you know, if your boss finds out, they can fire you. And people will start looking at you like you're a leper."

"Melinda wouldn't fire you for that, and you're not a leper."

"Thanks." Right now he was kind of lying on top of me,

and it felt *really* good. "Hey," I said. "Want to have sex?"

"Oh my God."

"Well, well, well. Who's the prude now?" I laughed. Really hard. "See? I didn't go boneless that time. Where are you going? Come back!"

He sat up to grab his phone. "I've got to look up narcolepsy and weed before I go crazy worrying about you. Hold on."

"Holding," I said, and looked up at the ceiling. It was green too. These nutty people were committed to the color green, and I had to admire that. Actually, this whole crazy house looked . . .

"Birdie!"

"What?" I said, jerking my head up. "I'm awake!"

"You sure?"

"Must've dozed off. How long was I out?"

"I thought that cataplexy thing was happening to you again, but you were snoring a little."

"Good grief," I mumbled. "I guess I didn't sleep so well earlier this morning. Must be catching up with me."

He stared at me and then said, "I looked up weed and narcolepsy."

"Am I going to die?"

"One day, but not tonight. THC may make you sleepier than the average person." He ran his hand over the side of my face while his eyes studied mine. "I wish you had told me."

"Guess we were both keeping secrets from each other, huh?"

He nodded slowly. "Guess we were."

"He-e-y," I said, leaning into his hand. "Weren't we talking about having sex?"

He snorted. "I'm not having sex with you."

"Ever?"

"We'll see."

We laughed a little, and then a lot. But I didn't go boneless again, thank goodness. He made me get up and walk around, just to check that everything was okay—which of course it was. I just felt a tiny bit weak. I couldn't concentrate on the movie anymore, so we tried looking through the record collection. Records, and records, and records . . .

Next thing I knew, I was waking up again, and Daniel was sitting me down on the coffee table so that he could spread out a sheet on the couch. The TV was off. The birdcages were covered up. All the lights were out except for a lamp next to the couch. "What's happening?" I asked, looking for a clock. "What time is it?"

"Three. You've fallen asleep four times."

Whoa. That was . . . more than usual.

"You're staying here with me tonight," he told me.

"Oh, okay," I said, still feeling good. "Where's my phone? I'd better text Grandpa Hugo. Oh, wait. I don't have to. He's gone fishing. Literally. Maybe I should make sure Aunt Mona isn't looking for me . . ." No messages. I was in the clear. I sent her a quick text to let her know I'd call her tomorrow and that I was turning in for the night.

"All good?" he said, when her reply came—a "good night" and lots of sugary emojis.

"All good."

"I'll take you back home tomorrow." He pulled me to my feet and gently tugged the flower out of my hair, tossing it on the coffee table, then pointed at my jeans. "May I?"

"You may."

He unbuttoned my jeans. "Don't get any ideas. We're just going to sleep."

"Together?"

"Is that okay?"

"Best idea you've had. Keep on doing what you're doing," I said, slinging my arms around his neck as he unzipped me and pushed my jeans down over my hips. Then he was urging me onto the couch and taking off his own jeans. And his shirt. Holy cow, I'd forgotten how nice he was to look at. He gave me a really good view of the front of his boxers when he leaned over me to turn off the light. And then he lay down with me on the couch, pulling me halfway on top of him to make room enough for the both of us.

"You okay?" he asked, and I felt the question rumble in his chest under my cheek.

"*So* okay." Strange silhouettes populated the strange room, but it was fine, because he had his arms around me, and something about the way his skin smelled made me feel happy. Safe. "I've never slept with someone else. I mean actual sleeping."

"Me either."

"Not even with that Emily girl?"

"Nope."

Huh. "Well, I'll let you know my verdict tomorrow, but so far I'm liking it. We'll just take a short nap, okay?"

"Sure. Just a nap."

"Hey, Daniel? Do you think if we fall asleep together, we'll have the same dreams?"

"I hope not. My dreams can get filthy. You might never want to speak to me again."

"My dreams might be filthier. I have super vivid ones. I could be dreaming right now."

"You should count your fingers."

"I can't see them. It's too dark."

"Guess you'll have to go on faith." His hand stroked up and down my back. "You scared me tonight."

"I didn't mean to."

"It's okay. I'm still glad you're here, even if we didn't run the gauntlet."

"We didn't fall in a perilous pitfall, did we?"

"If we did, we can pull ourselves out."

And for a moment, as I drifted off to sleep, listening to the soft thump of Daniel's heartbeat, I believed that we really could.

Until I woke up the next morning to find his mother standing over us.

"We always know when we are awake that we cannot be dreaming."
—Ruth Rendell, *One Across, Two Down* (1971)

24

"Get up," Cherry said. "Now."

Heart pounding, I flew off the couch and practically tripped over the blanket before I had time to realize that I wasn't wearing pants. Daniel made a loud noise and jumped, but he saw his mom and immediately covered his boxers. "Jesus Christ," he complained in a deep, sleep-rough voice. "What the hell, Mom?"

"What the hell is that you lied to me," she said angrily. "You said you were taking her home last night. Now I come over here to find you two sleeping together?"

I wanted to die. I also wanted to put on my jeans, but she was standing next to them.

Daniel groaned and pulled his hair back out of his eyes. "We weren't—we were only sleeping."

Cherry snorted. "Sure. That's what I'd tell Baba when I was your age. She didn't believe me either. And I don't think Dottie let you watch this place so you could have sex parties with your girlfriend."

"Did you not just hear me?" he snapped back.

"I heard you just fine." She pointed to the coffee table, where, next to the wilted lily from my hair, the box of condoms still sat. "And I see plenty fine too."

Chum bucket!

"I know what it looks like," Daniel said. "But it wasn't even opened. See for yourself. Go on. *Nothing happened.* I asked her to stay here because—" He glanced at me. "It doesn't matter. It was for her safety, and it's none of your business."

"I'm your mother. It will never stop being my business," she said, throwing his shirt at him. "Go get dressed in the back. I want a word with Birdie alone, please."

"Mom—"

She made a sharp hissing noise, and he relented, angrily snagging both pairs of jeans off the floor. As he handed mine over, he looked at me with big, sorrowful eyes, but I couldn't even hold his gaze. I just shoved my feet into my jeans and quickly pulled them up while he walked past me. I was breathing so hard, it felt like I might collapse.

Cherry walked to the kitchen. I followed, and when she got to the counter, she turned around. "What are you doing with my son?"

I shook my head. "We didn't do anything," I said, voice breaking.

"I don't care what you did or didn't do. I asked you a question. What are you doing with my son?"

"Um . . ." I didn't know what she wanted me to say. *We're solving a mystery together at work* didn't seem like the right answer. Neither did *I accidentally ate a bunch of weed candy last night and had a cataplexy episode*, or the one I'm sure every mother loves to hear: *I lost my virginity with your son, and now I might have feelings for him.*

After a few awkward moments, she finally gave me a clue about what was going on in her mind, saying, "I know he told you about his self-harm incident."

Is that what we were calling it? I nodded. "Yes, he did."

"Then you can understand why he doesn't need fair-weather girls in his life," she said. "He needs stability. If you're one of those girls who wants to have a wild weekend, find someone else. Because he's a good kid, and he doesn't need that right now."

"What? I don't even know what a wild weekend is," I said, perplexed and defensive.

"I don't know you, but I know my son. He's emotional. He gets attached. I'm trying to keep him steady so that he doesn't plummet into another depression. Do you really want to be responsible for that?"

How was I supposed to answer? I was confused and panicked, in a strange place with a strange woman. My eyes welled with tears. *Don't cry . . . Do. Not. Cry.*

Daniel rushed into the kitchen. "What the hell? What did she say to you?" he asked me. When I shook my head, he said to his mother, "Seriously? What is wrong with you? You can't keep pulling this shit. This isn't normal!"

"Don't tell me what's normal. I'm your mother. I'm responsible for your well-being. You weren't answering your phone."

"So, you broke in here to check on me—"

"The back door was open."

"—when I specifically asked you never to do that?"

"I will *not* talk about this now."

Not in front of me. That was the implication. I could take a hint; I strode away from the kitchen to gather up my things.

"Birdie," Daniel pleaded.

"It's fine," I said, feeling as if my heart were being shot with a dozen arrows—*prick, prick, prick.* "Talk to your mom. I'm going home."

"I'll take you," Daniel said.

I shook my head. *Prick, prick, prick.*

"Birdie—"

"I'm not a child. I can get home by myself." I quickly swiped at my eyes and found my purse as he begged me to stay. I couldn't. Everything inside me was screaming for me to run. Bolt. Flee the scene. I slipped into my shoes and bolted out the door, and when he tried to come after me, I stopped him and said, "I shouldn't have come. I'm sorry . . . for everything."

I somehow made it out of the neighborhood, avoiding stares as I tripped my way down the sidewalk, blubbering like a small child. But I managed to pull myself together long enough to board a morning bus. And when I was headed out of West Seattle, crammed against commuters headed to their jobs downtown, stunned and dazed about what had just happened, trying not to cry again—*Pull it together, Birdie!*—I realized that what I'd said to Daniel was a lie: I wasn't sorry in the least.

Sure, it was humiliating that I'd brought an entire box of condoms for Cherry to find, but I wasn't sorry that Daniel and I had talked about sex. And yes, it was embarrassing that I'd nodded off so many times last night, but I was honestly glad he knew about my narcolepsy now; it was a relief. And spending the night with him on the couch? I didn't regret that one single bit.

At least, not until Cherry walked in.

What are you doing with my son?

Good question. What *was* I doing?

I guess I needed to figure that out. But right now it was all I could do to hold back tears and try to stop my chest from feeling as if it were caving in and collapsing around my wounded heart.

It wasn't until I got back to Bainbridge Island that I remembered Grandpa was gone on his fishing trip with Cass. Instead of heading home, I walked past the harbor shops and hiked up the main drag to Aunt Mona's house while the sun timidly peeked through gray clouds. But when I spied the retro red letters of THE RIVERA on the marquee above the doorway, I also spotted a shiny black SUV parked in front of the door. My first thought was that the cops had come to arrest Mona for stealing that painting from Sharkovsky's house, but as I quickened my steps, hugging my purse against my ribs, I realized it was something far worse.

Leon Snodgrass.

He was putting something in the back seat of the SUV. When he shut the door and looked up, our eyes met. It had been more than a year since I'd seen him, and some things looked exactly as I remembered: pasty-white rich-boy complexion. Long nose. Stupid 1990s band T-shirt, in an attempt to look less like the stockbroker that he was.

But other things had changed. No longer clipped short, his chin-length light brown hair was tucked behind his ears. A matching beard covered the lower half of his face. And he was wearing jeans. I'd never seen him outside a pair of khakis.

If I had to profile Leon Snodgrass, it would look a little like this:

Suspect: Leon Snodgrass

Age: 39

Occupation: Investment banker

Medical conditions: (1) Allergic to mangoes. (2) Terrible yet frequent golfer. (3) Thinks "da bomb" is a funny way to describe things he likes. (4) Says Monopoly is better than Clue. (5) Possible foot fetish; always looking at Mona's feet.

Background: Born into an upper-middle class family on Bainbridge Island; great-grandfather owned a shipbuilding company in Scotland in the early twentieth century. Went to the University of Washington; has master's degree in finance and brags that he met former President Barack Obama in 2010 when the man made an appearance at a bakery in Pioneer Square, and that President Obama complimented his shoes. Won a bunch of sailing competitions after college. Started dating Mona four years ago; broke up. Then again two years ago, before going on a "break" a year later, during which time, seventeen-year-old Birdie Lindberg took photographs of him laughing it up over calamari with Cathy Wong inside Doc's Marina Grill. A month later he moved to Texas. Some of us wished he'd stayed there.

"Birdie," Leon said, blinking at me as if I were a figment of his imagination.

"Leon," I replied, hugging my purse more tightly. "Heard you were in town."

He nervously tucked his hair more firmly behind his ears. "Yeah. Decided to move back to the island. Austin was great, but it's sweltering, and the traffic is insane. And I got sick of waiting in line for breakfast tacos."

Did he say "move back"? As in permanently?

"Well, hoo-boy," I said. "You came back to a real restaurant mecca here, didn't you?" I said, unable to keep the sarcasm out of my voice. "Now you get to wait in line behind chatty Mrs. Carmichael at Pegasus Coffee."

He laughed softly and scratched the back of his head. "Believe it or not, I've missed all this. You don't realize how fresh the air is until you've gone."

"Like Murden Cove's tidal flats?" Farther north on the island, they start stinking like sulfur in the summer during low tide.

"Ugh, *Murder* Cove," he says, wincing. "Okay, maybe I didn't miss that. But the rest of it. Plus, the city is right across the water. I can zip over there if I'm missing nightlife."

"In your super-dope new yacht?" I said. "What was that you named it? *The Spirit of a Woman I Don't Deserve?*"

"Oof," he said, blowing out a hard breath. "Why are teens so vicious?"

"Because we haven't learned the art of being phony yet, Mr. Soundgarden."

He looked down at his T-shirt. "They were the first band I ever saw in concert."

"And what's with the hair and the jeans? Trying to relive your golden years? Is that why you're chasing Mona again? You know she doesn't fit in with your golfing lifestyle, right? That hasn't changed."

"I don't have a golfing lifestyle. I learned to play golf so that

I could schmooze my clients. It's called being good at my job."

"Now you're bad and bourgeois, buying yachts and making it rain?"

"I have no idea what that means."

"That doesn't surprise me in the least."

"Why are you throwing all this shade on me, Birdie?" He said this as if he were partly teasing, partly confused.

My patience was in tatters. Everything I'd endured over the last couple of days—Daniel's confession over sushi, our emotional talk in Green Gables, my accidental foray into stoner life, the cataplexy episode last night, and getting yelled at by Cherry this morning . . . It felt as if I were in the middle of a lake, trying to paddle a canoe by myself, and some unseen force was poking holes in the boat, letting in more and more water. My canoe was sinking, and Leon had the misfortune of being a fish in the wrong place at the wrong time.

I wanted to bash him over the head with my paddle.

"Why are you trying to take Mona away from me?!" I said, almost shouting, sounding like one of those loony-tunes, doom-and-gloom street preachers who wildly accuse innocent passersby of contributing to the fall of humanity. "Can I not have one good thing?"

"Birdie," he said in a pleading voice, holding out both hands as if he was trying to keep me calm. "I promise you—"

Whatever he was going to promise, it was lost when the door to the theater opened. Out came Aunt Mona, who trotted toward us wearing white pants, wedge heels, a blue-and-white striped shirt, and a navy blazer emblazoned with a hand-stitched gold crest that said AHOY! Over a bobbed white wig, she wore a glittery sailor hat.

"Darling!" she said to me, breathless. "Is everything okay? You didn't set the house on fire, did you? Are the two of you playing nice?" She gave Leon a questioning look.

"We're completely fine," he said, sounding like we were in the middle of a bank robbery and he was the level-headed one trying to keep us calm. "It's all going to be okay."

Speak for yourself, I thought.

"What's wrong?" Mona asked me. "Is everything all right between you and our Daniel?"

I shook my head once, self-conscious.

Aunt Mona held up a hand to Leon, telling him to wait, and then pulled me back under the theater's entrance. "Hey," she said in a low voice. "Tell me what's happened."

"This isn't a one-time thing anymore? You're dating Leon again?"

She closed her eyes briefly. "It's . . . complicated. We're talking. That's all."

"Talking about what? He told me he was moving back here to the island, but was that a lie? Did he only come back to convince you to move to Texas?"

"And sweat to death in the summer? Not on your life."

"Then what? I came over here because I needed to talk, and

there he is, standing outside in the morning sun like he spent the night here last night."

Mona groaned. "Okay, he did, yes. But it's not what you think. Trust me, there's nothing juicy going on. Not even so much as a French kiss. We just stayed up late talking and he slept on the sofa. I swear," she said, holding up three fingers.

I still didn't totally believe her. Or maybe what happened with Cherry this morning had completely stripped away all rational thought and turned me into a raving, panicking paranoid.

"Now, stop pouting," she said in a calming voice, "and tell me why you're here."

Blowing out a hard breath, I tried to put Leon out of my mind while I gave her the short version of last night's events: going to West Seattle, meeting Daniel's family, the stupid gummies.

"Sweet baby Jesus," she murmured with wide eyes. "Hugo's going to eat me alive for letting that happen on my watch!"

"Are you insane? Don't tell him! You want him to have a heart attack?"

"All right! All right," she said. "Go on. Tell me the rest."

And I did. About sleeping with Daniel on the couch. And about Cherry finding us.

"Jeez," Aunt Mona complained. "Uptight much?"

"Actually, I'm not sure she is." I certainly wasn't going to get into Daniel's issues while Leon pretended to watch late-Sunday-morning post-church traffic. "I think she's just overprotective about Daniel. She's actually . . . I don't know. You'd probably like her. I think she's a few years older than you. She was a magician's assistant back in the late 1990s. She had a stage name and everything—Black Butterfly."

Aunt Mona blinked at me. "No way. *That's* Daniel's mother? Holy shit. Hold on," she told me. And then shouted to Leon, "Just a second, okay?"

Before I could stop her, she was racing back inside the theater. And while I gave Leon an awkward lift of the chin that said *I acknowledge that this is holding up your plans and that I was a total jerk to you a few minutes ago, but please don't come over here and try to make good with me right now*. Then I stared at the cardboard movie standees in Mona's ticket window until she came back out—this time, carrying something.

"Look!" she said, holding out an old event flyer, affixed to a backing board and stored inside a clear plastic sleeve. The flyer's design was silk-screened in black ink on neon pink paper. It advertised an event at a Seattle club in 1999. The Jim Rose Circus Side Show, with opening act the Great Albini and Black Butterfly.

"That's her!" I said, pointing at the blurry, silk-screened people.

"I know! I saw this show with your mom when we were in high school! We were sixteen—I made us fake IDs to get inside, but they didn't even check them. I tore this flyer off the wall as we were leaving the show."

"You saw Cherry perform?"

"I did! I remember her outfit, the most amazing black corset with roses . . ."

"*You saw Cherry perform,*" I repeated, completely astounded. "She could have been pregnant with Daniel."

She was silent. I looked up to see glossy eyes. "What's the matter?" I asked.

Shaking her head quickly, she said, "I'm not sad. I was just thinking about when your mom was pregnant with you, and now my eye makeup is going to smear, so I'm going to stop being nostalgic and focus on what matters here. Because I think this is a sign. Destiny!"

"Destiny hates me, and so does Cherry."

"You said she was an overprotective mama bear. All you need to do is convince her that you're not a threat. Calm the bear down."

"How?"

"No idea, but you're the one who loves solving mysteries, Veronica Mars." She gave me a wink with gold-tipped eyelashes before shoving the flyer into my hand. "Here. Take it. It's yours now, and you can do whatever you want with it. All I know is when destiny calls, you answer. Right now I'm answering my own call."

"With Leon?" I said, making a face.

She kissed the top of my head. "We'll see. It's only a boat ride."

Right. I didn't believe that for one second. But she told me when to expect her back and promised—again—that we'd talk more later. And as I stood on the sidewalk, clutching the flyer she'd given me, Leon helped her into his SUV. Then he turned to me, hesitated, and then hugged me.

Hugged.

Me.

I froze, all my muscles stony, not knowing what to do. Then he pulled back to look at my face, holding my arms, while he said in a low voice, "We got off on the wrong foot today, but I want you to know that nothing will change. I get that Mona is practically a mother to you, and I wouldn't do anything to take her away from you, okay? So don't be worried. It's all going to be fine."

He sounded serious, and I was so discombobulated, all I could do was stare at him when he released me. Then he was jogging to his SUV and getting behind the wheel. Aunt Mona waved at me from her window as they pulled away from the curb and disappeared into traffic.

Nothing will change? What was happening? Did that mean they were officially a couple again? And if nothing was changing, then why was my stomach in knots?

My phone buzzed. I pulled it out and found a series of texts:

Daniel: I'm so so so so sorry.

Daniel: R u ok? Did you make it to the ferry? I went after you in my car, but u weren't at bus stop. R u home yet?

Daniel: Even if u r upset, lmk u r ok.

Me: I'm home.

Daniel: PRAISE ELVIS. R u ok?

Me: Physically, yes. Mentally, I'm sorry I left.

Daniel: Really? Bc I'm devastated u left.

Me: Yeah?

Daniel: Yeah. And I'm just so sorry it happened. Mortified. Please don't hate me.

Me: I don't. At all. Zero hate.

Daniel: Can't tell you how happy I am to hear that.

Daniel: Last night was the best sleep I've had. Ever.

Me: Me too. Wish I was still there.

Daniel: Wish u were still here too. (⁾□ˢ,)

I looked at the pink flyer Aunt Mona gave me. I didn't want to come between Daniel and his mother. What a disaster. A disaster upon disaster, considering all the events leading up to this morning's confrontation with Cherry.

Before I met Daniel, my life was a cozy mystery book in a small town with one quiet murder to solve. Now dead bodies were piling up everywhere, a serial killer was on the loose, and I was a brooding detective with a sleep disorder who'd fumbled all the evidence.

A good detective restored order.

So why was I leaving behind a trail of chaos wherever I went?

25

After a nap and a leftover cinnamon roll heated up in the microwave, things started looking . . . not exactly rosy, but less dreary. I still didn't know what to do about Cherry, but Daniel and I texted on and off throughout the afternoon about other things, including what Leon Snodgrass had said to me, which Daniel thought was no big deal.

And maybe it wasn't. I definitely regretted some of the stuff I'd said to Leon in the heat of the moment. I decided to let it go. I had too many other things to worry about, and I desperately wanted to see Daniel. I was hoping maybe he could meet me at the diner before work, but he was busy finishing some woodworking project for one his neighbors.

Once I got to work, he'd already been dragged into a security meeting with all the other employees who reported directly to Mr. Kenneth. It had something to do with SARG, the animal rights group. They'd staged another protest earlier today, outside the hotel, and this time the local news covered it.

"They dropped a huge banner from the second-floor windows," Daniel whispered at the side of the registration desk later during a rare interlude, checking to see that no guests or employees were in hearing range. A couple of businessmen lounged on one of the sofas in the middle of the lobby, but they were caught up in their own conversation.

"A banner?" I repeated.

"Apparently, during the protest out front, two of their members checked in under false names in adjoining rooms and hung a banner out the window that said 'Octavia Is a Prisoner,'" Daniel explained. "No one in the hotel noticed for an entire hour. Management says SARG is becoming a PR disaster, and we have to watch out for their members. Gotta admit, though—I'm sort of admiring what they're doing. They have pluck."

I felt the same way. Just before ten p.m., I'd checked out an entire women's soccer team, who were taking a red-eye flight back to Chicago, and their manager was fussy about every line item on the bill. They'd also rented five goldfish, and one of the players admitted that she'd knocked over the goldfish bowl and by the time she'd found the fish on the floor under the bed, it was dead, so she'd flushed it.

So, yeah. Maybe the animal rights group had some valid beefs with us.

"By the way," I said, a little hesitant. "I wanted to ask . . . How's your mom?"

"We're not speaking at the moment." He glanced at the guilt on my face that I couldn't hide and added, "Don't worry. We shun each other when we're fighting. I always let her make the first move, since she's supposed to be the adult. Anyway, it's a ton easier to do when we're staying in two different houses, so all hail Green Gables."

He was trying to sound nonchalant. I could recognize it now in the little double swish of his eyelashes. The mannered shrug of his shoulder.

"I'm sorry you're not speaking," I said. I felt awful about it.

His lips parted as though he was going to respond, but nothing came out. His eyes roamed over my face for a long moment—so long my heart started racing madly and my chest got warm.

"Want to see a trick?" he asked, digging a deck of cards from the inside of his hotel zip-up jacket. Impossibly quick fingers shuffled the cards and fanned them out for my perusal. "Pick one."

"Is this a marked deck?"

"You're not supposed to ask that," he said, mouth twisting upward. "Spoils the illusion. Just pick one."

My fingers hovered over the worn blue corners of the cards. I slid one out.

"Don't show it to me," he said, flicking the remaining cards back together and palming them. "Just look at it and memorize it."

I held my hands together, shielding the card from his eyes, and peeked.

"Got it?" he asked.

It was the two of hearts, and over the middle of the card were block letters, written by hand in Sharpie. It said: LOOK UP.

I did just that—right as his mouth pressed against mine.

Misdirection.

It was completely unexpected, and I kissed him back without thinking. His lips were soft and warm. He was still palming the deck of cards, and they were now pressing against the back of my neck. Pleasure flooded my limbs. Then he was pulling away, and when my hands left the mooring of his chest, I wobbled, cheeks hot, dizzy with the surprise of it all.

"We forgot to do that last night," he said in a gravelly voice.

All I could do was make a noise to answer him, but it sounded more like a whimper than an acknowledgment. "That was a mean trick. How am I supposed to work now?"

"Never trust a magician, Birdie," he said, smiling with his eyes. He dumped the deck of cards in a trash can behind the registration desk as he glanced over his shoulder. One of the businessmen sitting in the lobby was getting up and headed this way.

"See you after work," Daniel whispered. "Pie for breakfast. One positive about fighting with my mom is that she can't complain about when I come home."

I watched Daniel stride across the lobby, heat still thrumming through me, toes curling inside my shoes. These were not feelings I should be feeling in public.

The businessman approached the desk and asked me for a pen. I dropped it twice, right as Chuck was coming out of the back offices. "Dopey strikes again," he mumbled as he passed. "Wake up. It's going to be a long night."

Pasting on a smile for the guest, I waited until everyone was gone, and then quickly squatted in front of the trash can and fished out the cards Daniel had dumped. Every single one said the same thing: LOOK UP.

This was not how friends were supposed to act.

I imagined him marking all the cards, perhaps sitting on that old green couch, and wondered how long it had taken. Then I thought of him and Cherry not speaking, and it felt like my fault. If Daniel and I were going to be friends, I didn't want her hating me. He shouldn't have to choose me over his own mother.

What are you doing with my son?

Maybe I had a better answer for her now.

Maybe I needed to fix the problem I'd caused.

The next afternoon I took an early ferry into the city and hopped on a bus that stopped a bit beyond the International District. I'd never been out this way, and it took some time for me to get my bearings. But when I spotted the black-and-red single-story building across the street, I recognized it from its online photos. Salsa Dance Studio.

Nothing of note happened between me and Daniel after our shift last night. The Moonlight was surprisingly packed, and our normal booth was taken, so we ended up sitting at the counter, and that wasn't the ideal spot for intimate conversation. I didn't mind all that much. I was just glad to sit next to him and feel his shoulder against mine. We shared a slice of the Pie of the Day: *LIVIN' ON A PEAR, featuring spiced Anjou pears under an angelic cloud of streusel topping.* It was so spectacular, I wasn't even depressed when we talked about the Raymond Darke case and how neither of us could figure out any new angles to pursue. It was just one of a dozen things that wasn't going smoothly this week. The only thing that *was* okay—miraculously—was my relationship with Daniel.

And I needed to make sure it stayed that way. Which was why I was doing this right now as I fought down the overwhelming urge to turn on my heel and run in the opposite direction.

She's only an overprotective mama bear. You can do this.

As traffic sped by on Jackson, I warily entered the dance studio. An unoccupied reception area divided the entrance from a warehouse-like dance space. Polished wooden floors and brick walls surrounded a handful of sweaty people who were laughing as they headed toward the doors in a herd, probably after they'd finished their bachata dance lesson—that's what had just ended. The studio's dance classes were listed online, as well as the instructors; Cherry Aoki was easy to find.

And easy to spot, striding across the dance floor in loose, dandelion-yellow dance pants and a sleeveless T-shirt that read SHAKE IT! But when she spotted me in return, my mouth went dry, and I almost lost my nerve. What if this was a huge, GD mistake?

I could tell she thought I was some schlub off the street,

wanting to sign up for dance classes, or maybe a one-on-one instruction to prepare me for a prom or a wedding. The moment she recognized me, I knew it, because her high ponytail stopped swinging.

"Birdie? Is something wrong with Daniel?"

Too late to run now.

"No, not at all! I'm sorry. I looked you up online. Daniel doesn't know I'm here."

"Oh, thank God. Whew!" she said, holding her hand over her heart. Then her eyes narrowed. "Why *are* you here?"

"I just . . . wanted to talk. If you're busy—"

"I've got a few minutes before my next class." She gestured toward a corner of the dance floor. "Over here."

I followed her to a waiting area with a couch and two chairs. She took a seat, wiping her cheek on a towel around her neck. "What's on your mind?" She wasn't cordial, but she wasn't icy cold, either, and that made it easier for me to talk.

"I just wanted to apologize for upsetting you," I said.

She was silent for an impossibly long time. Then she said, "I appreciate that."

"I didn't have any intention of spending the night with Daniel. It just happened. I don't know what the protocol on this kind of stuff is." Or why my hands didn't seem to know what to do when I was nervous; I hoped she didn't notice.

She flicked a look at me, curious but wary. "Daniel said you met downtown."

"At the Moonlight Diner," I said. My nerves were jangling, and I was hoping I wasn't giving away anything about that first day I met Daniel. "I was shocked to find out we worked together, and I guess he was too. We started talking more, and . . . I don't know. I guess we've been confused about our relationship. But nothing happened that night I stayed with him."

She stared at me. "I can't figure you out."

"You aren't the only one," I said, scratching my neck. "I have no idea what I'm doing. Not with Daniel or anything else in my life, if you want to know the truth."

Something in her posture softened. "It never gets easier, just so you know. I've been floating from one thing to the next all my life. The only thing that's changed is that I gave up trying to make sense of things."

"I'd definitely like to stop trying. It's exhausting."

"It truly is." She sighed heavily and reclined against the couch.

"You asked me what I'm doing with your son, and I couldn't give you an answer. I've never . . . been in a relationship before. My grandmother—well, I guess because my mother got pregnant at seventeen—she had strong feelings about who I could see. Mostly who I couldn't see, which was everyone. And now I'm just trying to figure it all out as I go. I don't want to screw things up, and I'm sorry if you thought I disrespected you or your rules. That's the last thing I want. I . . . guess I don't know what I want, honestly. I didn't realize relationships could be so complicated."

A long moment stretched between us. Then Cherry said, "Has Daniel told you how I met his father?"

"Not really," I said. "Only that he didn't stick around."

She let out a single laugh. "Understatement of the century. I met his father by accident, when I was trying out for a dancing part in a production of the Vietnam War musical, *Miss Saigon*, at the 5th Avenue Theatre. Ever been there?"

I shook my head.

"Beautiful old theater. A landmark. I desperately wanted to work there, and I desperately wanted to be in an off-Broadway production—and *Miss Saigon* has a real helicopter that hangs from the rafters and descends onto the stage, really dramatic. It was everything I wanted artistically . . . and financially, because I was trying to supplement my magic income with something steadier. Anyway, I memorized every song in *Miss Saigon*, but I still didn't get the part. However, Daniel's father happened to be there, having lunch with one of the theater owners. He saw me, and the next thing I knew, we were meeting every week."

She sighed, long and slow, and then continued. "It was only a fling. I just didn't want to face it at the time. Here was this rich, important man who was educated and a decade older than me—I thought he was so sophisticated." She crossed her legs and sighed. "I knew he saw other women. He was very up front about that. But when I got pregnant, which was a complete surprise, I was scared and then happy. Because I truly thought I was crazy about this guy, and I made myself believe that the prospect of a baby would melt him. That he'd give up the other girls and realize he loved me. Or, at the very least, he'd sober up and take responsibility. I pictured myself living in his big mansion that overlooked the city, with a maid and a nanny, both of us in love. Do you know what happened?"

I did, but I didn't want to repeat what Daniel had told me, so I shook my head.

"None of that," she said, swiping her hand through the air. "Not any damn bit. His 'traditional' parents wouldn't accept me because I wasn't blond and Catholic. That's what he told me— that our relationship was doomed. But it was just a cowardly excuse. He didn't love me, and nothing could make him. If the prospect of a man caring for his own flesh-and-blood isn't enough to change his feelings, nothing is. People either gravitate toward each other or they don't. You can't force it. You can't control their feelings or yours."

"So, you're saying . . . ?"

"I'm saying that I've never seen Daniel so worked up about a girl before. Ever."

Several emotions raced through me.

"I can't tell you what to do," she said. "I'm completely biased when it comes to Daniel, and in my head I pictured the same dream for him. I imagined him being brilliant at something— maybe carpentry—and being successful and happy, and for one day, a sweet Japanese girl to come along and give me lots of grand-children with fat cheeks."

Something that sounded like an old mausoleum door creaked out of my mouth.

Cherry gave me a sheepish look. "Daniel's father put me off white guys for a *long* time," she explained. "But it doesn't matter, because it was my dream—not Daniel's. I can't plan his life. I try, believe me. I try *so hard*. But it's only because I can't bear to lose him again."

"I'm sorry," I said. "I can't imagine what you've all been through."

She nodded, stroking her fingers down a seam of her pants. "I just want him to be happy. And he was right—I promised him I'd give him some space, but I used a spare key to get into Green Gables, so technically I was being a jerk."

Oh, wow.

"I'm sorry I yelled at you that morning," she added. "I overreacted. When it comes down to it, I guess I'm just as emotional as Danny. We're both beautiful cinnamon rolls, too good for this world," she said wistfully.

I suddenly remembered what I'd stuck in my purse before coming out here. I wiggled it out and handed it to her. "My aunt Mona had this. When she found out who you were, she remembered seeing one of your shows when she was a teen. She and my mom saw you."

"The Showbox," Cherry said, staring at the neon pink flyer. "Oh God. I remember this show. I'd just found out I was pregnant with Daniel. I don't think I've ever seen this flyer."

"It's yours if you want it."

"That's . . ." She nodded a couple of times, gripping it tightly in her fingers as she stared at it. Then she looked up with a soft smile. "You're a good kid, to come apologize to me. That was respectful, and I appreciate it."

Finally. I'd done one thing right. At least, I thought so. Then I *knew* so when I got a series of texts from Daniel a couple hours after I left the dance studio.

Daniel: Birdie

Daniel: Birdie

Daniel: Birdie

Me: You rang?

Daniel: Mom told me you came to see her.

Me: Does that mean you guys are speaking now?

Daniel: Yes. Do you know how cool you are?

Me: Not very.

Daniel: Wrong. This is you: (❀ ‿ ︵)

Me: You flatter me, sir.

Daniel: This is me when I think about u:
(>‘-’)> <(‘_’<) ^(‘_’)\- \m/(-_-)\m/ <(‘-’)> _(.”)> <(._.)-`

Me: What is that? Someone having a stroke?

Daniel: It's dancing, Birdie.

Me: I warned you I wasn't cool.

Daniel: I never listen to warnings. Life is better when you wing it.

26

A lot of things were going right with my life now. I was back in Cherry's good graces (thank goodness). I was mostly sleeping okay (at least, I hadn't dozed off at work). And I was getting used to having the house to myself (Grandpa had texted me photos of him and Cass holding up armfuls of rainbow trout).

But there were also a few things that *weren't* right. Mona was always too busy to talk. The Raymond Darke case was stagnating. And after I went to see Cherry in the dance studio, two entire work shifts came and went and Daniel never once tried to kiss me.

Was he friendly? Yes. Was my stomach filled with butterflies every time he smiled at me? Yes. Were we sharing breakfast pie at the diner? Drivin' Me Cocoa (chocolate silk and whipped cream, dusted with cocoa), Buttermilk Kisses (buttermilk pie topped with candy kisses), and King of the Forest Fruits (a medley of berries topped with a crown of golden, spun sugar).

But were we kissing? Putting our hands all over each other? Whispering sweet nothings into each other's ears?

No.

Even our sleuthing gig had come to a sputtering standstill. We'd all but given up on the stupid spreadsheet. And when Tuesday rolled around, the day Raymond Darke normally visited the hotel, instead of us pulling another James Bond stakeout outside of room 514, Daniel texted me to say he had something to do in his cohousing community—that he'd asked other employees to keep an eye out for a man in a baseball cap at seven p.m. Turned out, Darke never showed. It wasn't a huge surprise. We knew Ivanov was flying out of Seattle since that day we followed him to Ye Olde Curiosity Shop, so I wasn't sure why this disappointed me so much. I think because the mystery that had bonded us together was now fizzling out.

And I worried *we* were too.

In fact, that was all I could think about after Raymond Darke was a no-show. I had the night off from work, and when I got up in the early afternoon to take a shower and found no texts from Daniel, an achy gloom settled into my bones. I began to wonder if I'd done something wrong. Maybe Daniel was reevaluating his feelings and had changed his mind about us.

When I finished blow-drying my hair, I heard a *ding* on my phone. My hopes rose, but it was only my fairy godmother.

Mona: Are you up?

Me: Up but not Adam.

Mona: Better get that way.

Me: Why?

Mona: This is ur only warning. Get up. Get dressed. Be ready. You hv 15 min.

Me: Ready for what?

Mona: This text will self-destruct in 5 seconds . . .

Me: Are you coming over here?

Mona: 5, 4, 3, 2, 1. You're welcome, btw.

And that was it. I continued to text her, but she didn't answer. So I got dressed. I pinned a stargazer in my hair. And I trotted downstairs right as the doorbell rang.

Aunt Mona didn't ring doorbells. She had a key.

When I peered through the keyhole, all my thoughts scattered.

I unlocked the door and swung it open, a little breathless.

"Hi," Daniel said, rocking back on his heels. His hair hung loose around his shoulders, and his hands were stuck firmly into the pockets of his jeans.

"What are you doing here?"

"Dropping off a bucket of apricots at your aunt's."

I squinted. "Um . . . what?"

"We've got three apricot trees in the Nest. Jiji picked them clean before Old Man Jessen could get them, so I guess you could say it was a revenge harvest. Anyway, we had three buckets of apricots, and most of them weren't even close to being ripe, but Jiji wanted to get rid of the evidence, and my mom suggested that I take some to Mona. In return for that flyer you brought her."

"Oh."

"I looked her up online and called her art studio, and she invited me over this morning. You told me about the theater, but wow. Amazing. All that vintage furniture and those Broadway posters— my mom would totally be into those."

"Her parents used to manage a local theatrical playhouse," I said.

"She told me. I met Zsa Zsa Gabor," he said, shaking white cat hair out of his T-shirt. "That is one friendly feline. Blueberry would crush her with one paw. Oh, and I met Leon Snotgrass."

"Snod. He was there?"

"You say snod; I say snot. He was actually pretty nice."

"Traitor," I said, pretending to shut the door. "You're dead to me."

"He was terrible! A monster!" Daniel said, pressing back against the door.

I peered through the crack. Our faces met, mere inches apart. He smiled at me, and I nearly melted into a pool of warm, giddy sap.

He knocked on the door without moving his face. "Hey, little pig, can I come inside?"

"If I say no, will you huff and puff and blow my house down?"

"No, but I'll wait here for hours until you feel sorry for me and let me in."

I opened the door and held out an arm, gesturing for him to enter.

"Jesus, Birdie. This neighborhood is . . ." He finished by whistling. "Are these, like, million-dollar homes, or what?"

I pointed toward the house next door. "*That* is a million-dollar home. What we have is a fixer-upper. We barely have modern plumbing."

He took off his shoes and set them by the door while looking around the living room. "I like it. Very homey. I saw the greenhouse outside and the koi pond."

"No koi for a couple of years, so I suppose it's just a pond now."

"Guess you don't need it since you've got the entire Sound in your backyard," he said, looking through the kitchen at the view through the back windows. "Holy shit. Mount Rainier looks huge out here. One day it's going to erupt, and we'll all be dead."

"Not from lava. The earthquakes will kill us first."

"I was hoping to be preserved like Pompeii. What's the point of living near a volcano just to be killed by an earthquake?"

He padded into the kitchen, and I followed. It was so strange to have him here in my house. I couldn't stop looking at him while he surveyed our beach.

After a while, he noticed. "It's okay that I'm here, right?"

"Of course. I'm happy you're here."

"Your grandfather—"

"Is still in Yakima," I said.

"I mean, he wouldn't want to bite my head off that I was here?"

"He wants to meet you. And he's pretty easygoing. Also, he's not here, so it doesn't matter, does it?"

Daniel chuckled. "Guess not."

"So?"

"So . . . ," he repeated. "We're both off today. Did you have any plans?"

"Zero plans. You?"

"Also zero."

I nodded, and he got quiet. So I said, "We could work on our case? I mean, the spreadsheet is a dead end right now, but maybe there's something else we haven't thought about."

"You have any ideas since we talked about it in the diner? I can't figure out how we pick up the thread if Darke isn't coming into the hotel anymore. Only thing I can think to do is try to go to Kerry Park again and trail him."

I didn't like that idea. He already nearly caught us once, and obviously there were cops patrolling that street. Then something hit me. "Maybe there's another way to get a different angle on this. Do you still have that video you took of Darke entering the hotel room?"

"Yeah, on my phone," he said, patting the pocket of his jeans.

"Excellent. We'll need to—well, it's probably easier to do on my laptop." I headed into the living room and remembered it wasn't there. "My laptop's upstairs," I said, suddenly self-conscious that it was in my bedroom. I started to suggest he wait in the living room, but he was oblivious.

"Lead the way," he said.

Feeling as if I had an entire hive of wasps buzzing around in my belly, I took the stairs two at a time. Daniel's heavier footfalls thumped behind me as we breezed across the landing into my room.

"Oh, wow," Daniel said, making me jump. His head turned as he looked around. "This is *Casa de Birdie*, huh? Did Mona paint all those? She showed me all the paintings in the theater. I see Sherlock. Who's that with the mustache?"

"Hercule Poirot."

"Duh. I should have guessed." He glanced at my vanity mirror, where the Elvis not-a-penny fortune was stuck into the frame alongside his LOOK UP! playing card. He quickly took stock of my vase of lilies and the vintage Smith Corona on my desk before his gaze jumped to the adjoining wall. "Oh my God, are these your mystery books? Shit. You weren't exaggerating." He squatted in front of the bookshelves to browse. "Hey, it's Nancy Drew. A ton of them."

"Two different sets."

"And who's this? Billie Holiday?" He stood back up to look at the framed poster.

"She's my style icon, with the big flower in her hair," I explained. "Supposedly she burned her hair once with curling tongs right before she was going onstage to sing, so her friend went and got flowers to cover up the singed spot."

"Didn't know that," Daniel said.

"And she was a great jazz singer, of course. No one could mistake that voice. The woman who owns the Moonlight, Ms. Patty—"

"The old woman who works the lunch shift? Really tall, husky laugh?"

I nodded. "She has a million old records. She used to let me listen to them sometimes when she babysat me. Anyway, I like how she sings all of these sad songs, like 'Gloomy Sunday,' but somehow her voice is comforting. It's sort of like she's commiserating with you."

He looked at the poster and said, "I love it when they play her and Ella Fitzgerald in the hotel. My mom dances to a lot of old jazz standards. Frank Sinatra, Sarah Vaughan. Billie Holiday's kind of the best, though. Very nice. I approve." He smiled at me, and I felt it in the bottom of my feet, warming me all the way into my chest. That smile was dangerous. I would know.

"Hey," Daniel said, inspecting a couple of framed photos on the wall. "Who's this? Same killer eyes. Not you."

"That's my mom," I said.

"Jesus, she was gorgeous. Is that Mona . . . and a toy monkey?"

"That was her Frida Kahlo stage."

"And this one," he said, pointing to the other photo of my mother by herself. "She was a waitress? Wait. Is that the Moonlight?"

I nodded. "Worked there until I was five, I think? Then she started managing stores at Westlake Center. Then she worked at Macy's . . . Then she was unemployed for a while. She sort of bounced around a lot." I pointed to another photo of her, when she was a year younger than me—seventeen. She'd gotten her first job behind the counter at the cinnamon bun café near the harbor. In this photo, she smiled at the camera, showing off her apron, her name embroidered at the top. This was the last picture of her taken by my grandmother, and you could almost feel her sense of pride from behind the camera. Oh, how that changed.

"My mother was already pregnant with me when the photo was taken, but she didn't tell them until much later, when she started showing," I told Daniel. "The only person who knew was Mona."

He squinted at the photo and then turned to me, a strange expression on his face. "Your mom's name was Lily?" he said, eyes flicking to the stargazer in my hair.

I nodded once.

The lines on his forehead softened, and he looked at me with so much tenderness, my chest became hot and constricted. Without warning, tears brimmed, stinging the backs of my eyelids.

"I'm sorry," I managed to say, talking around the knot in my throat. "I don't know what's wrong with me. It's been eight years. I should be past all this."

And I was, sort of? When I thought about my mom too much, my mind went into a horrible loop, because the thing was, I couldn't remember a lot about her. She was pretty and had a dry sense of humor, and she smelled good. She was always working, never around enough, and I remember always wanting more of her. More of her attention and time. But the rest of my memories had been trampled under everyone else's opinions of her. Grandma said she was rebellious and stubborn and never thought about conse-quences; Mona said she was loyal and determined and always tried her best. Maybe both of them were right.

"I can barely remember the real Lily anymore," I said. "My strongest memories from back then are of Mona. How is that pos-sible? How could I forget her?"

He didn't say anything. He just wrapped his arms around me. I laid my head on his shoulder and clung to him. It felt like holding sunshine in my arms. As if I was starving and he was nourishment. It felt like forgiveness. Relief.

Warm hands cupped both sides of my head. I cleared my throat, sniffled, and then laughed, as if I were some sort of malfunctioning cyborg. "I seriously don't know what's wrong. Ugh, I'm so embarrassed. I'm sorry."

"I'm not," he said, eyes shining. He swiped beneath my eyes with his thumbs. "You're a little bit of a disaster, Birdie," he murmured, but not unkindly.

"You have no idea."

"I don't mind. It takes a disaster to know one. And I'm a grade-A disaster."

"Daniel?"

"Yes?"

"What are you doing here? I mean, I'm happy you're here. Really happy. It's just . . . I thought everything was okay with Cherry."

"It is. Did I not just lug a bucket of apricots on a ferry across Elliott Bay?"

I huffed out a soft laugh and then said, "We haven't talked much the last couple of days. . . . I worried maybe you'd had second thoughts."

"About us?"

"Yes."

"I've had thoughts. Not second ones, though." He swiped at my cheek again. "I just realized some things."

"What things?"

He blew out a long breath. "All of this has happened so fast, and it's not like any other relationship I've been in before. And I didn't expect any of this at all. When we started, I just liked you, in the diner that first night. And then I just wanted to spend time with you. And then something changed."

That didn't sound good. I tried to pull away, but he gathered me more firmly against him. "Listen. I need you to listen to me, okay? Before I lose my nerve. Sometimes I feel a little sick to my stomach when I can't see you, and then when I do, I get so nervous, I worry I might vomit."

"You . . . never act nervous."

"I guess I'm good at hiding it."

"You are?"

"It's a skill." He rested his forehead against mine. "What I'm trying to say is that I didn't expect this to happen. I didn't sit around wishing for it. I didn't even realize what was happening until it had. It's like you walk into a convenience store to get bread and you hear a song playing over the speakers, and you've never heard it before, but it's so good, it blows your mind. And all you wanted was bread, but now it feels like you've just seen the face of God, and how did this even happen?"

"You haven't been eating more of those gummies, have you?"

He lifted his forehead from mine and shook his head. "Not a one, Birdie."

"Sure?"

"So sure," he said, sighing. "No one tells you about the yearning.

I've never yearned in my entire life—not once, Birdie. But here I am, yearning. It's awful."

Longing-pining-aching.

"Because of a metaphoric song you heard in a metaphoric convenience store?"

"Yep. It was one of those big moments in life that completely changes your head. And I know the exact minute it happened, too," he said, studying my face as if he were looking at me for the first time. "That's the weirdest part. It happened about thirty seconds after I hung up with my mom. She called on Monday to tell me you'd come to the dance studio, and I was happy—happy that she was happy and that we weren't fighting anymore. And happy that you cared enough to do that, and then . . . Then my entire brain just lit up."

"I don't understand what you're trying to tell me," I whispered.

"I didn't mean for it to happen."

"What to happen?"

"You're the song in that convenience store, Birdie. Do you understand? I've accidentally fallen in love with you."

Everything fell out of my head at once. My fingers started trembling. Then my arms. My internal organs were melting together, and a blazing wildfire spread through my chest. My frightened-rabbit heart tried to tear a hole through my flesh and escape.

"You don't have to say it back," he assured me. "But I had to tell you. That's why I came out here." He leaned in and whispered in my ear, "See, the funny thing is, though, I think you feel the same way."

I opened my mouth, but weird noises came out instead of real words. His confessional thrilled me . . . and terrified me. I didn't know how to answer, and I wasn't sure why. All I could do was cling to him like the floor was disappearing beneath my feet and I'd fall into a bottomless pit if either of us let go. All I could say was, "Kiss me."

And he did.

We kissed like we were desperate, separated for years and had only minutes to spare until the world ended, rushing, breathless, all roaming hands-teeth-tongue, and I was clinging to his neck, trying to pull him underwater with me. When I stopped for breath, he said my name against my open mouth, hips swaying against mine. And a dark, drugging heat spread through my limbs like a slow fire.

I didn't even care that he pressed too hard against me and made me jump—"*Sorry, sorry, sorry*"—or that I accidentally bit his lip and tasted blood—"*Are you okay?*" None of that mattered. Not until I felt my knees giving out. I pushed him away, worried I was going boneless again, waiting for the telltale feeling, that between-heartbeats moment when I knew I was going down.

"What's happening?" he said in a rough voice, sounding like he'd been chasing down a freight train. "Are you having an episode?"

My quiet room filled with the sound of our heaving breath. I waited to be sure, then shook my head. "I'm okay," I assured him.

"Sure?"

"False alarm. You made my knees turn to jelly."

"Yeah?"

My gaze lit on his bottom lip and the dot of blood there. I

wiped it away. He held my hand there and kissed my fingers. Then he said, "Wanna take a nap?"

"Not tired," I said.

"Me either."

We both laughed as joy rushed through my chest.

"Just a nap," he said, letting go of me to take off his socks.

I did the same. "Sure. Just a nap."

We took off our shirts. Jeans. His eyes all over me and mine on him.

He tentatively took my hands and pulled me toward my canopy bed, where we crawled on top of the covers together. "This is a small bed, Birdie."

"Big enough."

He snorted. "Better than the back seat of my car."

"And no creepy forest mural."

"Just this weird old bum staring out from this pillow. Is this Columbo? You have a Columbo pillow?"

I did. Beneath a screen-printed photo of the famous detective was his catchphrase, JUST ONE MORE THING. I yanked it from beneath Daniel's head and threw it on the floor. "Better?"

"Much. God, you feel good," he murmured, hands roaming over my hips.

"So do you."

"If you ignore it, it will go away. Maybe. Eventually. Jesus, that's . . . not helping."

"Should I not . . . ?"

"Depends."

"On what?"

"I forget?" He half smiled at me, eyelids heavy and blinking like his lashes were trapped in honey, until I stopped touching him. "Oh, that was mean." He shifted, half on top of me, pinning a leg to the bed with his. "Okay, listen, Birdie."

"Listening," I said, squirming against him.

"I propose a new plan. It's called the Nick and Nora Go Wild plan, and it involves us solving mysteries, eating pie for breakfast, *and* putting our hands all over each other."

"Sounds risky."

"It's completely risky, and I can't promise it won't fail. But before you say yes or no, I want to try something. You tell me to stop if you hate it."

What was not to like? He was kissing my neck again and then lower, moving down the bed to my stomach. His long hair was a curtain around his face, tickling my skin as he slid down my body, and then—

Oh.

Oh.

"Give it a chance, okay?" he said from a million miles away. And then I nearly blacked out. First from embarrassment, then from pleasure. If my body was going to pick a time to go cataplexic, it sure as heck better not be now! But it didn't, and the only thing interrupting the greatest thing that had ever happened to me in my entire life was Daniel, stopping to ask me questions. I tried to answer, but couldn't, so I was relieved that he seemed to understand what I only had a vague idea about.

And I was *doubly* relieved that after he made his way back up the bed, he reached for his jeans—and that the condom he managed to pull out of his pocket, after three tries and a cry of anguish, was not glow-in-the-dark.

"Do you want to try my Nick and Nora Go Wild plan?" he asked.

"I thought we just did," I said in a dreamy voice that didn't sound like it belonged to me.

He chuckled, and it was the most erotic thing I'd ever heard. "There's more."

"Is that right?" Frankly, if he'd asked me to bomb a building, I'd have asked which one.

"We can stop now. . . ."

"No, thanks," I said.

"No to stopping or no to continuing?"

"To stopping."

"You sure?"

I'd never been so sure about anything.

It was slightly awkward and fumbling. Certainly not bad for a second try. But it was the third try a little later that was—

Intense. Emotional.

Light-years away from what it was in the back seat of his car that first night. Those people were strangers. We were not. And what do you know? That made all the difference.

• • •

When we were done being wild, we lay side by side, all tangled up in each other. Daniel picked up my hand and placed it over his heart. Its powerful rhythm was unhurried and strong, pounding in time with mine. It felt like we were inside an invisible cocoon. As if everything we'd just done together somehow created a safe space that was just big enough for the two of us.

I exhaled a long breath and sank into the mattress.

"Hey, Birdie?"

"Yes?"

"Something fuzzy and purple is jammed between your head-board and the mattress. It has one eye, and it's staring at me."

I reached above his head and pulled out a stuffed animal. "It's just Mr. Flops."

"Mr. Flops is super creepy. Oh God, he only has the one eye."

"He's had a rough life," I said. "I've had him since I was a kid."

"Did your mom give him to you?"

I shook my head, petting the bunny's ear.

"I'm sorry you don't have a lot of good memories of your mother," he said.

I sighed. "It's okay. Mr. Flops is still a good memory. The Easter before my mom died was super rainy. My mom was gone—I can't remember why. Maybe she was seeing someone, I don't know. But I was upset about the rain because Mona was supposed to take me to an Easter egg hunt. Instead, Ms. Patty and Mona hid a bunch of clues around the diner in those pastel plastic eggs that break apart. Like, the first egg had a piece of paper inside that hinted where I could find the next one."

"A treasure hunt for young Detective Birdie," Daniel said, smiling. "A mystery hunt."

I smiled back. "Exactly. And I loved every second. And at the end of the hunt was Mr. Flops and a crapload of candy. I felt like I'd won the lottery."

"I love that," he said, then told the bunny, "Sorry I called you a creep, Mr. Flops. You're a fine bunny."

I smiled, and then said, "Hey, Daniel?"

"Yes?"

"I just realized. We don't have to work tonight."

"Nope."

"And we have the house to ourselves. Maybe you should just stay here."

"All night?"

"You could just text your mom and tell her you'll be home in the morning."

"Oh, she'd love that."

"Really?"

"That was sarcasm, Birdie."

"But you'll stay anyway, right? I'll let you sleep on Columbo or Mr. Flops. Gentleman's choice."

"Well, then. How can I say no?"

I closed my eyes, completely blissed out.

"Hey, Birdie? Truth or Lie. Do you believe in second chances now?"

I ran my fingers through his hair. "I believe in us."

"I do too," he whispered back.

"Curious things, habits. People themselves never knew they had them."
—Agatha Christie, "The Witness for the Prosecution" (1933)

27

"The video of Darke in the hotel!" I said as the tub drained, tightening a damp towel around my chest.

"Oh, shit." He paused in the middle of a vigorous hair-drying. "I knew we forgot something."

It was well past midnight. Over the past few hours, we'd napped—for real, this time—used up the rest of the condoms, listened to old jazz records, set off the kitchen's fire alarm when we accidentally burned grilled cheese sandwiches, and now bathed. That two people could comfortably fit in our old clawfoot tub was news to me and possibly the best idea we'd had all night.

Honestly, it was a miracle I even remembered Raymond Darke.

"The woman who was with Darke in the hotel," I said. "Can't we grab a still from the video and run some kind of reverse-photoscan thingy on it? See if we can search for her online?"

Daniel's head popped out from a floral-print towel that had

seen too many years. His dark hair was a chaotic mess. "Do you even know how to do any of that?"

"N-o-o-o," I drawled, giving him a guilty grin. "But it sounds easy."

It wasn't.

In the wee hours of the morning, we spent far too long searching, sitting cross-legged on the rug in my room, laptop propped on the Columbo pillow. We tried multiple stills, multiple ways. But it wasn't until we narrowed our photo search down to Seattle—duh—that we stumbled across an article in the newspaper.

Fran Malkovich, interior designer. There she was, showing off, standing in her own kitchen, in her historical home in the Queen Anne District, which she shared with her new husband, vaguely described as a writer named Bill.

"Bill Waddle," Daniel murmured. "That was the name he used at Tenor Records."

"Does it indicate where the house is? That's a big neighborhood."

He read the article out loud. No mention of an address, naturally. But what it did provide was a slide show of several rooms she'd designed in the home . . . and one photo of the exterior. We didn't even bother reverse-searching it. There was an entire website dedicated to historical homes in Seattle, and this eight-million-dollar pale-pink Victorian was right there, for all the world to see.

It was three blocks from Kerry Park.

"Got you, asshole," Daniel said, flicking his finger against the screen. "Good work, Nora. Looks like you and I need to return to Queen Anne and take a little stroll."

We couldn't go the next day. Daniel needed to get home and change, as he hadn't planned for a sleepover at my house and was still wearing yesterday's clothes. And then we both had to work, which was a little . . . nerve-racking. Not in a bad way. It was just that everything had changed between us in one night. I was positive every single one of our coworkers knew what we'd been doing.

Joseph knew for sure. Every time I saw him, he had a funny look on his face and gave me a little lift of his chin. And don't get me started on Chuck. First he asked me if I'd won the lottery because I was suspiciously "in a good mood." Then he made a joke in front of Mr. Kenneth about me having a look on my face as if I'd "spent the weekend in Las Vegas with a bunch of male hookers and a bag of cocaine."

I didn't care, to be honest. Every time Daniel swaggered toward the registration desk to log a van trip, he said "Hi" in a way that made my insides melt like the center of a chocolate molten lava cake, because no matter what anyone thought or guessed, they could never actually know what was between us. It was the most delicious secret, and it made work a thousand times better.

Harder. But better.

On Friday, all the stars aligned, and we were able to meet

before work and continue the Raymond Darke investigation. We decided it was better to just take a bus up to Darke's side of town and avoid the hassle of parking. Plus, it was gloriously sunny— the first real sun of the season. Walking outside was not optional, so we chose to get off the bus a few blocks from our destination to soak up every ray, as if our very existence depended upon it.

"Vitamin D, you feel so damn nice," Daniel said as we strolled along a city sidewalk, turning his face up to the blue above. When we passed Kerry Park, we didn't stop, because the grassy space was packed with other sun worshippers. And who could blame them? The sky was so clear, the dome of Mount Rainier rose over the city like a snow-capped guardian. It made you feel good about life.

And good about the future, too. Daniel's arm was slung around my shoulder, and we took our sweet time, sauntering past luxury apartment buildings and big houses with perfect lawns and perfect city views, every cross street flashing us glimpses of Puget Sound, glistening in the sun.

Perhaps we were too dazzled by the perfect weather. When we came closer to Darke's address, we got a little turned around. Problem was, the hillside homes facing the street were hidden behind gates and shrubs and columns. It was almost as though they were downplaying their assets, trying to look nondescript to passersby—nothing to see here, folks—while they showed their grand sides around back, facing the city. But while Daniel double-checked the address on his phone, I spotted the pale-pink Victorian behind a tall, deep green hedge.

"That's it," I said, gesturing across the road. "It's got three stories facing the street, but it's on a slope—"

"Four stories around back," Daniel said. "All the pictures online were taken in their backyard."

The house was perched on a corner. An iron gate between hedges guarded the paved front "yard," which was just empty space for several cars. "Doesn't look like anyone's home," I said.

"Unless there's a garage or something around back." He squinted into the sun. "Looks like there's a camera pointed at the front door, so let's steer clear of that and head around back."

An open, curved driveway led to a garage beneath the side of the home. Parked there was a white van with a richly scripted QUEEN CLEAN painted on the door. We paused behind a tree and watched as three uniformed maids emerged from a door near the garage. One of the women locked the door and pressed a code into the security panel before she got in the van. A minute later it was backing up, and we flattened ourselves against the hedge as it sped away.

"Shit," Daniel said. "That was close. Three maids? That's some kind of rich."

"This place is huge. I can't image what it takes to keep it clean. Just look at all the shrubbery and trees back here. His lawn has one of those golf course patterns mowed into it."

"Unbelievable," he murmured, something close to disgust in voice. "And what the hell are we doing? If the maids turned on the alarm, then no one's home. Which means this trip may be a bust.

I mean, we already knew he lived near here, logically, since he walks the dogs every morning. And we already knew he was rich. How does this help us figure out what he was doing in the hotel?"

"Detective work is slow," I said. "But there's lots to learn if you observe. It's four p.m. on a Friday, and he isn't home. Is he never home at this time? Is that why the maids are scheduled to come? They know the passcode, so they're used to working alone in the house. Where does he go during the day? He doesn't need a second job, clearly, and he doesn't make public appearances as a writer. Is he shopping? We know he likes to go to Tenor Records early in the morning. Is that because he's doing something else in the afternoon?"

"Whoa," Daniel said. "I'm impressed, Nora."

"Books are great teachers, Nick," I said. "But all of this is speculation. What would be better is if we could figure out a way to see inside the house."

Daniel surveyed the driveway. "A camera's above the garage. What about that gate in the bushes?"

It was next to a small shed on the far side of the driveway, perhaps used for lawn equipment. No camera. No lock.

I looked at Daniel. He looked at me.

"We'd need a cover story, in case we get caught," I said. "Maybe we should come back later with props or disguises or something."

He shook his head. "No way. Luck's on our side today. We need to go for it. What about . . . ?" He took out his phone and pressed the screen until he'd pulled up a photo of Blueberry the Enormous Cat and practiced an impromptu script. "So sorry to bother you. We're staying with friends down the street, and their cat escaped this morning. We've been helping them scout the neighborhood and thought we spotted it back here, but now it's disappeared, and, sir? Have you seen a cat that looks like this?"

"You are *really* good at lying," I said. "It's scary."

He kissed my forehead. "Misdirection, Birdie. While I say all this, you call out for Twinkle Toes, the lost cat, and we apologize for trespassing before leaving."

"Okay. It's not the worst plan. Let's see what we can find."

Heart hammering, I walked up the driveway with him, careful to keep away from the camera's eye. We moseyed on up to the side gate, and Daniel reached over it to lift the latch. Boom. We were in the backyard.

And what a yard. Beautiful grass. Lush trees. And the entire city of Seattle at our feet.

"Good God," Daniel whispered. "Now, *this* is what I call an eight-million-dollar view. Look at the Space Needle, Birdie. We see it every day, but how many times have you gone up top?"

"Once, when I was a kid."

"Exactly. Jaded hipsters would tell you that it's just a tourist trap, and maybe it is. But it's *our* tourist trap. It's weird and iconic, and it's a freaking engineering miracle with a flying-saucer deck on top, so it kicks the Eiffel Tower's ass any ol' day. Now, tell me you wouldn't want to go up there with me."

"I may, possibly, just a *wee* bit, see the appeal."

"Oh, you do, do you?" he teased. "What's changed your mind, Birdie?"

I gave him a brazen look, and he gave me one in return, and we were both smiling like idiots, so I blew out a breath and changed the subject. "Can you imagine the parties they have back here?" I said, shielding my eyes to take in the entire lawn. "Tea cakes and champagne. Pretty dresses. Classical music. Important people."

"Who all know him as Bill Waddle, the husband of Seattle designer Fran Malkovich? Why does he live like that? If I were a megaton author, I'd be wearing a sign around my neck that said, 'Yeah, it's really me, motherfuckers.'"

"He probably tells his maids to never look him in the eye," I said. "Oh! I wonder if that's why they come when he's away. Protecting his anonymity."

"What about all his awards or whatever? Wouldn't housekeepers see those and think, 'Hey, this is Raymond Darke's house!' I mean, don't they give writers giant gold books or some shit to hang on their wall? Musicians get Grammys. Actors get Oscars. What do writers get?"

"No idea. Whenever I see photos of a writer's office, it's filled with books and things they like, not awards."

Once we got over the thrill of standing around in Darke's backyard, we summoned the nerve to move a little closer to the house. The bottom floor was built into the hill; it had tiny windows, too high to see into, and a small patio flanking the back door. The top two floors had balconies. But the second floor had an enormous wraparound deck and tons of windows. It was accessible from a curved set of patio stairs that spilled onto the lawn.

Maybe it was all that sunshine rotting my brain, but I felt reckless and said, "Bet we could see straight into the house from up there."

Daniel hesitated, raised a brow, and said, "All right. Let's find out."

Trying not to laugh, we headed up the patio stairs to the second-floor deck while Daniel called out "Twinkle Toes" in a low voice as he searched for cameras or a sign of anyone inside. We were high up with a splendid view of both downtown and all the homes below. I felt like royalty.

"I think the coast is clear," Daniel whispered into my ear from behind, causing me to squeal. He grabbed me around the waist, pulled my body back against his, and pretended to eat my neck. After some hushed laughter and wrestling, I freed myself and swung around to give him a finger of warning.

"This is not cat-hunting behavior," I whispered.

"I could make a joke right now, but I won't. Jesus ever-loving Christ, look at this shit, Birdie," he said, suddenly distracted as he stared into Darke's window.

Just as I thought, we could see right inside a large, open living room with posh furniture, artwork, plants, and a grand piano. It was like something out of one of those *lifestyles of the you-can't-afford-it, so don't bother* magazines.

"Look," Daniel said. "In the frame, hanging over that chair.

It's the same artwork from that *Aida* opera album sleeve—the one I bought at Tenor Records."

So it was. And nearby it were several framed prints from local opera productions. I spotted the Paramount Theatre; I'd seen *Les Misérables* there a few years ago with Aunt Mona.

But it was the print hanging next to it that caught my eye. A chair sitting in front of the print prevented me from seeing the bottom half of it, but there was something familiar about the bold design at the top of the print: a yellow sunset on a red background with something black and swirly blocking the sun. Why did this look familiar? Maybe it was something I'd seen on another opera album cover in Tenor Records, like the Egyptian-temple *Aida* album Daniel had bought there. As I was squinting to make out the swirly mark blocking the sun—or the type below it—Daniel said from several feet away, "What do we have here? Recycling?"

He was on the side of the deck, peeking inside a built-in hutch that hid three plastic bins.

"He shreds a shitload of paper," Daniel noted, digging around. "Hey, what's this?"

It was an envelope that had been opened. Daniel rooted through the shreds and found its mate: a piece of folded paper. The envelope and letter were addressed to Bill Waddle. "What does it say?" I asked, peering over his arm.

"It's from the Seattle Opera. A written confirmation for the reservation of a private box for him and five guests. You think that's one of those balcony seats on the side of a concert hall?"

I nodded. "Probably very expensive."

"Well, seems as if the opera company is just reminding dear old Bill to let his guest know that they can pick up tickets the night of the opera by going to the VIP will-call window and letting the attendant know they're part of his party. They'll be shown up to the box."

I blinked at the paper. "They don't have to show ID?"

"Huh? Oh, nope. It just says to identify themselves as a member of his party. And they thank him for his continued patronage and generous donations."

"When is it?" I asked, taking the letter from him. "A week from now."

"So?"

"At the Seattle Center."

"Again, not following," he said, tugging his bad ear.

I repositioned myself so that he could hear me better. "Remember what Ivanov said when he was buying those shrunken heads?"

Daniel stared at me, realization dawning behind his eyes. "He was stopping in Seattle one last time to see a show 'uptown.'"

I nodded slowly, unable to stop smiling.

"Oh shit! Do you really think Ivanov is planning to attend this opera?"

"If so, he'll be with Darke. In his opera box."

"Both of them there at the same time. In public," Daniel said, blinking rapidly. "How does that help our case?"

All my mystery-loving senses were lighting up and blinking

inside my head, screaming, *Undercover*. "Don't you see? If this letter is right and all we have to do to get inside the opera house is mention we're with Darke—or Waddle, as the opera company knows him. And *voilà*! We're in. It's the perfect opportunity for spying."

"You're seriously proposing we should sneak into the opera and spy on him?"

"Who says we're not members of his party? We don't have to *actually* sit in the box. Maybe we can trail him. See if Ivanov shows up. Overhear some conversations that won't be behind a closed hotel door. Their guard will be down. They won't be expecting anyone like us to be spying on them."

Daniel grimaced. "I don't know. That seems . . ."

"Risky? Like what we're doing now, standing on the man's balcony? We could be shot for trespassing."

"Touché, Birdie."

"You don't have to wear a tuxedo or suit, or anything. I know boys hate that."

"*Au contraire, mon ami*," he said. "I look dope in a suit."

I laughed. "Dope?"

"So dope . . . *so* fly. I'll have you know, I've got a lucky suit."

I squinted. "It makes you lucky, or you got lucky in it?"

"Zero getting lucky. I was my mom's date at a fancy charity thing for Disney Cruise employees a few months ago, so she got me a new suit."

"Well," I said, smiling, "you're one step ahead of me, because I have no lucky dress in my wardrobe." I'd have to figure something out; maybe Mona could help. "But we have to go to the opera, Daniel. Don't you see? It's fate."

"Oh-ho-ho," he said, merry. "So, *now* you believe in fate?"

"Don't know about that, but you have the lucky suit, and this is the break we've been waiting for," I argued, trying not to get too excited. "Ivanov and Darke in the same place again? And not behind closed doors. They'll be relaxed, in Darke's element. They may loosen their tongues. We could overhear a conversation that could change everything. It's a detective's dream—investigating right in front of everyone. We'll be undercover—just a couple of young opera fans, there to see the show."

"Okay, Nora. If it means that much to you, we'll go. But if we end up in the slammer, my mom is going to be *pissed*."

As he stuck the letter in his pocket, I wanted to return to the wall of windows and take a second look at Darke's living room, to see if there was anything else there that could help us figure out what Darke could be doing in the hotel and perhaps study that framed sunset poster from another angle. But as I started to turn around, Daniel's head snapped toward the side of the house. My gaze followed.

A pickup truck filled with lawn equipment was pulling into the driveway.

If they saw us up here . . .

Alarm fired through my limbs. Daniel grabbed my hand and took off, racing across the deck and down the stairs, onto the back lawn. "What about the cat cover story?" I asked.

"Fuck that! Run for it, Birdie!"

The lawn maintenance truck was blocking our way out. Panicked, I glanced around for a place to hide.

"There!" Daniel said, redirecting our run to the back corner of the yard, where a waist-high gate sat in the bushes. It was locked, but easy enough to jump over. At least, easy for Daniel. He had to drag me over the top when I got stuck.

Breathing heavy, we sped down a narrow service walkway between Darke's house and the next row of Victorians farther down the hill. Once we were fairly certain we were clear, we found a sidewalk and headed as far away from the house as we could get.

"I think we're safe now," Daniel said, glancing down the street. "Whew. I nearly had a heart attack. Sleuthing is hard work."

And frustrating. I never got a second look at that framed sunset print on Darke's living room wall. Which shouldn't have bothered me; after all, we had our next clue in the letter about the opera box, a much flashier, more interesting clue.

But even the most boring TV detective knew better than that.

The devil is *always* in the details.

28

"Hol' 'till," Aunt Mona complained, pins clamped between her lips, while she adjusted the hem of my dress.

I stood on an upside-down wooden crate in the living room area of Mona's theater, wearing a simple white gown that once was part of Mona's ice princess outfit. Yesterday she'd deconstructed it to remake it into something I could wear to the opera, and now threads hung loose around missing sleeves and the hem was several inches too long. But at least it didn't have glittery snowflakes on the bodice anymore.

She removed the last pin from her mouth and stretched her neck while Zsa Zsa Gabor flipped over and rolled around on the dress's discarded chiffon sleeves. "I think that's straight. We've lost the daylight. Be sweet and go flip on the lamp, will you?"

I stepped off the wooden crate and shuffled over to a 1960s space-age floor lamp. Aunt Mona looked tired, or maybe that was because she was wearing no makeup or wig and was dressed in a pink satin robe, her natural short brown hair slicked back. Without all the glamour, she seemed smaller and a little vulnerable.

"You aren't mad about having to do all this sewing work on a Saturday night, are you? Because we've still got next week. The opera isn't until Friday night."

"Are you kidding?" she said. "It's one of my favorite things to do."

"I thought maybe I was keeping you from a hot date with Leon Snodgrass."

"You don't have to say his name like that, you know," she complained gruffly.

Yikes. "I'm sorry. I'll stop doing that." Clearly he was sticking around. I needed to be more supportive of her choices, even if I didn't agree with them.

She shook her head and sighed. "No, darling. I'm sorry. I've got something on my mind, and it's giving me a headache. I shouldn't be taking it out on you."

"What's wrong?" I asked.

"Just some stupid adulting details that I don't want to think about right now. Tell me something happy. Where's our Daniel tonight? Did he have to work?"

"Unfortunately so."

And because I was a sucker, I briefly entertained the notion of taking a ferry into the city to meet him before his shift started, but then Mona asked me to come over.

"Think you can go one night without him?" she teased.

"*Ye-e-es.* Probably."

Let me just say that two people who are carrying on a secret romance at work and live on opposite sides of a giant bay of water have it *rough.* Especially after you've spent an entire night engaging in erotic activities with no one else around but the two of you; it's unfairly sobering to realize you can't do that every night. And desperate people do desperate things, so I'm a little ashamed to say that we *may* have taken advantage of our working situation and made use of an unbooked hotel room on our lunch break after our trip to Darke's house.

And again during last night's shift.

I had no regrets. I was riding an intoxicating high that made all hurdles tolerable.

"When the two of you are sixty, kissing on your front porch, I just want you to remember that it was me who encouraged this one true pairing."

"Whoa. Let's not get ahead of ourselves."

"Have you said the L-word back to him yet?"

Ugh. I regretted telling her about Daniel's big love speech. "That's N-U-N-Y-A."

Just the thought of saying it made my frightened-rabbit heart wild with fear. Everyone I loved died. At least half of them did. Those were terrible odds. Did I really want to put that curse on Daniel? The rational part of me knew this was ridiculous, but something deep and feral inside my subconscious wasn't so sure. . . .

Aunt Mona squinted at me. "You guys are being careful, right? Every time?"

"Every time."

"Just one slipup and your entire life can change."

"Um, *very* aware of that. My entire existence is the result of one slipup," I said, gesturing to myself dramatically. "And I have no intention of repeating that cycle. I promise, hand on this coffee table book of . . . male bondage?"

Aunt Mona gave me a sheepish smile. "It was on sale. But see? This was a snap decision. In one fleeting moment, you've spent your entire electric bill budget on stupid things."

"Jeez, I've got it, for the love of Pete. I don't have an electric bill, so I think I'm okay for now."

"God, I'd give anything to be eighteen again," Aunt Mona said, falling back on the sofa and tucking her legs beneath her robe. "Not a care in the world. My entire future ahead of me."

"You're only thirty-six."

"Ancient, Birdie. I'm too old. And I'm terrified."

I sat down next to her, careful not to poke my legs with the army of pins that circled the hem of my dress. "Seriously, what's wrong? You've been keeping something from me for weeks, and it's clearly not Leon, because I already know about him."

"I don't want to tell you."

"Are you in trouble about *Young Napoleon Bonaparte*? Is that why you were meeting with a lawyer last week?"

"I wish. Sharkovsky's left me a million messages, but I've just ignored him. I posted all over the local art blogs about what he did. I hope he loses the Pioneer Square Gallery."

"Okay. So why were you seeing a lawyer?"

She curled tighter into her robe and hugged her knees. "Reasons."

"What reasons?"

Her eyes flicked to mine. "I'm pregnant."

I snorted. That was absurd.

But she wasn't laughing. In fact, the look on her face was very, *very* serious.

My thoughts tumbled around in my head like clothes in a dryer. "But . . . how?"

"I think we both know how, Birdie."

"You were just on your period—that day I brought over chocolate pastries."

She gritted her teeth. "No, you assumed, and I didn't correct you. That was shitty of me, and I'm really sorry. But in my defense, I was overwhelmed and had vomited all morning. I couldn't think straight."

"But wait. The father is . . . ?"

"Who do you think?" she said, sounding a little perturbed that I was slow to catch on.

"Leon Snodgrass? He's only been back in town for a few weeks!" I argued. "You said it was—you told me you hadn't even kissed."

"We haven't. Not since he's been back." She gestured loosely to her stomach. "All of this happened three months ago."

My brain spun through another cycle. "When you went to that art festival in Arizona?"

"He kind of, sort of, met me there."

"And got you pregnant?"

She held up her index finger and thumb in front of one eye and looked through them. "Just a little bit."

"I don't understand."

"That makes two of us. Three, if you count Leon . . ." She groaned and curled up on her side, laying her head on the back of the couch as she looked at me. "We'd been texting. One thing led to another, and we spent the weekend together in Scottsdale."

That sounded like the last place I'd want to have a romantic weekend. I was having trouble processing everything she was saying. I could feel panic and a little anger rising inside me. "And you're here lecturing me about slipping up?"

"We used condoms. One must have broken, maybe? We don't know. They're only ninety-eight percent effective against pregnancy, so . . . Please don't look at me that way—I can't take it."

"Why didn't you tell me?"

"I was embarrassed. And terrified. And . . . I don't know. I wanted to, but you were starting work at the hotel, and then Daniel happened, and I didn't want to ruin any of that for you."

She was going through all this, and I was prancing around with hearts in my eyes? My anger suddenly fizzled out. "We're not supposed to keep secrets from each other. We made a pact. We're gutsy gals."

"I know, I know," she said, eyes glossing over. "I was just scared is all. But I'm telling you now."

"Are you keeping it?"

She nodded. "I'm due in early December. I haven't even told my parents. Obviously Leon knows, and my doctor. But, you know, as far as friends and family, you're the first person I've told."

My head swam with all this new information. I was stunned. *Stunned.* I also felt ridiculous that I didn't figure this out on my own. I'd known she wasn't telling me something, but now that I thought back to all our conversations, it made sense. The signs were all there. I should have seen them:

Suspect: Mona Rivera

Age: 36

Occupation: Professional painter/artist; unprofessional costume designer

Motto: Glitter makes everything better.

Medical conditions: (1) Ambidextrous. (2) Broke her leg when she was 22. (3) Gives great hugs. (4) Obsessed with changing her appearance. (5) Addicted to spicy food and pastries. [Not a period craving, but a pregnancy craving.]

Personality traits: Cheerful. Dramatic. Original. Loyal. Supportive. Risk-taker. Good

sense of humor. Great sense of style. Recently
guarded. [Worried about telling me she was
pregnant.]

Background: Born on Bainbridge Island to Carlos
and Iris Rivera, who managed a local theatrical
playhouse before recently moving out of state.
No siblings. Became best friend of Lily Lindberg
when they were ten years old. Dated Leon
Snodgrass twice, her only serious boyfriend;
after second time, said she was done with
relationships and would never marry or settle
down, never have kids of her own. [Come to think
of it, every time she says she'll "never" do
something, she almost always does it: i.e., now
pregnant.]

Additional notes: Made excuses when Leon showed
up this summer, saying they weren't dating, yet
acting weird and avoiding my questions [because
she was secretly pregnant], and then Leon hugged
me and said nothing would change [because he
knew she was pregnant].

And, oh yeah: MONA IS GD PREGNANT.

My mouth tried to make words, but nothing came out for
several moments. When I finally found my voice, I asked, "And
Leon . . . This is why he came back? Because of the baby?"

"Yes and no? He was planning to come back anyway. He hates Austin. But yeah. He wants to be involved. And I've been trying to decide how I feel about that . . . and about him. We aren't getting married or anything. That's why I saw a lawyer. I wanted to know what options I had. Like, what if we don't get along and he wants custody in a couple of years?"

"Good grief."

"It's not like I expect that to happen or anything. I just . . . God, Birdie. I just don't know. I'm old and set in my ways. Look at me! I'm a fucking mess. My income is erratic, and I don't keep normal hours. I'm completely irresponsible—I just stole a painting in broad daylight!"

"It was *your* painting."

"I know, but responsible adults are supposed to behave, and I'm a terrible behaver." She sighed heavily. "The scariest part about it is trying to figure out how I feel about Leon. He's completely my opposite, and we've never been able to stay together for longer than a year or two. I mean, we're friends. Good friends. Great in bed together."

"Ugh," I complained. "I don't want to think about that."

"But the most important thing is that he seems completely committed. He's offering financial support—which I desperately need—and he bought a new condo in Winslow, less than ten minutes from here. He wants to change diapers and all that. He's a good guy, and I *like* him—I know you don't."

"I don't dislike him."

She lightly shoved my shoulder. "Liar."

"I don't like how he treated you, that's all."

"It wasn't just him. It was how we treated each other. Trust me, I'm not wife material. I'm not even mother material—look around! Can you see me raising a kid in here?"

"Well, yeah," I said, choking up. "You already did."

Tears pooled in her eyes. She reached for me, and I reached for her, and we held each other, both sobbing our eyes out. And then she cradled my face and said, "Nothing is going to happen to me. I'm healthy. The baby's healthy. I've already had an ultrasound, and everything's how it should be. And I'll take every single test the doctor offers me, and I'll go to all my appointments. I'm not Lily."

"I know that."

"I will never leave you."

"But I'm so scared you will," I admitted in a whisper.

"Birdie, when I say I won't, I mean it. I'm not moving away, and I will never desert you. *Ever*," she said, swiping beneath her eyes. "Besides, I may need you more than you need me."

"I doubt that."

"Are you kidding? I'm about to burden you with a lifetime commitment. I can't do this alone. This kid is going to need an aunt."

I sniffled and laughed. "That's insane. We can't both be aunts."

"We can do whatever we GD want, Birdie. I have to believe that," she said, hands cupping my face. "And I need you to believe it too, because I really need a friend right now."

I smiled back at her as a fierce sort of joy filled my chest. "Now, *that* I can handle."

29

The next few days zipped by like the monorail on an overcast day. If I wasn't busy reading pregnancy books with Aunt Mona, I was researching what I could about the Seattle Opera and texting with Grandpa—who was returning home this weekend. And when I wasn't doing all that, I was working at the hotel, trying to stifle the urge to throw my arms around Daniel every time he passed through the lobby.

During one of our post-work pie breakfasts at the Moonlight, I told him about Aunt Mona's baby. I checked with her first, and she said it was okay to tell him, as long as he kept it secret until she was ready to broadcast it. He was happy for her, but also freaked out about how she got pregnant.

"Whoa," he said. "I guess life really *does* find a way, huh?"

"I thought that was fate."

"So did I," he murmured. "Dear God, so did I. . . ."

I wondered if I should get on the pill. Just as a double safeguard.

I could handle aunt duty, but that was my limit right now. Maybe my mom was made of stronger stuff than I was. "You don't want to know what happens when someone gives birth," I told him, thinking of everything I'd recently learned from all those books Aunt Mona and I read. At this point, I was wondering how any woman ever in the history of time had survived childbirth. Better Mona than me.

By the time Friday rolled around, I'd gotten more used to the idea of Aunt Mona having a baby. My sleep had been more erratic than usual that week, so I was extra spacey, constantly nodding off for several seconds at a time. I never had to lay my head down, or anything. I just kept zoning out, constantly missing several words of any given conversation, which made me frustrated and unusually cranky. And that crankiness is what I blamed when Daniel and I got in a small tiff about going to the opera.

He was getting cold feet about trailing Darke there. He even suggested we should just drop the entire investigation: "We can find something new to investigate. There's always something weird going on at the hotel. What about the animal rights group? Joseph says he's almost positive he's seen SARG members sneaking around the parking garage. Maybe they're planning another banner drop or some other kind of publicity stunt."

I didn't care about the animal rights group. That wasn't half as interesting as Darke, and besides, we were already committed. "Detectives don't just give up," I told him. "We can't move from case to case without solving anything."

"I suppose you're right," he said. "But if I had to choose between regular Nick and Nora and Nick and Nora Go Wild—"

"You know the real Nick and Nora had both, right?"

"Birdie, my Birdie. I love it that you think they were real," he said, mouth twisting up. "Fine. We'll go to the opera."

Sometimes when people say things, it's easy to see that their mind is on other things. And that's what I saw in Daniel. It bothered me a little, but so did a lot of things, including that stupid red-and-yellow framed print I saw in Darke's house. Where had I seen it before? My mind wanted to connect to something I'd seen when I was younger—at the diner? In our old apartment? That wasn't quite right. At first I thought maybe it was a logo, but blindly searching for it online only made my eyes swim with beaches and palm trees. Then I thought maybe it was the words below the sunset that had my detective whiskers a-twitching. If I'd only had a few seconds to view the print from another angle, maybe I could have read those words.

I wished I could forget about that stupid framed print, but I couldn't. And on the night of the opera, on the ferry ride over to the city, I fell asleep in my seat and dreamed that I'd gone back to Darke's house alone—only to look inside his glass windows and see them turn into the glass of a Houdini water torture cell, and inside, Daniel was drowning. I broke the glass, and as the water streamed out, I caught a glimpse of Darke's sunset poster again—and tried to focus on the black, swirly mark that was blocking the sun. I saw something in that black mark! But when a foghorn blew in the soupy night air hanging over the Sound, I woke up and couldn't remember what Dream Me had seen.

Maybe I was just obsessing over something trivial. I tried to put it out of my mind, which was easy to do when I stepped out of the Seattle ferry terminal and saw Daniel waiting for me. He was right about that suit of his. It flattered him. He was polished and pressed, and the suit fit him like a glove. His tied-back hair gleamed under the streetlights.

He was dazzling.

"Jesus, Birdie," he said with tender eyes. "You look beautiful. Like a dream. Oh shit. Is this a dream? Let me count; hold on."

"I'll join you," I said, smiling, cheeks warm. And we both counted our fingers—one, two, three, four, five.

"All there," he reported as he touched my flower. "It's not a lily."

"It's a gardenia from our greenhouse. A hybrid called Mystery."

"For real?"

I nodded. It was the only bloom on the bush, and the white matched my dress, which felt a little like what Daniel would call fate. "It's my lucky flower," I told him. "To go with your lucky suit. We should play the lottery tonight. Our chances of winning are astronomical."

"I think I already won," he said, kissing my forehead.

I could have stood there with him forever. But we nearly got bowled over by a rude hipster on a bicycle, so we decided to get our lucky selves far away from the terminal. We piled into his car, and he turned on David Bowie. And then we headed out of downtown.

The Seattle Center was home to the World's Fair in the 1960s. Now it was a sprawling complex that was half grassy pavilion, half tourist attraction—museums, live concerts, and, of course, the Space Needle. The Seattle Opera's official home, McCaw Hall, was also here, and it looked beautiful at night, its modern glass exterior lit up in purples and blues. And when Daniel and I parked in a garage across the street and strolled over a connecting skybridge that overlooked throngs of people, I was just so happy to be doing something special, I forgot all about everything else.

So much so, in fact, that when we walked under scrims of glass and peered into the entrance—with its enormous modern sculptured chandeliers hanging above operagoers dressed to the nines—I was completely caught up in the fantasy that this was a date. A beautiful, happy date. Prince and princess, out doing glamorous things. It wasn't until Daniel pointed to a VIP sign that it hit me like a ton of bricks we weren't on a date at all: We were committing a crime.

Okay, maybe not robbing a bank. I wasn't even sure if it was considered illegal or just in poor taste to take someone else's free tickets. But we certainly didn't belong there, and we were lying like cheap rugs to get inside.

The VIP entrance was segregated in its own little portion of an interior promenade; this was where the big-money patrons entered, the ones who donated large sums of cash to the opera and Pacific Northwest Ballet. They had their own ticket window, coat check, and ushers.

We did not belong here.

You're undercover, I told myself. *Stay calm.*

Daniel blew out a long breath and headed straight to the woman running Will Call, confidently informing her that we were part of Bill Waddle's party, and were we the first to arrive? While they talked, I stood frozen, half zoned out, telling myself that sometimes even the best detectives must bend a couple of small rules to ferret out clues, and this might be the last clue we got on Raymond Darke. So, we weren't going to waste it, and it was fine. It was all fine. And WHAT WAS I THINKING, COMING OUT HERE? We were going to end up in jail, and who would bail me out? Mona? Cherry?

But I was freaking out for no reason: Daniel turned around with his hands full of tickets and printed opera programs . . . and a look of victory on his face. "I can't believe they fell for it," he whispered.

"Did you have to give our names?"

"I just made them up. We're Nick and Nora Washington."

"Washington?"

"I couldn't remember their last name!"

"Charles. But I'm glad you didn't remember. Might as well have signed in as Sherlock Holmes and John Watson!" I said, lightly slugging his arm.

"Ow!" he whispered, trying not to laugh. "Does it matter? She entered it in the computer and didn't blink. Must have been the suit. Told you it was lucky."

Indeed. All praise the suit. Maybe now I could relax and things would go smoothly.

We were the second to arrive in Darke's party, Daniel confirmed with the ticket agent, and there was still plenty of time before the opera. After noticing some of the guests strolling through a preshow art exhibit that had been set up in the lobby, Daniel asked if I knew anything about the opera being performed. I opened the program and skimmed the introduction. Tonight's show was a production of Puccini's *Madama Butterfly*—the story of an underaged Japanese geisha named Butterfly and a jerky US naval officer who gets her pregnant and runs off to marry an American woman. Devastated, the geisha kills herself.

"Jesus. This is . . . heavy," Daniel said, reading over my shoulder.

"It's pretty horrible," I agreed. "Why would anyone want to see this?"

I didn't want him watching a teen girl offing herself onstage. I didn't even want him knowing about it, but it was obvious when he spotted it in the program, because his shoulders stiffened.

"We're not here to see the opera. We don't even really have seats," I reminded him. "Let's go try to find Darke."

"Yeah," he said coolly. "Let's do that."

We headed past concession stands selling wine and *Madama Butterfly* T-shirts. Daniel's strides were purposeful and angry, and I struggled to keep up in heels that I wasn't accustomed to wearing. Why couldn't the production have been something nice and easy? What about *Carmen*? Doesn't everyone love *Carmen*? Was all opera problematic? I wish I'd spent more time researching tonight's performance than what clothes to wear to it.

Or maybe the whole thing was a dumb idea. The hall was filling up with people, and that made it harder to spot someone. We couldn't find Darke, not in the lobby or on the promenade. Not sipping on wine or chatting with other people in his circle, the ones who were wearing tuxedos and long evening gowns.

"It's getting swamped in here," Daniel said. "Let's split up. You make a pass back to ticketing, and I'll go upstairs to the mezzanine. We'll meet back here in five?"

I didn't want to split up, but one moment Daniel was squeezing my hand and the next he was slipping through the crowd.

Every detective has setbacks. That's what I tried to tell myself as I wandered through the crowd, eyes peeled for any sign of Darke or Ivanov. But after I'd covered all the ground we'd already walked, circled back around, and stopped at our designated meeting spot, I began to worry less about finding Darke and more about finding Daniel.

Five minutes passed. Ten . . .

I glanced at giant red banners cascading from the second floor. They were red and black, a dark silhouette of a woman in front of a red Japanese parasol that fanned out like the sun.

Like a sunset. Huh.

Something fired inside my head, and I remembered where I'd seen it before: at Mona's place, on her wall of Broadway posters. It was from a play.

But that wasn't why it was important. Because it wasn't the only place I'd seen it.

I pulled out my opera program and quickly thumbed through it, stopping when I got to right page.

It was suddenly clear to me now. That framed poster I'd spied inside Darke's house, with its yellow sunset inside a red border and its swirly, black shape blocking the sun . . . I was looking at it right now, reprinted in the opera program. The black shape I couldn't quite identify when we were spying into his windows was clear now: It was a collection of brushstrokes, a vague Asian-inspired script that also doubled as a sketch.

A sketch of a helicopter.

Cherry's words came back to me from when she was telling me about auditioning for a dancing role in an off-Broadway production at 5th Avenue Theatre: Miss Saigon *has a real helicopter that hangs from the rafters and descends onto the stage.*

Nerves jangling, I skimmed the text of the opera program as tuxedos and gowns passed me. The program said that *Miss Saigon* was a Broadway musical set during the Vietnam War, a tragic tale of a doomed romance between an American GI and a Vietnamese bar girl who has his child after he abandons her.

Based on the opera *Madama Butterfly*.

Everything swirled inside my head: *Madama Butterfly*. *Miss*

Saigon. Raymond Darke's framed print. Cherry's story of meeting Daniel's father while she was auditioning for *Miss Saigon* at 5th Avenue Theatre—*I pictured myself living in his big mansion that overlooked the city.*

My heart raced wildly. I didn't want to jump to conclusions. It could all be a coincidence.

It had to be . . . right?

Then where was Daniel now?

I glanced upstairs, where he said he'd be looking—which also happened to be where the private opera boxes were located. . . .

Hiking up the hem of my gown, I raced up the staircase and glanced around the mezzanine, where patrons clustered around a cocktail bar, drinking and chatting. No Daniel.

I spotted a side hall. An usher stood outside, but when she turned her back to help someone, I slipped past her and immediately found myself in one of the curving halls at the rear of the private boxes.

Red doors lining the hall. The performance hadn't yet started, but most of the patrons seemed to either be drinking at the bar outside or already in their seats. A lone woman was walking toward me, and as she approached, I recognized her face.

The interior designer, Darke's wife.

Her head was down as she strode past me, talking rapidly on her phone in a hard-to-place accent. She didn't even spare me a glance. I rounded the corner and peered through the open door of the first private box, seeing down into the theater below. An expansive curtained stage sat in front of an empty orchestra pit. The seats in front of it were buzzing with people, standing and talking, coming and going. The atmosphere on the floor was much livelier than it was up here. But because the private hall was so quiet, it made it easy to spot the only person standing in front of the door to the next booth. And easy to spot the only man strolling out of it.

I came to a stop a few strides away from Daniel and whispered, "Wait!" But he didn't even notice me. His gaze was squarely fixed on Raymond Darke, who stilled in the opera box's doorway, hands on the lapel of his tuxedo.

Darke looked at Daniel. Looked at me. And then he sputtered, "You're the goddamn kids who went through my trash!"

Words . . . I didn't have them.

Darke pointed an accusatory finger at Daniel. "Yeah, that's right. I've got you on video, you little delinquent. Perfect shots of both your faces looking straight into the window of my house."

Cameras were inside the house? Why had we been so reckless? I was going to have a stroke.

"That's trespassing," Darke said. "What are you doing here now? Trying to rob me?"

"I don't want a damn thing you've got, old man," Daniel said.

No, no, no! Why was Daniel confronting him? We should run now, while we could get lost in the crowds and escape. THIS WAS NOT PART OF OUR PLAN.

"Call the cops, then," Daniel said, defiant. "I'd expect nothing less from you, hiding in your big house, paying other people to take care of all your problems. Pretending to be someone else. Do you even write your own books, or do you hire someone to do that, too?"

A low-level panic prickled the back of my neck. I'd never seen Daniel act like this. He was inordinately aggressive, and Darke was teetering on fury, and I was on the outside of it all, overflowing with information that I could barely comprehend.

"Daniel," I pleaded, but he ignored me.

"Should I call you Bill or Raymond?" Daniel said to the man. "Or maybe you have another name you prefer?"

The author's neck and shoulders visibly stiffened. He waited until an extravagantly dressed couple passed, nodding politely when they greeted him. When they stepped into another box, he squinted at Daniel. "Do I know you?"

Daniel snorted. "Do you?"

"I've seen you before," the author said, his brow a ledge that shadowed his eyes. "Where?"

"Take a good, hard look, motherfucker," Daniel challenged. "Strain that memory. Strain it all the way back, twenty years ago, to the face of the girl you knocked up."

> "I just know that any time I undertake a case,
> I'm apt to run into some kind of a trap."
> —Nancy Drew, *The Clue of the Broken Locket* (1934)

30

Raymond Darke's face blanched. He looked as if he might be sick. I was feeling that way myself.

Daniel knew.

He already knew!

"Hello, Dad," Daniel said. "Surprise! Cherry didn't get that abortion that you wanted her to get. You *do* remember her, right?"

Darke's features turned stony. "I don't know what you want me to say. That was twenty years ago. Do you want money from me? Is that why you're here?"

"You can't buy my silence. I'm here to expose you for the fraud you are."

Darke struggled for words, scratching the back of his head, looking around the corridor as if someone would come save him. He finally said, "I have a right to use a pen name. I just want a peaceful life, and—"

"Why is that?" Daniel asked. "I keep asking myself why you'd want to be anonymous. See, my mom didn't tell me who you were. She kept it secret and said you weren't worth the hassle. It was my grandfather who spilled the beans to me last year. I've been trying to hunt you down for months. Imagine my surprise when fate dropped you right into the back seat of my van, and I overhear you yelling at your agent on the phone."

Fate. Imagine that, I thought, frantically trying to piece together what I knew and when I knew it and all the signs I'd missed. That afternoon I found Daniel in the market, in front of the magic shop. *I know a real-life mystery going on at the hotel.*

"Fuck," Darke mumbled, scrubbing his hand over his mouth, as if he could somehow rub away the conversation. "That's where I know you from. The Cascadia."

"Bingo, Dad."

"Don't call me that."

"Sucks that you didn't put a hat on your jimmy, but here we are. And yeah, you know me from the Cascadia. See, we followed you and your wife to room 514. We know you were meeting Ivanov there. We have evidence you left behind—your list from a Ukrainian company that doesn't exist? I'm sure a newspaper would love a juicy scoop about an illegal international sex ring."

"Sex ring?" Darke bellowed.

"Whatever nefarious thing you're up to with your 'facilitator,' Ivanov," Daniel said, throwing up air quotes.

"He's helping my wife and me adopt a child!"

The din in the theater below floated up through the private box as Daniel stared at Darke in disbelief.

"Adoption from the Ukraine," I said in a daze, thinking back to the list of the names we found. Males and females. Dates. *Birth dates.*

Darke glanced at me. "My wife can't have children, and I got snipped years ago, after . . ." His eyes flicked to Daniel. "Adoption takes time. We've been on a list in the United States, since last summer. They told us it could take five years for a healthy newborn. My wife and I aren't young. We don't have that long."

"Fran Malkovich. Your wife is Ukrainian," I said, suddenly placing her accent.

He nodded once. "She found Ivanov. He makes things happen quickly. There are too many laws about adopting newborns—it's complicated. And expensive."

Everything suddenly became clearer. "You've been giving Ivanov adoption payments every week. In room 514."

"It's none of your business," he snapped. "That's between me and my wife. It's personal, and you had no right to spy on me. I'll have you both fired."

"Oh, will you?" Daniel said. "Because what you're doing still sounds pretty fucking illegal. And there's the fact that we know who you are, Bill Waddle."

"What do you want from me? An apology? It was twenty years ago, and we only saw each other for a few weeks. I can't even remember her last name, for the love of God. But I was up front with her about our relationship. We weren't exclusive. I dated a lot of women. She knew I wasn't ready to start a family."

"But you are now," Daniel said. "Sorry I was such an inconvenience."

"Daniel," I pleaded in a low voice.

He tossed me a look, but I wasn't even sure that he saw me through the haze of anger and pain that tightened his jaw and made his eyes swim with emotion.

"Look, kid," Darke said. "I don't know what you want me to say. If I could go back and change things, I would have never seen your mother. I was young and foolish—"

"You were almost forty! Twice her age!"

"It takes two to tango. I never forced her to see me. And what difference does it make now? I have my life and you have yours. If you want money—"

"I don't want your goddamn money!" Daniel shouted, startling me with the level of explosive animosity in his voice.

Darke lifted his hands in surrender. "Fine. But if you change your mind, I can have my lawyer draft up an agreement. After a paternity test, of course. But you get nothing if you go public. And if you're going to threaten me with that, I'll beat you to the punch and do it myself. You've got nothing on me."

"We have Ivanov's spreadsheet."

Darke shrugged. "What does that prove? I never checked in at the hotel. I was just meeting a friend for a drink." He stuck his finger in Daniel's face. "You've got nothing. You're just a lawless kid who's making up stories."

Down the hall, Darke's wife was tottering toward us in

stilettos. "William?" she called out. "Is anything wrong?"

Yes, I thought. *Everything's wrong. All of this was a terrible, terrible mistake.*

Daniel leaned toward Darke. "You know what? I got what I wanted. The knowledge that my father is the asshole I've always imagined. I don't want anything to do with you, so you can keep your agreement and your money. Have a good life with your new, more convenient son," he said, giving Darke's wife a look of contempt before turning toward the exit. "By the way, if you fantasized about my mom pining away for you like *Madama Butterfly*, sorry to disappoint. She's doing great. Best decision of her life was to walk away from a monster like you."

And with that, Daniel stormed away.

He didn't even look at me. Maybe he'd forgotten I was there. I chased after him as the lights above us blinked to warn the theatergoers that the production was about to start. With every step, I went from bewildered to enraged. And as we entered the mezzanine lounge, I lost both my patience and ability to reason.

"You lied to me!" I shouted at Daniel's back.

His striding legs slowed. Then he stopped abruptly and swung around. I'd never seen him look like that, so angry and hurt all at the same time.

I repeated, "You lied to me," in a lower voice. "You knew he was your father all along. You roped me into helping you just to figure out what he was doing in the hotel? You used me? Was this all just one big misdirection?"

"No!" His eyes squeezed shut. "I didn't use you. I . . ."

"But you knew who Raymond Darke was when you first told me he was coming into the hotel. You knew he was your father?"

"Yes!" he shouted. "I knew. But I wasn't using you. It's just that you were treating me like I had the plague, saying you didn't want to have anything to do with me, and I thought—" He tugged his ear and made a pained face. "When you were talking about detectives and mysteries, I thought it was a way for us to spend time together—to get to know you. And yeah, okay, maybe I wanted to see what my father was like. I was curious, okay? And finding out about him with you made it seem less like something personal, not some big emotional risk. I meant to tell you eventually, but one thing led to another, and when we came here, I just wanted to confront him, and then it was too late to tell you."

"How could it be too late? You had a million chances to say, 'Hey, Birdie. This guy is my father.' In fact, you could have even said that after we walked into this building and I would have forgiven you."

"And you won't now?"

I didn't know, honestly. I was vaguely aware that stragglers heading into the theater were staring, but I was too upset to care that we were making a scene. "You got what you wanted out of me, didn't you? You got my help, and you got me to start sleeping with you again."

His face darkened. "Did *I* show up on *your* doorstep with a box of condoms?"

"Don't you dare shame me for that! I did that after you were all charming and sweet to me. Did you mean any of it?"

"Of course I meant it! How could you even say that?"

Tears stung my eyes. "Because I don't know what's a lie and what's not anymore."

He put his hands on the back of his neck, elbows bent, and paced away from me in distress before turning back around. "I told you the secrets that mattered. This doesn't. He doesn't."

"He's your father!"

"He's nothing. I'm sorry I didn't tell you. I'm *so* sorry. I'm a fuckup. I warned you. And I'm sorry I lied, but I was afraid if I told you, you'd run away like you did that first day. You're accusing me of using you, but didn't you use me?"

"I didn't use you—I freaked out. I've already told you this."

"But if I hadn't asked you to help me investigate Darke, would you even have had anything whatsoever to do with me? The way I remember things, you were telling me you didn't want to talk about what we'd done in my car. You asked me to forget it and pretend it didn't happen. Because that's what you do—when you're afraid of something, if it's just too hard for you to face, you'll do anything to avoid it. You didn't want to talk to me after we had sex that first time. You don't want to face getting treated for your narcolepsy. And now you're doing the same thing—because it's easier to just walk away from us than to talk about all this, right? I know I screwed up, but I screwed up because I was scared of exactly this—that you'd run away again."

"So this is my fault?"

"I told you I loved you, and you couldn't even say it back."

"You told me I didn't have to!"

"I wanted you to *want* to say it. But for some reason, you feel more comfortable having sex with me than making any kind of commitment that doesn't involve a stupid mystery!"

His words were a slap in the face. The telltale signs of bonelessness prickled in warning. It started in my face and neck, and then it spread to my arms. My hands stopped working. I dropped my clutch purse.

"Birdie?" Daniel said, rushing toward me.

But not fast enough. My legs gave out, and I collapsed on the floor like a puppet falling off its wires.

The problem with cataplexy wasn't the sensation itself, which was disconcerting, sure, but so far beyond my control that I had no choice but to endure it until my body decided to start functioning again.

The problem was that time didn't stop.

Everything around me moved and talked and breathed while I didn't. I saw Daniel drop to the floor to help me. I heard him calling my name and saw him touching the side of my head, and his fingers came away red with blood. I saw the panicked look on his face and on all the faces that were swarming around us. People shouting out commands to give me room. I spotted Ivanov, of all people, Mr. Adoption Facilitator. And then Raymond Darke was dropping to the floor alongside Daniel, asking him urgent questions about my health—checking my eyes, checking the blood on the side of my head, demanding that his wife call 911. Daniel's hands shaking as he fumbled with his phone. Were they bonding over my humiliation? That was some kind of cruel irony.

All of this was happening around me as I lay like a corpse. I wanted to answer Daniel. I wanted to scream.

All I could do was stare.

While Daniel drifted farther away, out of my dreams, out of my life.

And I was stranded on my island again.

Alone.

"Tears never bring anything back."
—Ole Golly, *Harriet the Spy* (1964)

31

After I regained control of my body, details from that night became fuzzy. I knew that my cataplexy fall had lasted only a few minutes, but it was the longest episode I'd ever had—long enough for an ambulance to come. And long enough for me to get poked and prodded by an EMT outside the opera hall while Darke and Daniel talked in the distance.

Daniel had phoned Aunt Mona immediately after calling 911. As luck would have it, she was in the city on Capitol Hill having dinner with Leon Snodgrass, and they rushed over and rode with me to the hospital. I'd cut the shell of my ear during the fall, not my head—my earring popped out and nicked me. At first they suspected a concussion, because I was having trouble staying awake and kept missing parts of questions they asked. Then Aunt Mona told them about Grandpa's narcolepsy. The ER doctor flashed a series of lights in my eyes and said I was experiencing something called microsleeps. Then she wrote up an entire series of referrals to other doctors that filled up three printed pages.

Daniel was there the whole time, but I just ignored him. Easy to do when nothing seems real and you keep losing consciousness. I remember him apologizing a lot, and I think he started crying at one point, but he walked away, so I couldn't be sure. I know I told him that I needed some space to think about what had happened. He didn't argue, so I took that as a sign that he needed space too. When I got released, Aunt Mona pulled him aside and talked to him alone, and then he left the hospital without saying good-bye.

Nothing that happened that night really sank in until the next day, after I'd slept for ten hours with the aid of a drug they gave me in the ER. Aunt Mona spent the night with me, sleeping next to me in my bed, and when I woke, Grandpa was back. Cass had driven him home in the middle of the night when Mona called, and he'd already heard the entire story from her. He was surprisingly calm. Not one word about the opera or why Daniel and I were there. When I tried to explain, he didn't even want to hear it. He said it was unimportant.

"I've failed you," he told me in the kitchen after I'd come downstairs. He leaned back against the counter, arms folded, while Mona sat next to me at the kitchen table.

"What? Of course you haven't," I said, tightening the belt of my robe. "It was just a bad night. It could have happened while you were here. I'm fine."

"You're not. And I've set a bad example. It's time we stop ignoring the sleep issues and did something about it."

"Do I have any say in this? It's my body."

"And my bad genes. Are you really going to follow in Lily's footsteps and ignore your health problems, hoping they go away until you end up dead in the ER?"

"She didn't know she was pregnant that time!" I said, suddenly angry with him for bringing Mom into this.

"Tell her, Mona. She needs to see things for what they are, not some dreamy, romanticized version of it."

I looked at Mona, confused. "What's he talking about?"

She sighed heavily. "Your mom knew she was pregnant that second time."

"What? No, she didn't. She thought it was food poisoning. I know. I was there." It was the strongest memory I had of her, that night when everything went wrong. I sometimes thought it weakened all my other memories, and I wished I'd been anywhere else but with her that night—at Ms. Patty's apartment, in the diner, sleeping over at a friend's house . . . anywhere but there. And that made me feel guilty.

"She'd known for several weeks. She'd told me," Mona said, fake eyelashes from the night before starting to peel off, dark makeup smeared. "She refused to go to the doctor. She didn't know who the father was, and she wasn't planning on keeping it, but she suspected something was wrong because she kept . . ."

Mona blinked up at Grandpa, but he just waved at her to keep going. "I've heard it before. Tell her."

"She kept spotting," Mona said. "And she didn't feel right. She was worried she was going to miscarry. We fought about it a lot. I was so mad that she wouldn't do anything about it. Either take care of it or go to the doctor—that's what I told her."

"What?" I said, absolutely stunned. This didn't match up with anything I remembered. "Why wouldn't she go?"

Mona shook her head slowly. "If I had to guess, I'd say she was running out the clock. I think she hoped it would take care of itself—that she'd miscarry, and then she wouldn't have to do anything. She'd be absolved from making a decision. You know how much I loved your mother—and still do. But she wasn't perfect. Lily was brave when she had to be, but she had to be backed into a corner *completely* and run down the clock until the very last moment before she'd take action. And that time she waited too long."

I stared at Mona, wiping away stray tears. "She could have lived?"

"We'll never know," Grandpa said, emotion brimming in his eyes. "Mona told me this a few months ago, after your grandma passed. I've thought about it a lot. I'm not sure I have any answers that will make either of us feel better, but I know one thing that gives me hope."

"What's that?" I asked.

"You have a chance to make different choices."

I cried a little. Mona held me, and while her arms were around me, I thought about her pregnancy and how she was taking all these tests and following all her doctor's directions, seeing lawyers, making plans with Leon . . . asking for help. Everything my mom didn't do. Maybe my memories of her were nebulous because Mona was doing all the work. Maybe she was more of a mother to me than Lily Lindberg ever had been.

And maybe I forgave Mom for that.

"Okay," I said firmly, done with crying and hurting. "Take me to the doctor."

Grandpa stood up from leaning against the counter, hand on his walking cane, and gave me a pleased look. "Good, because I already called Dr. Koval. She's meeting us at her office in thirty minutes."

The three of us piled into Mona's car and drove there together, and I told the doctor everything. About Grandpa's diagnosis. About my symptoms and how they'd gotten progressively worse since my grandmother died, but especially since I started working at the Cascadia. Dr. Koval asked a million questions, made me fill out a written sleep test, and took a lot of blood. Then she called another doctor in the city for a favor.

That afternoon I called into the hotel to let them know that I had to take emergency leave for a few days. And the next night Grandpa, Aunt Mona, and I walked into the University of Washington's sleep clinic. The technicians were all very kind, and they set me up for an overnight polysomnography test, in which they hooked me up to machines with wires and monitored my sleep. I thought I wouldn't be able to sleep in a lab, but I surprised myself.

The next morning I went straight into a multiple sleep latency test. For that they put me in room that looked like a bland dorm with IKEA furniture and a private bathroom. They made me take five naps and measured how often I entered REM sleep throughout the day. Sometimes I wasn't sure if I fell asleep, but the tech was always asking me what I dreamed, so I suppose I did.

Between a couple of the tests, I talked to Mona while Grandpa went to the lobby for coffee. "Hanging in there?" she asked, pulling a chair next to mine.

"All this napping is exhausting," I said, smiling a little.

She smiled back, then said, "Are you mad at me?"

"Why would I be?"

"Because I've been a terrible gutsy gal. I kept secrets from you about your mom. I shouldn't have, and I'm sorry."

"Why did you?" I asked, suddenly self-conscious. "You could have told me. I understand if you thought I was too young to understand back then, but, you know, it's been years."

It took her a long time to answer. "I used to think it was because I didn't want you to remember Lily in a bad light. Because she made some bad decisions—or didn't make any decisions at all, I suppose. Which was frustrating. But she was also sweet and wonderful and funny, and people never remember the good things. They remember the bad stuff."

"I already remembered some of the bad stuff."

"Not about her, about me," Mona said. "What if I had told somebody about Lily's pregnancy? What if I'd called Hugo and urged him to talk to Lily? What if I'd pushed her harder to see a doctor?"

"That's absurd," I said. "It's not your fault."

"I know that now. But I was worried you wouldn't. And that you'd shut me out for either making a mistake or keeping that mistake from you all these years. Maybe it sounds stupid, but I think I've been afraid you might do what Lily did and just walk away one day."

"I wouldn't do that."

"Darling, I sure hope not. But between your mom and your grandma's deaths, and everything else that's happened, I sometimes look at you and see the same coping mechanism I saw in Lily—a girl who protects herself by keeping people at a distance."

As I glanced at the sleep clinic technicians through a glass window, I thought about Daniel and our fight. He said he didn't tell me that he knew Darke was his father because he was afraid I'd run away from him. Was this who I was? Someone who ran away when the going got tough? Who pushed people away?

"I love my mom, but I don't want to be her," I said.

"Then don't," she said firmly. "Just be yourself."

It wasn't until the next day that I was able to get my sleep center results. With Grandpa and Aunt Mona, I sat in a tufted leather chair on the other side of the doctor's desk while he flung out phrases like "sleep latencies" and "sleep onset REMs." But when I heard "troublesome" and "narcolepsy with cataplexy, type one," I sat up straighter and listened to what the doctor was trying to tell me.

She said that there's some genetic disposition for the disorder, but that symptoms sometimes didn't appear until teen years, and they typically increase over time, which is probably why my sleep issues had been getting worse lately.

She said that it was a long-term neurological disorder, and I was never going to be cured or perfectly normal.

But.

I could manage it with changes in my routine and with medication. And that I'd need to make an effort and be willing to experiment with treatments, because it may take a couple of years to find the right balance of medication—to keep me awake when I needed to be awake and to sleep when I needed to sleep. And maybe that's where Grandpa went wrong after he got diagnosed: he didn't like how the medication made him feel, so he gave up. I needed to be more tenacious than that if I wanted this to work.

And I did. In some ways this felt like turning over a new leaf. No more running away. Time to commit to things that mattered and stop fearing the worst.

Armed with prescriptions and a series of future appointments to check on my progress, I emerged from the doctor's office feeling like Rocky Balboa, arms raised in triumph at the top of the famous stone steps in Philadelphia, ready to win at life. As if I'd accomplished something monumental. God as my witness, I'd never go boneless again!

Well, it was a start at least. And that wasn't nothing. I could finally set my eye on the horizon, where feeling better wasn't guaranteed but at least possible. It was a weight lifted off my shoulders—a spring-cleaning of the sticky cobwebs inside my head. And as we stood in line for a celebratory lunch of chicken sandwiches and strawberry-lemon bars, my newly cleared mind had space for thinking about other things.

Like Daniel. And that night at the opera.

And our fight.

I thought and thought, and I didn't understand how I could be so angry at him one second, and the next, miss him so much that my heart felt like it was shattering. But it wasn't until I got home from the doctor's office that I came to some realizations.

He was right when he said he'd tried to tell me earlier about Raymond Darke—at least, in a small way. Before the opera, when we'd argued about going. He wanted to call the whole thing off. He never flat-out said, *I knew Raymond Darke was my father this entire time*—which would have prevented all of this. At the very least, my heart wouldn't feel as if it had been punched repeatedly.

But I'd been so distressed about Daniel lying to me that I'd failed to realize how upsetting it must have been for him to face Raymond Darke. That was the point of the whole thing, right? It wasn't that Daniel was hell-bent on outing Darke's true identity to the world; he was trying to communicate with his father. And could I blame him? A couple years after my mom died, when I was twelve, I spent weeks trying to figure out who my father was, based on nothing but a nickname and a school that Aunt Mona had remembered. I looked online. I called people. I made lists. I never found out who it was, but it wasn't for lack of trying. And I'd done it all behind my grandparents' backs. I'd lied. I'd kept secrets. It wasn't because I didn't love them, but because it was *my* quest. They could never understand what it felt like.

Daniel shouldn't have lied to me. But I could understand how it snowballed into something he didn't intend. And I understood why he was afraid to tell me, because right now I was afraid too. Afraid that we'd both failed each other. Afraid of what I'd lose if I gave up on us and walked away instead of accepting his apology.

Afraid it might be too late for us to find a way to rebuild trust.

I hoped it wasn't.

That night I got up the courage to send him a text: Truth or Lie. Do you believe in third chances?

His response came several hours later: I believe anything's possible.

"Everything is connected."
—Officer Jim Chee, *The Ghostway* (1984)

32

Late the next afternoon, I took a ferry into the city. I'd been trying to call the daytime manager at work to see if she'd put me back on the work schedule after my emergency leave. I was a little worried Melinda would be miffed for making her shuffle everyone around to accommodate me—and more worried about what would happen when I told her my doctor wanted me to work in the day. But when I called, no one picked up the manager's line. So I called the main guest line repeatedly but kept getting a busy signal.

Which was strange. It should go straight to the automated menu.

After several fruitless attempts, I wasn't sure what to do. Then I got a text from Daniel:

The Cascadia is closed today for maintenance.

But u should go in anyway.

Maybe around 5:30.

Will u go? Y/N

I reread this several times. I had so many questions: Closed for maintenance? Why? Were guests still there? Employees? Was Daniel working? Did he want to talk? About us? Was he being terse because we weren't speaking right now, or because he was about to break things off with me?

In the end I decided to send a simple reply: Yes.

He never responded, and that made me worry even more. I was also hopped up on my new medication, and it made me feel anxious and weird. But I figured it was better to go face whatever was going to happen than sit around wondering.

When I got to the Cascadia, the entrance was roped off, and a big sign in the front said that the hotel was temporarily closed for repairs and for guests with bookings to speak to the doorman. Only there was no one there. The van was gone too. I headed around to the employee entrance in the alley and had to squeeze past massive trucks and people in hazmat uniforms.

And the smell. Dear God, the smell . . .

Before I could swipe my badge to get inside the employee hallway, the back door swung open and Chuck's blond head appeared. A surgical mask covered his mouth.

"Dopey," he said brightly, pulling down his mask. "Weird to be here during the Hawk shift, huh?"

"I've been trying to call. What's going on?"

"SARG happened. The animal rights group reported us to the city for the sewage leak in the garage. Think they sabotaged us too, because there's shit coming up inside the hotel toilets. It's an actual shit show on the fifth floor!"

"What?"

"City shut us down until it's repaired. We've been busing people over to the Fairmont and comping their stays. Guests are pissed, the management is stressed, and no one's in charge."

I blinked at the hazmat team. "What about Octavia?"

"What about her? SARG didn't take her, if that's what you're thinking. I think they're just trying to make us look bad. Roxanne says they've been trying to get the city to vote on making public aquariums illegal."

"When will all this be fixed?" I asked, holding my hand over my nose.

"They say to call in tomorrow and prepare to come in then, in case it gets finished tonight. But the cleanup crew says that's a crock of shit. See what I did there?"

"Who's the manager on duty?"

"Roxanne's in the parking garage right now. So, Tina? I think. She's crying in the manager's office, so I'd avoid her at all costs. Oh, and if you hadn't heard, Melinda went into labor last night, so she probably had her kid. Hard to find out because everything's in chaos."

"I see that."

My phone buzzed. I pulled it out of my pocket while Chuck called out to someone in the alley. The screen showed a new text from Daniel: Are you at the hotel yet? I typed a quick response: Just arrived. His reply came a few seconds later: Find Chuck.

I stared at my phone. Find Chuck? Why? No further replies clarified the message.

"Hey," I said. "I'm supposed to talk to you, I think?"

Chuck turned around, gave me a blank stare, then smacked himself on his forehead. "Duh, almost forgot. Daniel left something for you in locker twenty-seven."

"In the employee area?" I asked, my heart thumping madly. "Is he here somewhere?"

Chuck shook his head. "Nah. He was driving the van earlier today, helping the midshift driver haul guests and luggage. I think he's gone now. Oh, and I'm supposed to tell you to hurry before it closes."

"Before what closes?" I said. "The hotel? Isn't it already closed?"

He shrugged. "No idea. That's what he said. I'm just the messenger."

With my pulse speeding, I murmured a quick thanks, and as I slipped inside the hotel's back door, I paused and called back into the alley, "By the way, don't call me Dopey again."

Chuck blinked at me and opened his mouth, but he couldn't quite manage an immediate retort. And I didn't give him a chance to think of one. I just let the door shut behind me and made my way inside the hotel.

The employee hall was empty. No one in security. No manager. No one in the break room. I checked the schedule when I passed the time clock, but it just had a red line drawn through today and tomorrow.

I made a beeline to the employee lockers. Number twenty-seven was locked and had a note taped to the front that read: *You have the key.*

Did Daniel write this? It looked like his illegible scrawl. What did he mean? I have the key? I checked my purse, but of course it wasn't there. After glancing around in paranoia to make sure I wasn't being watched or filmed for some kind of cruel hidden-camera prank, I stared at the note again. I have the key. . . . My gaze flicked to the slits at the top of the lockers. Big enough for a key? I strode to my assigned locker, unlocked it, and what do you know? A tiny key sat on the top shelf.

Grabbing it, I went back to locker twenty-seven and stuck it inside the padlock. Success! I popped the lock, opened the locker, and peered inside. Empty. No, wait. Something sat on the shelf.

A book.

A single yellow sticky note on the cover read *Birdie* in neat handwriting.

I peeled it off and stared at the peach cover of an old Agatha Christie paperback—*The Body in the Library*. I'd read it many times. Not this edition, which looked to be from the 1970s or '80s and had a fifty-cent price tag on the front.

My heart raced. I looked around the locker room as if I'd find Daniel lurking in the shadows. But no. Why had he left this here? Just a random gift?

Or worse: another misdirection?

Never trust a magician.

Right, well . . . Too late for that, wasn't it?

I inspected the book, thumbing through the pages. No marks inside. Nothing unusual . . . except a receipt that fluttered out.

It was purchased at the mystery book shop in Pike Place Market. This morning. The name of the clerk who rang up the purchase was circled in red ink—the shop's dull-minded assistant, Holly. Three red question marks were written above it.

Was this a clue?

I looked through the book carefully but found nothing else.

Should I text him? Hold on. Did he want me to go to the mystery book shop? Should I wait here until he comes back and ask him?

He could have given me the book in person. Why go to all this trouble?

I thought about what Chuck had told me, to hurry before it closes.

Before the market closes!

Daniel was handing me a mystery to solve.

"Holy crap," I mumbled to myself as realization struck. Not a mystery—a mystery hunt, like the one Mona and Ms. Patty had given me in the diner that rainy Easter afternoon.

I glanced around the locker room, clutching the book against my chest, heart filling with joy. But before I broke down and got too emotional to think straight, I remembered the time. If I was going to find Daniel's second clue, I'd need to get my butt in motion.

It took me ten minutes to speed walk to Pike Place Market. Stalls were packing up, so I jogged through the crowds and down the ramp into the lower levels to the mystery bookshop. Still open! I was breathless when I pushed open the door, scanning the cramped store for Holly. She stood up behind the front counter, lifting a box of used books.

"Holly," I said.

Her head swiveled toward me. "Yes?"

"Someone left this for me, and they bought it here from you this morning," I said, flashing her the Agatha Christie book and the receipt.

"Oh, right," she said. "You're Birdie."

"Yes!" I said. "Was it a boy with long, dark hair?"

"Our customers are confidential," she said robotically, sounding as if she were reciting lines. I was a second away from grabbing her by her cat-with-ball-of-yarn T-shirt and shaking the answer out of her when she pulled something out from beneath the counter. "This is for you."

It was a ragged DVD box set of a British cozy mystery TV series, *Midsomer Murders*.

"What's this for?" I asked.

Holly shrugged. "No idea. I just do what I'm bribed to do."

I flipped the box set over, where it had a list of episodes. One called "The Magician's Nephew" had been circled in red with more question marks.

Magician. Magic. Magic shop?

Another clue!

My heart raced, and my feet followed. "Thank you, Holly!" I shouted as I headed out the door and ran across the hall.

I'm not sure what I expected, but Daniel was not there. In fact, I was the lone customer in the shop. An out-of-order sign had been taped to the Elvis fortune-telling machine. I guess even fate broke down once in a while.

"We're just about to close. Can I help you?" a middle-aged man said from behind the counter. I'd seen him before, showing kids how to walk an invisible dog on a trick leash that had a wire inside to make it stand up. I thought perhaps he was one of the owner's sons.

I showed him the DVD set and cleared my throat. "Um, hi. You wouldn't happen to know anything about this, would you?"

He stared at me.

I smiled back.

Nodding, he pressed a button on the register. It *ding*ed as the drawer opened, and he pulled out an envelope with my name written on it in red. "This you?"

I nodded. "Did Daniel leave this?"

He zipped his lips. "A magician never reveals his secrets."

I nodded excitedly and took the envelope from him. "Thank you."

Walking briskly, I left the store and stopped near the Swami fortune-telling machine to inspect the envelope. It had my name written on it, and it was sealed.

I impatiently ripped the side off the envelope and puffed it open to peer inside. When I tipped it sideways, a card spilled onto my palm. It was . . .

An Elvis not-a-penny fortune card.

I flipped it over and read the text:

> *I see that you will have a chance meeting with a dark stranger who will reveal great secrets to you. If you collaborate, a bold and dashing adventure will be in your future. But beware of perilous pitfalls that lead to ruin. It takes a level head and determination to survive a run through the gauntlet. In great attempts, it is glorious even to fail, because in conflict you will find common ground together.*

This was the same fortune! *My* fortune! Maybe not the exact card, because this one had crisp corners, unlike mine, which got bent when I jammed it into the frame of a bedroom mirror. And there was something else: the word "gauntlet" was circled in red with three more question marks.

Crazy emotions pinballed around my chest. Embarrassment over my stupid sex-gauntlet proposal at Green Gables. But also a shimmering, distant hope that he was acknowledging our private joke for a good reason.

And there were other clues on the card. When I squinted,

I could just make out a few words written in tiny print at the bottom.

Moonlight Diner. 8 p.m.

Did this note mean eight p.m. *tonight*? That was almost two hours from now. I flipped the card over several times and peered into the envelope but found no other information.

Was I going to follow the card's direction?

How could I not?

Trying not to hang too much hope on any of this, I decided to go ahead and walk to the Moonlight. I holed up in our usual booth and ordered tea from one of Ms. Patty's nieces who by some miracle I had never met. Then I used not only their free Wi-Fi and restrooms, but also the peace and quiet to think. Perhaps I did too much thinking, because I *may* have fallen asleep. But I didn't beat myself up over this. My doctor said managing narcolepsy was never going to be easy, so I should get used to losing a few battles now and then. But by the time it got closer to eight, I was fully awake again and began watching the door like a hawk.

And watching and watching . . .

Eight came and went. No Daniel. No nothing.

WAS THIS ALL AN ELABORATE SETUP?

"Get it together, Birdie," I mumbled to myself, blowing out a long breath.

I crossed my legs and brushed up against something under the table. When I bent to the side to peer underneath, I found not only my childhood crayon drawing of Ms. Patty, but also a note taped to the grain of the particle board. I ripped it off and quickly scanned more scrawled handwriting: *Ride the blue horse.*

My eyes darted around the diner. No blue horse here. Nothing outside, either. At least, none that I could remember.

I stared out the diner window, scanning the sidewalk, and noticed a blue Mustang idling loudly at the curb. Blue horse! But it wasn't Daniel in the driver's seat—it was Joseph, from work.

"Hey," a woman's voice said behind me.

I swiveled in my seat to face the bright red hair of server Shonda—aka TONY THE TIGER, according to her name tag today, taking off her coat, as if she was on her way to clock in or had just been on a break.

"You're supposed to get a ride from that guy in the Mustang," she said, pointing out the window. "That's what your lovebird tipped me to tell you. There was a note or something?"

"I just found it. Thank you!" I quickly left cash on the table for my tea, scooted out of the booth, and strode outside to the Mustang.

Joseph ducked his head to me through the window and gestured for me to get inside. I opened the passenger door and slid into the seat while the engine rumbled. "Hey," I said. "I'm supposed to get in the car with you. Sorry I'm late. I didn't find the note in time."

"No worries," he said. "I've only been here a few minutes. Had to drive around the block a few times to snag this parking space."

"What now?"

He checked his rearview mirror as I put on my seat belt. Then he put the car in gear. "Now you refrain from asking me where I'm taking you."

"Why?"

"Because I'm not supposed to tell you."

"Just a hint?"

"Daniel wanted you to wear a blindfold, but that's a little too kidnappy for my tastes, so just keep your eyes down, yeah?"

That was hard to do. And after a couple of blocks, I gave up. We were headed out of downtown as a purpled twilight fell over the city. I asked Joseph a rapid-fire series of questions, trying different angles to get him to spill the beans about this mystery hunt that Daniel had arranged, but he was buttoned up tight.

We sped down Second Avenue and turned north on Broad. After a couple of blocks, Joseph stopped at a red light and discreetly texted someone. When I asked if that was Daniel, he merely said, "You'll see."

I went through a dozen possible scenarios in my head, trying to figure out where we were going. Seattle Center was on the left, along with the opera house—something I wished I could forget—and then Joseph was taking a quick turn into a driveway marked with a valet-parking sign. We went around a fountain before coming to a stop. A middle-aged African-American woman in a blazer waved at us.

My heart pounded furiously.

I peered past the woman and stared at colossal, white metal legs that stood at the base of a towering urban structure I saw every day I came into the city. It was iconic and weird, an engineering miracle, and it kicked the Eiffel Tower's ass any ol' day.

It all happened so fast. One minute Joseph was stopping the Mustang and jumping outside. Then next he was talking with the woman in the blazer, and she was opening the passenger door and waving me out.

"I'm Martha," she said, smiling. "You're Birdie? You're to come with me."

I gave Joseph a look that said *I'm freaking out right now. Please help me.* And he gave me a shrug that said, *You're on your own now.* Before I could protest, I was briskly led away by Martha and swept into glass doors. We passed the gift shop, where tourists browsed T-shirts and glass cases, and then hiked up a curving ramp, skipping past lines of people. It was all I could do to keep up with her hurried gait as she swept me into an elevator and closed the door on all the people gawking at us.

Then we began ascending.

"So," Martha said as we rose over the city, flashing through the glass. "Normally I'd tell guests that we are climbing five hundred and twenty feet at five miles per hour. And that the Space Needle was built in 1962 for the World's Fair, and the total height is over six hundred feet, which made it the tallest building west of the Mississippi for a few years. This your first time up here since the renovations?"

"Since I was a kid, so yes. Also, my first time in a private elevator."

"My first time taking anyone up privately, so we're even." She unfolded her arms as the elevator slowed and then *ding*ed. "And here we are at the observation deck."

"But what am I supposed to do now? Is there an envelope you're supposed to give me or—"

"Enjoy," she simply said, urging me out of the elevator.

I stepped onto the round, flying-saucer section of the tower: the observation deck. An enclosed inner area that had been recently renovated with clean, smooth lines: white floors and ceilings, modern benches, and floor-to-ceiling windows that sloped outward to form the Space Needle's distinctive shape.

People meandered around the circular space. They snapped photos and headed through glass doors that led outside, to the outer ring of the deck and the darkening purple city, lights twinkling on while the last orange rays of the sun sank on the horizon.

I swung around, heart racing, looking for the next clue— anything recognizable. And when I turned back around, I found it right in front of me.

Leather jacket with the diagonal zipper. Hair pulled back into a samurai topknot.

Daniel.

My frightened-rabbit heart thumped wildly with joy.

"Hi," he said, stuffing his hands in his pockets. "You made it."

"You left a trail of bread crumbs," I said.

"I knew you were a good detective." He took a couple of steps and stopped in front of me, tugging his ear and looking more than a little nervous. Guess he couldn't always hide it. Or maybe I'd gotten better at recognizing it. "What do you think about it up here? Was I wrong? The view's not too shabby, yeah?"

I'm sure it was amazing, but I couldn't possibly look at the city right now. My chest constricted painfully, because suddenly all I could think was how much I'd missed him over the past few days.

I missed his cheerful smile and his jokes.

I missed the way he looked at me right before we kissed.

I missed the thud of his heartbeat under my palm.

I missed all of him.

"Birdie," he said in a low voice. "I'm sorry for everything. I was an idiot and I'm sorry. I should have told you right from the start about Darke. I was stupid. I know you have no reason to trust me, but I'm asking you to try, Birdie—please. No more secrets. Forgive me. I need you to forgive me. I need . . . you."

I stared at him. He stared at me. And then I nodded.

"Because if you wanted to bail again, I wouldn't blame you."

I shook my head.

"Is that a no, you don't want to bail, or—"

I blurted out, "I'm in love with you."

He stilled. His eyes became glossy. He blinked rapidly, shifting his gaze to the side, blowing out a quick, huffed breath. Then he reached for me.

His mouth came down on mine. He kissed me quickly—small, desperate kisses all over my mouth, until I flung my arms around him and kissed him back. Earnestly, rapturously. Like he might disappear at any moment.

Warm fingers cradled the back of my head. He rested his forehead against mine, breathing heavy, eyes teary, and whispered, "I love you too."

I let those words cascade through me, soaking them up like sunshine. "Are we going to be okay now?"

"We're going to be okay," he whispered back. "I told you fate would find a way."

"And I told you there's no such thing as fate."

"Sorry. Can't hear you," he teased, his mouth turning up at the corners. "Can you repeat that?"

"Listen," I said against his good ear, and then I told him I loved him again. And again. I couldn't stop telling him. I didn't care that we were standing in the busiest tourist attraction in the city and that people were gawking.

I didn't care about any of it; I wasn't afraid.

I didn't have to count my fingers; I was awake.

I didn't have to track down any clues; I'd already solved the mystery.

I'd never been so sure of anything in my life.

He hugged me tight. I pressed my face into his neck and my palm against his chest to feel his heartbeat, strong and confident: *Thump, thump. Thump, thump.* And my own heart bounded to meet it.

"And you call yourself a detective."
—Nora Charles, *After the Thin Man* (1936)

33

"Any more questions?" the woman on the other side of the diner booth asked. She glanced at her watch before peering out the raindrop-speckled window. Yesterday it had been hot and sunny. Today it had decided to rain. Late-October weather was unpredictable.

I scanned my notes one last time and tried to think of anything I'd missed. I didn't want to blow my big opportunity, but I was also aware that she was doing me a favor and that I wasn't paying her for her time. "I think I understand everything. It just seems unfair that I'd have to work in an agency before the state will allow me to take the test to get a license, but I can't work without a license? What kind of catch-22 is that?"

The woman crossed her arms, brown leather jacket creaking. "It's not an evil plot to stop you from becoming an investigator. It's to make sure you know what you're doing before the state gives you permission to start stalking people."

Dorothy McKnight was a frequent patron of the Moonlight. She was also the owner of McKnight Investigations and a licensed Seattle PI. A couple of weeks ago, we'd struck up a conversation at the counter, and I'd surprised both myself and her by boldly asking if she'd meet with me to answer questions about becoming an actual detective.

In her early forties and nearly an entire foot taller than me, she was strikingly pretty, no-nonsense, and sharp. I could see why she'd been drawn to detective work, because I could feel her sizing me up from the first moment we talked. Her eyes never stopped moving.

"I'm sure it's not a conspiracy against me personally," I told her, trying to block out the steady stream of people who were carrying presents, heading to the Moonlight's private dining room in the back. The diner was officially closed right now and would be for two hours while the shower was happening. There was a sign out front that informed potential customers. "I just don't understand why I can't take these criminal justice classes you suggested—"

"*And* computer science and forensic science."

"That's a lot of science," I said.

"It's a scientific world."

And one that I could now explore: I may not have an official diploma from my grandmother, but I'd passed the GED test with a nearly perfect score last month. "I'm just saying, why isn't there some kind of junior detective position that I can apply for to learn on the job before I take the license exam?"

"Because no PI needs a junior detective," Dorothy said, pushing an empty coffee cup out of the way to lean over the table. "What a PI *might* need is a receptionist. Someone to take calls and do data entry. Someone to keep the files updated and look up information when a detective calls into the office. You have that kind of experience, working at the Cascadia, do you not?"

"I do, yes." I was doing it only twice a week because that was all they could spare to give me during the day, since my narcolepsy doctor didn't want me working graveyard shifts. "But I already have that job. And how would that help me get my license?"

"At a hotel? It wouldn't. But working for me might. Because you'd get to learn a little bit about the business, and if you did a good job and took all the courses I suggested, I might be in a position to sponsor you for your license."

I blinked at her. "Are you . . . offering me a receptionist job?"

"My last girl left months ago to move to Oregon. Things are a little chaotic, so I wouldn't be able to babysit you. I'd expect you to take initiative and learn things for yourself. Ask questions. And being a good receptionist doesn't guarantee you shit. I can't help you study or get your license, do you understand?"

"Yes, but—"

"But if you're willing to come into Beacon Hill a few days a week, I'm willing to be flexible with hours so that you can take your classes."

"Seriously?"

"Can't pay much." Dorothy gave me an amount that was five

cents lower than what I was making at the Cascadia, but she was willing to give me full-time hours after a trial period. "You'd be working for all of us, another investigator working under me and the agency's attorney. Like I told you before, it's mostly corporate vetting and the occasional landlord who thinks his tenant is dealing coke. Exciting cases are few and far between. But I could use someone who's interested in the work. Don't see a lot of females wanting to be PIs. I can show you the ropes better than one of the big agencies can, and you won't have to suffer through dick jokes."

I chuckled nervously.

"What do you say?" Dorothy asked. "You need to think about it?"

"This wasn't my intention, asking to meet with you. I wasn't trying to beg for a job."

She smiled. "I know you weren't. I wasn't intending to offer you one. But sometimes you get a gut feeling about someone."

My own gut was getting the same feeling.

"Can I start in three weeks?" I needed time to give notice.

She stuck out her hand, and I shook it. "Call me in a few days to set up a date to come in. I'll introduce you, and we can start your paperwork. Sound like a good plan?"

It sounded like the best plan in the world.

"See you soon, Birdie. I've got a good feeling about this for both of us." She scooted out of her seat, and after I thanked her profusely, left the diner, heading out to another appointment.

Had that actually happened? I think it had! I resisted the urge to count my fingers for a few seconds and then gave in: one, two, three, four, five—all there!

I barely had time to do any internal squealing before I spotted a familiar dark-haired silhouette lugging something past the window. The diner door flew open, and Daniel walked inside backward, breathing hard as he carried one end of something heavy and wrapped in dark plastic. Jiji, wearing a bright purple-and-yellow Hawaiian shirt, was holding the opposite end. When they got it inside, they set it on the floor and both shook rain off their heads.

"You made it," I said to both of them.

"Told you we would," Jiji said, smiling.

"Hello, beautiful girlfriend," Daniel said, planting a kiss on my forehead. "Are you done with your meeting? How did it go?"

"She offered me a job."

"A job?" Jiji said.

"Full-time receptionist."

"Shut up!" Daniel said with a grin, knocking his shoulder against mine. "That is fantastic."

I quickly told them the gist of it, and they were both happy. "Better commute to Beacon Hill than downtown," Jiji noted.

For the time being I was splitting my time between living with Grandpa on the island and shacking up with Daniel in Green Gables. Roman and Dottie had decided to move in with their daughter and help her through the first year of raising her new baby, so we were house-sitting for them until they were ready to come back.

Daniel's mom, Cherry, was the one who actually suggested it. And after Grandpa met Daniel and his family, he gave me his approval—which was sort of a miracle. I think it was heavily influenced by Mona, who had become fast friends with Cherry over the last few months. Anyway, it was sort of nice to have Daniel's family close by. Also, I volunteered to weed part of the cohousing's garden in exchange for pink and purple zinnia blooms for my hair. Not a bad trade.

Don't get me wrong: I didn't want to live there forever. For one, the creepy forest mural in Green Gables was not something I wanted to see every day, and I missed cable television. Also, we'd already had a few minor family squabbles about privacy and freedom. But no one had chopped anyone's head off. Yet. And it gave me and Daniel time to get used to living together before we decided if we were ready to take the next step of getting our own apartment.

A boisterous group of people entered the diner, and I recognized a few of them as artist friends of Mona. They glanced at the handmade sign flanked in balloons—RIVERA BABY SHOWER—and followed the arrow to the private room in back while one of Ms. Patty's new servers gathered teacups and cleaned up the booth where I was sitting.

"Okay," I said to Daniel, poking the wrapping on the object they'd carted into the diner. "Let's see this artistic masterpiece."

Daniel pulled back the plastic, and I bent down to see inside. It was a wooden bassinet. A small, very simple one with slatted sides and a silvery, metallic stain. He'd spent a week making it in wood school, after class. On the top of the railing at the foot of the bassinet was a thin plaque, intricately cut with a scroll saw and painted with silver glitter. The first line was the name Aunt Mona had chosen for her baby, Paloma—"dove" in Spanish. Below that it said: DARING DAME AND GUTSY GAL.

"It's beautiful," I said, unexpectedly emotional.

"Are you sure?" he asked, almost shy.

I knuckled away a stray tear. "All this glitter? She's going to go crazy for it. Best baby gift ever."

Jiji patted his grandson on the shoulder, a big smile on his face. "Told you. You're a wood genius. That school will be paying for itself in no time."

Daniel rolled his eyes, but I could tell he was pleased. He'd quit his job at the Cascadia two months ago to focus on school. Though he joked that by enrolling, he was fully embracing his Jesus persona (carpenter, long hair), he enjoyed his classes. He wasn't sure that he wanted a long-term career in carpentry, but Jiji convinced him it was a skill to fall back on. And as long as he was in school, Cherry agreed that he could do street magic at the market on the weekends. Sometimes he even worked in the magic shop for a few hours. Last week he saw Raymond Darke there, but he didn't speak to him. The two of them had lunch once, a couple of weeks after the debacle at the opera. I think Darke was trying to make an effort to get to know his son, but Daniel thinks he was trying to feel him out and see if Daniel wanted money from him. Either way, they didn't strike up a fast friendship or bond in any way. Daniel says he's okay with that, and he doesn't regret tracking him down.

I didn't either. Sometimes mysteries turn up things you didn't expect to find. Like witty, beautiful boyfriends who may turn out to be the love of your life. You never know. Fate's funny that way.

My phone buzzed with an incoming text. "Leon says they're driving out of the ferry terminal, so they'll be here in a couple of minutes." I'd already seen the outfit she'd made for the occasion: a bejeweled fortune-teller with a cutout in the gown over her baby bump, which revealed spandex underneath, painted like a purple-smoke-filled crystal ball; when she rested her hands on top of her belly, it looked as if she were seeing into the future. "We should probably make our way back to the shower."

"Is Baba here already?" Jiji asked.

I nodded. "She's inside with Cherry."

"Hope they have good food at this shindig, because I'm starving."

"There's cake," I confirmed. "And punch."

Jiji made a face. So did Daniel.

"No pie?" he said mournfully, and then glanced at the Pie of the Day board: *STRAWBERRY'S BABY, featuring glazed bloodred strawberries scented with rosemary and piled into a devilishly dark chocolate-cookie crust.* "Are you freaking kidding me? I have to have that."

A tall, elderly African-American woman in a floral dress whistled at us from across the diner. "You gonna stand there all day?" she said in a husky voice. "Get your rumps in here."

"What about strawberry pie, Ms. Patty?" Daniel called back.

"It's back here, next to the cake, where you should be if you want a slice."

"You're a GD goddess, Ms. Patty," Daniel said.

"That's what they tell me," she said with a wink before gesturing to me. "Come on, Birdie girl. My ice ring is melting in the punch bowl, and I need your help filling the cups. Your grandpa is too slow with the ladle. And someone tell Gina to lock the door when Ms. Mona and her man arrive; otherwise people outside will ignore the sign and wander in."

"Yes, ma'am," I called. For one déjà vu moment, I was ten years old, back living above the diner, waiting on my mother to come home. Missing people is hard. Letting new people inside is harder. But the reward for making that effort was greater than I could have imagined. Family isn't always blood, and it isn't contained in a single tree. It's a forest.

It took me a long time to figure out that not everyone in my life was meant to stay. But using that as armor didn't shield me from future heartache. And even heartache felt a million times better than running away.

If I were to update my own case profile, it would probably look something like this:

Suspect: Birdie Lindberg

Age: 18

Medical conditions: (1) Narcolepsy with cataplexy; currently managing and under doctor's care. (2) Bookworm disease (incurable). (3) Recent struggle with grief, but getting better every day. (4) Madly in love and not seeking treatment.

Personality traits: Shy but curious. Less cowardly than she used to be. Excellent with details. Good observer. Just might make it.

"Hey, Birdie," Jiji said as he helped Daniel lift the bassinet out of its plastic covering. "Now that you're on your way to being a professional detective, I've got a whodunit for you. There's a young lady who walked into the baby shower, and I just remembered that I've seen her talking to Old Man Jessen in the grocery store in an intimate manner."

I didn't know exactly what he meant by that, but he was peering through the doorway into the baby shower, trying to find her. "Chances are it's not the same person. Why would Old Man Jessen know a friend of Mona's?"

"I don't know, but it's her. I'd bet my life on it. And I think Mr. Holier Than Thou Jessen is running some kind of flimflam on his wife."

"Flimflam?"

"Maybe he's having an affair, or maybe he's got a secret family. Whatever it is, it involves that lady. I need you to question her and figure out how she knows him so that I can throw it in his face the next time he tries to give me a citation for Blueberry pissing in the playground sandbox."

"Again?" Daniel said.

"Can't curb a cat's natural instinct," Jiji argued. "So how about it? Will you talk to the lady and see how she knows Jessen?"

"Why can't you just ask her yourself?" I asked.

"She might recognize me. Besides, you're the detective. You and Danny do it; then report back to me."

Daniel comically rolled his eyes at me as he hefted his side of the bassinet. "Come on, Nora. Let's go eat some pie and solve a mystery."

Acknowledgments

This book was difficult to write. Thank you to everyone who made it possible:

Laura Bradford and Taryn Fagerness (for representing and believing in me).

Nicole Ellul (for your patience, and for making this book a gazillion times better).

Sarah Creech (for recreating the Moonlight Diner on this amaaaaaazing cover).

The entire Simon Pulse and Simon UK teams (for being the best publishing team ever).

Early readers who offered critical technical/sensitivity advice but prefer to remain anonymous . . . You know who you are. (All mistakes are mine.)

Also many thanks to:

Karen, Ron, Gregg, Heidi, Hank, Brian, Patsy, Don, Gina, Shane, and Seph (for support).

Downtown Seattle, my home for two bewitching years (still miss it).

David Bowie (for title and musical inspiration).

Columbo/Peter Falk (for being the greatest of all TV detectives; don't @ me).

Librarians and teachers and booksellers (for being book heroes).

The online YA book community (for spreading book love).

And most importantly, thank *you*.

Sometimes to find the good,
you have to embrace the bad.

Read on for a sneak peek at Jenn Bennett's
latest heart-pounding romance.

WELCOME TO BEAUTY: This faux-colonial sign greets travelers entering the small seaside town of Beauty, Rhode Island. A popular summer resort, the historic harbor area connected to Narragansett Bay attracts well-to-do New England vacationers. *(Personal photo/Josephine Saint-Martin)*

February

There's a long-held belief in my family that all the Saint-Martin women are romantically cursed. Unlucky in love, doomed to end up miserable and alone. Supposedly, one of my early New England ancestors angered a neighbor—big surprise—who then paid the wise woman in the village to curse us. *All* of us. Generations upon generations. Like, *None of you will ever get your happily ever after, so mote it be, enjoy the heartbreak.*

I'm seventeen and have never had a boyfriend. Only had one true friend of any kind at all, really, and that was a long time ago. So I haven't had a chance to personally test the curse in action. But even though my family is ridiculously superstitious, I know that everything bad that's happened to us amounts to a bizarre series of unfortunate coincidences. Moving back here to the curse's place of origin isn't the end of the world, no matter what Mom may say.

As I stand in front of Beauty's city limit sign, taking the photo I always snap when we relocate to a new place, I ignore my mother's irrational *woe betides!* about love and instead focus my lens on what this sign represents to me—my future.

See, Mom and I move around a lot. And by "a lot," I mean seven moves in the last five years . . . seven different cities up and down the East Coast. We're pros. We can skip town faster than a mobster who got tipped off that the cops were on their way.

One place is like another, and after a while, they all start to feel the same.

Except Beauty.

It's the place where the all the important things have happened in my life. It's where I was born—the birthplace of every Saint-Martin woman, all the way back to that silly love curse. It's where Mom and I lived until I was twelve years old, and where I'll finish high school next year, fingers crossed.

But most importantly, if things go as I hope they will, it's also where my life is going to change. Monumentally. I have epic plans for the future, and they all start with this sign, right here. Everyone else may just see "Welcome to Beauty," but not me. I see:

Hello, Josie Saint-Martin. Welcome to the Beginning of Your Life.

"It's freezing out here, shutterbug," Mom calls from the small moving truck parked behind me on the side of the highway. Our car, aka the Pink Panther, a 1980s cotton candy colored VW Beetle with too-many-thousand miles on the odometer, is hitched to the back. "Haven't you taken this one before? Forget tradition. It's not going anywhere. Shoot it later."

"Don't rush me, woman," I call back, capping the lens of my vintage Nikon F3 camera before I settle it into the brown leather case that hangs around my neck. The City Limits photo is tradition, sure, but taking photos of signs is my artistic vision as a photographer. Some people like photographing landscapes or people or animals, but not me. I like billboards, snarky church signs, obnoxious neon diner signs, street signs riddled with bullet holes. They all tell a story. They communicate so much with so few words.

And Mom is right about one thing. Unlike people, signs are always there, twenty-four seven, waiting for you to take their picture. You don't have to text them to ask if they're coming home for dinner. You don't have to be mad at yourself for being disappointed when they text back: go ahead, order takeout and eat without me. Signs are dependable.

I climb back into the moving truck, and as I pull on my seat belt, some rare emotion flickers behind Mom's eyes. Whatever the opposite of excited is, that's what she looks right now. Her anxiety over our move to Beauty started with Mildly Stressed, and on the drive here it escalated to High Anxiety, but now I do believe we're up to Scared Shitless.

And Winona Saint-Martin isn't scared of anything, so that leads me to believe that something big is waiting for us here— something Mom has failed to tell me about. Again.

Whatever it is, it must be *bad*. Worse than an old family story about doomed love.

"Seriously, you're starting to freak me out," I tell her. "Why are you so nervous about moving back here?" The reason we left when I was twelve is temporarily gone: the matriarch of the Saint-Martin family, Grandma Diedre. My mom's mother. They had a major falling out. Shouting. Tears. Police were called. Huge drama, and some of it was about me. They've since made up . . . sort of? But whenever we come back to visit, it's never for more than a day or two, and things are always strained.

Our family is kind of messy.

Mom's distracted and not listening to me, as usual. "Crap. Think that was one of your grandmother's friends who just passed us," she tells me, eyes on the rearview mirror. "She's probably on her phone right now, calling up half the town to alert them that Diedre's harlot of a daughter is crossing the border."

"You're being paranoid. Grandma would never call you that." Probably. Fifty-fifty chance.

Mom snorts. "Oh, to be young. Be glad I shielded you from that old bat the past few years. Thank God for Mongolia."

"*Nepal*. You know Grandma's in Nepal."

My grandmother and my mom's older sister, Franny, joined the Peace Corps and left to teach English in Nepal last week. Just like that, Grandma temporarily gave up the independent bookshop that had been in our family for generations and handed over the keys to my mom—someone she doesn't trust to post a letter in the mail, much less run an entire business. And between you and me and this bargain-priced moving truck, my mom isn't exactly the most reliable person in the world.

Which was why Grandma and Aunt Franny running off to Nepal and leaving us as stewards of the family bookshop was a shock to all. Aunt Franny's daughter, my nineteen-year-old cousin Evie, is currently minding the store and will be helping my mom run it while attending college and shacking up with us in my grandma's above-shop apartment.

"There's no reason for you to be nervous. Grandma's gone. Aunt Franny's gone. You can make a fresh start here in Beauty—"

"Dream on, baby." Mom rummages through her purse for a tube of lipstick labeled Ruby Kick. Bright lipstick and pointed cat-eye glasses are the two things my mother wouldn't be caught dead in public without. "You have no idea what we're about to walk into. You were twelve years old when we left this wretched village of the damned. You don't remember what it's like. Beauty is a viper pit for people like us, Josie."

"Then don't give them a reason to gossip."

"What's *that* supposed to mean?"

I clutch my camera case tightly. "You know what it means." Blame the stupid Saint-Martin love curse if you want, but my young-and-single mom never has long-term boyfriends. Never brings men home. But she swipes right and sneaks out to meet guys . . . a lot. I used to keep track of the numbers, but it got depressing. I mean, hey. We aren't living in eleventh century feudal France: I know women can and should have whatever sex life they want. But it's my mom, and I know she's not happy. Also, the lying. If it's no big deal, why lie about it?

If I end up with trust issues, this is why.

Anyway, Mom did imply that she'd cool it with all the online hookups if we moved here. It's not something we *directly* discussed, because we don't talk about anything uncomfortable, so it wasn't a firm promise. But she gave me a silent nod that said: *I will not sleep with everyone in our small hometown, where people know us and our family, and gossip is currency.* And I gave her a return nod that implied: *Okay, cool, but mostly because I'm tired of you lying to me.*

I can tell by the way she's biting a hangnail that I've hurt her feelings by bringing this up right now—the forbidden subject of the dates she doesn't really have. And because I'm always forced to be the adult in the room, I opt to cool things down and switch subjects before we end up in a fight before we even get into town.

"Now you've got me all freaked out about vipers and pits and black holes," I say, trying for lighthearted. "Is it really going to be that bad here?"

"Worse, shutterbug. So much worse. It's not too late. We can turn back around and go right back to Thrifty Books in Pennsylvania."

Mom has managed every chain bookstore on the East Coast, along with some amazing indies . . . and a couple of complete hellholes. The one she just quit in Pennsylvania was in the hell-hole category.

"You emailed your district manager that 'Take This Job and Shove It' song and walked out on your staff in the middle of your shift," I remind her.

The corner of her mouth tilts up. "Okay, sure. Pennsylvania may technically be what people call a burned bridge. So we'll drive straight through town and head down the coast to Connecticut instead. You liked Hartford, remember?"

"Too many murders, too expensive. We lasted five months and got evicted."

"We could go farther south. Maryland?"

"Or we could just stay here in Rhode Island and do what we planned. Live in Grandma's apartment rent-free for a year and save up money for Florida. It's your dream, remember? Palm trees and white, sandy beaches? No digging cars out of snow?"

"Palm trees and white, sandy beaches . . . ," she murmurs.

"And you promised I could finish high school here. Henry said—"

"Oh my God, Josie. Seriously? Don't bring up your father when I'm in the middle of a panic attack."

"Fine," I say, protectively crossing my arms over the soft leather of my camera case. One of the few gifts he's ever given me, the Nikon is my most prized possession . . . and a point of contention between Mom and me. My parents hooked up in college, when she was enrolled at a prestigious state art school for a couple of semesters. He was a thirty-something photography professor, and she was a rebellious nineteen-year-old student who did some nude modeling for him that turned into a one-thing-led-to-another situation.

I'm not sure how I feel about that, but I try not to think about it too much.

Regardless, they never lived together, much less married. And now Henry Zabka is a famous fashion photographer in Los Angeles. I see him every year or so. I think Mom wishes I would forget he even exists. "Look," I tell her diplomatically. "There's no need for panic. This is easy. It's not a viper's pit. Besides, even if it is, Evie is counting on us. She's alone. Support Evie. Save money. Let me finish high school. Then you can head down to Florida, just like you've been dreaming."

"I'm not going alone."

I let out a nervous laugh and hope she doesn't notice. "Both of us . . . Florida . . . yep. That was implied." Wow, that was close. Gotta be more careful.

"Okay, you're right. We can do this," she says, calming down as gabled buildings and picket fences appear up ahead. "And Beauty is just a town, right?"

"Like any other."

Only it isn't. Not even close.

Beauty is a strange place with a long, dramatic history that stretches back to colonial America. It was founded in the late 1600s by a man named Zebadiah Summers, who helped King

Charles III of England "purchase" the "goodly" waterfront land here from two warring New England tribes, the Narragansetts and Pequots. A large quarry of high-grade marble at the edge of town made the English settlers stinking rich. And the postcard-blue harbor—which stretches beyond our U-Haul windshield as Mom drives the curving main road around the coast—later attracted other members of New England high society, who built their summer homes here in the 1800s and helped make this one of the most affluent communities in Rhode Island.

Being a harbor town, Beauty has a lot of boating action. A private yacht club. Racing cups. Boating festivals . . . A public pedestrian path called the Harborwalk circles the water for several miles, and if you like sandy beaches and saltwater taffy, you'll find that here too.

But it's the kooky parts of Beauty that I like. Things like that the town nickname since the 1920s has been—no lie—"Clam Town," because it has more fried clam shacks per capita than any other New England town. (Suck it, Providence!) Or that a slightly famous gothic nineteenth century American poet lived here and is now buried in Eternal Beauty Burial Grounds, a historical cemetery—and here's the weird part—inside the grave of one of the original female colonists who was found to *not* be a witch when she drowned in one of those "if she floats, she's a witch" tests given by Beauty's early paranoid townspeople.

Graveyards and clam shacks aside, the beating heart of Beauty is its historic harbor district. Hazy childhood memories surface in the setting sun as Mom drives us past a horse-drawn carriage trotting alongside gas streetlamps. I crack my window and breathe in the familiar briny air. Along Goodly Pier, sailboats bob in their winter moors, and tourist shops along the waterfront begin closing up. Glassblowers and candlemakers sit across from a row of gated historical mansions, some of which are occupied by families whose kids go to Ivy League schools.

It's another world here. A strange mix of money and weird.

We make our way to the southern side of the harbor, down a one-way street still paved with eighteenth-century granite setts. The South Harbor is the working- to middle-class side of town. It's pretty here. Quiet. A few shops. Waterfront warehouses. But Mom parks the U-Haul in front of the best thing in the South Harbor.

The Saint-Martin family business.

SIREN'S BOOK NOOK

OLDEST INDEPENDENT BOOKSTORE IN THE SMALLEST STATE.

Our street-facing family shop, known to locals as "the Nook," occupies the ground floor of a white bay-windowed house that's on the National Register of Historic Places because of its Revolutionary War connection. A private living space is on the second floor—an apartment that's accessible around back via an exterior flight of rickety wooden stairs above a three-hundred-year-old cobblestone alley. Mom and I lived here with Grandma until I was in sixth grade, but since Grandma Diedre and Mom do a lot of bickering every time they spend quality time together, we stay with Aunt Franny when we come to town, which isn't often.

Still. The quaint shop looks the same.

Generations of Saint-Martins all lived in this one building.

A large, paned window holds a display of books about ships, and over the recessed doorway, a wrought iron mermaid holding an open book juts horizontally from a pole over the sidewalk.

"Salty Sally," Mom says cheerfully to the mermaid, earlier anxiety left behind. "Mermaid boobs looking perky, as always. Guess we're stuck here together again. At least for the time being."

Pushing open the shop door, I'm engulfed by scents of old and new paper. Musty foxing on parchment. Ink. Worn leather. Orange wood polish. It smells inviting, and the New England folk music playing over the speakers is familiar and haunting; my Grandma Diedre collects recordings of traditional sea shanties and local broadside ballads.

Back during the Revolutionary War, this building housed both the Beauty post office and a printshop—I come from a long line of people who worship the printed word—which not only published the local newspaper but also seditious leaflets urging the rebels that lived in our Crown-supporting Loyalist town to "rise up against our redcoat overlords." Several of those leaflets are framed on the walls, and the original eighteenth century printing press crouches in the middle of the shop, now used as a prop to display books about Rhode Island history.

The shop appears empty of customers as Mom and I circle

around the old press and head toward the shop counter. Behind the register, lounging on a stool that squeaks loudly when she moves, is a nineteen-year-old community college student with her mother's long legs and her late African American father's warm brown skin. Her nose—which is dusted with the same pattern of splotchy freckles that all the Saint-Martin women have inherited—is buried in a historical romance paperback with a pirate on the cover.

Evie Saint-Martin.

"Credit card only. No cash. We close in two minutes," Evie says in a bored voice from behind her book in the same way a spooky butler would sound answering the door in an old-dark-house horror film. A ceramic cup of tea steams at her elbow, her own private fog machine.

"I need to pay half in a sock full of pennies, half in a check that looks like it's been dug out of a trash can," I say.

She lowers her paperback until big eyes outlined dramatically with Cleopatra-style makeup peer at me from beneath thick bangs that have been chemically straightened and smoothed with a flat iron.

"Cousin," she says brightly, her grin broad and slow as she pulls me into a hug over the counter. We nearly knock over a display of mermaid-topped writing pens near the register. She grasps my shoulders and pulls back to look me over. "See? This is why you should post more selfies. I had no idea your hair is longer than mine now. You should let me snip-snip it into something strange and beautiful," she says, eyes twinkling like a mad scientist.

Evie cuts her own hair. She's strange in a very good way and a million times cooler than me. And though her parents moved back and forth between Beauty and a couple hours away in Boston, causing us to miss some time growing up together, we've developed a long-distance friendship over the last few years.

She shoves me softly. "Can't believe you're here. Thought you'd be arriving after dark?"

"We downloaded an app to avoid police radar," Mom explains, sliding around the counter to wind long arms around Evie. "You've never lived until you've been in a U-Haul going eighty in a fifty-five zone."

"It was terrifying," I inform my cousin. "Seriously thought the Pink Panther was going to disconnect and fly off."

"How you and my mama are sisters is a complete mystery, Aunt Winona," Evie says as she leans around Mom's shoulder to peer out the front window. "Um, you know you'll get ticketed if you park there without a permit. Massive fine."

Mom groans. "Ugh. Beauty. Nothing changes—even the Nook's counter stool still squeaks. What the hell am I doing back here again?"

"Saving up for palm trees and white, sandy beaches," I remind her.

"And saving me," Evie says. "Grandma Diedre left too many instructions—the store window has to be changed out to her exact list of boring books every month, because God forbid anything changes around here. And even though I've counted everything a hundred times, the safe has somehow been $6.66 short for two days, because the vengeful spirit of the town is smiting us for selling fiction with dirty words in a town settled by puritans and yachting fanatics."

"Ah ha! Knew it!" Mom says. "I was *just* reminding Josie that this place is built over an actual portal to hell, and everyone who lives here is a minion of the dark lord."

A creaking floorboard near the old printing press makes us all turn our heads at once. A boy about my age stares back at us—at *me*.

Big, black Doc Martens. Black leather jacket. Dark waves of hair eddy and swirl around his face like fog circling a lamppost, overlapping a network of scars that mark one side of his face and forehead. Part of his eyebrow is missing. A tiny black cat is tattooed on his hand between his thumb and forefinger.

Carrying a book, he grips the strap of a brain-bucket style motorcycle helmet with the words LUCKY 13 curving around the back in a wicked font. He squints at me through a fan of black lashes—first at the camera case hanging around my neck, then at my face.

He stares at me like I'm the ghost of his dead dog. Like he's surprised to see me.

Like we're old friends . . . or enemies.